T0221584

CRACKS
BENEATH
THE
SURFACE

Also by Mary Ann Miller
Bones Under the Ice

CRACKS BENEATH THE SURFACE

A JHONNI LAURENT MYSTERY

MARY ANN MILLER

OCEANVIEW PUBLISHING
SARASOTA, FLORIDA

Copyright © 2024 by Mary Ann Miller

All rights reserved. No part of this book may be reproduced in any form or by any electronic or mechanical means, including information storage and retrieval systems, without permission in writing from the publisher, except by a reviewer who may quote brief passages in a review.

This book is a work of fiction. Names, characters, businesses, organizations, places, and incidents either are the products of the author's imagination or are used fictitiously. Any resemblance to actual events, businesses, locales, or persons living or dead, is entirely coincidental.

ISBN 978-1-60809-539-1

Published in the United States of America by Oceanview Publishing

Sarasota, Florida

www.oceanviewpub.com

10 9 8 7 6 5 4 3 2 1

To my three granddaughters,
Lucy, Emory, and Ella
What joy you bring to the family

ACKNOWLEDGMENTS

Thank you to Bob and Pat Gussin, Faith Matson, and Lee Randall for their excellent editing suggestions and promotion of *Bones Under the Ice* and *Cracks Beneath the Surface*.

Thank you to my agent, Dawn Dowdle at Blue Ridge Literary Agency, for her advice and support.

CHAPTER ONE

"ON YOUR MARK. Get set. Go!"

Sheriff Jhonni Laurent dropped her arm and stepped back as a hundred and fifty screaming elementary school kids raced across the soccer field in search of hidden Easter eggs. The turnout for the annual egg hunt sponsored by the sheriff's department had grown every year since Laurent had become sheriff.

She and all her deputies were up that morning before dawn to transform Webster Park into a giant Easter event. Ages one and two were roped off under the oak trees where parents could hold the basket as toddlers bent over to pick up an egg and put it into the basket without doing a face-plant into the wet grass.

Children, ages three, four, and five, crowded into the area around the band shell and the playground equipment as parents sat on picnic tables, shouting encouragement to the kids while chatting with friends and neighbors.

Her favorite was the group of kids ages six through ten. Mid-April was always wet, the grass slippery, and the kids knew to wear grubby clothes. Laurent watched as a younger boy's feet slipped out from under him and he plopped on his bottom. He grinned up at his big sister as she stopped to help him up before running to join her friends.

Public works had cut the grass in the park on Friday afternoon before Easter, and Laurent breathed in the lingering scent. As the last group of children finished their search for eggs, she strolled to a nearby picnic table to join Lisa DuVal, the owner of Big Al's Diner.

Lisa had donated and prepared twelve hundred hard-boiled eggs this year. On the two Saturdays prior to Easter Sunday, Laurent, her deputies, and anyone over the age of eleven was invited to color eggs at the diner between lunch and dinner. Originally, any age was welcome to help decorate the eggs, but when one seven-year-old boy drank the vinegar, water, and dye solution and then threw up, she'd raised the age. Yesterday, groups of boys and girls along with a few moms were dropped off at Big Al's to dye eggs. For some families, it had become a tradition.

"Great job, Sheriff," Lisa said. "Jake, my oldest grandson, was boasting this morning about how this was his last year with the 'little' kids. Next year, he gets to color the eggs for his brother and younger cousins. In a few years, he'll be helping me boil and dye them, and after that, he'll be working at the diner. Where does the time go?" The cheerful, chubby diner owner shook her curly brown hair.

"I can't believe this is my twentieth year in Field's Crossing with the sheriff's department," Laurent said as she eased a hip onto the picnic table, one foot resting on the ground. She'd dressed too warmly for the day and the back of her shirt was damp. She picked up her long black braid and held it away from her neck.

Field's Crossing was the largest town in the rural farming area of north central Indiana. The small community was made up of residents who lived in town and farmers who kept watch on the mid-April weather. When the spring rain slowed, tractors would dot the countryside and the smell of freshly turned dirt would linger in the air.

"I thought your daughter might come today," Lisa said. "What does she do for a living?"

"She teaches high school calculus and plays violin in the Indianapolis Symphony Orchestra. We're having dinner tomorrow night." Laurent shoved her hand in her pocket and hunched her shoulders.

Thirty years ago, she had given up her daughter for adoption. A month ago, her daughter asked to meet. Laurent's first reaction had been to ignore the request, but she changed her mind after the death of Stephanie Gattison, an eighteen-year-old local high school senior.

During the capture of Stephanie's killer, Laurent was shot in the shoulder and still had not fully recovered. During the murder investigation, she had been embroiled in a bitter reelection campaign and was sure that the discovery of an illegitimate daughter would hand the election to her opponent, Deputy Mike Greene. On the contrary, she won. Whatever Laurent had expected from the residents of the quad-counties, it hadn't been acceptance.

"What are you doing for Easter?" Laurent asked.

"Heading to Aubrey's as soon as the kids find their eggs," Lisa said. "I tried to get the family to turn today into a picnic, but you know Aubrey. Gotta be able to brag about making Easter dinner—and at the same time complain about it."

"I hear ya. We'll be finished cleaning up by one o'clock, and then I'm having dinner with Starr and a few friends. Have a great day with your family."

Laurent picked up a Styrofoam cup of coffee from the picnic table manned by Deputy Bill Poulter and strolled among the participants. The Easter egg hunt was winding down and happy, muddy families trooped to the parking lot. Laurent waved to Starr Walters as her best friend exited Webster Park, sixties music blaring.

Laurent walked through the parking lot, admiring eggs in baskets as children lifted their treasures to show her. She stopped at Aubrey Holmes' car to chat with Lisa's grandson, Jake. "Your grandma tells me this is your last year to hunt Easter eggs. Next year, you're helping to decorate them."

"I'm not a little kid anymore," Jake said. "Grandma says when I start high school, I can work at Big Al's—learning how to make sandwiches and stuff like that. I already know some."

"What's your favorite sandwich?"

"Peanut butter and bananas. Sometimes I add potato chips on top."

"I don't think that's on your grandma's menu," Laurent said.

"It should be. Me and my friends eat it, like, every day," Jake said, glancing toward the Ford Explorer that had pulled alongside them. "Here's Dad."

"Hope you got all the mud off!" Doug Holmes snapped at his son. "Get in the back. Justin's in your mom's car. Your little brother decided to splash in that mud puddle near the edge of the woods with his buddies. Your mom's pissed." He pointed a finger at Laurent. "Next year, Sheriff, if you see a big puddle, rope it off. One of Justin's friends decided to wash his hair with mud. Thank God we remembered to bring the camping blankets. Justin's sitting on those in the back seat of Aubrey's car."

Laurent raised her eyebrows. *Doug's in a bad mood.* "I'll remember that. Enjoy the rest of the day."

* * *

"Jhonni. Have you seen Lisa recently? Aubrey called me looking for her mom," Starr Walters said as soon as Laurent answered the call. Starr worked for the village of Field's Crossing as an accountant and had also been injured in the previous month's murder investigation. The killer had pushed her down a flight of concrete steps at the village hall, injuring Starr's neck and breaking her wrist.

"Nope. I'm still at Webster Park. I talked to Lisa earlier in the day, but the parking lot's empty. We're about to close the gate. Why do you ask?" Laurent wasn't surprised Aubrey had called Starr. Laurent's personal cell phone number was known only to a handful of people. When she was off duty, she valued her privacy.

"Aubrey's been trying to reach Lisa for the last hour, but Lisa's not picking up, and Aubrey's mad as a wet hen. She says Easter dinner was at one o'clock and it's ruined and it's all her mom's fault."

"Think those two will ever get along?" Laurent asked.

"You and Randi get along better than Lisa and Aubrey, but you two haven't got any history built up. That counts for something."

"True," Laurent admitted. "Would you call Aubrey back and tell her I'll swing by the diner to check on Lisa on my way to your house? Sorry about the call."

"No worries. You know Aubrey. She thinks she's the cat's meow. Her mom donates the eggs, so you, the sheriff, can track her down and tell her to call her daughter. Like you've got nothing else to do today. I hate Aubrey's entitlement attitude. On the other hand, how many dozen eggs did Lisa donate and dye this year?"

"One hundred dozen," Laurent said. "When we started, Lisa cooked ten dozen eggs. Five years later, we've got at least a hundred and fifty kids hunting Easter eggs. I offered to pay for them, but she hung up on me. I think I offended her."

"Jhonni, that's eight eggs for each kid. You need to limit the number of eggs one kid can take home," Starr said.

"Maybe you're right. I'll be at your house after I stop by Big Al's. Did you forget anything? Do I need to swing by 7-Eleven?"

"Sour cream."

Laurent tapped the END button and slid her cell phone into her pant leg pocket. She flagged down Dak Aikens, her favorite deputy from across the parking lot.

The bald Black officer jogged over to her. "Everyone's gone," he reported. "Caleb's emptied all the garbage cans and picked up the sawhorses, and I've pulled up all the markers and tape. We're ready to close."

"I'll leave you to it. Thanks for taking the sixteen-hour shift. Holiday pay plus overtime pay. You're making more than me today."

"And someday, I'll have your job." Dak grinned at her. "Not for another twenty years, I hope."

"Damn straight." Laurent waved and slid behind the wheel of the black police SUV. Turning south on Field Street, she headed toward Big Al's Diner. She'd stop at the convenience store for Starr's sour cream after she found Lisa.

*　*　*

Laurent parked in the front lot of Big Al's Diner and walked to the door. Twisting the doorknob, she found it locked. As she peered through the window, she noted the blinds were closed and no light shone from the rear of the diner. She strolled along the side of the building, passing a row of arborvitae that surrounded the dumpster and continued to the circular driveway in the rear of the diner. She paused and glanced at the parked catering vans, rear doors facing the back of the diner.

Laurent sniffed. Wet grass, damp pavement, and something else. Eggs. Hard-boiled eggs. A few must have broken during the day. She headed to the back door and turned the knob. Unlocked.

"Lisa?" Laurent flicked on the light and saw no one. Wandering down the hallway, she glanced in the tiny office. Empty. Same with the employee break room. Dining room, food prep area, and walk-in cooler, all empty. Where was the owner of Big Al's Diner? Laurent retraced her steps and stopped at the back door, her gaze taking in the green garbage dumpster, the glistening circular black-top drive, the two white catering vans.

"Shit." Laurent bolted toward the farthest van and yanked open the driver's door. Lisa DuVal's head rested on the steering wheel, face turned toward the window, her ear pressed against the spoke, eyes closed. Her right arm hung down, the fingers dangling midair. Her left arm lay in her lap. Laurent poked Lisa's shoulder. "Lisa?" No response. Quickly, Laurent reached across Lisa, her fingers searching for the release button on the seat belt.

Click.

Lisa's body tilted away from Laurent and she grabbed Lisa's left arm, holding her in the middle of the seat. Glancing down, Laurent found the buttons to adjust the driver's seat. With one hand, she pushed the button moving the seat back while cupping the back of Lisa's head. She gently lowered Lisa's head against the head rest and pressed two fingers on the carotid artery. Nothing.

She touched the radio on her shoulder. "Dispatch. Send an ambulance to the rear entrance of Big Al's Diner. Circular drive off Delaney Street. Advise female patient, unconscious, no heartbeat, approximate age fifty-five. Beginning CPR."

"Ten-four."

Laurent slid one arm behind Lisa's lower back and nestled the unconscious woman's shoulder into her shoulder. Lisa's head dropped forward and her brown curly hair tickled Laurent's nose. Sliding the other arm under Lisa's knees, Laurent tugged the body out from behind the steering wheel. She took three steps back and bent over, settling Lisa's butt on the ground. *That's gonna hurt.*

She gently lowered Lisa's upper body to the pavement and slid one hand under Lisa's neck, tilted her mouth, and breathed two quick breaths. In the distance, a siren cut through the air.

Locating the sternum through the long-sleeve T-shirt, Laurent placed the heel of one hand on top of the other, interlaced her fingers, and began CPR. One, two, three ... *What the hell?* Laurent glanced down. Blood gushed from Lisa's left side, soaking Laurent's pants. She leaned back on her heels and stared at the woman on the ground.

Lisa lay dead at her knees.

CHAPTER TWO

"Sheriff, let me confirm." The voice of Keke King, a paramedic with the quad-county fire department, spoke to Laurent's left.

"She's all yours." Laurent continued CPR until Keke's partner took over. She scooted back, pushed to her feet, and stood next to Dak who had arrived at the same time as the ambulance.

Keke stepped past her and knelt. He pulled a stethoscope from under his coat and pressed it against Lisa's chest. A minute passed. Easing back on his heels, he shook his head. "Nothing I can do for her."

"Dak. Call Creighton," Laurent said as she moved a few feet away from Lisa's body. It was midafternoon and the sun hid behind gray clouds. The wind had picked up, the temperature had dropped, and the damp April air cut through her light jacket. She shivered and shoved her cold hands into her pockets.

"He's on vacation," Dak said.

"I forgot. Who's covering for him?"

"Some rookie at Columbia Hospital."

"Give him a call." Laurent touched Keke on the arm. "Did I kill her? Push out what little life she had left? She had no pulse. She wasn't breathing. I started CPR. Please tell me I didn't kill her."

"Calm yourself, Sheriff. The coroner will be here in a minute. He'll tell you what he thinks, but I doubt very much that you killed her," Keke said. "You did exactly as you were trained to do. You weren't trained to search the body first and then administer aid." He lifted Lisa's long-sleeved T-shirt and pointed. "Stab wound. And I can tell from looking at her, she's been here for a bit. See how gray her face is?"

Laurent exhaled. "I didn't see any blood. I didn't notice it until my knees were wet and then I smelled it. Maybe if I had, I would've looked first."

"Don't jump to conclusions. Wait for the coroner. I'm sorry you've had such a lousy ending to your day."

Laurent knelt next to the large young man and peered down at the body. *Stab wound? Who'd murder Lisa?*

CHAPTER THREE

"DEPUTY, I'M GOING to turn her over now. Will you grab the feet?" Dr. T'ara Romero, a recent graduate in forensic medicine from Indiana University and the assistant coroner for the quad-counties, was in her late twenties and petite, weighing in at one hundred pounds. She wore two pairs of gloves. A turtleneck showed through at the collar under her dark blue scrubs, and when she knelt, black long johns peeked out at the ankle.

"Yes, ma'am." Dak leaned back on his heels, gloved hands on his knees.

Laurent had watched as the young Black doctor took control of the crime scene. Dr. Romero brought her own camera and wasn't interested in Laurent's ten-year-old, out-of-date digital Nikon. Laurent typed a note into her phone to add a new camera to the budget.

"Are you able to ID the victim?" Dr. Romero slid a preservation bag over each hand.

"Everyone knows Lisa. She's been making sandwiches at Big Al's for the last two decades, maybe more. My first day on the job, I came in to eat and she wouldn't let me pay," Dak said.

"Her daughter contacted me earlier in the day," Laurent said. "Lisa didn't show up for dinner. Now we know why." She snapped a few more pictures and then stood back as the young doctor completed another round of pictures. Laurent massaged her shoulder. At her last visit to the orthopedic doctor, he had allowed her to remove the sling, but warned her too much activity would put a strain on her injured shoulder. She had been so glad to get rid of the sling, she had promised not to overdo it and take ibuprofen before the pain started. Not after. She had forgotten this morning and a dull ache was spreading across her shoulder blade and down her arm.

Dak gestured toward Laurent. "You just got that sling off and I can see you're hurting. Put it back on."

Laurent wasn't going to admit to Dak her arm was killing her. *Damn physical therapy. When's it going to end so I can get back to normal?*

"I heard you were wounded, Sheriff." Dr. Romero slipped Lisa's blood-soaked shirt into an evidence bag and marked it with her black Sharpie. "And that you caught the killer. How'd you do that?"

Dak grinned and pointed to Laurent. "She shot him. In the forest. Through the snow. By the time we got there, he was screaming like a two-year-old."

"I was hit in the shoulder. More of a flesh wound, but it went deep enough to nick the bone. The doctor released me for limited active duty after my last physical therapy session but said I might be sore for a few more weeks," Laurent said.

"Don't get behind the pain."

"I wasn't expecting to take so long to heal."

"The older you get, the longer it takes. For everything. Take some ibuprofen. It'll reduce the swelling and help with the pain.

There's no need to be a hero." Dr. Romero took a blood sample. "I've got the victim's body temperature and enough for a preliminary cause of death. Let's slip her into the body bag and go inside where it's warm. If you'll help me load her onto the gurney, I'll get out of your way."

"Appreciate it. I'm doing my best not to speculate on the cause of death, but Keke showed me the wound," Laurent said.

Laurent stood next to the back door of the diner and watched as Dak and Dr. Romero slid Lisa's body inside a black bag, zipped it up, hoisted it onto the gurney, and locked it into the rear of the coroner's vehicle. She stepped inside as Dak and the tiny coroner slipped past her into Big Al's. Laurent shut the door and instantly the hallway felt warmer. "Let's sit in the eating area."

Laurent followed Dak and Dr. Romero into the dining room and pulled out a chair. She dropped her headband on the table before sitting down.

"The preliminary cause of death is a stab wound under and to the side of the left breast." Dr. Romero rolled off her gloves and folded them inside each other. "It looks as though the weapon penetrated on an angle up and toward the victim's right shoulder, going through the left lung and maybe hitting the heart. I'm placing the time of death between noon and four today."

"What can you tell us about the murder weapon?" Laurent asked.

Dr. Romero sighed. "I'm pretty sure the wound was caused by a knife. The opening is a slash or a cut. If the knife was pressed all the way in, the part of the knife closest to the handle measures approximately one to one-and-a-half inches wide. Once I get back to the morgue, I'll be able to give you the length of the knife, if it was serrated, the spacing of the serrations, and if the tip was tapered. That should narrow down the weapon you're looking for."

"She didn't have a chance."

"When vital organs are injured, the victim's only chance is immediate surgery, and even then, she would have had a tough fight. You can't mess with internal organs," Romero said.

Laurent gazed at the rookie coroner. "I didn't see any blood when I opened the driver's-side door. What do you think about that?"

"It's possible all the blood oozed or leaked from the stab wound and was absorbed by the T-shirt or her jeans," Dr. Romero said. "Whoever killed her may have blood on his or her hands or gloves. When the knife was yanked out, some blood would have escaped with it. You might find traces on a pair of shoes or pants, possibly the seats, especially if they were cloth, and the floor or the mats, maybe the running board."

"Good to know. Do you need any more help?" Laurent asked.

"It'll be Tuesday before I've got more information for you."

Laurent followed the young doctor to the rear door of the diner and watched the coroner's van pull onto Delaney Street before heading north on Indiana Street. She closed the back door and joined Dak in the eating area. "Get Poulter over here. Have him take Lisa's computer and the security video back to the office, make a copy, and look at it. Someone stabbed Lisa between noon and four. I know she spent most of the day at Webster Park. I helped her unload the van around eight this morning and I chatted with her around eleven. We're going to need to track her movements during the Easter egg hunt today. Who was the last person to talk to her before she left? Was anyone else in the van with her? Did someone leave the park before Lisa and wait for her at Big Al's?"

"Another homicide? Crap. This time, everyone in Field's Crossing knows the victim." Dak ran a hand over his bald head. "And likes her."

"*Liked*. Me, too." Laurent sighed. "Dak, pull the work schedule off the board in the employee break room and have dispatch call anyone scheduled and tell them not to come in. We don't need a bunch of gawking, gossiping employees. After that, start bagging evidence. There's got to be fifty knives in the prep room. Dust for prints. After I get back from the next-of-kin notification, we'll work outside before we lose the light."

"You want me to do it? You look a little peaked," Dak said.

Laurent shook her head.

"Then take the damn ibuprofen."

CHAPTER FOUR

LAURENT PARKED ON Cardinal Street and sat, engine idling. *Was it only six weeks ago she had done this exact same thing? Tell Owen and Theresa Gattison their daughter was dead? How was Keith DuVal going to react to the news of his wife's murder?* She shut off the engine, wincing slightly at the pain. She had stopped at the twenty-four-hour pharmacy and bought more ibuprofen. Picking at the plastic seal with her teeth, she opened the bottle and pulled out the cotton ball. *Why do they make it so hard to get the pills out?* She downed four ibuprofen with a swig of tea from her Yeti and climbed out of the police SUV.

Lisa and Keith Duval owned a home in the residential area west of downtown Field's Crossing. To the east was Field Street, which was lined with businesses and was the main north/south street with Big Al's Diner occupying an entire block on the south end of town close to the school campus.

Laurent glanced down Cardinal Street. The houses had been built one by one, no tract housing or subdivision-looking homes. A few mounds of dirty snow were heaped at the end of driveways, shoveled there after the long winter. The weak April sun was trying to break through the cloud cover, and a chilly wind snuck down Laurent's collar. She shivered. She was ready for spring, ready to shed the heavy winter clothing, ready to plant more annuals and perennials in her flower garden. But the nighttime temperatures were still falling into the thirties, and it was too soon to plant.

Laurent stopped on the sidewalk and looked at the DuVal house. It was painted the same color as Big Al's Diner. Barn red with white trim and black shutters. The driveway was shiny black asphalt. She remembered the grumbling among Field's Crossing residents when the popular diner had closed for a week to put in a new parking lot. It looked as though any exterior upgrades to the diner were also done to the owner's house. *Looks like one of the many farmhouses I was raised in.*

She trotted up the front stairs and knocked. Stepping to the side, Laurent glanced into a large ceramic pot, empty, awaiting spring planting. She counted twenty pots of varying sizes on the front porch. *Did Lisa grow her own herbs? Was that the secret to making mouthwatering sandwiches?* A two-person swing hung from one end of the porch, lightly dusted with snow. As the front door opened, Laurent's stomach tightened.

Keith DuVal was in his mid-to-late fifties. A potbelly hung over the waistband of flannel pajama bottoms and his terry cloth robe hung open, the ends of the belt stuffed into the pockets. The almost-white wifebeater T-shirt was stained, the neckline stretched allowing a few gray chest hairs to show.

It's Easter Sunday. Did he go to dinner at Aubrey's looking like that?

"Thank you for seeing me," she said.

"Come in. Aubrey called me looking for Lisa and then called back and said she called you. I guess it can't be good news." Keith folded his arms across his chest and spread his legs wide as though he was getting ready to take a blow.

Shutting the door behind her, Laurent paused and took in the cluttered mess. The neatness and tidiness on the exterior didn't match the interior. The tired carpet in the living room showed worn, well-traveled paths around furniture, and the cushions on the couch were faded with torn or ripped seams. The newest item in the living room was a huge flat-screen TV above the brick fireplace. The sound bar on the mantel was covered in dust and a cobweb hung from the ceiling and stuck to the corner of the TV. College basketball blared and the smell of bacon and beer hung in the air.

"Are you sure you don't want to sit down?" Laurent asked.

"Spit it out."

"Your wife's dead. I found her body at Big Al's this afternoon."

"Shit." Keith looked down, his arms falling to his sides. "You're sure it's her?"

"Both myself and Deputy Aikens recognized her, but as next of kin, I'll need you to make the positive identification. Not now."

"Serves her right. Killed with her own knife." Keith plopped into a worn leather recliner.

"Why do you say she was killed with her own knife?"

"You told me."

"I said she was *dead*. You said she was *killed*."

Keith shrugged. "The security at the diner sucked. Everyone in town had a key. It was only a matter of time before someone decided to rob her. She must have got in the way."

Laurent stepped further into the living room and perched on the edge of the sagging couch. And waited. No tears from Keith

DuVal. Was he in shock? Overwhelmed? *How did Keith DuVal know his wife was killed with a knife? Did he kill her?* "Can I call someone for you?"

He lifted his head. "Are you going to Aubrey's house?"

"I was planning to. Would you rather I call and ask her to come here?"

"No. No." He waved a hand. "Go on. I'll be fine."

"May I ask a few questions?" Laurent pulled her notebook out of her pocket and clicked her pen. *He's not upset. May as well get a feel for the guy.*

"Shoot."

"When did you last see your wife?"

"Friday after she got home."

"Time?"

"After nine. We had a big-ass fight. I filed for divorce a year ago, and we were still arguing over the damn details." Keith clenched a fist.

"What details?"

"She wanted half of my 401(k) but wouldn't give me any money from Big Al's."

Laurent jotted a note. Keith and Lisa were getting a divorce. "How long have you been married?"

"Thirty-five years."

"How long have you owned Big Al's?"

"There's the hitch. Lisa claims my name isn't on the title and I own no part of the diner and I told her that's bullshit. You couldn't have bought it without me. The bank used this house for collateral. Don't tell me I get nothing from that goddamned restaurant!" Keith's knuckles were white.

"The divorce was about money?" Laurent asked.

"It sure as hell wasn't about anything else. We haven't slept together for the last ten years."

"You argued about Big Al's and the divorce. Then what happened?" Laurent asked.

"She got in her big ol' Escalade and left."

"Where'd she go?"

"I'm assuming either Aubrey's or Vickie's." Keith leaned forward, opened the drawer on the side table, and pulled out a pack of cigarettes and a lighter. "At least now I can smoke in the house."

"Who's Vickie?"

"Victoria Scott Wright. Lives on Corn Belt Road on the south side of town. Lisa slept there a lot."

"How often?"

"How the fuck do I know? She never bothered to tell me a goddamn thing," Keith snapped. "I'm done answering questions. I got people to call." He shoved to his feet.

Laurent closed her notebook and stood. "I'm sorry for your loss. I always enjoyed chatting with your wife."

"You and the entire town. Too bad she gave all her energy to complete strangers." Keith turned his back on her and stalked into the kitchen. "Don't bother going to Aubrey's. I'll call her."

Laurent closed the front door behind her and jogged down the stairs. *That was weird.* No grief. Only anger mixed with greed. With his wife dead, there was no more fighting in court. Keith would get it all. *How much money are we talking about? Enough to kill? Wonder where he's been all day. I don't remember seeing him at Webster Park.*

CHAPTER FIVE

"WHERE DO YOU want to start?" Dak asked. "Poulter is fast-forwarding through the security video and should be back soon."

"Let's start at the van and work outward. Van, driveway, diner," Laurent said. "The light is fading fast. It'll be dark by seven o'clock. Dak, see if you can find the light switches for the outside lights around the entire building. After that, wind crime scene tape through the handles on the front door. We'll make the rear entrance the only ingress and egress until we can finish investigating the inside of Big Al's. Call Caleb Martin from public works and ask him to bring some sawhorses so we can block off the circular drive. He probably headed to his folks' house for Easter dinner after he finished at Webster Park."

"Ten-four."

Laurent stared at the chalk outline of Lisa's body. The woman had always been kind to her and all of Field's Crossings' first responders, frequently waving away payment for her fabulous sandwiches. She plucked her pant leg away from her skin and the scent of blood floated up. She pulled out her cell phone. *Better call Starr. Tell her I'm not going to be there for dinner and to forget about the sour cream. Maybe she'll bring me a clean pair of pants.*

The exterior lights flicked on.

"Caleb said he'd be here in a half an hour or so." Dak held up the digital camera. "Let me make a complete circle around the van and then I'll start on the interior of the vehicle."

"Don't forget underneath the van. I'm gonna sweep the drive." Laurent slowly shuffled toward the street. Bits of gravel, a few dead leaves, scrape marks from the snowblower, a flattened pop can. She bent over. Dog poop. Stepping around it, she reached Delaney Street, backtracked, and searched the other half of the circular drive. Nothing out of the ordinary.

Laurent heard the crunch of a vehicle and swung around to see Starr's GMC Yukon pulling up on Delaney Street.

"What happened? You're not gonna make it for dinner?" Starr's armful of bangles jangled as she handed clean jeans out the window.

"Lisa's dead." Laurent tucked the jeans under her arm.

"No shit. Heart attack? She was carrying some extra weight."

"Don't know yet."

"Then why do you need clean pants? Is that blood?"

"Nothing gets by you. Thanks. I'll call later if it's not too late." Laurent waved. She jogged into the diner and changed in the public washroom and placed her blood-soaked pants into an evidence bag before rejoining Dak.

"Exterior complete," he said.

"I'll open the driver's door and wait until you're done before I start searching." She swung open the door and stepped back. As Dak snapped pictures, she studied the inside of the catering van. It was well used. The floor mats were filled with bits of white paper, a French fry, twigs, and a straw was lodged alongside the gas pedal. The dashboard was dusty, and a pair of sunglasses perched in the cup holder. The victim's purse and jean jacket lay on the passenger seat.

"No one drove from the park to the diner with her," Laurent said.

"Why do you say that?" Dak asked.

"If someone rode back with Lisa, she'd have put her purse and coat on the floor between the seats."

"You don't know that."

"That's what I would have done. That's what Starr would have done. I'd never ask a passenger to hold my purse," Laurent said. "But we won't rule out that there might have been someone in the passenger seat. My assumption could be wrong."

Dak snorted. "You're right and you know it. Mimi'd do the same." He paused. "Why aren't there any sliding doors on the sides of the van?"

"Shelving. Let's open the rear doors and take a look." Laurent glanced toward Delaney Street as Poulter parked on the street blocking one end of the circular drive and waited until he joined her and Dak. "What did you see on the security tape?"

"I checked the exterior cameras first. It started off with a bunch of kids and Lisa loading the vans with trays of eggs. Then some of the kids left, but two boys stayed behind. Lisa drove one van, and the two boys were in the other van. Then, there's a big gap of nothing and then those same two boys come back, park the van, and walk out of sight of the camera. And then the camera shut off. One o'clock. That's when Big Al's closed today."

"Dr. Romero puts the time of death between noon and four today. With the camera shutting off at one, we might be able to narrow the time of death between one and four." Laurent tapped the flashlight against her leg.

"We were just about to look inside the rear of the vehicle." She strode to the back of the catering van, opened one side, and pulled it wide, the smell of eggs wafting out. Laurent liked hard-boiled eggs, but now the odor would be associated with Lisa's murder. *Gonna be a while before I eat another hard-boiled egg.*

Dak and Poulter joined her, all three flashlights splaying over the inside of the van. Both sides were lined with adjustable stainless-steel wire mesh shelves and connected to the wall behind the driver and passenger seats. The center aisle was shoulder-width, and the floor was a non-skid bare metal.

"That answers one question," Poulter said. "You can't get from the driver's seat or the front passenger seat into the back of the van. The only way is through these doors. Someone could hide here, and no one would know."

"Somebody had to close the rear doors. Is it possible to shut them from the inside?" Laurent ran her flashlight over the interior rear door.

"Looks like." Poulter pointed to a handle. "Probably a safety feature so you can't get locked inside, like a walk-in cooler."

"Wouldn't she notice if someone was hiding back here?" Dak asked.

"Depends. After all the eggs were hidden at Webster Park and we put the trays back, the doors were closed. Were they locked? Did someone hide in here? Would Lisa or any of her staff open the rear door and look inside before driving off? I wouldn't," Laurent said.

"How many doughnuts you think it holds?" Poulter took off his baseball cap and raked a hand through his brown hair, the short stubble sticking straight up.

"Five pounds went straight to my thighs just looking back here," Laurent said.

"Please tell me you don't eat that crap." Dak put his hands on his hips.

"All day long, Mr. Health Nut," Poulter said. "All day long. I love me some sweets."

"In a fair world, I'm with you, Poulter. But after the age of fifty, I find myself eating more and more rabbit food."

"Good for you, Sheriff. Mimi says the lack of proper nutrition stunted her growth," Dak said.

Laurent smiled at the thought of Dak's pint-sized grandma.

"Boss, what are we going to do about the dumpster?" Poulter asked. "I sure as hell don't want to comb through it."

"Let me put in a call to CSU," she said. "They've got more technicians and space. Maybe I can get them to come out today or tomorrow and haul the thing to Indianapolis or look through it here." She pulled out her phone. "Dak, keep taking pictures. Poulter, grab evidence bags and markers from the back of my SUV. We're going to concentrate on the front seat."

Laurent walked to the open driver's-side door of the white catering van. *The stab wound was on Lisa's left side so the door had to be open for the assailant to stick the knife in and take it out. I'm five-ten. How high is the seat? Where would Lisa's butt sit? I need a ruler.*

Laurent texted Caleb Martin. *He'll have a measuring tape in his truck.* She shoved her phone back in her pocket. *Okay. The murderer stabs Lisa, steps back, and closes the door.* She mimicked the action. *The murderer could be either right-handed or left-handed.* She opened the door again and looked down at the running board. *Is that a spot of blood?*

"First marker, right there." She pointed and waited for Poulter to place the yellow cone. "Scrape it. Then let's bag both floor mats, everything in the glove compartment, and any other loose items like the sunglasses. I'm going to search her purse and tag everything in it individually."

"Ten-four."

Laurent picked up Lisa DuVal's purse and walked to her SUV. Lifting the rear hatch, she pulled a tarp from the evidence kit, spread it, and laid it down. She placed Lisa's purse on the left side of the tarp and snapped several pictures with her cell phone. Pulling out one item at a time, she laid the keys, wallet, a roll of cash, tissue, pen, paper clip, receipts, and reading glasses on the tarp and photographed and tagged them. There was nothing in Lisa's purse that Laurent didn't carry in hers—except for the roll of cash. She counted the money. Three thousand dollars. *Must be from the diner.* Big Al's had a cash-only policy.

"Find anything?" Dak asked. "I finished taking pictures and dusted the door handles for prints. I also got a few prints from inside the back of the van, off the shelving units. The mesh baskets were useless."

"Everything other than the roll of cash looks normal to me."

"Did CSU call back yet?" Poulter carried two boxes of evidence. "Open the door, dude. My scrawny arms are aching."

"If you spent some time in the gym, you wouldn't have scrawny arms." Dak opened the rear door of Laurent's SUV.

"That's why we got you." Poulter laughed.

"I'm not expecting to hear from CSU for a while. Limited staff on Sunday, and it's a holiday for most folks."

"Got it."

"Let's close up and move inside," Laurent said. "Dak, you and me and Caleb were the last ones to leave Webster Park. When he gets here ask him if he saw anyone get into the catering van with

Lisa when she left. We need to reconstruct Lisa's day. Set up a time-line. Who she talked to and when and what the conversation was about. Who wanted her dead? Who would she let get close enough to stab her? We need the employee list and who worked today and who those two boys were in the other van. What did they see? Any strangers or cars loitering around when they left?"

"It sounds like you don't think either of those two boys stabbed her," Dak said.

"I could be wrong, but I think either someone drove back with her, or someone was waiting for her. When I got here, the front door was locked, but the back door was open. Did the killer wait inside? Was the back door unlocked all day?" Laurent glanced at the deputy standing next to her. Poulter was smoothing his mustache, forehead wrinkled.

"Town's been empty all day long. Every time I passed through, it was a ghost town. Stores all closed. The only thing happening today is the Easter egg hunt. I think someone knew that and capitalized on it. Ain't nobody around to see anything," Poulter said.

Honk. Honk.

"Here's Caleb."

The three officers walked toward the road commissioner as he popped out of the orange county pickup.

"What took you so long?" Dak asked.

"Mom made strawberry shortbread," Caleb said. "You think I'm gonna leave it for Dylan? He'll eat it all."

"I think the better question is—did you bring us any?" Laurent looked at Caleb. Two months earlier, Dylan Martin had been a suspect in his girlfriend's murder and eventually cleared of wrong-doing. Since then, Laurent had become friends with the entire Martin family, including Caleb's crazy uncle, Vern.

"Maybe."

"Yesss." Poulter fist-pumped several times.

"Where do you want these sawhorses?" Caleb asked. "Here's the measuring tape. Why do you need it?"

"Dak, Poulter, move our vehicles and block off both ends of the circular drive," Laurent said. "I don't want anyone back here. At least not until we know what we're going to do with the dumpster." She took the tape measure from Caleb. "I need to measure the height of the driver's seat."

"What am I missing?" Caleb asked.

"Lisa DuVal's been murdered."

CHAPTER SIX

THE BACK DOOR of the diner had been propped open with two cinder blocks and a fifty-pound bag of flour, now slightly damp. After photographing and dusting the van, the three officers moved inside the diner. Laurent was grateful for the warmth. A slight drizzle had started, and the damp had chilled her to the bone.

She moved the cinder blocks and the flour and closed the back door. Her conversation with Caleb had been short. He hadn't talked to Lisa the entire day and didn't see her leave Webster Park.

Laurent slipped on clean booties and gloves. She had been a customer at Big Al's dozens of times during her twenty-year career with the sheriff's department, but today was the first time she'd entered through the back door. *Make that the second time today.* Off to her right was an eight-by-eight office holding a desk and chair, tall filing cabinet, shelves, and a coat stand with two sweaters hanging from it. Two metal folding chairs sat in front of the desk and behind the door, and a large corkboard hung on the wall with various OSHA regulations tacked on it.

Farther down the hallway and off to the left was an enormous workspace, walk-in refrigerator, four microwaves, a double oven, and two sinks. All the workstations were pristine. Each sandwich-making station held a box of gloves, one or two knife blocks, a tray of plastic knives, forks, and spoons, wrapping paper, Styrofoam carry-out cartons, and lids. It was a large, open space with a drain in the middle of the concrete floor.

Dak and Poulter had pulled a table and two chairs into the center of the prep room. Dak sat at the table, laptop open, typing in the evidence list while Poulter stood next to him, assigning an item number and description. After finishing each item, Poulter placed it in a box at his feet.

"What did you find?" she asked.

"Every workstation had at least a dozen knives. We're taking all the butcher blocks and knives except the plastic ones. We could have a lot of knives that fit whatever Dr. Romero finds," Dak said.

"Did you get Dr. Romero's number?" Laurent asked. "Or is it email these days?"

"What? No. That would've been unprofessional."

"Who's Dr. Romero? Are you blushing? I've never seen a big, Black dude turn red," Poulter said.

"Dr. T'ara Romero is the assistant coroner and smart as a whip," Laurent said. "You're gonna give her a call, aren't you?"

"Maybe." Dak's shoulders were hunched over the laptop, his long fingers flying.

"I'll sic your grandma on you if you don't."

"You wouldn't."

"Watch me."

"That's blackmail." Her deputy glared at her.

"Damn straight it is." Laurent grinned at Dak. She liked both of her deputies and enjoyed messing with them. The atmosphere after she won reelection had been relaxed, easygoing, the way she always envisioned her department to be. "Dr. Romero gave me a couple of business cards." She handed one to the now-flustered deputy and watched as he shoved it in his back pocket.

"After you're finished in this room, dust for prints," she said. "Concentrate on the employee areas and the rear of the diner. Out where the customers eat, we could end up fingerprinting all of Field's Crossing."

"I'll dust the surfaces—especially the door handles and the cash register. What do you want to do about the refrigerator?" Poulter asked. "Do you want the food dusted?"

"I don't think we need to do anything inside the walk-in fridge. Big Al's will be closed until we figure this out. If we need to, we can always come back, but I don't see the killer spending time in the refrigerator. He was waiting for Lisa. Peering out the back door," Laurent said.

"I'd have made myself a sandwich," Poulter said. "Eat, stab, and run."

"You would," Laurent said. "Has Marissa contacted all the employees? You need to schedule them for prints and interviews. Start with anyone who worked the last shift on Saturday and this morning." She leaned against the stainless-steel counter and folded her arms across her chest. "I've been thinking. Lisa knew her killer. The front door was locked when I got here and still is. The killer was already here and waiting for her."

"Or hid in the back of the van and jumped out when she pulled in," Poulter said. "Probably scared the shit out of her."

"Who wanted her to die and why?" Laurent asked.

"Was she married? Kids?" Dak asked.

"Husband, Keith. Grown son and daughter. Four grandkids in elementary school. After I finished the NOK, I called Aubrey to confirm something her dad said. Keith and Lisa were getting a divorce, but it was dragging on in court because they couldn't agree about money. Aubrey also claimed her father was sleeping with another woman."

"Did she know who?" Dak asked.

"She claims she didn't, but I'm going to talk to her again. Her kids were nearby, and I got the feeling they didn't know, or she didn't want them to know about the divorce, especially now that it's a moot point."

"Who inherits the diner and what would have happened to Big Al's if the divorce had gone through?" Poulter asked. "Maybe Keith killed Lisa so he could get the diner. Maybe Lisa wanted to leave the diner to her kids and Keith didn't want that."

"Or Keith's girlfriend, if she exists, wanted the diner or the money and killed Lisa." Dak stopped typing. "We've got two good suspects already."

"Keith said Lisa's name was the only one on the title to the diner, but the bank used their house as collateral, and he's half-owner of the house. So, in his mind, he's half-owner of Big Al's and that's what was holding up the divorce. That and his 401(k)," Laurent said. "We need a copy of Lisa's will."

"How'd the NOK go?" Dak asked.

"I don't think Keith DuVal gives a shit about his wife, let alone his deceased, murdered wife." Laurent unzipped her jacket, reached in, and massaged her shoulder. "He seemed relieved."

"That puts him at the top of the suspect list," Poulter said.

"He wasn't shaken up when I told him Lisa was dead," Laurent said. "He made a snarky comment about how one of her own knives stabbed her."

"How does he know she was stabbed?" Dak asked.

"Good question. I didn't tell him. He claims the diner was a great target for a robbery and Lisa must have gotten in the way. We're assuming one of the knives here is the murder weapon, and I'm guessing he made the same assumption, but I've got a few more questions for him. When I got there, he was still in his pajamas."

"What a bum. No wonder Lisa wanted a divorce," Dak said.

"He's getting higher and higher on my list," Poulter said.

"We're going to follow the money. But keep in mind this might have nothing to do with who inherits the diner. Who would want Lisa dead and why? It might be personal and not related to Big Al's," Laurent said, frowning at her two deputies. "What about the security tape for the inside of the diner? Could you see anything?"

"The interior security system was programmed to turn off when the diner closed and on again when Big Al's opened. There are no cameras in the work area or office or walk-in cooler. Everything was geared toward the front of the restaurant and the cash register." Poulter pulled out a chair and sat. "You can't even tell who's making sandwiches."

"So not all of the employees show up on the video?" Laurent asked.

Poulter nodded.

"Maybe an employee wanted the day's proceeds and got caught and stabbed her and ran. Big Al's has been cash only for as long as I've been here," Dak said.

"Then why didn't the killer take the three grand in her purse?" Laurent asked.

"Her jacket was on top of her purse on the passenger seat. Maybe the killer didn't see it," Dak said.

"So, the would-be thief killed her and didn't take the money? That makes no sense," Poulter said. "Unless he or she knew about the safe in the office, which points to an employee. I dusted it for prints, but I didn't open it.

"I'll check it out while you finish up here."

Laurent pushed away from the countertop, grabbed a couple of evidence bags, and headed down the hallway. After pulling on another pair of gloves, she flicked on the office light. Fingerprint dust lay on the arms of the chair, the top of the desk, and the doorknobs. She settled behind the desk. The top of the desk contained very little. Poulter had taken the laptop, power cord, mouse, and mouse pad. She opened the middle drawer. Pens, pencils, scissors, paper clips, ring of keys, and a couple of envelopes. Laurent slipped the scissors and keys into separate evidence bags and laid them on the desk. She picked up one of the envelopes. Utility bill from Field's Crossing. Next envelope. Return address was the Internal Revenue Service. Laurent slid the paper out, smoothed it on the desk, and snapped a picture before reading. Big Al's Diner was being audited. The owners were required to send income verification and proof of deductible expenses for the previous five years. After the records were reviewed, a determination would be made. The entire process could take up to six months. Penalties would apply from the time of the infraction. *Is this normal? Do restaurants get audited on a regular basis? Does this have anything to do with Big Al's being cash only? Has Big Al's been audited before? Is this connected to Lisa's murder?* She refolded the paper, slipped it back into the envelope, and slid it into an evidence bag.

Laurent opened the left-side top drawer. Paychecks, tape dispenser, stapler, staple remover, Post-it notes. The bottom drawer was a built-in filing cabinet, arranged alphabetically. Laurent flipped through. Paid bills, current invoices, commercial insurance policy for Big Al's. No will. No ownership papers. She turned to the right side of the desk. One door, locked. Laurent pulled the ring of keys from the evidence bag. The second key she tried worked. Behind the door was a safe. Taped to the top was the combination. *Unbelievable. Keith was right about security. There is none.* She dialed the numbers, pulled down on the handle, and the door swung open.

Empty.

Relocking the safe, Laurent picked up the evidence bags and scanned the rest of the small room. After turning off the light, she walked to the prep room and handed the bags to Poulter.

"What did you find?" Dak asked.

"Pair of scissors. Bunch of keys. Empty safe and a letter from the IRS," Laurent said.

Dak and Poulter snapped their heads around to stare at her.

"Say that again?" Dak said.

"Our favorite diner is being audited by the IRS. Nothing good ever comes from the IRS contacting you," Laurent said.

"Any way this was a suicide?" Poulter asked.

"Don't think so. The angle of the knife doesn't work," Laurent said. "I'm contacting the bank to see when the last deposit was made. A deposit on Saturday night would explain an empty safe on Sunday. We'll be able to rule out robbery as a motive, but I'd like to know who made the deposit. Theoretically, that should be the last person in the safe."

"So, Lisa leaves the egg hunt, parks back here, goes inside the diner, grabs today's deposit—the three grand in her purse—comes out, climbs into the van, and is killed?" Poulter asked.

"Something like that."

"We're done in here," Dak said. "I'll start boxing everything up and sticking them in your SUV."

"What do you want us to do with all those milk tins and jugs in the eating area?" Poulter asked.

"Leave them for now. They're just for decoration. The killer might have dumped the knife in one of them, but I don't see it. Lisa was killed outside. I doubt he'd return inside and put the murder weapon in a milk stool. Why traipse through the diner to hide the weapon? Why not take it and shove it into the dumpster or in your own vehicle or inside the van or take it with you and get rid of it someplace else? He'd risk getting caught."

The front door rattled. A face peered in.

"Who's that?" Poulter asked. "The closed sign is still up."

Laurent unlocked the front door and cracked it open. Dak had wound the crime scene tape extremely tight. "Can I help you?"

"We're here to pick up our paychecks." The teenage girl wore a bright yellow Big Al's T-shirt.

"I'll be there in a minute." Laurent closed the door and relocked it. "I'm going out to the front. There's a couple of teenagers asking for their paychecks." She exited the diner through the back door and strolled to the front.

Laurent pulled out her notebook. "Names?"

"Brooke Cunningham."

"Hunter Anderson."

"Should we, like, come back in fifteen minutes?" Brooke asked.

"Big Al's won't be open today."

"Why not? Lisa always let us pick up our paychecks at six on Sunday night," Hunter said.

"How did she usually handle that?" Laurent asked.

"The checks are in the top left-hand drawer of her desk. You go in and she hands it to you." Hunter hitched his backpack higher on his shoulder.

"What's wrong? Why are the cops here?" Brooke asked.

"I'm sorry to tell you, but Lisa has passed away."

"She's dead?" Brooke's eyes widened.

Laurent nodded. "When was the last time you saw her?"

"Yesterday. I open on Saturday and Sunday. Obviously, not today," Hunter said. "Did she have a heart attack? She was kinda chunky."

Brooke smacked him. "Shut up. You're gonna be chunky like that when you get old. Just look at your mom and dad."

"Genetics isn't everything."

"If Lisa didn't have a heart attack, how'd she die?" Brooke asked.

"That will be up to the coroner to determine."

"Coroner? Why do you need a coroner? Was she murdered or something?" Brooke asked.

"No comment." Laurent glanced past the heads of the two teenage employees and saw two more cars pull into the parking lot. *More employees?*

"We're the first ones here," Hunter said. "I gotta text Jaime."

And this is how it starts. With a text from a teenager to another who tells his mom and dad who tell their friends. In a few hours, the entire town of Field's Crossing would know Lisa DuVal, owner of Big Al's Diner, was dead. Murdered. Technology was a blessing and a curse. *More a curse.*

"What about my paycheck?" Hunter asked. "What should I do with the keys?"

*   *   *

Even though it was Sunday, Laurent called the president of Farmers Bank and Judge Jenkins. She had found the paychecks in the top left-hand drawer of the desk and wanted outside confirmation that it was okay to distribute them. Laurent, Dak, and Poulter took turns verifying driver's licenses, passing out paychecks, and making every employee sign the clipboard. It was after eight at night before they finished.

It was interesting to note who did not show up for their paycheck. Four people. Laurent listed those names and matched them against this week's work schedule. All four worked the lunch hour. Monday through Friday. Stacy Simmons. Ruby Rae Evans. Diane Wells. Hannah Burton. All females. Considering the time of day they worked, Laurent assumed the women were moms, part-timers. High school kids from three o'clock to close during the week and Saturday and Sunday. *Looks like Lisa employed two different workforces.*

Laurent confiscated twenty keys from employees. "Keith was right about Lisa being loose with security."

"You think? Paychecks in a drawer, every high school kid has a key to the building, and the combination to the safe is taped on top of it." Dak snorted. "It's amazing she wasn't robbed."

Woodruff Street in front of Big Al's had become a virtual drive-thru. Employees picking up checks and curiosity seekers hanging around the diner. The sun had set, and the overhead streetlights flickered on. Laurent, Dak, and Poulter had finished their preliminary search and inventory and were getting ready to lock up the diner.

"CSU called back and they're expecting us. Who wants to drive all this down to Indianapolis? Whitmore's going to give me a call in the morning about the dumpster and vans. If we have to, we'll finish up with them tomorrow. Let's hope he sends a crew," Laurent said.

"I'll drive the stuff down," Dak said.

"That'll give you time to call that hot coroner." Poulter slipped out the back door, jogged to his cruiser, and shot out of the parking lot, his goofy laugh lingering in the air.

Laurent pulled the last box of evidence toward her.

"Don't you dare." Dak pointed a finger at her. "The doctor told you not to lift anything heavier than a gallon of milk. That box weighs more than a gallon of milk. Take some ibuprofen and go home. I got this." He turned off the exterior lighting and motioned for Laurent to exit in front of him before locking the back door.

Laurent held up both hands in defeat. Her shoulder did hurt.

CHAPTER SEVEN

"CAN YOU TELL me Lisa's schedule for the weekend?" Laurent followed Keith DuVal on a winding path through the living room. She stopped in the doorway leading to the kitchen. Two of the maple cabinets were missing their doors and a curtain hung in place of a pantry door. Congealed bacon grease coated the bottom of a frying pan and eggshells lay on the countertop. The sink was filled with unwashed dishes. Big Al's coffee mugs were piled next to the full sink and the stovetop was stacked with dirty pots and pans.

"I told you yesterday," Keith snapped. "I don't know if she even slept here."

"What do you mean?" Laurent pulled out a chair, unzipped her jacket, and laid her notebook on the slightly greasy table. Keith was her first interview on Monday morning following the death of his wife, Lisa. The NOK didn't count as an interview.

"I told you about our marital difficulties. The ongoing divorce. The endless compromises I made. The shit Lisa put me through." He lit a cigarette and blew smoke toward the ceiling.

"Can you be more specific?"

"We've had separate bedrooms for the last ten years, so I've got no idea if Lisa slept here this weekend. Hell, for all I know, she's got a cot in that damn diner," he retorted.

"Let's assume she slept here."

"If she was here, she was already gone by the time I got up on Saturday. She receives a delivery late on Friday afternoon and sticks it in the walk-in refrigerator. Then she goes in early to sort and repackage so she's ready for the lunch crowd and any special events. People order from Big Al's for graduation parties, bar mitzvahs, stuff like that. She's been doing it for years."

"Her weekend schedule was well known?"

"She'd even let customers pick up before Big Al's opened if they needed to. The customer was everything to her. Me, the kids, not so much."

"What about Sunday?"

"This weekend was a little different because of the egg hunt," he admitted. "I'm assuming she was at Big Al's early in the morning to load the vans and get to the park. I hope you appreciate all the time she donated to your pet cause."

"Did you help her this weekend or do you know who helped her?"

Keith grunted. "I never worked at Big Al's. That was all Lisa. Check the work schedule. Ask Aubrey."

"What was your schedule this weekend? Start with Saturday morning."

"I made coffee. Ate breakfast. Got gas in my car. Came home. Put on the basketball game. Love college basketball."

"How long did you watch TV?" Laurent resisted the urge to slap away the smoke. She hated the smell and the stench it left on her clothes. *Cigar smoke doesn't bother me, so why does cigarette smoke annoy me?*

"Most of the afternoon."

"Did you leave the house? Have anyone over to watch the game?" Laurent asked.

"Doug came around two on Saturday and watched the game with me."

"Aubrey's husband? What time did he leave?"

"Four thirty or five."

"Then what did you do?"

"Showered. Shaved. Got ready," Keith said.

"For what?"

Keith laughed. "I had a date and no, it wasn't with my wife. You've lived in Field's Crossing long enough to know what's going on."

"Why don't you spell it out for me?" Laurent scooted her chair closer to the kitchen table, pen poised over her notebook. She wanted to capture the exact phrases out of Keith's mouth. His attitude toward his wife was dismissive as though he didn't care about her, the diner, even his grown children. *Am I sitting at the killer's table? Was Keith so fed up with Lisa that he killed her?*

"Monica and I have had a relationship for the last six months. Lisa and I haven't had sex in forever. She shut down a few years after Andrew was born."

"That's when you started seeing other women?" Laurent frowned. *Who told me Lisa's husband was cheating on her? Where did I hear that?*

"Not right away," he said. "But soon after that. A man's gotta sow his oats. Get some every so often." Keith leaned back on two legs of the kitchen chair and smirked at Laurent. "I had a date with Monica on Saturday night. I picked her up at that crummy apartment complex on First Street at six thirty. We went to Jalapeños for dinner and saw *Captain Marvel* and then I slept over."

"Where did you go after you left Monica?"

"Here. Home."

"You didn't go to Webster Park for the Easter egg hunt? Watch your grandkids? Go to Aubrey's for dinner?" Laurent watched Keith's face as a red blush crept over it. *At least he's embarrassed about not spending time with his family.*

Keith sucked on his cigarette.

"What was Lisa's reaction to your date on Saturday night?" Laurent asked.

"She didn't give a damn. Told me ten years ago to get a vasectomy and then I could screw anyone I wanted. She killed our marriage and then she bought Big Al's."

"Did you cheat on her before she bought Big Al's?"

Keith looked away. "Maybe. I don't remember."

"What year did Lisa buy the diner?"

"Sometime around 2009, maybe 2010. She signed a buyout agreement with Al Jr. I let her use the house as collateral."

"Very gracious of you." The sarcastic comment slipped out before Laurent could stop it. She understood why Lisa didn't care about her husband anymore. His attitude toward women was revolting. *He should have lived during the Stone Age.* "So, you're both sleeping in separate bedrooms. Was Lisa seeing anyone?"

"That bitch had better not have been fucking some asshole." The front two legs of Keith's kitchen chair slammed to the floor; his fists bunched. "She's my wife."

"But it's okay for you to sleep with any woman you want?"

"Yeah. She even said so, but I never said she could sleep around. I'd kill her for that. Making a fool out of me."

And there's motive. Laurent took her time in capturing Keith's exact words in her notebook. She looked across the table. "Where were you on Sunday?"

"I woke up in Monica's bed. Fortunately, that pain-in-the-ass manager was out of town for the weekend. Old fool posted it everywhere. He's lucky he didn't get pranked or spray-painted by a bunch of high school kids."

"What time did you leave?"

"Late morning. Eleven or so. Came home. Threw in some laundry."

I was chatting with Lisa about that time.

"Then what?" Laurent asked.

"Monica came over. I turned on the basketball game. She brought Chinese. We ate. Aubrey called looking for Lisa and then she called again later saying you were coming here. The rest you know." Keith slumped in his chair and closed his eyes.

"Let's talk about the divorce proceedings."

"I filed for divorce a year ago, and we haven't been able to come to terms with our assets," Keith said.

"What does that mean?"

"I want my half of that fuckin' diner." Keith straightened up and pounded his fist on the table.

"What's the holdup?"

"Lisa claims because I make the same income as the diner, I don't get anything, and since I never set foot in the place, I'm not entitled to a penny. What the diner nets is the same as my net income. Now that she's dead, Big Al's belongs to me."

"What does the divorce judge say?" Laurent asked. *Keith expects to inherit Big Al's. Who legally owns Big Al's now?*

"He hasn't said anything yet. He expects us to act like adults and settle it ourselves. Lisa's such a child. She wouldn't budge."

"The divorce becomes moot now, doesn't it?"

"Thank God. I get it all. Goddamn lawyer'll charge me an arm and a leg, but at least I can sell." Keith settled back in his chair and laced his fingers behind his head.

"You didn't want to buy the diner?"

"Hell, no. Restaurants are nothing but time-consuming enterprises that don't make money. After Lisa bought the diner from Al Jr., she was never home. Opened the diner in the morning and closed it every night."

Laurent looked at Keith. "Who do you think killed your wife?"

"I got no idea. Someone who's hard up for cash. Maybe one of those high school kids."

"Have you received any threats? Any strange phone calls?"

He shook his head.

Laurent heard the front door slam and, a few seconds later, a young woman appeared.

"Sheriff, this is Monica Sun, my girlfriend. We figured we'd kill two birds with one stone."

CHAPTER EIGHT

BOTTLE-BLONDE DOESN'T REALLY *work. Maybe bottle-white.*
Laurent scooted back in her chair, rose, and stretched out her hand.
Monica Sun briefly touched Laurent's fingers. Not a handshake.

"For the record, would you state your name and address."
Laurent picked up her pen and looked at the young woman sitting
on Keith's lap, arms draped around his neck. Monica, girlfriend
of Keith, was in her mid-twenties, but trying to look twelve. Her
almost-white hair was tied in a high ponytail and the army boots
had three-inch platform heels. Her lips were painted bright red and
both ears lined with little silver hoops from the lobe to the top of
the cartilage. Her nose was pierced. A motorcycle jacket hung to
her waist and a dirty white T-shirt topped black leggings. As she
straddled Keith, Monica gave him a long kiss, running her fingers
through his gray-brown hair. Laurent waited for Monica and Keith
to finish their lengthy embrace.

"No tape recorders." Monica slid off Keith's lap. She moved a
white plastic chair next to Keith and sat.

Laurent held up her pen.

"I suppose you can take notes. My name is Monica Sun, 501
First Street, Apartment 2-A, although not for long."

"Are you moving?"

Monica rolled her eyes. "I packed up my apartment this morning and told that asshole manager I was leaving. Jerk wouldn't prorate the month."

"What's your new address?"

"Right here."

Laurent narrowed her gaze at Keith. "Your wife is murdered on Sunday and the next day your girlfriend moves in?"

"I was moving in anyway. Lisa agreed to move out this past weekend, but then she went and died. Even better," Monica said.

Keith frowned.

"Do you know where Lisa was planning to live?" Laurent saw a few wheels starting to click in Keith's head.

"Who gives a shit? Lisa didn't give a crap about her family. All she cared about was her stupid little diner, and she still wouldn't give him his half of the restaurant. Who do you think supported her when she was low on cash? And now, the whole thing is ours."

"You might want to wait until the will is read. Aubrey and her brother, Andrew, may inherit part or all of Big Al's," Laurent said.

Monica flicked her fingers as though Aubrey and Andrew were gnats. Not worthy of mentioning. "The building doesn't matter. It's the recipes that count."

"I'm guessing Aubrey's got them memorized," Laurent said.

"If she uses them, we'll sue," Monica said.

Laurent looked at Keith. "Sue your daughter?"

"It won't come to that. If I have to split Big Al's with the kids, I'll pay Aubrey to manage the diner and Andrew will get a percent of net proceeds," he said.

"Have they agreed to this?"

"Not yet, but they will."

"Why?" Laurent stretched the fingers in her writing hand. *I'm going to need another notebook.*

"You think this is motive for getting rid of that bitch," Monica snapped. "We worked this out before she wound up dead in the driveway."

"Who's *we?*"

"Me and Keith."

"Aubrey and Andrew knew about this?" Laurent asked.

"We were just planning, dreaming about our future one night. That's all," Keith said.

"Don't go thinking this is motive for murder, 'cuz it's not." Monica pointed a long, manicured fingernail at Laurent.

"Let's get back to Lisa's murder. Monica, can you tell me your schedule for the weekend?"

"I worked all day Saturday and then we went to dinner and a movie and fucked each other the rest of the night. Want to know the details?" Monica smirked.

Laurent pointed her pen at Monica. "The two of you are claiming to alibi one another for Saturday night." She made a note to ask the apartment manager if he had security cameras in his building. "Where do you work?"

"Cutting Edge Salon, right on Field Street. I do hair and nails."

"How long have you worked there?"

"Couple of years."

"Was Lisa a customer?" Laurent asked.

"I never saw her at the shop."

"How long have the two of you been dating?" Laurent wasn't exactly sure how to ask that question. A married man dating his girlfriend.

"Six months," Monica said.

"Where'd you meet?"

"At the salon. Keith came in for a haircut and walked out with a date." Monica smoothed the hair behind Keith's ear.

Laurent glanced at Keith. His demeanor hadn't changed since Monica waltzed in. Goofy smile, gaze never leaving the large bosom, one hand running up and down Monica's back, a finger dipping under the thong, peeking out just below the tramp stamp.

"What about Sunday?"

"My sweetie left around eleven and I started packing. Then I drove here and spent the afternoon. Curled up on the couch. Watching basketball. Screwing."

"You weren't here when I arrived to give Keith the news about his wife. Where'd you go?" Laurent asked.

"Aubrey called and said you were on your way. That's when I left."

Monica and Keith alibi each other for most of Sunday.

"That's all for now. Please text me your cell phone number." Laurent looked at Keith. "I'd like to see Lisa's bedroom."

"What about Big Al's? We need to get in there." Monica laid both manicured hands on the table.

"The entire building is a crime scene," Laurent said. "Anyone caught in, on, or around Big Al's will be tossed in jail and charged with trespassing and interfering with a murder investigation."

Monica sniffed. "You can't keep it closed for long. We need the money."

"What do you need money for?"

"To pay bills," Monica snapped.

*   *   *

Laurent pulled on gloves and opened the door to Lisa's bedroom, leaving Keith and Monica in the kitchen. The bedroom smelled of mold and mildew. She stepped over the threshold, switched on the overhead light, and closed the door. She gazed around Lisa's almost empty bedroom.

The room was small and dark. Heavy black curtains covered the window, not allowing any sunlight to touch the room. The faded pink walls matched the stuffed chair sitting in the corner. A double bed was pushed up against the far wall, completely stripped, the box spring and mattress yellowing and sagging. The dusty outline of a lamp showed on top of the nightstand.

In the closet hung one pair of black pants and one white shirt. An old pair of tennis shoes lay on the floor. Laurent bagged every item of clothing. The dresser drawers held one pair of underwear, one bra, and one pair of socks. No pajamas, no sweaters, no slippers. It was clear to Laurent that Lisa had moved out. Were these clothes meant to be worn on Sunday? Did Lisa intend Saturday night to be her last night in this house? Did Lisa know her husband had a date that night and expected the house to be empty? The house on Cardinal Street was less than half a mile from the diner. If Lisa knew about Keith and Monica's date, she could have been planning to sleep here and would have been gone before Keith returned. She wrote a note to herself. *Where did Lisa sleep on Saturday night? Where's her stuff?*

Laurent opened the drawer to the nightstand and pulled out several sheets of paper clipped together with the name "Andrew" written on the top page. She flipped through. Moonshine recipes. She slid the papers into an evidence bag and labeled it.

A few minutes later, Laurent finished her search and paused at the door looking at the sad room. No photographs, empty walls.

What was she expecting? Laurent shook her head. The chubby, cheerful Lisa from Big Al's did not exist in this room.

*   *   *

Laurent trudged to her police SUV, climbed in, and reread her notes. *Pay bills, my ass.* Monica was at least twenty-five years younger than the married man she was dating. *Wonder if that's a pattern with her?* The hair stylist had been unzipping Keith's jeans as he slammed the front door behind her. Laurent shoved the thought away.

It was a safe assumption Keith would get all or part of Big Al's, but deciding how to divvy it up before Lisa was dead indicated he had a plan. Premeditation. Did Keith kill his wife so he could inherit? Did Monica help Keith kill his wife? Monica certainly didn't like Lisa, and in fact, seemed to loathe her. Laurent wasn't sure she believed anything either one of them said.

The next item she wanted to check was Keith's credit card. There should be a charge for dinner at Jalapeños and the local movie theater. If there were no charges on his credit card, Keith and Monica could claim they paid cash. There were still some jobs that received cash tips and Monica as a hair stylist was one.

Laurent put the SUV in gear and flinched. She glanced at the dashboard clock. *Time for ibuprofen.* She stopped next to Monica's Toyota as she dug in a pocket for the medicine. How long does it take to pack up an apartment? The back seat of the old Toyota was filled to the roof with clothes, shoes, and blankets, while the front passenger seat held a laundry basket piled high with makeup, blow dryer, curling iron, sprays, and bottles of shampoo and conditioner. She saw no furniture. Or food. Did Monica live off takeout?

Everybody's got ketchup and mustard and mayo in the fridge. Salt and pepper.

Monica was definitely moving up in the world by moving in with Keith. The question was what did she do to make it happen? Was she guilty of murder? Did she kill Lisa with or without Keith's knowledge or assistance?

Monica said they needed money to pay bills. Whose bills? How much did hair stylists / manicurists make? Was Monica in debt and expecting Keith to help her out? Laurent sighed and shoved the bottle of ibuprofen back in her coat pocket. She eased her foot off the brake. It was time to interview Aubrey Holmes.

CHAPTER NINE

"I DON'T GIVE a crap who you've got scheduled. My mom is dead, and I need my roots touched up before the funeral. I don't give a shit about someone who's been coming in every Thursday morning for the last twenty years. Bump her."

Laurent stood in the foyer of Aubrey's house and waited for her to finish her phone tirade. From the front door, she could see all the way to the rear of Aubrey's house and into the backyard.

"These people don't understand." Aubrey waved her phone in the air and motioned Laurent to follow her into the kitchen. Five baskets of laundry were stacked into each other along the back kitchen wall, near the laundry room. "I don't know why my cleaning lady can't get more done. She works for four hours and always leaves me the folding. I hate folding laundry," Aubrey complained. "A lot of people will be stopping by in the next few days and the house needs to look immaculate. I'm making her come again. Maybe this time, she'll actually clean something."

"What a beautiful kitchen." Laurent perched on a stool at the island counter.

"Thank you. I just love the farmhouse look. I think the shiplap ceiling is my favorite feature. Some mornings I sit in the breakfast nook for hours," Aubrey said. "I absolutely love the farmhouse sink. I don't have to run the dishwasher every day."

"How do you feel about the gray cabinets?" Laurent asked. "I'm thinking of redoing my mudroom and kitchen. Enlarging the window over the sink and adding a counter next to the dryer so I can fold clothes there."

"Love 'em. They hide all Jake and Justin's fingerprints. Abby at 'Tiques and Things gave me the name of her decorator. She's fabulous. Let me send you her info." Aubrey whipped her phone out of her back pocket. The young woman had pencil-thin eyebrows and wore a black turtleneck, her blonde hair spilling over her shoulders, and the skinny jeans had a worn rear pocket where her cell phone sat.

"Thank you. I'll write it down in my notebook." Laurent copied the decorator's information, knowing she would never call. She glanced down. "Whoa. Who's this?"

Aubrey scooped up a tiny white dog. "This is Dolly. She's mine. I take her everywhere."

"I've heard about purse dogs but never seen one. May I pet her?" Laurent waited until Aubrey nodded. "What breed is she?"

"Bichon frise. She weighs just under five pounds."

"She's so pretty." Laurent stroked the top of the little dog's head and scratched behind the ears. "How long have you had her?"

"Two years. She's been such a comfort to me."

Laurent opened her notebook and picked up her pen. "I've got a few questions. Do you think you can answer them?"

Aubrey nodded.

"Why don't you tell me about your mom?" Laurent settled onto the uncomfortable counter stool.

"Mom started part-time at the diner when Andrew and I were in elementary school. Lunch only. As we got older, she took on more responsibility. Full-time manager. After school, my brother and I would run to the diner. Mom made the best after-school snacks. My friends were jealous. Mom always donated food for my class and Andrew's class for field trips and holiday parties."

"I would have liked to have been in your class," Laurent said. "Tell me about the relationship between your parents."

"Thank you for not saying anything in front of my kids. They didn't know anything was wrong between Grandma and Grandpa, and now, obviously, it doesn't matter." Aubrey put Dolly on the floor, opened the dishwasher, and began putting clean glasses into the upper cabinets. "I think they both had had enough. Dad was tired of being second fiddle to a diner. Mom was always thinking about Big Al's, jotting notes to herself, trying out recipes on us."

"I'd have been a guinea pig when she tried a new recipe," Laurent said.

"We all enjoyed that. She had a knack," Aubrey admitted. "Her chocolate cake was the best."

"My mom made a cake like your mom's. She used mayonnaise. Said it kept the cake moist."

"That was Mom's secret ingredient," Aubrey said. "I didn't think anyone knew about it."

Laurent tipped her head. "It was a long time ago. You mentioned your parents were getting a divorce. Were they faithful to each other?"

Aubrey slid the top rack back into the dishwasher and pulled out the lower rack. "No."

"Would you elaborate, please?"

Aubrey ran her manicured nails through her long blonde hair, a red flush dotting her cheeks. "Dad's been cheating on Mom for the last twenty years. Could be more. I really didn't catch on until I was in high school."

"Same person?"

"God, no. The older he gets, the younger the woman. Such a cliché."

"Name?" Laurent clicked her pen.

"Monica something or other. I don't keep track anymore."

"What do you know about her?"

"The bitch is younger than me."

"You've met her?" Laurent raised an eyebrow.

Aubrey groaned. "Doug and I have a standing date night. First Saturday of the month. We went to Jalapeños for dinner, and right after we ordered our margaritas, my dad walked in with Monica. She was hanging all over him and he was loving it. Patting her on the fanny. He didn't need to look down her blouse. She had on a spaghetti strap top that showed off her nipples and she looked like a hooker. Everyone stopped talking and stared at her and then Dad saw me and Doug and came over. I wanted to crawl under the table. I was so embarrassed. Doug told him we were on our date night and didn't want to talk. So, they got a booth and spent the entire dinner kissing and squeezing each other's private parts. They ruined our night out."

"Did your mom have an affair?"

Aubrey grimaced. "If she did, she hid it well. I never saw her with anyone other than Vickie. They've been friends for years. Went to Sam's Club and Costco every week. Mom never let her pay when she came in for lunch. I'm glad Mom had such a good friend. Every woman needs a Vickie."

Agreed. Laurent's best friend, Starr, was a loud, boisterous person, but she was loyal. And opinionated. She gave Laurent advice. Advice Laurent didn't want to hear.

"A divorce was pending? Who filed first?"

"Dad."

"On what grounds?" Laurent furrowed her brow. She would have expected Lisa to file for divorce based on infidelity.

"Unfixable breakdown. But we all know they were fed up with each other."

"What was holding up the divorce?" Laurent asked.

"Dad expected Mom to pay him alimony because he thought Big Al's made more money than he did. Mom said he wasn't getting a penny from the diner, and she wanted half of his 401(k)."

"What did the lawyers say?"

"When they looked, they found Mom's name was the only one on the title to Big Al's, but the bank used their house as collateral for the loan and buyout period. Dad and Mom own the house on Cardinal Street jointly. The lawyers were fighting it out in court." Aubrey shoved the lower rack into the dishwasher, removed the silverware tray, and placed it on the marble countertop. She opened a drawer and dropped forks, knives, and spoons into their slots. Black-handled knives were slid into the butcher block.

"What does your father do for a living?"

"He's in IT at Columbia Hospital."

"How do you think they would have resolved the issue?" Laurent asked.

"All-out war."

"Meaning?"

"It would have dragged on and on. Years. The judge may have had to step in and decide," Aubrey said.

"Was your father angry enough to do something about it?"

"You think my dad killed my mom to speed up the divorce and get control of Big Al's?" Aubrey pointed a finger at Laurent. "How dare you say that. Are you nuts? Where would you get such an asinine idea? They may have had their differences, even separate lives, but my father would never kill my mother."

Laurent laid her pen on the counter and sat back. "I'm trying to find your mother's killer. I have to ask a lot of questions that may appear offensive or accusatory. That's my job."

"Find a better way to say it," Aubrey snapped. "I've been through enough."

"Other than Vickie Wright, who was your mom friends with?"

"She was on good terms with all the other women business owners."

"Who else?"

"I'm sure she considered the women who worked at lunchtime and on the weekends to be her friends," Aubrey said. "They certainly worshipped the ground she walked on."

"Any other friends?" Laurent asked.

"I think that's everyone."

"Who came to dinner at your house on Sunday?"

"Obviously, my entire family, including Andrew and Michelle and their two kids. My dad, get this, asked me if he could bring his girlfriend. Of course, I said no, what are you thinking? He didn't show up at all. Probably spent the day with the bitch. How could he do that to me? All the trouble I go to making Easter dinner." Aubrey plucked a tissue out of the box and wiped her eyes. "Dad said Mom was stabbed. Who would do such a thing?" Aubrey burst into tears and sank onto the built-in bench in the bay window. She picked up Dolly and hugged the dog to her chest.

Laurent picked up the tissue box and set it next to the distraught woman before returning to her seat at the counter. "What time did you get home from the egg hunt?"

"Noon."

"What time did everyone arrive?"

"We all left Webster Park about the same time. Andrew and Michelle brought their kids to the egg hunt. Doug and I drove separately because the boys always make such a mess. Jumping in mud puddles. We put down towels so they wouldn't trash my car." Aubrey reached for another tissue.

"What time did Andrew and Michelle leave? Was everyone here the entire time?"

"Around six," Aubrey said. "The kids played in the backyard most of the afternoon. We adults sat around drinking and sneaking Easter candy out of the kids' baskets."

"What happens to Big Al's with your mom gone?"

"I'm assuming Dad gets it all or he has to split it with me and Andrew," Aubrey said. "Like I said, Dad assumed he owned half of Big Al's. Mom said, 'You never worked a day in the diner, you get nothing.' Dad said, 'I supported you all these years, you owe me.' After Mom bought Big Al's, she rarely took a day off. One day for my wedding, and one for Andrew's."

"What about Andrew?" Laurent asked.

"My sister-in-law's family paid for their entire wedding. Michelle wanted a big, fancy reception at some country club in Indianapolis. The reception must have cost fifty thousand. There's no way Mom and Dad could afford that kind of wedding for me and Doug. Michelle comes from money. That's how Andrew was able to open Cityscape, his rooftop wine bar. They've never had to struggle to make ends meet. Must be nice."

"Are you and Doug having financial difficulties?"

"What? No. No way. I just meant it would be nice not to have to juggle paying bills. I'd like to pay them once a month and then forget about it. We're fine."

"You worked at Big Al's. What were your hours?" Laurent circled a dollar sign in her notebook with *AH* and *DH* next to it.

"Monday through Friday, eleven to three."

"Twenty hours a week. Great part-time job," Laurent said. "What does Doug do?"

"Service manager at the Ford dealership."

"May I ask how much Doug's annual salary is and your hourly wage?"

"Doug makes ninety thousand dollars a year and I make fifteen dollars an hour, but my job was more than a part-time job. I helped Mom develop new recipes. I made bank deposits. I worked more as a manager than the cashiers or sandwich-makers."

"Who else worked with you?" Laurent asked.

"I don't remember all the high school kids I've hired and trained. The only regulars are the women who work during lunch and serve alcohol on the weekends. I'll write their names down for you. Stacy Simmons was there every day like me. She managed the alcohol and dessert bar. I managed the rest."

"Walk me through the process. What happens when I come in and order an Italian sub on white?" Laurent asked.

"I'd give you the first-responder discount, write down your order, and pass it through to the prep room. One of the sandwich-makers in the back grabs the paper, makes your sandwich, and brings it out to you," Aubrey said.

"Kind of old-fashioned."

"Mom liked it that way. There was no paper trail for the IRS to follow. I think Al Jr. taught her that. The man probably under-reported his income his whole life. Same as his dad."

"Did your mom underreport her income?"

"I have no idea," Aubrey said. "Ask Vickie. She's the accountant Mom hired."

"Did you know about the IRS audit?"

"Mom told me the IRS was checking Big Al's income for the last five years and she needed to send in copies of a whole bunch of things in the next sixty days."

"What was her reaction?" Laurent asked.

"She didn't want anyone other than me and Vickie to know."

"Why?"

"Her reputation. Everyone knows that Al Sr. and Al Jr. sold illegal moonshine out the back door and she didn't want people to think that she was cheating the IRS and not reporting income the way those two did. I think those first two years she almost went under."

"She wasn't upset or scared about the audit?"

"I don't think so."

"You made bank deposits Monday through Friday. Before or after your shift?" Laurent asked.

"After."

"Who made deposits on Saturday and Sunday?"

"As far as I know, Mom put all the cash from the weekend in the safe in her desk. I made the deposit on Monday for every-thing the diner brought in from three in the afternoon on Friday until the same time on Monday."

"Can you give me a rough estimate of how much money would have been in the safe after Big Al's closed on Sundays?" Laurent asked.

Aubrey put Dolly on the floor. "Weekends were crazy busy. If I had to guess I'd say double, maybe triple of a weekday."

"Got a dollar amount?" *Why is Aubrey evading the question? She's got to know I'm gonna subpoena the bank. Monday afternoon's deposit should be the largest of the entire week. I wonder if those bank deposits she claims to have made were really made. Maybe Aubrey dipped her hand in the till before she got to the bank.* "Did you count the cash at the diner or at the bank?" Laurent asked.

"Bank."

"Did your mom suspect?"

"Suspect what?" Aubrey tossed her long hair over her shoulder. Laurent waited.

"Are you insinuating I stole money from my mom?"

"Not insinuating. I'm asking outright. Did all the money your mom asked you to deposit make it into the bank account?" Laurent stared at Aubrey.

"Every. Single. Dime." Aubrey shot to her feet and stalked to the kitchen counter. She leaned against it and folded her arms across her chest.

"We found a roll of cash in your mother's purse," Laurent said. "You just said your mom put the cash from the weekend in the safe in her desk. Do you know why she was carrying so much money?"

"I have no idea."

"Were there any bills or local vendors that she paid in cash?"

"She may have decided to buy more of those stupid milk stools and tins that she's got everywhere in the dining room. God, I hope not." Aubrey rolled her eyes.

"Who do you think killed your mom?"

"My first guess would be Stacy Simmons."

"Why do you think that?"

"Mom and Stacy were friends in high school, but something happened after Mom and Dad got married. I don't know what. After that, they both worked at Big Al's and hit another bump in the road. Al Jr. decided to retire and both Mom and Stacy submitted bids to buy Big Al's. Obviously, Mom won."

"And she kept Stacy on?" Laurent narrowed her gaze at Aubrey. *There was no way Lisa kept Stacy as an employee because they used to be friends. Why would Stacy continue to work at Big Al's instead of finding another job? Something's not right. What does Stacy have on Lisa? Blackmail?* "Why did Al Jr. accept your mom's bid and not Stacy's?"

"Mom said the reason Al Jr. accepted her bid was because Stacy had no collateral. She was living with her parents, but until they died, Stacy didn't own that home. After Mom took over, they had a big, hairy fight, but Stacy and Mom were stuck. Mom didn't dare fire Stacy while she was taking care of her parents because she knew if she fired Stacy, she'd lose business and tarnish her reputation. Everyone knows everyone else's business in a small town. I think it was a relief to both Mom and Stacy after Mr. and Mrs. Simmons died. And Stacy lives a few blocks from the diner and could walk to work, rain, snow, or shine, which Mom needed."

"Your mom worked from open to close every day," Laurent said. "Stacy was there to give her a break?"

Aubrey nodded. "Mom did all the ordering and paid the bills. She needed a few hours every afternoon to keep up with the paperwork, especially payroll. I don't know why she didn't use QuickBooks or some accounting software. It would have been so much easier and saved her so much time, but she liked to do it by hand."

"Does Stacy have any children?" Laurent asked. Friends through high school, then both women bid on the same business and then the winner doesn't fire the loser. *A bit of an insult to the loser. How did Stacy feel about Lisa? Another suspect.*

"Divorced."

"Doesn't mean you can't have kids." The minute she said the words, Laurent wished she could take them back.

"I forgot. You kept your daughter hidden for quite a while," Aubrey said. "How's that going? Does she like you? Does she speak to you? What does she want?"

"It's going," Laurent said. "What do you think Stacy's motive would be for killing your mom?"

"Revenge."

"For what?" Laurent asked.

"Being humiliated."

"Any chance Stacy will inherit Big Al's?"

"Not a snowball's chance in hell."

Laurent slid off the uncomfortable stool and pulled on her windbreaker. She slid her pen and notebook into her pocket. "That's all for now. I'm calling Judge Jenkins to see what the procedure is if your mom died with a will or without a will."

"When can we reopen Big Al's?" Aubrey picked up Dolly before leading the way to the front door.

"I have no idea. I think we have to locate the will and ask Judge Jenkins to read it and decide about reopening. I'm taking another walk-thru in case I missed any evidence, but I'll have to wait for the judge's decision. Or possibly the executor's decision."

"You know, I really need your personal cell phone number. I have a right to know what you're doing to find out who killed my mom."

"You can always leave a message at the non-emergency number. Dispatch will contact me if it's important."

No way you're getting my cell phone number. You'd call me day and night to complain. I don't need that.

Laurent trotted down the front stairs. It was nice to see someone in the DuVal family who was upset about Lisa's death. A few of the high school employees had cried when Laurent told them about Lisa, but that was it. Keith wasn't upset, more relieved. Laurent wondered whose fingerprints would be on the murder weapon when they found it and hoped it wasn't one of the high school kids. She wiggled her shoulders. Just the thought gave her the creeps.

She started the SUV and headed north. The snow was almost completely gone, and the trees held the early yellow-green buds waiting to burst open. *April showers bring May flowers.* Laurent smiled. The old saying was so true. Certainly, in Field's Crossing, Indiana. Laurent was looking forward to planting more perennials and flats of annuals. Working in her garden should help mend her shoulder injury.

Turning onto Field Street, she pulled into a parallel parking spot and put the SUV in park and gazed down the street. Field Street dated back to the 1850s when Field's Crossing was a small, rural farm community. When automobiles were first introduced, the skinny tires got stuck in the muddied street where the wagons had formed deep ruts. As farm machinery grew in popularity, the founding fathers decided to permanently widen the street to accommodate the large farm equipment.

In the early 1950s, the town council changed its mind and forbade large farm machinery from driving down the middle of town. Too many businesses had sprung up and too many people inhabited the residential area. The Field's Crossing Garden Club was formed, and over the next several decades, the downtown area was transformed. The street was wider than normal with parallel parking on both sides. A greenway ran between the lanes of traffic and a gazebo cemented the middle of the parkway. Twelve- to fifteen-foot purple wisteria grew on all four sides of the gazebo and the vines hung over the corners. Groupings of azaleas and rhododendrons and day lilies flowered in the spring and the rose bushes bloomed in the summer.

Sidewalks were well traveled and stone benches were scattered along the ten-block greenway. On warm summer evenings, the line at the Dairy Ripple stretched for half a block and retail merchants were open late, some pumping music into the street.

Laurent radioed dispatch to inform them she was walking along Field Street for the next half an hour. Her next interview was with Victoria Scott Wright, Lisa's best friend.

CHAPTER TEN

"WHAT CAN YOU tell me about Lisa?" After interviewing Keith and Aubrey, Laurent had driven to Victoria Wright's house on Corn Belt Road. The two women sat in Vickie's home office, coffee cups on the end table between them, steam rising.

"Such a kind, friendly soul." Behind wire-rimmed glasses, Vickie's eyes were bloodshot. "We met years ago when she put in the bid for Big Al's and won. The bank required an audit of the diner's books before they financed the business loan, so she hired me."

"How did that audit turn out?" Laurent asked.

"Excellent. Al Jr. kept good records and paid his taxes. As an auditor, I can't ask for more."

"No financial issues when Lisa took over?"

"I conducted an audit every year for Big Al's until the loan was paid off. No problems. Ever." She sipped her coffee.

"How'd you become friends?"

"My husband passed away years ago, and I found myself dropping by Big Al's more and more. Lisa was very unhappy with her marriage and didn't know how much longer she was going to put up with Keith and his cheating. About a year ago, Keith surprised her by filing for divorce. As you know, Indiana is a no-fault divorce state. All the parties have to do is agree there is an unfixable break-down of the marriage. It's the settlement that takes forever."

"What was Lisa's opinion about the settlement proceedings?" Laurent asked.

"Keith wasn't going to get a penny from her restaurant." Vickie's knuckles turned white on the handle of the coffee cup.

"She said that?"

"More than once. In fact, she thought she deserved half of his 401(k) but was willing to let that go if he would drop his request for alimony."

"You think Lisa was going to be ordered to pay Keith? Not the other way around?"

"I think the judge was going to rule that neither party would pay alimony. Keith's income from Columbia Hospital was slightly more than the net proceeds from Big Al's. Lisa and Keith were on equal financial footing."

"Except for Big Al's and its potential to make more money than Keith," Laurent said.

"Exactly. Keith wanted financial reassurance for the future, but that's not how divorce works. If Lisa started making buckets of money, then Keith could take Lisa back to court and demand alimony, but as things stand today, they're financial equals."

"With your years of auditing Lisa's books, you made sure Big Al's net income was close to Keith's income." Laurent glanced at Vickie.

"You're very sharp, Sheriff, but I did not cook the books," Vickie said. "And Lisa never asked me to."

Laurent could think of no reason why Vickie would conduct an improper audit for Big Al's. There was nothing for her to gain. She nodded. "I had to ask."

Vickie picked up her coffee cup and sipped. "As long as we're talking about money, let me mention something that upset Lisa. Her daughter, Aubrey, skimming money every day."

"How did Lisa know Aubrey was stealing from her?"

Vickie laughed. "Sheriff, this is a small town. If Aubrey thought she could park in front of Farmers Bank every day with cash laying all over the passenger seat and think no one would notice and not tell her mom, then she's an idiot."

True. Aubrey, you lied to me. Still, that's no reason for you to kill your mom.

"Sounds like Aubrey needed her mom for the money." Laurent paused. "There was a letter from the IRS on Lisa's desk. What do you know about that?"

"Lisa mentioned it to me, and I told her to send me a copy of all correspondence from the IRS and I'd answer it. Let the government know right off, they're dealing with a professional."

"You weren't worried about the IRS? Just the thought makes my heart race," Laurent said.

"Businesses are audited all the time by the IRS. Over the years, I've gotten used to it," Vickie said.

"How does the IRS decide who to audit?"

"Cash-only businesses are audited more than other businesses because so many people abuse it. Big Al's has never been audited in the time that I've been the auditor. Sometimes, it's just the luck of the draw."

"Is there any way to tell if someone tipped off the IRS to audit Big Al's?"

"No. If someone reported Lisa, the identity of the whistleblower is protected."

Laurent sipped her hot tea. *Aubrey wouldn't report her mom. Did someone report Lisa to the IRS or is this a random audit? Why didn't they report Aubrey? Same issue. Not reporting income.*

"Who do you think killed Lisa?"

"I've been thinking about that since I heard, and the only person with that much anger or anything to gain is Keith or his latest girlfriend."

"Monica Sun," Laurent said. "Does Keith know about Aubrey stealing money?"

"I assume so. She probably hit him up for money every so often, too."

"What about Stacy Simmons? What was Lisa's relationship with her?"

Vickie hesitated. "I don't know Stacy very well, but they seemed to have a love-hate relationship. Something happened back when they were in high school, and now they're stuck with each other. I never asked."

"Anyone else?"

"I'm absolutely positive none of the high school kids killed Lisa. They loved her, but that may be because she fed them for free. It was a badge of honor to work at Big Al's, back then and even more so today."

"Did Lisa ever tell you she was afraid? What was her mood the last few days?"

"She loved to cook, even hundreds of hard-boiled eggs. I think she was tired but looking forward to the Easter egg hunt. Gave her a chance to get outside. Enjoy the sunshine. It was a beautiful April day," Vickie said. "She never said a word to me about being afraid or fearful, not even of Keith."

"Did you go to the egg hunt? Talk to Lisa on Sunday?" Laurent asked.

"I was there for about an hour. My husband and I never had children, but I do enjoy the little kids. They're so excited. Lisa watched her grandkids, so we chatted a bit and then I left."

"Did you help load or unload the eggs?"

"A couple of high school boys who worked for Lisa did most of the work."

"What time did you leave?"

"Around noon. Lisa said she'd be here after dinner at Aubrey's. She had the rest of her belongings in the back of her Escalade."

"Why was Lisa moving in with you?" Laurent asked.

"She'd had enough of Keith and Monica. She said she came home three nights this past week and found the two of them snuggled up on the couch watching TV. The first time, Lisa pitched a fit, screaming, ranting, and raving and Monica left. Then Lisa and Keith fought. The next day she asked me if she could move in until she found somewhere else to live."

"Why didn't she ask Aubrey?"

"I asked her the same question. She said the time may come when she has to move in with one of her kids, but it wasn't now," Vickie said.

"Did Aubrey and Lisa get along?"

"For the most part. They spent three to four hours every day together at Big Al's. I never heard or saw them argue in front of customers, but I was only there for lunch a few times a month. Ask the staff."

"What do you think they'd fight about?"

"Keith or the divorce. I think Aubrey was humiliated by her father and his girlfriends, but Lisa had either gotten used to it or didn't care, especially after Keith filed for divorce. I think Aubrey wanted her mother to be embarrassed by Keith's behavior, but Lisa had given up on the marriage. She didn't care anymore and didn't believe Keith and his girlfriend were a reflection on her. I think Aubrey saw her father's behavior as a reflection on her and wanted her mom to get mad, but Lisa brushed it off like a flea. But they both loathed Monica."

"Monica or all of Keith's girlfriends?" Laurent asked.

"All of them."

"How long has Keith been cheating on Lisa?"

"Years."

"What did Lisa say about Keith?" Laurent asked.

"She ignored him, which was probably worse. If Keith thought Lisa was going to make a scene or anything like that, he was disappointed. She never talked about him with customers. Aubrey was the one who was upset by the gossip and finger-pointing," Vickie said. "I think Lisa was also a little pissed with Aubrey. I heard Aubrey say one time money was tight, and Lisa told her to manage her budget better. Jake and Justin don't need the latest Xbox or gaming system and they certainly don't need any more games. Lisa also questioned why Aubrey and Doug drove brand-new cars and took expensive vacations every year."

Laurent closed her notebook. "That's all I have for now. I'm sure I'll have more questions later on. May I see where Lisa was moving into?"

Vickie stood and motioned to Laurent.

Laurent followed Vickie out of her home office, placing her empty cup in the kitchen sink before winding her way through the living room to the en suite.

"My mother-in-law was supposed to come and live with us, so when we built the house, we added the en suite. After my husband died from the second heart attack, she decided to move in with her other son," Vickie said. "So, no one has lived here." She opened the door and stepped back. "I'll be in my office if you need anything."

Laurent hesitated in the doorway of the en suite. The living room was small but comfortable. Two La-Z-Boy recliners flanked an end table and goose-necked reading lamps peered over the shoulder of each chair. The fireplace was clean, no soot, and looked as though it had never been used. On one side of the mantel sat three candlesticks and above the mantel hung a flat-screen TV, the remote sitting directly next to the sound bar. The walls were bare of pictures.

Laurent wandered into the bedroom. The room was large with a king-size bed in the middle. The bed was made, the down comforter a pale gray geometric pattern. Nightstands stood on either side of the bed, and on an opposite wall was a chest of drawers and dresser with attached mirror. Laurent walked to the closest nightstand and picked up the framed family photo. Aubrey and Doug had their arms slung around each of their boys. She didn't recognize the background. She picked up the other framed picture and saw a look-alike Keith smiling at her. *Must be Andrew and his family.* She returned both pictures to the nightstand. Stacked against the wall to Laurent's left was a row of boxes, neatly labeled, and two bulging suitcases.

A short hallway with walk-in closets on either side led to a full bathroom. Separate toilet room, bathtub, shower, and double sink vanity. Two boxes sat on the floor next to the vanity. Laurent opened the linen closet. Towels, sheets, cleaning supplies. *Lisa was all set to move in. Just hadn't unpacked.*

Laurent left the bathroom and opened the nearest closet door. Pants and shirts hung on hangers, shoes on the floor, and a stack of sealed boxes took up most of the back wall. More boxes filled the shelf above the hanging clothes. The image of Lisa's bedroom on Cardinal Street floated in her mind. *Such a difference.*

After searching the closets and bathroom, Laurent plopped into the chair next to the bay window and stared out. Vickie's house sat on five acres with the entire lot lined with huge old trees. From the en suite bedroom window, she looked at the empty cornfield and a circular drive in the rear of the house. Two rectangular garages, each large enough to house six cars, sat on either side of the drive. Enough for twelve vehicles. Laurent wondered if Vickie or her husband collected cars. Glancing at her watch, she decided to call it quits for the day. Pizza with Randi, her daughter, was next on her schedule.

CHAPTER ELEVEN

LAURENT GAZED AT her reflection in the bathroom mirror. A touch of mascara, some lipstick. After her shower, she had left her long black hair unbraided and it lay on her shoulders in waves. *I don't understand why I'm so nervous.* Ever since Randi had contacted her, Laurent realized that getting to know her daughter was a gift, a rare opportunity for which she was grateful. She intended to grab it.

*   *   *

"Tell me about my father."

Laurent gagged on her pizza and held up a hand. After swallowing a mouthful of ice tea, she swiped a napkin across her mouth. It was Monday night. She had driven south to Charlotte's Pizza, and after spending the day interviewing suspects, she was happy not to think about murder for the evening. Randi's demand caught her off-guard.

"You didn't list a name on my birth certificate. Do you even know who my father is?" Her daughter leaned back in the chair and crossed her arms over her chest.

The silent accusation hung between the two women.

There's no good way to answer her question. Laurent shredded the paper napkin in her lap. "I know who your father is."

"Is he alive?"

Laurent nodded. "I'm not sure telling you is a good idea."

"Shouldn't I be the judge of that?"

"I'm trying to protect you," Laurent said.

"I don't need protecting," Randi shot back.

"He left me, pregnant and broke. He got me thrown out of the orchestra. I don't have anything good to say about him."

"He's a musician?"

Laurent stared at the plastic tablecloth. She wanted to reach over and squeeze Randi's hand but was afraid of the response. So far, she and Randi hadn't touched or hugged or even shaken hands. "I think you and your parents are very brave. It takes courage to seek out biological parents without hurting the adopted parents' feelings. I admire them. That being said, they may be afraid they'll lose you."

"Mom and Dad are not insecure. They know I love them and always will. Adding you into my life doesn't change that, and knowing who my father is won't change that either."

"It might."

"He can't be that bad." Randi picked up a breadstick and dipped it into the marinara sauce. "Did he ask you to marry him?"

"He was selfish and arrogant, and I doubt he's changed. And no, he never asked."

"I think I should be the judge of that." Randi wiped her chin. "You don't trust me."

"We haven't known each other for very long. I have no idea how you'll react."

"Is he in prison?"

"Nothing like that."

"Why are you so reluctant to tell me his name?" Randi asked.

"I'm afraid he'll be cruel and mean to you."

"You're just *afraid*."

Laurent pushed her plate away, appetite gone. She had hoped to build on their previous lunch date and now it looked as though she'd lost Randi before she ever had the chance to know her.

"David Lucroy."

"My biological father is a world-renowned violinist?"

* * *

That did not go well. After finishing their meal, the two women said goodbye with no mention of a future meeting. Laurent walked slowly back to her little red pickup truck and started the long drive north. *Now what? I guess I'll have to wait for her to contact me and hope and pray Lucroy is the same selfish bastard he always was. What if he sweet-talks her and she believes him? He can be charming if he wants to. What if he carries a grudge against me? Sees this as a way to hurt me even more. Why should he carry a grudge? He got off scot-free. What would happen if I contacted him first? No. I'm not calling that asshole.*

What am I going to do if Randi decides she doesn't want to see me anymore? That she doesn't need me in her life? That I was just a curiosity? An itch? And I haven't even told her about the mess of a family she'd inherit. Her adoptive parents have been good to her, and she doesn't need me or Joelle or Lucroy. Well, no one needs him.

What's he going to say about me? That I'm stupid? Delusional? Untalented? What if he offers to further Randi's musical career? If he does that, I've lost. Again.

Laurent clicked on her right blinker and pulled off the road onto the shoulder, her tears blurring her vision. She drew in a sharp breath. *I love my daughter. I always have. What am I going to do?*

CHAPTER TWELVE

"AUBREY, I GOTTA talk to you." Doug Holmes put the fireplace poker in the holder and sank onto the couch.

"What now? Can't you see I'm exhausted?" Aubrey said.

"I know you are, but this can't wait."

"How much is it this time?" Aubrey dropped into her corner chair and pulled the throw pillow to her chest. These conversations with Doug never went well and were always about money.

"Thirty thousand."

"What the fuck?" She threw the pillow at him.

"College basketball."

Aubrey stared at her husband; her breath caught in her chest. *This is not happening.*

"I was positive Michigan State was going to take the whole ball of wax. It was Izzo's eighth appearance in the Final Four, and they were the most talented team. Everybody said so. And the odds were only seven-to-four."

Doug's mouth was moving, but she couldn't hear his words over the roaring in her ears. The rushing, pounding blood. *How could he do this to me? He promised!*

"It's your mom's fault. She wouldn't loan me the money, and I'm cashed out all over town."

"Don't you dare blame my mother." Aubrey shot to her feet. "Every time you couldn't pay your gambling debts, you ran to her and begged for money, and she never gave you a dime. She told you time and time again, she wouldn't pay. Did you kill her?"

"No. No. No. How could you think such a thing? You know I can't kill my own spiders."

"Where'd you go Sunday afternoon? I saw you leave." Aubrey glared at her husband.

"You sound like the police. How could you doubt me?"

"Answer the question."

"I took your stupid dog for a walk. She was whining by the front door. I think the kids running around the backyard screaming and yelling scared her," he said.

"Doug, you know we have no money. How can you do this to our family? What is it that makes you think you can put us in financial jeopardy over and over? I don't understand. Just stay away. Your addiction makes no sense to me. Where are your priorities? Why don't the kids and I come first?" Tears flowed down Aubrey's face. She had said the same thing last time. And the time before. And the time before that. It was only by stealing from her mother's daily cash flow at Big Al's that she was able to cover Doug's gambling losses and keep the bills current. Thirty thousand dollars was too much.

"I just want one big score. Then I'll stop." Doug sat on the couch, shoulders hunched, face in his hands. "He says he'll put me in the hospital if I don't pay up."

"Who says?"

"My bookie."

"When?"

"End of the week."

Aubrey slumped back in the chair. "We've got the reading of the will coming up. After that, we'll go to the diner and grab the key to the safe deposit box and go to the bank. Mom always kept a bunch of money in there."

"Will there be enough to cover this?" Doug cleared his throat.

"I think so."

"You think so? Yes or no? I don't want to get beat up."

"You should have thought of that when you were betting on stupid basketball," Aubrey snapped. "You have to stop. Not even Big Al's can cover these kinds of losses."

"Thanks, Aubs. This is the last time, I swear."

"Where have I heard that before? Get out of my sight."

Aubrey stared into the fire and listened to Doug's heavy tread on the stairs. *Maybe I should let Doug get beat up. Maybe that'll stop him from gambling.* Aubrey pounded the armchair. *He has to stop. There's no way the diner can support Doug's gambling addiction. After I inherit Big Al's, I'll probably have to share the profits with Andrew, and he's such a stickler. He'd probably audit me. The only thing I've got going for me now is that Andrew has no idea what the diner brings in. As long as the bills are paid, I shouldn't have a problem taking the rest. At least now I don't have to hide it from Mom. I wonder how much I've borrowed over the years?* She flopped back in the chair. It seemed like yesterday was the first time she had taken money out of the cash register at Big Al's.

*   *   *

Aubrey remembered she had been on edge all that day. She and her high school friends had been planning a sleepover, including alcohol. Except no one had any money. Her friends expected her to shove a few twenty-dollar bills into her pocket as she'd worked that day.

It was the last ten minutes of her shift, and the diner had been empty, the lunch staff leaving, the dinner staff not yet clocked in. She had it all figured out. Her mom usually removed the cash from the drawer around three in the afternoon and put it in the safe in her desk.

Aubrey walked the few steps to the hallway and peered down it.

"Looking for your mom? She's in the bathroom. I'm clocking out. See you tomorrow."

With a wave, Aubrey watched several employees leave the diner through the rear door. She shot to the cash register. Opening it, she snatched three twenties and shoved them into her jean pocket.

"What do you think you're doing?" Her mom had caught her. "That money doesn't belong to you."

Aubrey's heart jumped. "You know my sleepover tonight? I'm eighteen—and the only one who can buy beer, except I used all of my last paycheck to buy that new makeup I wanted to try, and none of my friends have any money either. I told them I'd buy the beer. They think I'm rich because we own the diner." Aubrey's words came out in one big breath and her heart pounded so hard she remembered feeling it knocking against her ribs.

"Stealing from me is your answer? You spend all your money on clothes and hair and makeup and when that's not enough, you steal. Give me your car keys. You can walk home." Lisa slapped the countertop.

"Mom, no. Look. I'll put the money back." Aubrey reopened the cash register and threw the twenties back in. "We'll skip the beer."

"Car keys. Now. Go home. I don't want to see your face."

Aubrey threw her keys at her mother, grabbed her coat and backpack, and stomped to the back door. She wrenched it open and began the six-block walk home, fists clenched at her sides. *I hate you. All you care about is this stupid place. Dad'll give me money. Might even buy the beer for me. I should have asked him first. And he'll let me go to the sleepover. Mom won't be home before ten, and by that time, I'll be gone, and she'll have forgotten about me. I bet she doesn't even check my room. That's how much she cares about me.*

*   *   *

Now, Aubrey pulled herself out of the La-Z-Boy and walked through the living room and kitchen to the mud room. Plucking her purse off the hook on the wall, she scrounged around for the deposit ticket from Friday afternoon. The balance in the account should be listed. With Friday's deposit, there was about ten thousand in the account. Not enough to pay Doug's bookie. *Wonder how much Mom shoved into the safe over the weekend? The deposit I make on Monday afternoon is usually five grand, maybe six. It'll be less because the diner was closed for Easter.*

She plopped into a kitchen chair and stared at the receipt. *I'm going to need that money to pay next week's wages and suppliers, which means I'll have to take the cash out of the safe deposit box. Mom kept fifty thousand in cash there. Just in case. I always complained that the money could be earning interest, but she said she wanted a few thousand on hand. Guess I'm lucky she didn't listen to me.*

Big Al's is locked up tight because it's a crime scene, but the reading of the will is on Wednesday. After that, the sheriff will have to remove all that yellow tape and the first thing I'm gonna do is change the locks. All those high school kids and Moonshine Mamas have access to the diner, day and night. Mom was so lazy about security. Trusting fool.

Aubrey wiped a tear. She would miss her mother terribly, but now she could make the diner into something she would get credit for. A new look. New sandwiches. New décor. Get rid of all those old milk tins and jugs. And the color. *I'm tired of barn red. I'm gonna jack up the price of moonshine and all the liquor, and with the money I'll rake in, I'll be out of this dumpy little house in no time. Maybe I'll build a country mansion like Vickie.*

CHAPTER THIRTEEN

"I'M RELEASING LISA'S body to the family tomorrow," Dr. Romero said. "The autopsy report is on its way. Check your email in a few minutes."

"Thanks, Doc." Laurent tapped END on her cell phone and leaned back in her chair.

"Well?" Dak strolled into her office with Bill Poulter right behind him.

"Dr. Romero emailed her report to me. Everything she told us on Sunday was spot on. The stab wound was on Lisa's left side. Because she was sitting behind the wheel of the van, the killer could be either right-handed or left-handed and it was close up. No blood spray pattern, so the killer is someone Lisa knew.

"I asked about the force necessary to go through the T-shirt, skin, and the upper body. She said that piercing the fabric would require little force. The blade was ten inches long and serrated; the handle, a standard five to six inches. The serrations were one-eighth of an inch apart. The knife was long and sharp enough to slice through the thoracic cavity, going through the lung tissue there and then on to the heart." Laurent clicked on the mouse.

"Dak, I'm forwarding the autopsy report to you. Check the size of the knife wound and see if you can match it with any item on the inventory list. If you find something, call CSU and ask them to put a rush on the fingerprints."

"What was the height of the driver's seat from the ground to Lisa's butt?" Poulter asked. "Any way we can figure out how tall the murderer is?"

"The seat is forty inches off the ground. When we were at the crime scene, I used Caleb's measuring tape to check that." Laurent stood and pointed to her waist. "About here. Imagine I have a knife in my hand." She thrust upward. "I'm five-ten. If I were five-two, I'd still be able to insert the knife, but the angle would be different."

"If the murderer was shorter than you, would the angle be flatter or sharper?" Dak asked.

"Flatter," she said. "The knife would have cut through the liver."

"The killer could be anywhere between five-two and six-two," Dak said. "All the suspects are in that range, so we're back to someone who Lisa would let stand next to her."

"The woman knew everyone in Field's Crossing," Poulter said.

"Family, friends, and coworkers are our prime suspects in that order," Laurent said. "Linville's Funeral Service is picking up the body tomorrow and Rina Yoshida called and told me she has been appointed by Judge Jenkins to open and read the will. She's setting up a meeting with the heirs this week. I'm not expecting anything to come out of it."

"I'm guessing Aubrey or Keith will get Big Al's," Dak said. "Sure hope it's Aubrey."

"Me, too," Poulter said. "I never saw Keith in the restaurant. He probably doesn't know the first thing about making a sandwich or running a business. Aubrey's been there for years."

"Don't forget Aubrey has a brother. Andrew. He'll probably inherit something. I don't know anything about him." Laurent glanced at her two deputies.

"Me, neither."

"Ditto."

"Thank God CSU took the vans and the dumpster, or we'd still be sorting trash," Dak said.

"Amen to that." She looked at Poulter. "How many people do you have left to fingerprint?"

"Getting the high school kids to come in and get fingerprinted has been a piece of cake. What they don't realize is that now we have their prints on file for the rest of their lives. Suckers." He tucked his thumbs into his belt. "I should have all the current employees printed by late this afternoon. All the lunch ladies stopped in this morning."

"That leaves family and friends," she said.

"Keith's prints were already on file with the state because he handles IT issues at Columbia Hospital, which receives state and federal funding. Dr. Romero took Lisa's prints, which leaves me with Aubrey and Andrew. I'm assuming you don't want the grand-kids' prints."

"I highly doubt a ten-year-old or an eight-year-old stabbed their grandmother."

"I'll call Aubrey and Andrew and ask them to stop by before going to the reading of the will, and I'll ask who Lisa's friends were," Poulter said.

"Vickie Wright is the only name I've heard mentioned," Laurent said. "She's a partner with Baylor, Scott, and Wright. Check with the state of Indiana. Her prints may already be on file because of her auditing and accounting fiduciary responsibilities."

Poulter nodded. "Any other friends?"

"I'll keep asking," Laurent said.

"Don't forget the girlfriend," Dak said.

"Monica Sun. Fingerprint her. Even if she's already got one on file. Get a copy of her professional license and attach it to the case file," she said.

"Why?"

"Habit. Make a complete file. Can you think of anyone else?"

"How about Aubrey's husband, Doug, and Andrew's wife, Michelle?" Dak asked.

Laurent stood. "Print them, also."

"What about the blood we scraped off the driveway?"

"Dr. Romero sent a sample to CSU."

"You think it's Lisa's blood?" Poulter asked.

"I do, and I'm hoping the killer walked in it," Laurent said. "But, if the killer has Lisa's blood on their shoes or clothing, it's going to be miniscule, assuming we find the clothes."

"We're looking at boots," Dak said.

"We're not going to find our killer that way," Laurent said. "Too many people trampled through there, including you and me. I think the blood belongs to Lisa, and considering it was late in the day, the blood was almost gone when we scraped the asphalt. The sample's going to come up with tar and gravel and crap."

She perched on the edge of her desk. "When I interviewed Keith and Monica, I checked Lisa's bedroom in the house on Cardinal Street, and then after I interviewed Vickie, I walked through the in-law suite Lisa was moving into at Vickie's house," she said. "What a difference."

Dak arched an eyebrow at her.

"On the outside, the house on Cardinal Street looks like the diner. Same paint colors, driveway looks like it's a few years old, but on the inside, it's a pigsty," Laurent said. "The carpet is threadbare, the couches are sagging, and, in the kitchen, there's old, plastic furniture. The cheap stuff from a garage sale. The place smells of mold and bacon. Lisa's bedroom was empty except for one day's worth of clothing, which I bagged and tagged, and there was dust everywhere. You could see the outline of stuff that had been sitting on the dresser and the side table."

"What about Vickie's house? The one on Corn Belt Road?" Dak asked. "I've driven by it lots of times and love the look of it."

"It's a beautiful red brick country mansion," Laurent said. "According to Vickie, her late husband and his partner started the auditing firm of Baylor, Scott, and Wright in Indianapolis. After his first heart attack, he built that house, complete with a twelve-car garage as a place to relax. After he died from a second heart attack, Vickie opened the local firm of BS&W in Field's Crossing. She's been the only managing partner." Laurent slid off the corner of her desk and retrieved a bottle of water from the mini fridge. "The en suite has never been lived in."

"Twelve-car garage? Did he collect cars?" Poulter's eyebrows met his hairline.

"I didn't ask. I only noticed the buildings," she said. "There are two garages, and they face each other with a huge driveway in between. Each garage is red brick to match the house, and from the street the buildings look like an extension of the house. You don't realize they are garages until you get to the back of the house where the in-law suite is located."

"Does it have a separate entrance?"

"I didn't see one and I asked Vickie about it. She said her husband didn't want his mom wandering around the countryside. If the en suite had its own entrance, she could have left, and they never would have known."

"Maybe that's why the mother-in-law didn't want to live there," Poulter said. "They'd watch her like a hawk. No freedom."

"Maybe she didn't want to live in a rural farm community," Dak said. "Country living's not for everyone."

"Either way, Vickie's house is a big step up from the house Lisa shared with Keith and where she raised Aubrey and Andrew," Laurent said. "I don't know what that tells us or how it relates to her murder."

"Do you think she knew about Keith and Monica?" Poulter asked.

"She knew. Vickie told me Lisa came home from work several nights recently and found Keith and Monica snuggled up on the couch and pitched a fit. She also said Aubrey knew about her father's girlfriends and was embarrassed for her mother."

"Lisa didn't care," Dak said. "Keith's been cheating on her for years. Everybody knew it. I never heard her talk about him. In fact, I never heard a negative word out of Lisa. Bubbly and bright. All the time."

"Maybe she was emotionally covering up a deep hurt," Poulter said.

Laurent glanced at him. "You sound like a psychologist. We're not going to be able to ascertain Lisa's emotional state at the time of her death. Even if we could, I don't know what help it would be in apprehending the killer. I talked to her a few hours before I found her. She seemed okay to me."

"What's the relationship between Aubrey and Andrew? Any conflict there?" Poulter asked.

"Aubrey didn't say a word about her brother, but it sounded to me as though she was jealous of Michelle, Andrew's wife," Laurent said. "She made a comment about how Michelle had to have the wedding reception at some fancy country club in Indianapolis while she and Doug were stuck in Field's Crossing with her mother providing the food." Laurent sipped her water.

"Judge Jenkins signed off on the subpoena for Farmers Bank this morning," she said. "When I asked Aubrey how the cash was handled at the diner, who made the deposits, and when and how much, she stalled at first and then got mad at me. I asked if she was skimming off the top. She said no. According to Vickie Wright, Lisa complained about Aubrey stealing from her. As far as I'm concerned, Aubrey lied to me. Poulter, I want you to find out how much money was deposited in Big Al's bank account on Mondays versus the rest of the week. Aubrey made the daily deposit, and Lisa kept all the cash from Friday night through Sunday in the safe in her desk. Monday's deposit should be the biggest of the week. Make a chart. What was Big Al's cash flow? List the vendors and amounts, tax payments, et cetera. You like messing with numbers. Have at it."

"If Aubrey took money before she made the deposit, she's got no reason to kill her mom." Poulter pushed away from the doorframe. "That makes her a liar and a thief, not a murderer."

"She claims she deposited every penny, but when I walked through her house, I noticed some very expensive items, mainly the theater room with a movie screen and surround-sound, which she was very proud to show me. Her kitchen had a marble waterfall countertop. Doesn't really fit with their income."

"Everybody's got something they spend extraordinary amounts of money on," Poulter said. "Soundproof music room, anyone?"

Laurent laughed. "You got me there. But I've been playing the cello since I was ten years old. Theater rooms and gourmet kitchens haven't been around that long. Doug makes ninety thousand a year and Aubrey pulls in fifteen an hour, but maybe they bought the house that way. With all the upgrades."

"Did Aubrey have any idea who might have killed her mom?" Poulter asked. "Anyone with a chip on their shoulder?"

"At first, she said she couldn't think of anyone. Said everyone loved her mother. Later in the interview, I asked again, and she said Stacy Simmons."

"Who?"

"A friend from high school. Aubrey thought Lisa and Stacy had a falling-out when Lisa got married but wasn't sure. Then, when Al Jr. retired, Lisa and Stacy put in bids to buy the diner. Obviously, Lisa won. Aubrey said Stacy has hated her mother ever since but didn't know why she continued to work for Lisa. I'm interviewing Stacy this afternoon." Laurent glanced at her computer screen. "Email from Dr. Romero's here."

"You ask her out yet?" Poulter punched Dak in the arm.

"None of your damn business."

*   *   *

"Hey, boss. You got a minute? It's not related to the DuVal murder." Poulter closed the door to Laurent's office after Dak left.

"What's up?" Laurent looked up from her desk where she was adding notes to Lisa's murder file.

"I talked to the bigwigs from the union, and they hate settling matters between officers. They'd rather fight city hall or the state. After they viewed the security video from Bubba's Steakhouse, they've decided to back you." Poulter plopped in the chair in front of Laurent's desk. Deputy Bill Poulter was the local union rep for the sheriff's department in the quad-counties.

"What happens to Greene? Does he get to come back to work?" Laurent didn't like Deputy Sheriff Mike Greene who had been her opponent in the recent election for sheriff. He and Ralph Howard, reporter for *The Crossing* newspaper, had falsely accused her of campaign fraud and conspired to try and defeat her.

"The union would like to end his suspension until the civil lawsuit is settled. After that, they'll reassess and discuss options," Poulter said.

"Do I get a say or is it a done deal?"

"Done deal."

"Can he be reassigned to another county?" Laurent threw her pen down and pushed back in her chair. She didn't want to see Greene's sneering face or listen to his subtle and not-so-subtle digs.

"I recommend you assign him to the county road patrol route and no overtime. Keep contact with him to a minimum."

"Damn."

Poulter pushed to his feet. "Off the record. No one wants him back either. What he and that asshole reporter Ralph Howard did was unforgivable. We're all glad you kicked the shit out of him in the last election. I just wish we could prove it was Ralph who broke into your house."

"The security cameras at my house were unclear. Ralph's attorney could put a mask and baseball cap on anyone the same height and weight as Ralph and no one would be able to tell the difference," Laurent said. "But I'm with you. I would have liked to put his ass in jail, too."

"I wouldn't expect Ralph to back off reporting about you," Poulter said. "He'll lay low for a while, but he was as humiliated as Greene. After Greene is reinstated, I bet in the first edition of *The Crossing*, Ralph starts his attacks on you again. And now, we've got another dead body."

"Don't remind me." Laurent pointed at her deputy. "The only people allowed access to the DuVal file are you, me, and Dak, and I know you and Dak won't say a word about the investigation when Greene is anywhere in the vicinity."

"Hell, I don't even want to say hi."

CHAPTER FOURTEEN

"WHAT CAN I do for you, Sheriff? We're completely booked this morning, but I can squeeze you in this afternoon." DeeDee, the owner of the Cutting Edge Hair Salon, was in her late fifties. Her face was lined from years of tanning and cigarettes. The wrinkles around her eyes, mouth, and neck were filled with tan silicone foundation that sank into her pores, creating a pasty effect against a splash of bright red lipstick. The shiny silver lame tank dress was belted at the waist with a black rope and stopped just short of her knees. Black leggings were tucked into UGGs, and her nicotine-stained hands were busy folding towels. Her hair was blonde and streaked with red highlights, and the scent of nail polish remover reached Laurent from the door.

"I'm not here for a haircut even though I need one. I'd like to ask you a few questions about Monica Sun, one of your stylists. Do you have a minute? What can you tell me about her?"

A slight frown crossed the salon owner's face. "She's punctual, well liked by our male clientele. She embraces all the new courses offered by the state."

"New courses?"

"The latest trend is hair extensions. There are several types, and they all require different techniques. She's the only one in the shop certified in all techniques."

"Hair extensions?"

"Not something you have to worry about, Sheriff. You've got long, beautifully thick hair, but God knows you need a trim and a root touch-up. I'm seeing more gray than I used to."

"I thought it was just me."

"Last month certainly wasn't easy on you. That jackass Mike Greene trying to oust you as sheriff and that scum-of-the-earth lawyer taking all our taxpayer money—it's no wonder a few more gray hairs showed up," DeeDee said. "And getting shot—how's your arm?"

Laurent hadn't been expecting this show of support and found herself momentarily choked up. "Arm's coming along. PT hurts like hell." *What is it about hair stylists that make you want to spill your guts? The proximity? The intimateness of someone combing through your hair? The head massage?* Laurent had her hair trimmed once a year and guarded against speaking too personally. Everyone was curious about police officers, and she was careful to impart only general information. She tried to steer these conversations to her cello concerts in the summer or the stylists' children. Safe topics. Easy topics.

DeeDee picked up a towel from the basket by her feet and snapped it. "I get it. My mom fell this winter, broke her hip, and spent six weeks at Turtle Lake Farm. She hated every minute of it. Said she hurt more after they were done than before."

"Exactly. I don't like taking medication, even something as common as ibuprofen," Laurent said.

"Keeps the swelling down."

"About Monica Sun?"

"Let's go back to the office. Liz, would you keep an eye on the door and answer the phone? I'll be a few minutes."

Laurent rounded the front counter to follow DeeDee but found herself stopped every few feet as women in various stages of salon services expressed their support and asked about her arm. But the main question was who killed Lisa. Did Laurent have any suspects? Any leads? How long was Big Al's going to be closed? Who was going to run it?

After squelching potential rumors and answering questions about her arm, Laurent pushed aside the dangling beads that constituted the door to DeeDee's office and stopped. The walls were painted bright pink and old album covers framed in black adorned the walls. A boom box sat on a shelf in the corner next to a stack of cassette tapes.

The salon owner perched on an exercise ball behind her desk. An air cleaner ran quietly in one corner, but the faint smell of cigarettes hovered under the strong smell of peroxide.

"What do you want to say about Monica that you don't want anyone else to hear?" Laurent eased gingerly into a contour chair with spindly legs expecting to be uncomfortable.

"Sit all the way back. It'll hold you," DeeDee said. "There's nothing specific I can point to, but my years in the business have given me a feel for people. I can tell by the way you're holding yourself you're in pain. You got some ibuprofen in one of those pockets? If not, I have some."

Laurent sighed. "Got a bottle of water?"

DeeDee pulled one out from the mini fridge behind her desk. "Sheriff, you've got the support of every woman in the four counties. Use us. We women got to stick together."

After swallowing the ibuprofen, Laurent looked at DeeDee. "Spill it."

"Like I said, it's nothing I can put my finger on. Monica doesn't report any cash tips, but that's common. Damn IRS takes more than their fair share as it is, and because all my stylists receive tips, I only have to pay minimum wage. Maybe it's because all the men ask for her specifically. Since she's been here, our male clientele has doubled. Now, mind you, I'm not complaining, and neither is Earl. He's getting on in years and standing on your feet all day doesn't help. He's been talking about closing shop in the winter. But people still got to get their hair cut, so my business will tick up a bit."

"Earl, the barber down the street. It looks to me like every guy who comes out of his shop has the same haircut," Laurent said.

"That's 'cuz they do. Earl never went to school to learn how to cut hair. His father taught him and that's why they all look the same."

"Do you think Monica offers services outside your salon?"

"Don't get me wrong. We all cut our family and friends' hair for free or at least cheaper than here. That's not what I'm talking about. If you'd been injured so bad that you couldn't come to the salon, I'd have driven to your house and trimmed your hair and covered up your roots right there in your kitchen. No. It's almost as though she's scoping out the men. Finding out how much they're worth. Who's got money and who doesn't. Who's tightfisted and cheap and who gives it away. She's a predator, and her prey are men with money. That's how she picked up Keith DuVal."

Laurent crossed one ankle over her knee. "What happened?"

"What do you think happened? Keith is a very vain man even though his hairline starts behind his ears."

Laurent chuckled.

"Keith and Lisa have been customers for a long time, same as Aubrey and Doug and their two boys," DeeDee said. "About six months ago, Monica had another customer in her chair and Keith was at Liz's station. Monica finished her appointment and then sat down in her chair and chatted with Keith for the remainder of his appointment. When he came to the front to pay, he scheduled his next appointment with Monica."

"Not Liz? I thought customers were loyal to their stylists. You're the only one who's cut my hair," Laurent said.

"When a customer finds the stylist who gets it right, they stick with that person. Some customers will follow their hair stylists to a new salon, especially women. Men aren't as fickle, but then men aren't judged on their appearances, are they? When do you suppose that shit will go away?"

"Not in my lifetime."

"After that, Keith was in here every four weeks for a trim with Monica," DeeDee said. "I didn't think much about it until Monica rushed in one morning carrying a coffee mug from Big Al's."

"I didn't know Big Al's sold coffee mugs." Laurent squinted. *Where have I seen those?*

"They don't." DeeDee rolled back and forth on her exercise ball. "Where do you think she got it?"

Laurent clicked her pen. "Keith and Lisa's house. You think Monica targeted him?"

"Like I said. She's a predator."

"Monica said she's worked here for the last two or three years. Did she pick up any other married men?" Laurent asked.

"She tried with a few others, but they shut her down pretty quick."

"Keith was her first choice?"

"Here in Field's Crossing, he was her first choice. I don't think she realized that farmers have their wives cut their hair. Only the professional guys come in here, and they're pretty much no non-sense. They saw her coming from a mile away," DeeDee said.

"Did you conduct a background check?"

DeeDee shook her head. "I confirmed her license with the state and that was it. Hair stylists change salons frequently. You know how the grass is always greener on the other side. I never bother to contact previous employers. Background checks are expensive and not worth my time."

Laurent was quiet. This was not what she had been expecting. Monica moved higher on her suspect list. Right next to Keith. "What time do you close on Saturday?"

"Five. We always run late, but I usually lock the door by six, and we're closed on Sunday."

"Did Monica work last Saturday?"

DeeDee nodded. "She was the last stylist out the door. Told me she had a dinner date at six thirty with Keith."

Same story. Keith and Monica. Did they spend Saturday night planning how to kill Lisa instead of going to dinner and a movie?

"What are you thinking, Sheriff? Am I going to lose an employee?"

*   *   *

Laurent paused on the sidewalk in front of the Cutting Edge Salon to tuck the appointment card in her wallet. DeeDee wouldn't let her leave without an appointment and made her put it in the calendar app on her phone. Laurent's cell phone vibrated. *Farmers Bank*. "Hello?"

"Vincent Walker. I don't believe we've met. I took over for Bob Kane as president."

"Did you receive the subpoena?" she asked.

"I've saved everything to a flash drive unless you need it in print."

"I'd like both. The courts in some counties don't have electronic filing," she said. "Did you read through any of it? Is there anything you can tell me?"

"From my standpoint, Big Al's broke even, but didn't make a huge profit," Walker said. "There were daily cash deposits ranging from fifteen hundred dollars up to two thousand dollars, Tuesday through Friday and up to several thousand dollars on Mondays. Very common for restaurants. All the checks written on the account seem to be to suppliers, vendors, and employees."

"Thanks. I'll send a deputy to pick everything up." Laurent stopped on the sidewalk. "Was there a late-night deposit on Saturday or early Sunday morning?"

"The last deposit was made Friday around three thirty in the afternoon."

"Who made the deposit?"

"I'll ask the tellers. As long as there's a deposit slip with the cash, we don't care who makes the deposit. Withdrawals are different," Walker said.

"Were there any recent withdrawals that don't look like business expenses?"

"Like cash? No. Electronic checks are processed every day."

"Who are the signers on the account?"

"Lisa DuVal, Aubrey Holmes, and Victoria Scott Wright."

"Only one signature is required for a cash withdrawal?"

"Correct. Any one of those three women can write checks on the account, make deposits, or withdraw cash. Cash withdrawals require a photo ID," Walker said. "There were very few cash withdrawals."

"Whose signature did you see the most?"

"Lisa's signature was the only one on the checks to suppliers and employee paychecks. I saw in the notes from Bob Kane that he tried to get Lisa to issue paychecks electronically and pay vendors the same way, but she resisted. His notes said she liked to write everything out. See it in black and white," Walker said. "Aubrey's name was on the cash withdrawals, and Victoria Wright's name was added last year, but there was no activity under that name."

"Aubrey made cash withdrawals? When?"

"The cash withdrawals were sporadic, but the restaurant was a cash-only business. They may have needed quarters, nickels, and dimes or five, tens, and ones. That would be standard operating procedure for Big Al's."

"Is there a limit on the dollar amount that can be withdrawn from this account?"

"No."

* * *

According to Vickie, Aubrey skimmed money off the top every day. How much was Aubrey stealing from her mom and why does she need it? What did she use the money for? Was Aubrey being blackmailed? If so, why would the blackmailer want Lisa dead? The money dries up. Laurent's forehead wrinkled. *Keep thinking.*

CHAPTER FIFTEEN

"Where were you on Sunday?"

"Batting cages."

"Softball season doesn't start for another month."

"I didn't get to be the all-time home run leader by waiting for the season to start," Stacy Simmons snapped. "I never had kids, and I've been divorced for years. I do as I please."

Stacy lived west of the downtown area in an ancient bungalow. The roof over the porch drooped and a rusty downspout lay on the ground. Dead thistles stuck up through a dirty pile of snow next to the front sidewalk, and the wooden steps sagged. Several spindles surrounding the porch were broken with dangling jagged edges and the chipped and peeled paint curled up in large swaths. The screen door was missing, and a plastic chair lay on its side tucked in the corner of the porch as though it wanted to hide from its owner.

"How'd you hear about Lisa's death?"

"One of the women who works at lunchtime has a kid in high school. Whoever showed up to get their check on Sunday sent it over Twitter or Facebook or some other dumb site, and her kid told her, and she texted the rest of us," Stacy said. "There's no secrets in a small town, although you did a pretty good job hiding your daughter. 'Course, you didn't live here thirty years ago."

Is Stacy taking a shot at me?

"How long have you known Lisa?"

After standing outside on the dilapidated porch, Stacy had finally allowed Laurent inside her home. The wood floors creaked but they shone as Laurent stepped over the threshold. The small house smelled of lemon furniture polish and bleach and cigarette smoke. Laurent followed Stacy to the kitchen at the rear of the house. *The outside might look like crap, but the inside is as neat as a pin, albeit sparse. So different from Lisa's home.*

"We went to high school together." Stacy snapped her fingers and a beagle trotted to her side. "We was friends until she got married."

"May I pet him? What's his name?"

"Sure. Mooch."

Laurent crouched and held her hand palm up to the tri-colored dog and waited until he licked her hand. "What a nice pooch." She stood and pulled out a kitchen chair, sat, and scooted closer to the table. "Where did you go to high school?"

"Field's Crossing."

"What happened after Lisa got married that broke up your friendship?" Laurent asked.

Stacy picked up a pack of cigarettes, pulled one out, and tapped it on the kitchen table. "We drifted apart. Happens all the time."

"When was the last time you spoke with Lisa?"

"Last week."

"Please be more specific."

"Friday."

Laurent sighed. Getting Stacy to say more than necessary was going to be work. "What did you talk about?"

"The usual."

Laurent stared at the woman sitting opposite her and said nothing. Not only was a picture worth a thousand words, but so was a look.

Stacy inhaled on her cigarette. Fine lines on her upper lip told Laurent Stacy had been a longtime smoker even though the ashtray was empty.

"It's no secret Lisa and me didn't get along, but I didn't kill her. If she could have fired me, I think she would have."

"Why?"

"Are you fuckin' kidding me? Miss Popular in high school didn't want to ruin her 'I'm the nicest person in the world' reputation. She kept me on because she felt sorry for me along with all of Field's Crossing."

"Why do you think people feel sorry for you?" Laurent asked.

"My parents sucked the life out of me. First, Dad's stroke, and then, Mom's dementia. Medicare and social security paid squat. I went through their savings in three years. Barely got this piece-of-shit house paid off before they died." Stacy crossed her arms over her chest and stared at the ceiling, smoke from her cigarette drifting up.

"People feel sorry for you because you took care of your parents until they died?" Laurent said. "I think that's an incredible amount of devotion and dedication."

"Well, you're the only one." Stacy ground her cigarette in the ashtray. "Last time I saw Lisa was Friday afternoon. I told everyone to have a nice weekend. Emptied the register and put the cash in the bank bag and gave it to Aubrey, and then I sat down and dyed Easter eggs. Lisa joined me, and we chatted about stuff."

"What stuff?"

"You talk to Vickie yet?"

"Why do you ask?"

Stacy tilted her head. "You're gonna find out one way or another. The IRS was auditing Big Al's."

"How do you know this?" Laurent's grip on her pen tightened.

"Saw the letter sitting on Lisa's desk."

"Did she know you saw it?"

"Yep," Stacy said.

"So, on Friday afternoon, you and Lisa are dying eggs—did you mention the upcoming audit? How'd she respond?"

Stacy slapped the table. "She got pissy and told me to stick my nose where the sun don't shine. She acted like she didn't care, like it wasn't a big deal, and then I reminded her about Aubrey skimming money off the top. There's no way I can prove that short of taking a video while Aubrey's sitting in her car outside the bank shoving twenty-dollar bills in her purse. Neither one of them counted the money at the diner before making the deposit, which left Aubrey free to snatch a few bills. Every day. Monday through Friday. For the last ten years. How in the hell do you think Aubrey and Doug can buy new cars every two years? Ski in Aspen every spring break? Vacation in the Caribbean every winter holiday? They was always flashing cash around town. But, if the IRS came in here and actually counted the money, Lisa'd have to pay all sorts of fines and penalties on money she didn't report, and which Aubrey stole."

Again, no reason for Aubrey to kill her mom, but why would Stacy kill Lisa? Revenge?

"You think Lisa kept you on out of pity. Why'd you stay?"

"I had nowhere to go. All I had was this dumpy little house. And I can walk to the diner. Don't even need a car."

"What hours do you work?"

"Nine to five, Monday through Friday."

"Big Al's is open until seven during the week and nine on the weekends," Laurent said. "Who served the alcohol?"

"Wasn't much call for alcohol during the week. After I clocked out, Lisa managed the alcohol sales. The Moonshine Mamas rotated Friday and Saturday nights. Lisa handled Sundays."

"Who are the *Moonshine Mamas*?"

"The women who sold the alcohol at the diner. We sell a lot of moonshine, and someone came up with the nickname," Stacy said.

"Nine is early for the weekends," Laurent said.

"Lisa didn't want to deal with drunks. Let the bars handle them."

Laurent flipped through her notebook where she had listed her questions. "Tell me about the bidding war between you and Lisa."

"It's not Al Jr.'s fault. He had to make a business decision, and at the time I had no way to secure the debt. Lisa did. The house on Cardinal Street, although why Keith agreed to let the bank use it as collateral is beyond me."

"You seem to know a lot about Lisa and Keith and Big Al's." Laurent settled back in her chair.

"I was born here, grew up here, got married and divorced here, and laid my parents to rest at Field's Cemetery," Stacy snapped. "Whad'ya expect?"

"What else do you know?" Laurent leaned forward and put her elbows on the table.

"I told her I knew all about her and Andrew developing recipes for his new rooftop moonshine bar in Indianapolis. I overheard Andrew tell her that competition was picking up and two new country bars specializing in moonshine were opening in the downtown area before the end of the year," Stacy said. "Lisa told him she wasn't going to add any items to Big Al's menu until her divorce from Keith was final."

"Andrew's opening a new bar? When?"

"I don't know, but he's been dropping by every so often. He already owns a rooftop wine bar, but maybe he didn't have the money to start up another bar. Who knows?" Stacy said.

Something's off here. "Lisa is testing new recipes for Andrew, but she wanted to wait before adding them to the menu at Big Al's. Why?"

"Keith wanted half of the net proceeds from Big Al's, and if Lisa added more specialty drinks to the menu, profits would go up. She wanted to prove to the court she and Keith made the same amount of money so she wouldn't have to pay alimony to him," Stacy said. "I agreed with her on that."

"Sounds as though you don't like Keith."

"That's an understatement. Guy's a jerk. Asshole. Cheating, lying scum of the earth."

Laurent heard the venom in Stacy's voice. *What was the story here?*

"Guy screws anything in a skirt. Before his current squeeze, he was having an affair with Ruby Rae Evans," Stacy said. "Made her late for work a couple of times."

"Ruby Rae works for Lisa? Any reason she'd want to kill her?"

"Nah. They broke it off and Keith started up with the chick from the hair salon."

"Do you know anyone who had a grudge or wanted Lisa dead? Did you overhear any arguments with anyone?"

"I think Keith's latest slut talked him into it." Stacy lit another cigarette.

"Talked him into killing his wife? Why do you think that?"

"I think both Lisa and Keith were tired of each other and the divorce. What would it take to push Keith's button? His latest squeeze saying no sex?" Stacy leaned back in her chair. "Both Keith and Lisa had their obsessions. Keith's was to see how many women he could screw. He started counting the week before he got married. Him and his brother. What a couple of assholes."

"What was Lisa's obsession?"

"Big Al's and all that shit she and her mother collected," Stacy said.

"What did Lisa and her mom collect?"

"Beanie Babies. I think her mom collected Hummels. Ask Keith."

Laurent made a note. "You colored Easter eggs but didn't go to the egg hunt. Why?"

"No reason."

"Anyone with you at the batting cages?" Laurent asked. *This is one lonely woman. She's lived in Field's Crossing her entire life and thinks people feel sorry for her. She doesn't want their pity. What does she want? Recognition. That's why softball is her baby. Home run leader. First thing she told me.*

"I practice by myself."

"Any park district employees around to verify?"

"I don't need an alibi. I didn't kill Lisa. That's like killing the golden goose. I may not like the woman, but she provided jobs and income for a bunch of people. Including me," Stacy said. "When can we reopen the diner?"

"It'll be a while. It's still a crime scene. I understand the reading of the will is taking place tomorrow. After that, I'll have a better idea when Big Al's can open up again." Laurent stood. "I'll be in touch."

*　*　*

After sitting in front of Stacy's house making notes for a few minutes, Laurent pulled away from the curb. *How does Stacy benefit from killing Lisa? Was she stealing, too? If she was, then there's no reason to kill Lisa. Stacy doesn't like Lisa, but I didn't get a sense of hatred. Resentment, all day long. What am I missing? Big Al's is cash only. Stacy said Aubrey made the deposit during the week. What if Aubrey, Stacy, and Lisa were all skimming money off the top? How much money wasn't reported to the IRS? What's the motivation for an IRS audit assuming the IRS didn't initiate it? Revenge? Put Lisa behind bars? Why kill her? Maybe someone wanted to take over.*

CHAPTER SIXTEEN

"HOW LONG HAVE you worked with Keith?" Laurent asked. She had parked in the visitor's lot at Columbia Hospital and rode the elevator to the basement to interview Ken Sakamoto, Keith's boss.

"We were colleagues until my promotion five years ago." Sakamoto, the IT manager, wore a button-down shirt with jeans. "We both interviewed for the manager job. I got it. He didn't."

"How'd he react?" she asked.

"He gave me the cold shoulder for a week or so, but eventually he got used to me telling him what to do."

"How would you describe his work ethic?" Laurent pulled out her notebook and balanced it on her knee.

Sakamoto leaned back in his chair. "At first, he was lazy. Took days instead of hours to get anything done, so I switched him to problem-solving on the floor."

"Which is?"

"Hospital staff call here every day, all day long. It's usually a simple fix like a loose cable or someone unplugged something. I have one person dedicated to running all over the hospital and the outpatient facility fixing all the simple stuff. Operator-error stuff. Up until Keith, everyone in IT hated the assignment so I rotated my staff. Keith, however, loved the job and requested it permanently."

"Why?"

"At first, I thought he was tired of keeping up with technology or fed up with how slow the hospital administration moved on budget items, like upgrades and stuff. And then, the first complaint came in."

Laurent clicked her pen. "Go on."

"One of the head floor nurses found Keith and a nurse screwing in an empty room."

"Did the nurse file a sexual harassment complaint?"

"Nope. It was mutual consent. Reprimands were placed in both employees' files."

"And that was it?" she asked.

"There's a huge shortage of nurses," Sakamoto said. "The nurse didn't file a complaint, was on her lunch break, and patient care wasn't compromised. As long as neither one didn't claim sexual harassment or assault, there's not much that can be done."

"When was this? Did you speak to Keith about it? What's the nurse's name?"

"It happened a few months after I was promoted. I figured he was testing my authority. He claimed he was on a break and the other party was willing."

"No harm, no foul."

"Exactly." Sakamoto wrote on a Post-it note. "I'll check with the legal department to see if I can release the nurse's name."

"Then what?"

"Since then, every task I've assigned to Keith has been completed on time and done correctly, but the scuttlebutt in the hospital is that he's very careful about who, where, and when. When he screws another employee, they don't use an empty hospital room."

"The janitor's closet?"

"This hospital has been added onto and renovated several times and has a lot of nooks and crannies and small unused spaces. He knows them all."

"How do you know that?" she asked.

"I can tell where he is in the hospital by what computer he's working on and the hospital cell phone he carries has GPS. When he clocks out for lunch, I'm able to find the closest cubbyhole."

"Any more complaints?"

"None."

"So, despite this one complaint, you continue to send him all over the hospital fixing stuff?" she asked.

"No one on the staff wants that job. It's stupid simple. I keep track of him and if anyone else files a complaint, I'll sack him. But since that one incident, he hasn't been a problem," Sakamoto said.

"Keith learned how to hide his sexual activity during work hours?" she asked. "Did you see a pattern?"

"I didn't spend time analyzing it. As long as the work is done and done right, I'm happy with that."

Laurent glanced at her list of questions. "Did you know Lisa DuVal, his wife?"

"Never met her, but Keith did rave about his wife's sandwiches."

"I can attest to that."

"Sheriff, what happened? Keith was short with me when he called. All he said was my 'wife is dead.'" Sakamoto leaned forward, elbows on his desk.

"Lisa was killed on Sunday."

"Killed? As in murdered?"

Laurent nodded. "What else did he say about Lisa? Did he ever talk about problems at home? Kids?"

"It's only been the last year or so that he's even talked about Lisa. It seems they were getting a divorce, and he started bad-mouthing her. Knowing his reputation at the hospital, I don't blame her."

"Can you recall exactly what he said?"

"Like, 'I'm gonna kill her'?" Sakamoto shook his head. "Nothing like that. More along the line of how much money he was going to get from selling her restaurant or how much debt she would have because he was demanding half of her income from the place. He seemed happy to hurt her. Financially."

"What's his salary?"

"Eighty thousand a year."

"Is there anything else you'd like to add?"

"Check with HR. Keith asked some questions about his 401(k), and I didn't know the answers. It sounded like he wanted an early distribution."

"Did he say why he wanted the money?" she asked.

"I didn't ask. I consider those types of questions to be out of my area of expertise, and I certainly don't want to steer anyone wrong, especially when it comes to money."

"Would you pull up Keith's tasks and locations for the last six months? There's a few more people I need to talk to."

"I'll need a warrant for that."

"I'll have it in an hour."

CHAPTER SEVENTEEN

"Monica was always crying poor," Wes said. The elderly apartment manager shuffled across the tiny office and plopped into a well-worn swivel chair behind his desk. Tufts of white hair stood straight up, but behind wire-rimmed glasses, his blue eyes were sharp.

"What do you mean?" There were no other chairs in the little office, so Laurent stood, notebook in her left hand, pen in her right. She unzipped her jacket. The old guy kept his office very warm. A bead of sweat ran down her back.

"Rent is due on the first of the month, but I'll accept money through the fifth without charging a late fee. Monica always showed up on the night of the fifth with cash, but it was never the full amount," Wes said.

"What did you do? How much is rent every month?"

"The first time, I let it go. After that, I gave her five more days, but I charged her the late fee." Wes pulled out a laminated piece of paper with apartment numbers and the corresponding rent amount. "The rent depends on which apartment you're leasing. I only have one three-bedroom apartment, and I usually rent to a family. The one-bedroom and two-bedrooms are the most popular.

The difference in rent is one hundred dollars a month. Tenant pays all utilities, but I provide internet access. Parking is free."

"What did you do when she showed up and didn't have the full amount?" Laurent pulled out her phone and snapped a picture of the rental price sheet.

"Told her to get the rest. She went back to her apartment and got it. Tryin' to cheat me."

"She had the money, but didn't want to pay?"

"Yep." Wes rocked back and forth. "I've been around the block a few times. I know a two-bit cheater when I see one."

"Why'd you rent to her?" Laurent asked.

"The only way I keep my head above water is with one hundred percent occupancy. I raised the rent last year and lost five tenants. Took me six months to get back full again. There's not a lot of people who want to rent apartments in Field's Crossing. There's only me and the owner of the complex on the south side of town, and Ollie who rents a couple of apartments over the stores on Field Street. We're all in the same situation. We keep our rents real close."

"Sounds a bit like collusion," she said.

"Ain't no one gonna file a lawsuit against us. We're small potatoes."

Laurent tilted her head. "You've got a point there. I'd like to ask you about last weekend."

"My granddaughter got married down in Indy. I left here on Friday around three for the rehearsal dinner. The wedding was on Saturday afternoon. I drove home on Sunday morning."

"When you're gone, who's in charge? What if a pipe breaks or someone's locked out?" she asked.

"I rarely leave the building or Field's Crossing, but I've got contracts with the plumber, the electrician, anybody I need, and nowadays you can buy anything off the internet. My arthritis is kicking up and some days my joints hurt so bad all I can do is sit. If I have to leave the area for any length of time, I let the residents know at least a month in advance. I put a flyer in their mailboxes, and I post it on the community bulletin board. I also tape the notice next to every elevator and stairwell. I send an email blast a few days before I leave and give them the name and number of who to contact if there's a problem." Wes heaved himself out of his chair and waddled to the desk. Plucking a piece of paper out of the inbox, he handed it to Laurent. "Here you go."

"Thanks." She folded the paper and tucked it in the back flap of her notebook. "Were there any issues?"

"None."

"Does your emergency contact live here?"

"No."

"Do you have surveillance cameras?" she asked.

"Too damn expensive." Wes plopped back into his chair.

"Can you give me the names of the residents who live on either side of Monica?" Her pen was poised above her notebook.

"I'll write them down for you along with their phone numbers." Wes scooted his chair closer to the desk and pulled out a pack of Post-it notes.

"What do you think of Monica?" Laurent asked.

"She's a loser. Always looking for a free ride. Wanted her money prorated for the month and called me a bunch of names before she left. I'm afraid of what I'm going to find when I inspect the apartment."

"Do you require a security deposit?" she asked.

"Damn straight, I do. Never had a tenant who didn't do some damage."

"Ever return a security deposit?"

"Hell, no. Not gonna start now."

"Did you ever meet any of the men she dated?" Laurent asked.

"A couple. She's been renting from me for the last two or three years. Seems to hang on to one guy and then gets rid of him. The latest guy she's been with for a while."

Laurent pulled out a photo of Keith DuVal from her notebook and handed it to the apartment manager. "Ever met him?"

"Once. A bit old for her."

"What's your opinion of him?"

"Goofball."

"How so?" she asked.

"Monica has him wrapped around her little finger. God knows what sexual favors she does for him."

"How'd you know they were sexual partners?" she asked.

"Got a few complaints about him parking his car overnight in the lot. I don't allow that. You gotta live here to park here, and Monica has her little piece-of-shit Toyota. Since she's the only one listed on the rental agreement, she gets one parking space. I knocked on her door one morning when I saw his car, and he answered wearing a bedsheet around his waist. I told him to get his car out of my lot or I was calling a tow truck."

"What'd he do?"

"Got dressed and left. Apparently, the asshole parked here while I was gone this weekend. Got a few complaints in my email on Monday morning."

"No one called the emergency contact?"

"He's only for emergencies, not stupid stuff like that."

CHAPTER EIGHTEEN

OPINION/EDITORIAL PAGE
HISTORY OF BIG AL'S DINER

April 23, 2019
Field's Crossing, Indiana
Ralph Howard

*Al Jensen returned home from WWII missing one leg
and opened Big Al's Diner in downtown Field's Crossing.
A year later, he built the current site of the diner at the
corner of Indiana and Woodruff Streets. Throughout the
late forties and early fifties, Big Al sold moonshine and
sandwiches—cash only—from the front counter. Sheriff
William Atkins, father of recently retired sheriff Glen
Atkins, was a regular customer and refused to enforce the
sale of illegal liquor. In the small farming community, it
was rumored that William Atkins was taking a weekly
bribe from Big Al to look the other way; however, that
claim was never proven.*

The diner remained essentially the same for decades, but after forty years in business, Big Al's health deteriorated to the point where he was forced to retire. In 1984, he handed the diner over to his son, Al Jr., who added a dining room and an asphalt parking lot and continued the cash-only policy.

When Al Jr. retired, a bidding war ensued. Lisa DuVal's bid beat Stacy Simmons' and, in 2009, the diner had a face-lift, was renovated, and expanded to its current size. Several liquor licenses were acquired. The diner now occupies the entire block of Woodruff, Delaney, Field, and Indiana Streets. DuVal added many of the diner's signature sandwiches.

With the death of Lisa DuVal, who will inherit? Will the DuVal family continue to run the diner or sell? What does the future hold for Field's Crossing's favorite diner, but more importantly, how long will Big Al's be closed? This reporter's favorite sandwich is the Waldo.

CHAPTER NINETEEN

IT HAD BEEN twenty-four hours since Randi had stalked out of Charlotte's Pizza. Laurent stood motionless in her kitchen, staring at the small frying pan filled with scrambled eggs. The toaster dinged. She plucked out two pieces of rye toast and slathered butter on each slice. Shutting off the cooktop, she slid the eggs onto the plate, picked up her cup of tea, and carried them both into the living room. After settling into her favorite, well-worn chair, she clicked on the Bose in-home sound system and chose classical piano solos. She scooped up a forkful of eggs. They were bland. She had forgotten salt and pepper.

How did last night's dinner with Randi end so badly? What happened? Maybe she thought I was lying when I told her who her father is. I'd have a hard time believing it, too. In the small world of classical music, David Lucroy was the next Isaac Stern. Younger, hugely popular, and far better looking than the elderly violinist.

But why would I lie? I told her the last time we had lunch that her biological father and I met at college, and I played cello in the orchestra. That's easy to confirm. Did she think I'd pick a name out of thin air?

Laurent dropped an uneaten piece of toast on her plate. *I should have listed his name on the birth certificate. That was a mistake. Even then, I was trying to protect her. That's why I left his name off. So he'd have no control over my decision. I did the right thing and now it's coming back to bite me.*

CHAPTER TWENTY

"You brought this skank to the reading of Mom's will? What the hell is wrong with you, Dad?" Aubrey kicked the leg of the chair next to her. She and Doug had arrived early at Rina Yoshida's office and had been hoping for a few minutes alone with the young attorney, but Andrew and his wife, Michelle, showed up almost at the exact same time.

"Knock it off, Aubs," Andrew said. "It's not like the entire town of Field's Crossing won't know what's in Mom's will in the next day or so. This town is a leaky spring. Everyone knows everybody else's business."

"I bet the gossip starts with her." Aubrey glared at Monica. *You think my dad's gonna be your meal ticket? Guess again.*

"Good morning, everyone. My name is Rina Yoshida, and I am the executor of the will of Lisa Marie DuVal. Why don't we get started? I'll begin by listing everyone in attendance. Keith DuVal, Aubrey and Doug Holmes, Andrew and Michelle DuVal, Victoria Scott Wright, and Monica Sun." Rina laid down her pen. "Ms. Sun, I'm going to have to ask you to wait in the lobby of the building. This meeting is only for people named in the will. Spouses of people named in the will are allowed, especially if minor children are named."

"Good riddance," Aubrey said. "Let me open the door for you." She shoved her chair back, hitting the wall, and stalked to the conference room door. She wrenched it open and smirked at Monica before slamming the door and returning to her seat.

"The actual will is quite short, seven or eight pages." Rina Yoshida, a recent graduate of Notre Dame Law School, was in her mid-twenties and the daughter of the local high school principal.

"Just give us the highlights. Who gets what?" Keith's hair was slicked back and a tiny ponytail held with a rubber band was starting to grow.

"Judge Jenkins read the will and believes it to be legal, valid, and binding, and has named me as executor of Lisa's will." Rina smoothed out a few sheets of paper. "'Special bequests are as follows: to my four grandchildren, I leave each of them their favorite milk tin and Big Al's aprons embroidered with their names. I also leave to my grandchildren, to be divided equally among them, the Hummel collection dating back to my mother, Beanie Babies, Pokémon cards, and any other items I may have collected.

"'To my daughter, Aubrey Holmes, I leave my recipe box containing the recipes for my signature sandwiches.

"'To my son, Andrew DuVal, I leave the sum of one hundred thousand dollars and all the new moonshine recipes I developed. These recipes are as follows, but not limited to: Peach Moonshine, Watermelon Moonshine, Honey Moonshine, Apple Pie Moonshine, Lemon Drop Moonshine, Key Lime Moonshine, Pumpkin Spice Moonshine, and any other moonshine recipes developed after the signing of this will. These recipes are the sole and exclusive property of Andrew DuVal and are not included in the recipes given to my daughter.

"'As per waivers signed by Lisa DuVal and Keith DuVal, Keith DuVal is to receive the property located at 822 Cardinal Street, Field's Crossing, Indiana, and all the proceeds from the joint checking account at Farmers Bank.

"'Victoria Scott Wright is to receive the property known as Big Al's Diner located at 410 Woodruff Street, Field's Crossing, Indiana, and the banking account at First Federal minus the one hundred thousand dollars given to Andrew DuVal. The land and building are free and clear of any liens and pass to Victoria Scott Wright via the aforementioned waiver. Any and all alcohol permits and licenses may transfer to Victoria Scott Wright per federal, state, and local laws and ordinances.

"'Signed and dated this nineteenth day of March in the year 2018.

"'Lisa Marie DuVal.'"

"Any questions?" Rina asked.

"What kind of bullshit is this?" Aubrey's hands gripped the arms of the chair. She glanced at the red, shocked faces around the conference room table.

"What waiver? I didn't sign no waiver." Keith slapped a hand on the table.

"I'm gonna fight this," Aubrey said.

Rina raised her voice. "Let's review some basic inheritance law. In Indiana, a spouse cannot disinherit a spouse. Indiana is unique in its interpretation of the 'one-pot' theory, but there are exceptions. First, abandonment, which obviously doesn't apply here. Second, via waiver, which applies, and third, statutory elective share in probate.

"Spouses are entitled to a portion of the probated estate. If you do not leave anything that has to pass through probate, the spouse will not receive anything. So, what has to pass through probate? All assets the deceased owned in his or her name alone need to go through probate, unless a waiver is signed. If Keith and Lisa had not signed the waivers, then Keith would be entitled to a portion of Big Al's, but because he did sign the waiver, Keith agreed to relinquish any rights he had to Big Al's Diner.

"Keith and Lisa executed wills, ten years ago, and both signed individual waivers. Keith agreed to take nothing from Big Al's and Lisa agreed to take nothing from the home on Cardinal Street. A fair market appraisal was conducted of both properties and the values were within fifty thousand dollars of each other, making the properties financially equitable and the signing of the waivers legal.

"I've made copies of the waivers, the appraisals, and Lisa's will." Rina passed stapled copies around the table. "I will be opening Lisa's estate and filing her will in court this coming Monday, which means that her will becomes public information. The waivers and appraisals will not be made public unless the will is contested. Until then, I recommend you only talk about this amongst yourselves."

"I never agreed to that bitch inheriting," Keith said.

"I understand your confusion," Rina said. "By signing the waivers, you and Lisa agreed to relinquish any and all ownership of the two properties. Once the mortgage to Big Al's was paid off, Lisa added a codicil to her will, changing the heir. There's nothing that says she has to inform you of any changes to her will. Also," Rina raised a hand, "any mortgage left on the house on Cardinal Street belongs solely to you, Keith."

"I'm selling. I ain't staying in that dump," Keith said.

"When did she change the heir?" Andrew asked.

"Last year. The codicil is dated June 10, 2018. The codicil also made the provision for the hundred thousand dollars and the new moonshine recipes and the collectibles."

"Andrew, what the hell is going on?" Aubrey asked. "Why did Mom leave you money and not me? Why am I getting shortchanged?"

"I'm opening a moonshine bar, like my wine bar, so Mom and I have been working on recipes. I knew she was leaving those recipes to me, but I didn't know about the money, I swear," Andrew said.

Keith stood up. "She coerced me into signing that waiver. I'll contest it."

"That is certainly your right," Rina said. "Since I am the executor of Lisa's will, it is my job to uphold it. I will be unable to assist anyone in this room should you choose to contest any portion of the will."

"Lawyers are a dime a dozen," Keith sneered. "We don't need you."

"Give me one good reason you should get Big Al's and don't give me that best friend crap." Aubrey glared at Vickie.

"I'm as shocked as you are. I had no idea Lisa was leaving me Big Al's. I'm a terrible cook. I don't want to run a diner." Vickie twisted her earring.

"Then you'll have no problem turning Big Al's over to me," Aubrey said.

"I need to think about this," Vickie said. "Is there anything else?"

"You're all free to go."

* * *

"What the fuck, Dad! You signed a waiver? What in the hell were you thinking?"

An inch of snow had fallen overnight, and in the early afternoon, the sun melted the snow, making rivers in the parking lot, the water draining into storm sewers. Aubrey and Doug, Keith and Monica, and Andrew and Michelle stood in a loose circle in the parking lot behind the professional building.

"Back off, bitch. We lost more than you," Monica said.

"*We*? Who's *we*? You've got no stake in this." Aubrey stepped directly in front of her father's latest girlfriend and shoved.

Monica fell back on her butt.

"What is this bimbo doing here? Have you no respect?" Aubrey screamed in her father's face.

Keith helped Monica to her feet. "Aubrey, Monica. Stop fighting. I'll tell you why I signed that stupid waiver. I never thought Big Al's would be profitable. I never thought Lisa would pay off the mortgage. By signing, I got the house and your mom assumed all financial responsibility for the diner. If we got divorced, I'd be off the hook for the diner's mortgage. I thought I made a pretty sweet deal."

"Yeah? How about now? Still think it's a good deal?" Doug asked.

"When you saw Mom was doing okay and making a profit, why didn't you hire a lawyer and rescind the waiver?" Aubrey pounded her fist into her father's chest.

"I forgot about it."

"Jesus H Christ. I get nothing, Dad. Nothing. Because you forgot, I get nothing." Aubrey buried her head in her husband's shoulder, sobbing.

"What did Vickie do to deserve inheriting Big Al's?" Keith cleared his throat and shuffled his feet. "Where'd she go? She's nothing more than a greedy bitch."

"Don't try and change the topic," Aubrey hissed. "You and your laziness and your sluttiness have ruined my life. Aren't you even going to apologize?"

"I think Vickie went out the front door," Andrew said. "Dad, how was Mom able to buy Big Al's?"

"She had a ten-year buyout with Al Jr. plus the mortgage."

"What did the bank use as collateral?"

"The house."

"You didn't know Mom paid off the diner and Al Jr.?" Aubrey asked.

"She must have paid it off early," Keith said. "She never said a word."

"After the buyout period, did you execute a new will?" Andrew asked.

"I didn't. The old ones are identical except for the special bequests and the codicil she added. I have no special bequests in my will. I think your mother was silly with hers. You think the grandkids are going to care about a stupid white apron? Or a milk tin? Or those goddamn dust collectors?" Keith snorted.

"The value is in the recipes," Monica said.

"Shut up," Aubrey said. "The recipes belong to me."

"Where are they?" Doug asked.

"They're in that little box on the shelf behind Mom's desk in the diner," Andrew said. "The new moonshine recipes she was working on for me are at the house. Dad, I'll stop by later in the week to pick those up."

"Andew, why are you opening another bar?" Aubrey asked. "Aren't you making enough money as it is?"

"Yes, Aubs, I make plenty of money," Andrew said. "But in order to keep up with the other bars and to compete, I have to offer new drinks, specialty drinks. Lots of people make their own beer, but no one makes their own moonshine. It's hugely combustible, which is why it's so highly regulated. People will pay big bucks for it, especially since it can be flavored."

Monica waved a hand. "Yeah, yeah, yeah. What I want to know is what would happen if the old sandwich recipes disappeared or were changed? You're not gonna be able to make moonshine with Lisa dead. The police will shut that down right away."

"You can't wait to soil my mom's reputation, can you? She was already humiliated by Dad's cheating and now you want the diner to serve crappy food. That'll put it right in the ground." Aubrey glared at Monica.

"Don't be such an idiot. You've got those recipes memorized. Why do you want a little box filled with index cards? No one uses that crap anymore," Monica said. "You want Big Al's or not? Talk to Vickie. I'm betting she doesn't have the recipes for your mom's sandwiches memorized." Monica smirked.

"You sneaky little bitch," Aubrey said. *But she's right. Without Mom's recipes, Vickie can't run Big Al's. Only I can.*

CHAPTER TWENTY-ONE

"YOU FUCKIN' IDIOT!" a woman's voice shrieked. "How could you be so stupid?"

Laurent paused at the door of Roses 'N More. *Who's screaming?* Her hand dropped off the doorknob of the floral shop as she strode to the corner of First and Roosevelt. Rounding the corner, she slipped behind a pickup truck parked in the rear lot of the professional building. Six adults, three men, three women, were gathered in a semicircle in the middle of the lot. Laurent recognized Aubrey and her father, Keith, and his girlfriend, Monica.

Aubrey shoved her father. "You asshole! You lost our inheritance."

Laurent strolled out from behind the pickup and watched the entire group stiffen up. "Problem here?"

"We were just leaving," Aubrey snapped. "Come on, Doug."

Keith and Monica turned their backs and walked away.

"Andrew DuVal and my wife, Michelle. Please forgive my dad and sister. They've received a bit of a shock."

"Your mom died, too." Laurent saw tears form in the man's eyes.

"Yes, but I don't need to inherit anything, and I wasn't expecting to." Andrew pulled out a handkerchief and wiped his eyes.

"Would you care to share the contents of your mom's will with me?" she asked.

"Mom left Big Al's to Vickie Wright, not to Aubrey or Dad or me."

"It seemed to me Aubrey was blaming your father."

"You'll have to talk to the lawyer." He gestured toward the building. "The way I understand it, Dad signed some document years ago which gave him the house and Mom got Big Al's."

"I assume Aubrey expected to inherit the diner." Laurent shifted from side to side. She hadn't worn her heavy boots today and was now wishing she had. The cold of the icy slush in the parking lot seeped into her shoes.

"Can you blame her? She's worked part-time at Big Al's since she was in high school. It's where she met Doug. She took off a few years to have Jake and Justin, and when they went to first grade, she worked there every school day," Andrew said.

"What do you do for a living?"

"Michelle and I moved to Indianapolis five years ago and opened Cityscape Rooftop Wine Bar." Andrew pulled out his wallet, extracted a business card, and handed it to Laurent. "The bar's number is on the front. Our home number is on the back. We need to head out. I've got a shipment of wine arriving at two. Call me if I can help."

Laurent watched as Andrew and his wife climbed into their Lexus and drove away. She glanced at the professional building. *As long as I'm here.*

*   *   *

Laurent found the female attorney on the second floor of the professional building. "Rina. Welcome home. Judge Jenkins told me you were opening up your own practice." She held out her hand to the young woman.

"Thanks, Sheriff. The landlord was happy to rent to me. It fills up the building."

"How's your dad? I haven't seen him in a month or so. I'm glad he puts up with me when I show up at school unannounced."

"You underestimate yourself. All the teachers appreciate it. The music staff love it when you sell tickets for a concert and the kids fight over your free private lessons," Rina said.

"I like kids."

"Can I get you something to drink? I assume you're here about the fracas in the parking lot just now. I'll admit to being nosy. I stood at the window and watched." Rina motioned to a chair. "Vickie shot out the front door so fast, I barely had time to get her phone number."

"Got any hot tea?"

"Coming up."

Instead of settling behind the enormous desk, Rina moved the chairs, so the women faced each other.

"Why don't you give me an overview?" Laurent sipped the hot tea and felt the warmth spread. She wiggled her toes and relaxed.

Rina crossed her legs. "I have been appointed by Judge Jenkins as executor of the will. I can't be hired by anyone named in the will or anyone who benefits from the will or anyone remotely connected to the will."

"You told them that?"

Rina nodded. "The will is not very long. Since this is a murder investigation, send me a records subpoena and I'll make a copy for you."

"What was your reaction when you read Lisa's will?"

"What a mess. I remember when Lisa bought the diner from Al Jr. and everyone in town thought it would go under. Then she got the liquor licenses and business was great. Long lines out the door. I was completely surprised when Lisa left the diner to Vickie. I'm sure everyone in town expects Aubrey to inherit. She's the only one in the family who worked there." Rina paused. "I didn't realize Keith had a girlfriend. I had to ask her to wait in the lobby. Depending on her influence on Keith, he may contest the will."

"What about Aubrey and Andew? Do you think they'll contest the will?"

"I doubt Andrew will. He seemed to me to be the only one upset about Lisa's death. I don't have a clue how Aubrey will react. She was extremely upset and I can't say I blame her."

Laurent took notes as Rina explained the terms of Lisa's will. "What are the points of contention? The waivers, obviously. Anything else?"

"The recipes for the sandwiches."

"I don't understand. You said Aubrey gets those."

"What about copies?" Rina said. "An argument can be made that Lisa's intent was for Aubrey to inherit the recipes, including copies. But another argument can be made that the printed copies that are in my house and everything in my house belongs to me. Or Lisa gave these to me. Yesterday, years ago. What happens if Vickie has a copy in her house and decides to run Big Al's without Aubrey?"

"Talk about hell breaking loose," Laurent said. "I overheard part of the conversation in the parking lot before they knew I was there. Keith claims Lisa used the house they owned together as collateral for Big Al's. Would that change anything?"

"Not sure. I'd have to do some research. It's possible a judge might rule since Keith and Lisa owned the house together and the bank used it as collateral that put undue pressure on Keith. The judge might also say the terms of the waivers were unequal, but then the fair market value appraisals that were done back then would refute that argument. However, a fair market appraisal today would show Big Al's to be worth significantly more than the house on Cardinal Street."

"What about the liquor licenses? What happens with them?"

"The state will allow Vickie to transfer the ownership of the liquor licenses assuming she meets their requirements," Rina said. "Again, I'd have to do some research to find out the specifics."

"What about the IRS audit?" Laurent asked.

"This is the first I'm hearing of an audit. What makes you think Big Al's was being audited?"

Laurent pulled out her cell phone and scrolled to the snapshot of the letter. She held out her phone to Rina.

"Vickie has to deal with the IRS, one way or another. She's the accountant hired by Lisa and now she inherits Big Al's, but I suspect the IRS will give her an extension," Rina said. "Do you know if Lisa had a financial planner? All the heirs stormed out of here before I could ask about a life insurance policy."

Laurent shook her head. "This could get messy. What's the next step?"

"I'll file the original will with the court and petition for Letters of Administration, which will allow me to change the ownership of Big Al's to Victoria Scott Wright, manage the current bank accounts, and disburse money. It's mostly paperwork. I'll do a physical inventory of Big Al's and the storage unit where the deceased had a collection of items and there were a few special bequeaths to grandkids.

"Keith gets the joint bank account at Farmers and Vickie gets the money in Big Al's bank account at First Federal minus the hundred thousand dollars to Andrew," Rina said.

"That's a lot of money in a checking account." Laurent set her empty cup of tea on the huge desk. "How long will this take?"

"If no one contests the will, it'll take a minimum of six months. Notices have to be placed so that creditors have time to file their claim," Rina said. "If someone contests any part of the will, it could take a year or more."

Laurent closed her notebook. "So, until Vickie is declared the owner of Big Al's, the diner has to stay closed. What about the utilities? Keeping the lights on in the parking lot? Heating the building so the pipes don't freeze? Eventually air-conditioning?"

"I'll pay those bills from the diner's bank account," Rina said. "But, sadly, yes, the diner has to stay closed."

"Damn. I love the Italian sub."

CHAPTER TWENTY-TWO

THE SCENT OF jasmine permeated the flower shop as Laurent swung open the outer door to Roses 'N More. The door was painted sunshine yellow with white trim and the storefront display was filled with roses of all colors. White, peach, pink, and red roses dominated the window, and as she closed the door behind her, Laurent's shoulders relaxed, the aromatherapy seeping in. She knew Dak's grandma kept a jar filled with soothing scents above the front door on a tiny shelf, and every time a customer entered the flower shop, their troubles melted away. At least that's what Mimi claimed.

"I hear you got my grandson a date with that new coroner at the hospital in Columbia. Thank the Lord." Dak Aikens' tiny grandmother, Mimi, stood in front of one of the refrigerated cases, holding the glass door open while adding water to a vase crammed full of flowers.

"Has he called her?" Laurent asked.

"Here's hoping. I want grandkids before I die."

"You've got time." Laurent pulled off her headband and gloves before settling onto a barstool next to the cash register.

"How come you shoot out of here so fast?" Mimi gently shut the glass door and set the watering can on the polished wood floor. Picking up a bottle of Windex, she squirted the glass and began to wipe.

"I heard yelling in the parking lot behind the professional building and that's never a good sign."

"Who was making all that racket?"

"You heard about Lisa?"

Mimi nodded.

"It seems Aubrey and her father were having an argument, and then Keith's girlfriend chimed in, and she and Aubrey got into a shoving match."

"Cat fight in the alley?" Mimi asked. "What did the cheatin' husband do?"

"Sided with the girlfriend."

"Not his daughter? That's gotta hurt." Mimi squirted the next door. "I 'spose they was arguing about Big Al's?"

"Why do you think that?" Laurent picked up a bag of potpourri and sniffed. *Nice.*

"There's not a lot of female business owners in Field's Crossing, so we get together every now and then," Mimi said.

"Who's *we?*"

"Me, Lisa, DeeDee at the hair salon, Abby from the antique store, Vickie from that auditing firm, sometimes the pastor's wife. We meet for lunch at the Skillet, and Karen—she's the waitress there—would join us. Kind of like an old-fashioned coffee klatch. Sit and bitch about stuff," Mimi said. "We was gonna ask Rina to join us seeing as she just hung out her shingle."

"Why do you think they were arguing about the diner? Did Lisa say something to you?"

"Said she wasn't going to leave it to Aubrey. That no-good son-in-law of hers would gamble everything away, and she wasn't going to let that cheatin' husband of hers get it. One of his whores would rob him blind."

"Doug has a gambling problem?"

"Always asking Lisa for money. He came in here the other day to buy flowers for the funeral and all three credit cards were declined. He finally went to his big ol' Explorer and came back with cash. All small bills. Ones and fives."

"When was this?" Laurent pulled out her notebook. Doug Holmes' gambling problem was news to her.

"Couple of days ago. Wanted me to deliver and set up for free. Henry, over at the funeral home, gave me a hand."

Laurent watched her favorite florist polish the glass windows. *What else does Mimi know?*

"How long has Doug had this gambling problem?"

"Started right up after he married Aubrey. Seems he thought Lisa was a pot of gold."

Was Doug a gold digger? Did he marry Aubrey to feed his addiction? Did Doug kill Lisa? Laurent frowned. The pool of suspects for Lisa's killer just got larger. *Doug and Aubrey, Andrew and Michelle spent Easter Sunday together. First, the egg hunt and then dinner. Any one of the four adults would have been missed if they had left for any length of time. That alibi is sound. But maybe Monica and Keith aren't the only ones in need of money.*

"Anything else you wanna tell me about the DuVal family or Big Al's?" Laurent closed her notebook and shoved it into her coat pocket.

Mimi pointed her finger at Laurent. "How long you gonna keep Big Al's closed? I want me some Sweet Tea Moonshine."

"How long have you been buying it?" Laurent grinned at the tiny grandmother.

Mimi swatted the air. "That ain't none of your business, but it sure soothes the aches and pains I got every night. I ain't no spring chicken anymore."

Laurent laughed and slid off the stool. "You can outwork anyone in this town with the exception of the farmers, and even some of them I bet you can beat."

"Damn straight I can. Especially these young kids. Got no work ethic. No sense of responsibility. Always on the phone."

CHAPTER TWENTY-THREE

VICKIE WALKED QUICKLY, head down, hands stuffed into her pockets. It was mid-April and Mother Nature was showing signs of releasing her grip on winter. She had scurried out the front door of Rina's office while the DuVal family was arguing. After hearing the angry voices coming from the parking lot behind the professional building, she decided to retrieve her car later.

Who killed Lisa? Was it one of those little old biddies who stopped by every day to fill their growler with Sweet Tea Moonshine? Vickie could think of a few old ladies who carried a .22 in their purse or a shotgun in the back seat of their decades-old Lincoln Town Car.

Maybe that sneaky, gambling son-in-law of Lisa's killed her. Always begging for money. *Wonder how much he's in for at the casino? Should I call the manager at Gray Fox Casino? See if I can get a number in case that jerk tries to blackmail me or worse, ask me for money. Like I would give him money when his own mother-in-law wouldn't.* Vickie wondered if Aubrey knew how much her husband gambled.

Maybe it was the age-old problem of the husband lusting for a younger wife. Keith killed the old wife to get a new wife. Vickie knew Lisa and Keith had been fighting over the terms of the divorce. Every time Lisa thought the situation was resolved, Keith came back with a new demand or rejected a previously agreed-upon condition. Vickie suspected Keith's latest girlfriend was responsible for his frequent changes of mind, and she didn't doubt that Keith or his girlfriend would hesitate to kill Lisa.

Vickie strode down Field Street, breathing in the spring air, before pausing on the corner and looking across the intersection at Big Al's Diner.

The building was old. Al Sr. started the diner after WWII and passed it to his son, Al Jr. The original building was one story, square, painted concrete with a pitched metal roof. When Lisa bought out Al Jr., she had tripled the size of the diner, turning it into a T-formation. During the buyout period, Al Jr. and Lisa had agreed to split the cost of updating both the inside and outside. A new, larger parking lot was created, but no drive-thru, and the old section was now the prep area, walk-in cooler, office, and employee area. The long axis of the T was the dining room for customers. The exterior paint color changed every few years. It was currently a combination of barn red, white trim, and black shutters.

Lisa had continued the cash-only policy. A credit card went nowhere in Big Al's. If a customer wanted one of Lisa's tasty sandwiches or homemade root beer or Sweet Tea Moonshine, they had to park the car, walk in, and stand in line. And sometimes, the line was long. Very long. Very old-fashioned for 2019.

Vickie crossed Woodruff Street. Yellow crime scene tape was wound around the handles on the front door and taped across the door at eye height. The police would know immediately if either seal was broken or cut. She walked south on Field Street and saw the back door was trussed up the same way.

Vickie frowned at the building. *I need to get the key to the safe deposit box out of the recipe box before Aubrey gets the recipes. How can I get inside without anyone knowing?*

Vickie walked around the entire diner, staying on the sidewalk. She wasn't going to be able to retrieve the safe deposit key without alerting Sheriff Laurent. She pulled out her phone, dialed the non-emergency number, and was put through to Laurent. "Can you meet me at the Skillet?"

CHAPTER TWENTY-FOUR

"In the last hour, I've drunk a gallon of coffee and read these documents four times. Lisa left me Big Al's and now everyone in the DuVal family hates me, including Keith's latest girlfriend. I have no idea what her name is, but she looked like she wanted to use her laser-long fingernails and gouge my eyes out and that was before the will was read." Vickie wiped her eyes with a tissue. "When Rina called me about the will reading, I assumed Lisa had left me a trinket or something. Not Big Al's."

"Why did the girlfriend show up at the reading?" Laurent asked. The Skillet Restaurant was the only building in town older than Big Al's Diner. It had recently been renovated by the grandson of the original owner. The grandson had sold all the family's farmland to make the Skillet a profitable business. It was the gathering place for early morning risers and old geezers who liked to talk the day away.

"I'm sure she thought Keith would get the diner. Maybe she wanted to gloat. Maybe she wants to be a cook. Maybe she expects him to sell, and she'll benefit from the sale. Maybe she needs money. I don't know, but I'm glad Rina made her leave. I think everyone expected Aubrey to inherit Big Al's, including me. You should have heard them at the lawyer's office," Vickie said.

"Who was there?"

"Keith, Aubrey and Doug, Andrew and his wife, me, and Rina Yoshida."

"Is there anything else that surprised you?" Laurent asked.

"Apparently, Lisa was developing some new moonshine recipes for Andrew, and she left him one hundred thousand dollars. He told everyone he was opening a moonshine bar similar to his wine bar and he and Lisa had been working on recipes for the last year. He claims he knew nothing about the money."

"Do you believe him?"

Vickie nodded. "He was shocked. Not about the recipes, but the money."

Laurent made a mental note. *Why didn't Andrew say something when we were talking in the parking lot? A hundred thousand dollars is a lot of money.* "Did you know about this?"

"Lisa didn't say a word to me."

"Is there enough money to pay the hundred thousand?" Laurent asked.

"I assume so," Vickie said. "I'd like to retrieve the recipe box and give it to Aubrey. It's more of a memento. The recipes are all written in Lisa's handwriting. Maybe it'll mollify her a bit. I really don't want bad feelings between me and Aubrey, especially if I decide to keep Big Al's. I'll need her to run it."

"Let me confirm with Rina, but I've got no problem with that. Dak is confiscating keys from employees and family members. So far, twenty-seven keys. Big Al's wasn't very secure."

"Who'd rob a sandwich store? If you were homeless or couldn't pay, Lisa'd give you the food. She was truly one of the most generous people I knew." Vickie sipped her coffee.

"Why did Lisa leave Big Al's to you and not Keith or Aubrey or Andrew?" Laurent asked.

"I don't know. I can't cook. Maybe she did it to spite Keith."

"Did you know what was in the will before today?"

"No. I don't want the diner. Lisa spent twelve to fourteen hours a day there and still brought work home. She hasn't been on a vacation in years."

"Any idea who wanted her to die?" Laurent asked.

"My first instinct is Keith's girlfriend. She's hiding something."

"How much influence do you think she has over Keith?"

"You think the two of them killed Lisa to get Big Al's?" Vickie said.

"It's a possibility."

"Men are idiots when it comes to screwing younger women," Vickie said. "She struck me as a money-grubbing little bitch and that was before Rina asked her to leave. It seemed to me that Lisa was fed up with everyone in her family except Andrew. Aubrey was stealing from her every day, Doug begged for money at least once a month, and Keith humiliated Lisa with a new floozy every few months. I think Lisa had had it with her family. That's why she left a bucket of money to Andrew. He never asked for a dime. He just wanted help in creating new recipes, which was Lisa's specialty."

"She never mentioned leaving Big Al's to you?" Laurent asked.

"No. But after I think about it, I guess I was a logical choice given her other options."

"She could have left Big Al's to Andrew. He's in a similar business."

"His wife, Michelle, would never leave Indianapolis, and she'd resent every minute he spent here in Field's Crossing," Vickie said. "He could have hired someone to run it, but then he'd have to get someone he trusted."

Andrew didn't trust his sister to run the diner? Laurent sipped her Diet Coke. "Does Andrew know about Aubrey stealing from Lisa?"

"I don't know."

I'll send Dak down to Indy to interview Andrew. Give him a list of my questions. Get him some experience. "Does Lisa have a life insurance policy?"

"The only insurance policy she had was for the diner. Slip-and-falls, that kind of thing. It's required for retail, especially restaurants. Fire damage, roof leaks. She also carried auto insurance for the catering vans, but no life insurance. She canceled it when she paid off the diner. Said her kids were old enough and didn't need the protection anymore and she wasn't leaving a dime to Keith," Vickie said. "I told her to get a lawyer who handles estate planning, but I don't think she ever did."

"Would you tell me about your financial situation?"

"I don't need the income from Big Al's. My husband died years ago and left me well off."

"What happens when you retire? Who gets the firm?" Laurent was curious. She had no idea how law firms or any type of professional company stayed in business for a hundred years. Surely, those who started the company were dead. *Why is their name still on the door especially if they had no children who followed them into the business?*

"Since I have no children, I'm hoping one of my partners' kids will buy me out. If no one wants to, then I'll negotiate a price for my retirement."

"Like a retirement bonus?"

Vickie nodded. "My clients pay a fee for my services so my retirement package will reflect the money they pay to BS&W. I'll ask for five years of fees and we'll settle at three years."

"How much money do you think that will be?"

"Half-a-million."

Laurent arched her eyebrows. "I'm hoping after thirty years of service, my pension will be around that. Pension plus IRAs."

"I've got IRAs from decades ago. When 401(k)s were first allowed, I started one also. I'm not worried about retirement. The house is paid for, and I estimate I'll have two million, possibly more, in retirement vehicles."

"That's a big house for one person," Laurent said. "I know Lisa was planning to move in. Before that, how often did she sleep over?"

"She rarely slept at the house on Cardinal Street. Keith's such a condescending jerk. She couldn't stand him. Lisa told Keith she was moving in with me and he could have the house. She said she'd sign over the title if they could just finish the damn divorce," Vickie said.

"Why was she holding up the divorce if she had the waiver?"

"Lisa assumed Keith remembered the waivers. Apparently, he didn't. That's what he claimed in Rina's office this morning. Even with the waivers, Lisa's name was on the title of the house, and she'd have to sign off. Anyway, the fight was over retirement assets. Keith wanted his entire 401(k) and she wanted half. He didn't want to give her half. He claimed she'd withdraw the money and use it on Big Al's and no way was his retirement savings going to that dump. It's possible Keith killed her to get the whole ball of wax. House, restaurant, retirement money. He could sell Big Al's and retire with his latest floozy. Maybe move to a warmer climate. I don't know. He's got the best motive."

"What are you going to do?" Laurent asked.

"I have no idea."

"It'll be a few more days before I can release the crime scene."

"Keep it closed as long as you can, but I think I should change the locks. Lisa was very lax about security."

"Call a locksmith and have him meet us there in an hour. He can change the locks while I look around a bit more," Laurent said. "Rina is the executor. I'll call and ask her if she can meet us this afternoon. She said she has to do an inventory of Big Al's and some collectibles Lisa owned. She can take any special bequests, and I'll write a receipt for her file. Anything else you want to add?"

"Sheriff, maybe I'm overreacting, but do you think whoever killed Lisa will come after me?"

CHAPTER TWENTY-FIVE

"Sheriff, the locksmith's arrived. Is it okay if I scoot under this yellow tape and let him in the back door?" Vickie had retrieved her BMW from behind the professional building and parked in the rear parking lot of Big Al's. She called Laurent from her cell phone.

"Go ahead. I'll be there in two minutes," Laurent said. "If I need to, I'll retape it when I leave."

Vickie waved to the white van and waited for the locksmith to tromp through the slushy parking lot. She unlocked the rear door to Big Al's and ducked under the yellow crime scene tape, holding it up for the locksmith. "Why don't you use the main dining room? You can hang up your coat and use one of the tables for your toolbox and stuff."

"That'll work great." The locksmith followed Vickie.

"The sheriff will be here in a few minutes. I'm going to turn up the heat." She rubbed her hands together.

"Thank you, ma'am."

As soon as the locksmith turned his back, Vickie walked to the office. She needed thirty seconds to get the recipe box and shove it into her tote. *Yes. The box is still here.* In four steps, she was around the desk. She grabbed the recipe box off the shelf and slipped it into her enormous tote. She quickly rounded the desk and was walking down the hallway when the breeze from the back door reached her. Vickie swung around. "I turned the heat up, but it'll be a few minutes before we can take off our coats."

"No problem. Where's the locksmith?" Laurent pulled off her gloves and shoved them into her pocket.

"Right here, Sheriff. Now, Mrs. Wright, what are you thinking of doing here? Those locks you got on are twenty or thirty years old. No sense replacing them with old stuff. People these days start their cars with their phones. Is that something you're thinking of?"

"I don't think I need to be that modern. I want a dead bolt on both front and back doors and a keypad." Vickie watched out of the corner of her eye as Laurent wandered away from the discussion about locks.

*   *   *

Laurent walked away from Vickie and the locksmith and stood in the doorway of the prep room. She remembered thinking it looked like Lisa had two different staffs. Lunchtime moms and nighttime and weekend high schoolers. All the kids she and Dak had talked to who worked the Saturday night shift or helped transport the eggs on Sunday morning said the same thing. Lisa was alive, happy, chatty, her usual self. None of them remembered locking the back door. The front door wasn't used.

Anyone could come in through an unlocked door. The safe was empty and, according to bank records, there was no deposit on Saturday night or Sunday morning. Laurent assumed whoever killed Lisa stole the money from the safe. Which meant someone who was familiar with the diner, closing procedures, security cameras, and bank deposits. Was the safe left open all day? What happened when the cash register got too full? Who emptied it? Laurent briefly flashed back to a video from Beaumon's Hardware store when Theo Tillman was accused of stealing from the cash register. The hardware store was forty thousand square feet and had a vacuum tube system for the cashiers. Big Al's did not. Someone, possibly Lisa, removed the cash from the register and either put it in the safe or someplace else. *Was one of the employees a thief?* They had confiscated twenty-seven keys to Big Al's. *That's a lot of people with access.*

Lisa had no defensive wounds. Whoever stabbed her caught her by surprise and the murderer was someone she knew and wasn't afraid of. *And the murderer didn't know she had three grand in her purse. I wonder if it was normal for Lisa to carry around that much cash?*

Laurent listed the suspects in her mind. Keith, followed closely by his girlfriend, Monica. Vickie, who inherited Big Al's but claimed she didn't know Lisa was going to leave the diner to her. The disinherited—Aubrey and Andrew. And, possibly, their spouses. Basically, everyone in the family.

How about coworkers, staff, employees? Laurent put the high school kids at the bottom of her list. Steal the money, yes. Stab Lisa, no. She sighed and strolled back to the eating area.

"You're all set, Mrs. Wright," the locksmith said. "You need to choose a passcode. Then, we'll settle up and I'll get out of your hair."

CHAPTER TWENTY-SIX

BEEP. BEEP.

Laurent glanced behind her and saw Vern Martin's beat-up old pickup truck swing into Big Al's parking lot. He pulled alongside her. "Afternoon, Sheriff. I hear you're keeping busy."

Laurent laughed. "Did Art and Dutch tell you that?" Art and Dutch were Laurent's favorite old guys. Since retiring from farming, they met every morning at the Skillet, drinking coffee and chatting like little old ladies.

"You know they're always good for gossip even though they deny it. They call it local news," Vern said.

"What's their theory?"

"Which one? Either the husband did it, the girlfriend did it, or one of those high school kids did it. They were all over the place and enjoying every minute of it. I think the real question is who do you think did it?"

"This family is so messed up. They're either letting each other down or finding some way to hurt each other. And it's all about money. I found them fighting in the parking lot behind the professional building this morning."

"Money has been ruining families for centuries."

"I think a lack of trust is also partly responsible."

"Care to explain?" he asked.

Laurent looked into the familiar blue eyes of the farmer and felt a knot around her heart loosen. Vern had probably guessed much of her story already. "How much time you got?"

"All damn day." Vern put his truck into park, climbed out, and leaned against the door. "What's weighing you down? Finding Lisa's killer or something closer to home?"

"I had dinner with Randi the other night and it didn't go so well. Not like the first time." Laurent scuffed the ground with the toe of her shoe.

"What did she want?"

"To know who her father is. I didn't want to tell her. He's such an asshole. She doesn't need him in her life."

"You told her that?"

Laurent nodded.

"And she told you she's grown up and can make her own decisions," Vern said.

"Right again."

Vern tilted his head. "She's right. You can't protect everyone you love. Pain is a part of life. I know you lost both of your parents at a young age, so the protective instinct is strong in you, but your daughter's a grown woman. She didn't get there without a few of her own battle scars."

"That's what she said."

"What did she say after you told her about her father?"

"She didn't believe me."

Vern's eyebrows shot up. "Why not?"

"Because he's a world-renowned violinist. We were at Indiana University together."

"Is Randi going to contact him?"

"I think so."

"You're afraid she'll choose him over you," Vern said.

"I'm afraid he's going to hurt her."

"Like he hurt you."

"I don't think she really knows what she wants. According to Randi, she just found out she was adopted," Laurent said.

"Why now?"

"I don't know."

"Well, maybe you ought to ask," Vern said. "She contacted you for a reason. Find out why. Her life might not be as great as you think."

CHAPTER TWENTY-SEVEN

"I SEE YOUR incompetence is rearing its ugly head again." Deputy Sheriff Mike Greene lounged against the doorframe to Laurent's office. "Got another murder on your hands and no way to solve it."

"Welcome back." Laurent shoved to her feet and refused to take the bait. She was not going to discuss Lisa's murder case with anyone other than Dak or Poulter. Every piece of information she'd gathered in Stephanie Gattison's murder investigation had found its way to Ralph Howard whose family owned the local newspaper, *The Crossing*. Ralph's nasty comments and insinuations fed the newspaper's opinion page the month before the election and pitted Greene against her for the job of sheriff. She had learned her lesson. Never divulge anything to Mike Greene or it was bound to appear in the paper the next day.

"Spare me," Greene snapped. "You don't want me here any more than I want to be here."

"So why are you here, then?"

"Gotta eat."

Laurent looked at the reinstated deputy. He had put on weight and the buttons around his stomach gaped, showing a black undershirt. His corn-colored hair stuck out from all angles reminding her of the scarecrow from *The Wizard of Oz*.

She had seen him around town during his suspension, and even after the election was over, there were still GREENE FOR SHERIFF signs. Local ordinance required him to take them down forty-eight hours after the election, but he had failed to do so. Laurent assumed she'd have to ask Caleb Martin from public works to send someone out. She wondered if she could send the bill to Greene. She knew she could fine him. *Do I really want to start a fight?*

Laurent opened the top right drawer, pulled out Greene's badge and weapon, and handed them across the desk. She waited until he re-pinned his badge and checked his weapon before sliding it into the holster on his hip.

"Now what? Want me to solve this murder for you?"

"Go downstairs and see Naomi. She'll reset your password and issue you a radio and phone. The Wi-Fi in the building has been upgraded. She'll give you the office password. After that, head to the firing range and put in an hour of practice. Take lunch and then sign out a cruiser and work the county road route."

"Banishing me to the country?" Greene sneered. "Don't want me around? Good thing I don't want to be in this office either."

Laurent continued as though he hadn't spoken. "Per your agreement, the GPS will be activated on any vehicle you use during your shift, and Naomi will track your password and keep a list of what websites you access during your shift."

"Yeah, yeah."

"Once the civil lawsuit is settled, the union will make recommendations," she said. "After that's done, you can expect to be fired."

"You're gonna find yourself funding my retirement." Greene smirked. "My lawyer tells me it's a slam dunk. You violated so many of my rights."

"I'm not discussing any aspect of the lawsuit with you, and I'm sure your attorney has told you not to discuss it with anyone else. I'd follow his advice. That's what you're paying him for."

"He's gonna get that security video from Bubba's Steakhouse thrown out and you'll be left with nothing. I'm tacking on punitive damages, especially for libel and slander. You ruined my reputation. The minute the judge sides in my favor, I'm filing a petition for a special election, and you'll be out on your ear. I'm gonna win and be sitting behind that desk."

"We'll let the judge decide." Laurent turned her back on Greene. "Now get out of my office." She waited until he slammed the door before picking up the desk phone. "Naomi, Mike Greene is on his way to see you. I want to know where he is every minute he's on duty."

"Ten-four, Sheriff."

I don't trust that bastard. Not one bit. I need to remind Dak and Poulter not to say a word about Lisa's murder investigation when he's around. Greene will tell Ralph and the next day it'll be all over town. I'm not going through that again.

CHAPTER TWENTY-EIGHT

DAK TAPPED ON Laurent's office door. "CSU sent some results."

"Have Poulter join us." Laurent pushed away from her desk to retrieve a bottle of water from the mini fridge.

"I'll start with fingerprints." Dak stretched his long legs and slouched in the chair in front of her desk and waited until Poulter settled into the chair next to him. "The first thing CSU wanted to remind us of is that people who work with food are required by law to wear gloves.

"We submitted fifty-four sets of prints from employees, the deceased, and her family and friends. We got a bunch of matches in the food prep area, office, bathroom, and employee break room. Every current employee had prints in the diner that matched something we sent to CSU, including the knives." Dak flipped a page. "We sent one hundred and two knives to CSU and none of them had blood on them. CSU says these knives come in sets and there were a few knives missing, possibly broken or stolen, and one of them could be the murder weapon. One of the missing knives matches the specs from the stab wound. Serrated, approximately ten inches long. A bread knife."

"At least we know what we're looking for," Poulter said.

Laurent leaned forward, elbows on the desk. "Does CSU give an estimate of the amount of force necessary to penetrate the skin and chest cavity?"

"I talked to the tech who ran the specs, and he wouldn't say the knife cut like butter, but it slid through tissue easily. Very little force needed," Dak said. "Whoever killed Lisa stood right next to her and slid the knife in all the way to the hilt and pulled it out.

"According to the autopsy report, fibers and threads from Lisa's shirt were found in the wound. The knife entered beneath the victim's left breast and headed upward and diagonally into the left lung, nicking the heart. The victim lost a great deal of blood and was unable to breathe. Dr. Romero lists the manner of death as homicide and the cause of death as stabbing," Dak said.

Laurent sipped her water. "Lisa didn't stand a chance. How much blood could the killer have on his clothing?"

"Not much. It's possible the killer pulled the knife out and walked away, without a drop of blood, but Dr. Romero thought we might find a drop or two on a pair of gloves or pants or shoes." Dak closed the manila folder and tossed it on Laurent's desk. "The samples we scraped off the circular drive had gravel, tar, leaves, and dog poop. No blood."

"The killer stabs Lisa and closes the driver's-side door. Then what? Opens the back door of Big Al's, walks down the hallway to the cash register, takes the money, and then steals the cash from the safe in the office?" Laurent saw the entire scenario in her mind. "Or vice versa. Takes the cash first and then kills Lisa. Either way works for me. If he already had the cash from the safe, he didn't need the money in her purse and didn't bother to look. That fits."

"Think he was parked in the back?" Poulter asked.

"Yep."

"The grocery store's parking lot is across Delaney Street, and they were closed on Easter Sunday," Poulter said. "Ain't no one to see if there was a vehicle sitting in the circular drive."

"I called the manager, and he sent over the security video. The camera angles are all facing the parking lot. Big Al's doesn't even show up," Laurent said.

"The other possibility is that the killer was in the van with her," Dak said.

"Then why didn't he stab her in the right side?" she asked. "After Lisa put the van in park and shut off the engine. Much easier, no one can see what's going on. Why open the driver's-side door and stab her and shut the door? I think the killer was waiting for her at the diner. Opened the door. Stabbed her. Closed the door. Stole the money and walked away. Or was in the process of stealing the money, heard the van pull up, and panicked. Grabbed a knife, stabbed her, and left and took the knife."

"Did the van have any fingerprints?"

"The steering wheel and door handles had multiple prints," Dak said. "Lisa's, Stacy's, and all the lunchtime ladies, and the two boys who drove on Sunday to load and unload the eggs, but we expected those. The one set of prints that surprised me was Vickie Wright's. I thought she didn't have anything to do with Big Al's other than being the auditor. Her prints were on the driver's-side door and the rear back doors."

"Vickie told me she was at the Easter egg hunt. I'll clarify."

"Out of all of the people we suspect, whose prints didn't we find, but should have?" Poulter asked.

"Keith admitted he never set foot in the place. Same with Monica. Did we find prints for either of them?" Laurent asked.

"There were no prints for Keith, Monica, Doug, Andrew, or Michelle."

"They could've worn gloves," Poulter said.

"Was the diner left unlocked on Sunday?" Laurent asked.

Poulter nodded. "The two boys who helped load the van on Sunday morning said Lisa left without locking the back door. One of them asked her specifically if she wanted him to lock it, and she said no. She was going to be back and forth all day."

"Anyone who worked at Big Al's could have walked in and taken all the money out of the cash register and safe," Dak said.

"Anyone driving by could have robbed Big Al's. All they had to do was walk through an unlocked door. Someone could have been watching from across the street and noticed that no one locked the back door. Another possibility is one of the high school employees said something to someone else and that person stole the cash," Poulter said. "You know how much those kids text each other. I reviewed Big Al's bank account and the Monday afternoon deposit always ranged between five and six thousand dollars. Except for last Monday. No deposit at all."

"Someone got away with a bucket load of money," Dak said. "Any way we can track it?"

"We could ask the merchants in town who's been spending more than normal, especially if it's a high school kid," Poulter said. "Doesn't necessarily lead us to the killer, just the person who stole the money."

"But maybe that person saw something," Dak said.

Laurent sipped her water. "You've got a point there. Anyone could have taken the money at any point on Sunday, especially since the back door was left unlocked. Lisa got to Webster Park around eight and after we unloaded the van, the two high school kids drove back to the diner, loaded the van again, and returned to Webster Park. Either kid could have taken the money or one of their buddies. Five or six grand isn't worth killing for, but getting control of Big Al's. That's worth killing for."

"So, follow the money, but don't follow the money," Poulter said.

"Exactly. What if Keith and/or Monica waited at the diner for Lisa to return and one of them stabbed her?" Laurent asked.

"Lisa would find it odd if Keith was there because he never stepped foot in the diner and she'd find it even odder for Monica to be there. But would she suspect they were there to kill her?" Dak asked.

"Lisa might have opened the door to the van and one of them stepped up, stabbed her, and closed the door. Quick and easy," Laurent said.

"Would Lisa let Monica stand next to her?" Poulter asked.

"You mean without belting her?" Dak said. "I doubt it."

"I think if Lisa saw Monica waiting for her, she'd have run her over with the van," Laurent said.

"Lisa might not have seen her killer," Poulter said. "The killer could have been waiting behind the trees or the dumpster and after Lisa parked the van, the killer came out and stabbed her."

The three officers were quiet.

"I think we're looking for an adult and the motive is control of Big Al's," Dak said.

"I'm with you on that one," Laurent said. "Let's run a deep financial background check on Keith. I only did a cursory check. He's got a solid job at Columbia Hospital. Bills paid every month. Nothing extravagant shows up on the credit cards. Income looked good. Go deeper. Check retirement savings, money market accounts, that sort of thing."

"Will do." Poulter pulled out his phone and tapped in a note.

"Next. Monica." Laurent laced her fingers behind her head. "She struck me as greedy."

"Hair stylists rely on tips to make a living," Dak said. "But most people put the tip on the credit card so now the IRS gets its share, whereas with a cash tip, no one knows."

"The financial check I ran on her came up pretty bare bones. She spends every dime she makes, but I didn't find any overwhelming credit card debt or debt of any kind. She obviously doesn't own a home and has no car payments," Laurent said. "I was interviewing Keith when she showed up. Her car was filled with her stuff. She moved in with Keith the day after we found Lisa. She said she and Keith and Lisa had already talked about it. But she did make an odd statement. She said they needed Big Al's to reopen because they had bills to pay."

"Who's she talking about?" Dak asked. "Her and Keith, or just herself? And what bills does she have to pay, especially if she's living with Keith? I bet he buys the groceries and pays the utilities and mortgage. Can't see him charging her rent."

"Agreed. What bills does she have to pay? Especially now. Maybe I missed something. Add her to your list. Go back at least ten years. She may also have changed her name."

"What about Aubrey? Talk about someone with a right to be upset," Dak said.

"No shit. You work for your mom for years. Your dad never sets foot in the place. Your brother's making buckets of money from a wine bar and is opening another one. Of course Aubrey expected to inherit. But kill her mom to get Big Al's? I don't see it." Poulter shook his head. "What's Aubrey and Doug's financial situation?"

"On the surface, everything's fine. Doug's a service manager at the Ford dealership. Aubrey makes about a grand a month at the diner. Mortgage is current, but three credit cards are maxed out. Utilities all current," Laurent said. "The only wrinkle is Doug might have a gambling problem."

"Who told you that?" Dak asked.

"Your grandma."

Dak slapped his bald head. "Mimi. I forgot about her women's coffee klatch."

"Vickie also mentioned that Doug frequently asked Lisa for money, but she never gave him a dime," Laurent said.

Dak waved a hand. "Wait a minute. Doug couldn't have killed Lisa. He was home with his wife, his brother- and sister-in-law, and four kids. Unless those four adults are in on a conspiracy, they're last on my list."

"I'll ask Keith if he knew about Doug's gambling." Laurent leaned forward and added another note to her growing list of questions.

"Where was Stacy Simmons on Sunday afternoon? I don't remember seeing her at Webster Park," Poulter asked.

"Stacy claims she was at the batting cages."

"The batting cages are at the other end of Webster Park," Dak said. "Stacy could have kept an eye on the egg hunt and driven back to Big Al's and waited for Lisa. She's got keys, and Lisa would have let Stacy get close, even open the door."

"Stacy is about as bitter as a person can get," Laurent said. "She claims Lisa kept her on at the diner because she didn't want to tarnish her reputation."

"How does Stacy benefit from killing Lisa?" Poulter asked.

"Revenge," Laurent said. "Maybe Stacy thought she could buy the diner from Keith. She's got collateral now for the bank loan."

"Killing Lisa's a bit of a stretch if revenge is the motive," Dak said. "I'd want to sit around and watch Lisa and the diner fall apart."

"I like that theory." Laurent looked at Poulter. "Run a financial check on Stacy Simmons, too."

"Will do," Poulter said. "What about the IRS audit?"

"Aubrey knew. Vickie knew. Stacy knew," Laurent said. "When I interview the Moonshine Mamas tomorrow, I plan on asking them."

"Who are the Moonshine Mamas?" Dak asked.

"That's what Stacy called the women at Big Al's who served alcohol."

"Why would they want Big Al's audited?" Poulter asked.

"I don't know. I can't figure out how anyone benefits from an IRS audit unless you're the whistleblower," Laurent said. "There may be a reward or something like that."

"That could take years," Dak said.

"What if the audit led to fines or jail time?" Poulter asked. "Who would have taken over the diner? Would Lisa have had to sell? What if Lisa couldn't afford the fine?"

"I'll ask Rina," Laurent said. "What else did CSU find? Anything interesting in the dumpster?"

"The dumpster contained every kind of animal shit known to man. Cats, dogs, squirrels, raccoons, turkeys, deer, rabbits—you name it, CSU found it." Dak wrinkled his nose. "Nothing stands out about the dumpster. A broken lawn chair, deflated soccer ball, reading glasses, uneaten food, plastic silverware. They did find a kid's mouthguard."

"I doubt the parents want it back."

CHAPTER TWENTY-NINE

"WHEN YOU GONNA hire another deputy?" Dak stood in the doorway of Laurent's office. It was eleven at night, and her long day was almost done.

"Pumping that caffeine already?" Laurent responded. The large Diet Coke from McDonald's looked small in Dak's hand.

"I'm pulling a double shift. I went home after our murder discussion this morning but didn't really sleep. I don't know if I'll ever get used to the graveyard shift." He plopped into a chair in front of her desk.

"It was hard for me, too," Laurent admitted. "My brain and body said it was time to sleep, not patrol the streets." She clicked and closed all the open windows on her computer. "I was planning to interview a few people this week, but with Lisa's murder, I've pushed back the interviews."

"How many new deputies are you planning to hire?"

"At least two, possibly three. We were short-staffed before Greene was suspended, but now that he's back, I'm keeping him to the county roads. I know you, Poulter, and Ingram like the overtime, but you're all looking a bit worn around the edges."

"Speak for yourself."

Laurent laughed. "I am."

"Tracking down murderers sucks," Dak said. "Who do you think did it? Professor Plum in the library with the candlestick?"

"I always loved that game. I think there's a Homer Simpson version now," she said. "We've got a lot of suspects, and they all have a motive to want Lisa dead, and the motive for all of them seems to be control of Big Al's."

"But who wanted Big Al's so bad they killed her?" He pointed his finger at her. "The more important question is how soon will Big Al's reopen? I can't even imagine what the first day will be like. What a zoo."

"Vickie's got a lot of options. She could sell. She could hire Aubrey to run it or negotiate a buyout agreement with Aubrey, but I don't see Vickie running it herself." Laurent put her computer to sleep.

"Maybe Vickie killed Lisa." Dak sipped his Diet Coke.

"I don't think so. Vickie complained Lisa spent twelve to fourteen hours a day at the diner. Killing Lisa serves no purpose, and she told me, she doesn't need the money."

"Vickie could give it to Aubrey. Free."

"Wouldn't that be nice? Nothing changes. My favorite sandwich still on the menu." Laurent sighed.

"Keith's got the biggest motive to get rid of his wife. Divorce, new girlfriend. Men can be so stupid."

"He said they were having difficulties in dividing their assets. In his words, 'I want my half of that fuckin' diner,' and they were fighting over the division of his 401(k). Lisa thought they should split it in half."

"How much was in his 401(k)?"

Laurent pulled out her notepad and wrote down Dak's question. *Money, money, money.*

"I'm leaning toward the girlfriend. She was furious Vickie inherited. Maybe Monica killed Lisa so she could get her hands on Keith and Big Al's. Maybe she's tired of cutting hair and doing nails." Dak ran a hand over his bald head. "Go over this waiver thing again."

"Ten years ago, Keith signed Big Al's over to Lisa with no right to inherit and Lisa signed over the house to him, again, with no right to inherit. Estimates of fair market value for the two properties, at that time, showed a discrepancy of less than fifty thousand dollars."

"The waivers mean?" Dak wiggled his eyebrows.

"Keith gave up his rights to Big Al's and Lisa gave up her rights to the house on Cardinal Street. Whoever died first was not leaving the property to the surviving spouse. Since Lisa died first, Keith does not get Big Al's. If Keith had died first, Lisa would not have gotten the house on Cardinal Street. Aubrey and Andrew would have inherited the house on Cardinal. That's how Lisa was able to leave the diner to Vickie. Keith had, in effect, signed it over to Lisa's heir. He made the assumption he would be her heir automatically, but the waivers changed that."

"Who would ever want to be a lawyer?" Dak said. "Can Keith claim he didn't understand what he was signing?"

"I doubt it, but I'll ask Rina," she said. "I'm with you on Keith being the primary suspect and his girlfriend, Monica, in second place. I put Stacy in third place. Aubrey and Doug and Andrew and Michelle are at the bottom of my list even though Aubrey's motive is the same as her father's. She says her dad's been cheating on her mom for years. If Aubrey was that upset, she should've killed her dad. I can see Aubrey stealing money from the cash register and the safe. She certainly had access." Laurent yawned. "What did the employees have to say? Anyone stick out as angry with their boss?"

"Nope. Aubrey was in charge of training employees, and she wasn't very well liked by the high schoolers. That being said, they're high schoolers. Anyone in authority pisses them off. I did talk to the two kids' parents' who drove the van on Sunday. Said they were home eating Easter dinner and never left," Dak said.

"Keys to the building?"

"Lisa's lucky she wasn't robbed. Not only is there no list of who has a key, apparently if you worked there twenty years ago, your key would still unlock the front door."

"How many keys did you confiscate?" she asked.

"We're up to twenty-nine. They're all tagged and listed on the evidence list."

"I wonder how many other business owners have poor security." Laurent looked at Dak. "You got a key to Mimi's?"

"Yep."

"Me, too." Laurent pushed to her feet. "I'm going home."

The radio on Dak's shoulder crackled. "Unit one. Possible break-in. Big Al's. Caller reports the front window smashed in." Dak jumped to his feet and wagged his finger at her.

"I'm going," Laurent snapped. "But if there's any chasing to be done, you're the one doing the running." She followed him out of her office, slamming the door behind her.

"Sheriff, this is not my idea of desk duty." Laurent and Dak jogged across the squad room, flew down the stairs, shot through the rear door of the police station, and slid behind the wheels of their police vehicles. As Laurent climbed into the SUV and switched on the lights, she smiled at Dak's voice in the radio on her shoulder.

"Desk duty, Sheriff. Keep saying that to yourself."

CHAPTER THIRTY

THE TWO VEHICLES raced silently south on Sycamore Street.

"Dak, cut over on Delaney." The surge of adrenaline had shattered Laurent's exhaustion. Braking lightly, she squealed around the corner and sped east on Oak Street.

"Ten-four."

Who wanted to break into Big Al's? What are they looking for? Everyone in town knew the police had removed anything of value from the diner. *Is the culprit a high school kid playing a prank? A definite possibility.*

Swinging into the parking lot, Laurent screeched to a stop blocking the front door. She touched the radio on her shoulder. "On scene. No vehicles in sight. Glass all over the sidewalk. And a chair." She slipped out of the SUV and ran to the corner of the diner. With her back brushing the concrete wall, she sidestepped to the broken window, squatted, and pulled out her Maglite. Crouching next to the smashed-in front window, she clicked on the flashlight, rose, and shone it into the diner. She ducked back down. And whispered into the radio, "Front dining room trashed. Possible intruder behind cash register."

"Ten-four. Back door open, tape cut, no vehicles."

Laurent flitted past the broken window, her shoes crunching on the broken glass. Reaching the front door, she twisted the knob. "Front's door locked. Tape intact." She glanced around the darkened parking lot. "Where are you?"

"Behind my cruiser."

"I'm coming around the west side of the building. We'll enter through the back door. If he tries to go out the front window, he's going to get scratched to pieces."

"Ten-four. Be careful, Sheriff."

Laurent trained her Maglite along the outside wall of the diner. The corner streetlights didn't reach the diner's parking lot and no light shone from the neon sign. Big oak trees filtered the moonlight casting the diner in and out of darkness. With her back scraping the cold exterior wall, she approached the first window. Interior blinds were down. Crouching, she duck-walked under the window. Next window. Same thing. Creeping around the corner, she spotted Dak squatting behind the tire of his police cruiser. He had turned off the red and blue roof lights on his cruiser and the interior dome light.

He pointed at her. "I'm lead."

Laurent gave him a thumbs-up. *There's no arguing with him when he's like this.* Sliding past the area where the dumpster used to stand, Laurent flattened herself against the wall and slipped behind the open back door. She motioned to him. In three steps, Dak stood next to her. His right hand gripped his weapon.

Quietly, Laurent pulled out her Glock and pointed it at the ground. "Ready?"

Dak's left hand reached inside the open door and hovered over the bank of light switches.

Click.

The first light switch was the hallway light. Tiny specks of water dotted the floor. Laurent glanced up at the ceiling. No water damage. She shone her flashlight down the hallway. The trail of water led past the prep area, the office, and the employee break room into the eating area. All the rooms were pitch black.

"Follow the puddles," Laurent whispered.

Dak stepped inside and slid past the panel of light switches; his broad shoulders flattened against the wall.

Laurent flicked the second switch and light flooded the prep area. She snuck a quick peek before stepping inside. The bright light glared off the stainless-steel counters. She squinted as she shone her flashlight under the counters. Nothing. Laurent yanked open the huge door to the walk-in cooler and shivered as cold air poured over her. She flicked on the light. Two tall carts filled with food blocked the rest of the refrigerator. She slammed the door and strode back to the hallway.

Pausing in the doorway, she waited as Dak cleared Lisa's office. *That room isn't big enough to hide a child.*

Laurent slid along the hallway, her back pressed against the wall, Dak mimicking her on the other side of the hall. He squatted and shone his flashlight into the employee area before reaching up to turn on the light. No one. Empty. Tables, chairs, hooks on the wall. Nowhere to hide.

Last room.

Laurent squatted at the end of the hallway. The large dining room lay before her, dark and filled with overturned chairs and tables. The blinds were down, but a little moonlight filtered through the slats casting slivers of light on the floor. She shone her flashlight around the room, the light reflecting off the shards of glass on the floor. Nothing. The wet tracks led to the cash register where a puddle of water had formed on the floor in front of the open register. She motioned toward the counter where alcohol and dessert were served.

Dak crept around the corner. A quick glance. Nothing.

"Where is he?" she whispered. She lowered the volume on her radio and waited until Dak copied her. She pulled her headband down around her neck. And listened.

Screech.

Laurent spun and aimed her weapon at the hallway. "The walk-in cooler. We got him trapped."

Dak ran down the hallway, Laurent on his heels.

"Get the door." He stood, both hands on his weapon, arms extended, gun trained on the heavy steel door.

Laurent grabbed the handle and swung the door open. The cold air from the walk-in cooler escaped out forming a mist as it met the outside air. Moonlight streamed in from an open door in the back of the cooler. Laurent shoved one of the two racks of food to the side. "What the hell?"

Dak shot out the hidden door and crouched next to his police cruiser. Laurent dashed to join him.

"Quiet. Maybe we can hear him running."

"Hear that?" The faint sound of pounding footsteps.

"That way." Laurent pointed west.

"Get in your vehicle, Sheriff. I'll run the bastard down." Dak holstered his weapon and took off running, his sneakers silent on the pavement.

Laurent ran back to her SUV, slid behind the wheel, and switched on the red and blue lights. She shot out of the parking lot, tires squealing, as she yanked the SUV onto Woodruff Street. *Where's Dak?* She didn't like chasing anyone, let alone her favorite deputy at night. She pushed away visions of the intruder pulling a gun and shooting him.

"Dak, what's your twenty?" Laurent turned the volume up on her radio.

"Delaney and Sycamore."

"Stay on Delaney. I'm on Woodruff." *He's in the residential area.*

"Ten-four."

Damn. Dak didn't even sound winded. Laurent raced through the residential area before turning onto Delaney. Dak was four blocks ahead of her. "Do you see him?"

"Negative. Sonofabitch is gone."

CHAPTER THIRTY-ONE

When Vickie walked through the door of Big Al's at two in the morning, Laurent almost didn't recognize her. No makeup, missing eyebrows, age spots, flattened hair. The normally put-together middle-aged woman wore gray sweatpants tucked into rubber boots and a black raincoat.

"What did they take?" Vickie asked.

"As far as we can tell, nothing. Whoever broke in had a key to the back door, threw a chair through the front window, and escaped through a door in the walk-in cooler. Did you know about this hidden door?" Laurent was angry. Her shoulder ached, her ibuprofen was at home, and the intruder got away. Dak was cruising the side streets, but she knew he was gone.

"I probably should have told you about that." Vickie righted a chair and flopped into it.

"You think?" Laurent glared at the disheveled woman.

"Lisa told me it was used when Big Al and Al Jr. sold illegal moonshine. Since she got a liquor license, that door is usually locked."

"Who has keys?"

"I only know of Lisa, Aubrey, Stacy, and Ruby Rae. I wouldn't be surprised if there were a few more," Vickie said. "I forgot that cooler door even existed, otherwise I would have had the locksmith change that lock, too. I'll call him tomorrow and have it replaced."

"How do you know all this? I thought you were just the accountant for the diner."

"Even though Lisa was moving into the in-law suite at my house, we talked almost every day. Keith never listened. Lisa talked about the diner all the time. It was her passion. I guess I picked up on most of it." Vickie slumped in her chair. "What should I do about the window?"

"Dak woke up Caleb Martin and he's bringing plywood from public works. They'll board up the window for you."

"Thanks, Sheriff. I'm sorry about this."

"I've got a few more questions." Laurent picked up an overturned chair and plopped into it. "Ruby Rae Evans. What's her role in the diner?"

"She's one of the Moonshine Mamas. There's only four of them. Stacy Simmons, Ruby Rae Evans, Diane Wells, and Hannah Burton. Stacy handled everything at the diner and Ruby Rae was in charge at the garage."

"What garage?"

Vickie straightened up in the chair. "Let me explain. It's all related to the liquor licenses. First, Lisa needed an FDSP. Federal Distilled Spirits Permit."

"Lisa had a distiller permit?"

"And the moonshine was made in one of the garages at the rear of my property."

"The Excise Police let you make moonshine in your garage?" Laurent's jaw dropped.

"With a few modifications, the garage met all the regulations. The first couple of years, they inspected us every six months, but we were perfect. No tickets were issued, no health regulations were violated. In fact, after a few years, Lisa said one of the inspectors made a comment about how the moonshine garage was cleaner and more compliant than some of the bigger distilleries. That made her happy."

"Who else did she sell to?" Laurent asked.

"No one. Big Al's was it. Everything was within the county limits, especially for transportation. It also kept demand up."

"Then what?"

"After she got the distiller permit, she needed another one for the distilling equipment and two or three different permits from the Indiana Alcohol and Tobacco Commission. One was for the manufacture, transportation, and sale of alcohol to retailers. Then she needed a permit to be a retailer. Then there was all the licensing for the servers, and finally, Field's Crossing wanted their share of the pot. The last step was the FDA. Food includes alcoholic beverages. It took almost two years and cost five thousand dollars."

"Did Lisa suspend sales while going through the permit process?" Laurent asked.

"Ah, no. She kept selling from the back of the diner like Al Jr. and hoped and prayed you and your staff wouldn't catch on."

"When was this?"

"2010–2011."

"I wasn't sheriff then, only a deputy." Laurent crossed her ankle over her knee. "Any reason any of the Moonshine Mamas would want Lisa dead?"

"No. They were paid very well. In addition to their hourly wage, Lisa paid them cash under the table based on sales," Vickie said.

"That's illegal."

"It is and I told her not to do it. Just increase their wages by the same amount. She said then they have to pay taxes and social security and all that crap. This way they could make a few bucks on the side free and clear."

"Unreported income," Laurent mused. "A bit like tipping your hair stylist or putting money in a jar at the Chinese take-out place."

"That's what Lisa said."

"Would one of these women turn Lisa into the IRS?"

"Doubtful."

"Why do you say that?"

"An IRS audit always carries the possibility of fines and even shutting down the business," Vickie said. "Who in Field's Crossing wanted Big Al's to close?"

"You've got a point there. Now that Lisa is deceased, I assume you're applying to transfer ownership of the licenses and permits, or do you have to start over?"

"I can apply to transfer all the necessary permits so long as I, Victoria Scott Wright, am eligible. Which I am."

"What do you mean?" Laurent asked.

"There's a bunch of individual requirements like living in the state for the past five years, not being convicted of any felony on any level. Stuff like that."

Laurent looked at the woman sitting opposite her. "If Lisa hadn't died, but ended up owing the IRS, what do you think she would have done?"

"Get a loan from the bank."

"What happens with the IRS audit now that Lisa's dead?"

"After the death certificate is issued, I'll send a certified letter to the IRS along with a copy of the death certificate and ask that the audit be postponed until the executor has transferred ownership and I've been given time to prepare."

"How long will the IRS give you?" Laurent asked.

"Six months to a year."

"Does the family know about this?"

"After the will was read, I scooted out the front door. I think they went out the back door into the parking lot, so I have no idea if they even know about the audit," Vickie said. "Technically, it's my problem, not theirs. Not only was I the accountant for Lisa while she owned Big Al's, but I also inherited the diner. I don't believe I'm under any obligation to tell them, but if I had to guess, Aubrey probably knew."

"Would the IRS keep a record if someone complained?" Laurent asked.

"Yes. But that individual may be protected by whistleblowing laws."

So, if someone turned Lisa in, I'd have to get it out of them. The IRS isn't going to tell me. Who wanted Big Al's audited? What does anyone gain from an IRS audit?

"We found your prints on the catering van. Can you explain that?" Laurent asked.

Vickie shrugged. "When I got to the Easter egg hunt, I met Lisa at the van. I probably touched it. Opened the door for her. I probably opened one of the van's rear doors. It's one of those things you do without thinking."

The radio on Laurent's shoulder squawked as headlights flashed through the broken front window. "Just me, boss."

"Any luck?"

"Nope. Caleb's pulling up. We'll get the window boarded up."

"Who do you think broke in tonight?" Vickie asked.

"No clue," Laurent said. "I'll call you tomorrow if I have any news."

*   *   *

Laurent slammed the hidden door to the walk-in cooler and moved a couple of racks of food back in place. She clicked off the light. Returning to the main dining room, she slid into a booth and watched Caleb and Dak as they pounded the plywood over the broken window. She sighed and rubbed her eyes with the heels of her hands.

God, I'm tired. Who busted into Big Al's and why? I hope it was just a teenage dare. Graduation's a month away. Stupider pranks have been pulled.

Moonshine made in a garage. Laurent shook her head. *Busy day tomorrow.*

"Dak, I want you to pull Lisa's permits tomorrow and look at the records and reports from the Tobacco and Alcohol Commission. Talk to the inspector from the Excise Police," Laurent said. "Check and see if the permits transfer on death and who it can transfer to."

"What are you talking about? Lisa's got a retailer's permit tacked to the wall in the diner," Dak said.

"Lisa made the moonshine in Vickie's garage."

"How'd she get by with that?"

"That's what I want you to check." Laurent slid out of the booth and stretched. "Vickie says nothing's missing. Let's hope we interrupted the intruder. I also want you to call the IRS and see if they'll tell you how the audit was initiated. Did they do it or did someone complain? See if you can get a name."

"Will do," Dak said. "Go home. I can see your shoulder's killing you. Me and Caleb got this."

"I don't need to be told twice."

"Sometimes, you do," Dak muttered.

CHAPTER THIRTY-TWO

LAURENT STAMPED HER feet on the rubber mat outside the moonshine garage as she waited for Vickie to key in the passcode. Last night's break-in of Big Al's and her failure to catch the intruder still rankled. She had been shocked to learn the moonshine was made locally and not shipped from somewhere else. Moonshine was big business. *I wonder if any of the Moonshine Mamas wanted to make and sell and distribute like Lisa. What would they do to put Lisa out of business?*

"You have two six-car garages here. Enough room for twelve vehicles," Laurent said. "Are they both used to manufacture moonshine?"

"Just this one. The other six-car garage is where the Moonshine Mamas park their cars when they work and it's where I park when I'm home. From Corn Belt Road, the two garages look like they're part of the house.

"Let me clarify. Lisa only made moonshine for Big Al's. She didn't sell to anyone else."

Vickie opened the door. "She didn't want the hassle or paperwork or a huge operation. She was a small-town girl."

"How much moonshine did she make?"

"Ten thousand gallons per year are allowed under the FDSP. The Moonshine Mamas made about half that every year," Vickie said. "Feel free to look around."

Laurent stepped inside and moved her sunglasses to the top of her head. Her gaze wandered around the garage. There was no evidence of the early morning sunshine, but the inside temperature was warmer than the April air. She estimated the converted six-car garage to be eighty feet long by sixty feet wide with fire extinguishers every fifteen feet. She counted eighteen. Overhead, fluorescent lights flickered on.

In her head, Laurent had envisioned huge copper kettles, rows of barrels, and a dark, dingy interior. *Maybe that's for big distillers. If Lisa only provided moonshine for the diner, how much equipment and space would she need? Vickie said Lisa didn't manufacture all ten thousand gallons. Is that the motive? More moonshine equals more money.*

Along the wall to her left was a row of lockers and hanging on hooks next to the lockers were goggles and heavy-duty rubber aprons. Gloves were stacked in a four-cubicle shelving unit. Small, medium, large. The side wall was shelving. Laurent walked slowly, reading the labels. Distilled water. Cornmeal. Yeast. Sugar. The next section of shelves held clean Mason jars and the last section contained Mason jars filled with a clear liquid and labeled with a date. Moonshine.

The far back wall had two enormous dishwashers and a sink labeled "industrial waste." Opposite the shelving walls were six locked and closed garage doors and down the middle of the room stood four stainless steel stills.

"Why is it so dark in here?" Laurent asked.

"Moonshine has to be stored in a cool, dark place. If it's kept in the sun or a hot spot, it'll explode," Vickie said. "I'm heading to work. Who's meeting you here?"

"Stacy Simmons."

* * *

"How did you get started?" Laurent asked.

Stacy had shown up almost immediately after Vickie left. Laurent propped one foot on the running board, leaned against the closed door of the black police SUV, and waited for Stacy to light her cigarette and drop the match on the ground.

"After Al Jr. sold to Lisa, the moonshine sales dropped off the charts. I came across Lisa one night in her office, crying. She asked me how in the hell did Al make ends meet? So I told her." Stacy exhaled a stream of smoke into the biting April air. "The real reason Al Jr. sold to you was that he was afraid of getting caught and going to jail. The sheriff before you, Glen, caught one of our customers speeding through town and the growler was on the floor next to him. Al told everyone to throw a coat over the growler if you were going to keep it on the front seat or lock it in the trunk. Well, this asshole didn't and now the sheriff and all of you started eating at Big Al's on a regular basis. So, he sold and took all his customers with him. They liked his rot-gut stuff. Lisa tried making moonshine, but it wasn't any good, so she gave up. Then she remembered my mama's Sweet Tea Moonshine. My mama was dead by then, but I had the recipe."

"Go on," Laurent prodded.

"You all know Lisa is a great sandwich maker, but that wasn't what kept Big Al's in the black. It was the moonshine. After Lisa got all the permits and licenses and crap, we was back in business. And that's how the Moonshine Mamas were born. It was slow at first, but picked up real quick when all the little old ladies realized it took away their aches and pains and let them sleep some at night and it tasted good. The first few weeks we used my mama's recipe, we gave out free samples. Kinda like they do at a beer garden."

"The caffeine didn't keep them awake?"

"Alcohol tops caffeine every time."

"So, Lisa uses your mother's recipe and makes a bucket of money. How'd you feel about that?" Laurent asked.

"It was good business. Lisa paid us an hourly wage and some cash under the table based on how much we sold, so letting her use my mama's recipe made me money. Lisa didn't try to cheat us, and she was very generous at Christmastime."

"How much money did you make?" Laurent asked. *Lisa might have been generous at Christmas, but you still resented her. Do you want to start your own moonshine gig?*

"We all raked in about a thousand dollars a month under the table. A couple of the Mamas put their kids through college with it."

"That's a lot of money."

Stacy blew out smoke. "Yep."

"Now what?"

"I got no idea, but it don't matter. Vickie's in no hurry to reopen so there goes our money."

"Any of the Moonshine Mamas upset about that?"

"We was all upset, but not enough to kill someone. It's not like any of us expected to inherit Big Al's," Stacy said.

She's got a point. The Moonshine Mamas knew when Lisa died and Aubrey didn't inherit, their days were numbered. No more cash under the table. *What if one of them wanted to run the moonshine business? Maybe one of them killed Lisa to take over. Steal all of Lisa's customers the way Al Jr. took his customers. Who else sells moonshine in Field's Crossing?*

CHAPTER THIRTY-THREE

"How long is this gonna take? I've got things to do."

"Hopefully not too long." Laurent pulled out a conference room chair and laid her notebook on the table before sitting across from Ruby Rae Evans. The Moonshine Mama wore a Jameson baseball cap, her ponytail pulled through the hole in the back. She wore Nike tennis shoes, black leggings, and a zipped-up windbreaker.

"Are you a runner?" Laurent asked.

Ruby Rae nodded. "Just finished my loop around town."

"Where do you live?"

"Near Webster Park."

"What's your running route?"

"I head east on Webster Street and then south on Seventh. I run home any number of ways. Today I cut over on Roosevelt, so I'd be here on time." Ruby Rae unzipped her jacket and pushed up the sleeves.

"When was the last time you saw Lisa DuVal?" Laurent picked up her pen.

"Friday afternoon. I left while she and Stacy were coloring Easter eggs."

"You didn't work on Saturday?"

"It was Easter weekend. Not a lot of business on Saturday or Sunday. We had minimal staff."

"Where were you on Easter Sunday?" Laurent asked.

"Home. Making dinner."

"Anyone with you?"

"My husband."

"Anyone else?"

"Just me and him having a lazy day. We're not churchgoers, but I do like to cook."

"How about last night?"

"Same. Home."

"Stacy tells me you're in charge of making moonshine for Big Al's. Take me through the process. I've never made it." Laurent leaned back in the chair and laid her pen on the table.

"Not much to tell. Making moonshine's easy when you've done it a few times," Ruby Rae said. "We started out with these little stovetop pieces of shit. Now we use only twenty-gallon stills and we've got four stoves.

"First, you make the mash. Boil ten gallons of distilled water. Stir in two-and-a-half pounds of cornmeal. Boil for five to seven minutes. Use a wooden spoon to stir. Reduce the heat to one hundred fifty degrees and add ten pounds of sugar and one-half ounce of yeast. Mix. Now you have to cover the mash and let it sit for four or five days. When you see big bubbles floating on top, you're ready to distill and filter the mash. Pour it all in the still and bring the mash up to one hundred and seventy-two degrees. The pipe on the top collects the vapors from the pressure and condenses into moonshine. The moonshine runs through the pipe and into the clean pot. Cool the mash. Filter it with cheesecloth and store it in clean, clear Mason jars. Throw out the impurities, especially the foreshots. They're high in methanol, which is poisonous. Label the jars and stick them on the shelf. That's it."

Sounds like a helluva lot of work. Which is why it's so popular in Field's Crossing. "All four of you do this? Day after day after day?" Laurent asked. "What else do you do while you're at the garage?"

"All the returned growlers and Mason jars have to be washed and the stills are cleaned every day. That's why there's two dishwashers," Ruby Rae said. "Most of my time was spent labeling and transporting the moonshine to the diner."

"What door did you use at the diner?"

"The walk-in cooler door. It's closest to where the customers pick up their alcoholic beverages."

"You have a key to this door?"

"I got keys to the entire diner. So does half the town." Ruby Rae snorted.

"Did you ever work at Big Al's? Serve liquor?"

"When I first started, I worked in the dining room pulling beers and making moonshine drinks. After a couple of years, Lisa asked if I wanted to work out here and I said hell, yes. Not have to deal with the public."

"What's your relationship with Keith DuVal?"

Ruby Rae's gaze fell to the floor. "That was a mistake. Asshole's interested in only one thing and I fell for it."

"Does your husband know?"

Ruby Rae shook her head. "He's oblivious to me."

*   *   *

"How'd your interviews go?" Dak rapped on the window to Laurent's office.

She motioned him inside. "Boring. Although I now know more than I ever wanted to about how to make moonshine. Diane Wells and Hannah Burton are nothing but glorified dishwashers. Lisa used Stacy Simmons' mom's Sweet Tea Moonshine to get started, but Stacy wasn't mad about that. Using the recipe made her money. Same with the other Moonshine Mamas. None of them have any motive for killing Lisa. She provided all of them with jobs and cash under the table. The most interesting tidbit is that Ruby Rae Evans had an affair with Keith DuVal prior to his affair with Monica Sun."

"Ruby Rae Evans? Is her husband that loudmouth drunk we lock up about once a month?" Dak asked. "Lives near Webster Park?"

"The one and the same."

"I've seen her running in town."

"We all have."

"Wonder if she was running last night?" Dak asked.

"She said she was home."

"Do you believe her?"

"No. And she said she had keys to the walk-in cooler door. It's where she delivered the moonshine. But why bust up Big Al's?"

"Pissed off?" Dak said. "Open the back door, throw a chair through the front window, search for money, and hide in the cooler when we get there, take off running. I can see it."

CHAPTER THIRTY-FOUR

"ARE YOU SURE about this?" Doug asked.

"You got any better ideas?" Aubrey glared at her husband. "Then shut up. It's the best I can do. Let's hope your bookie's greedy." She slammed the car door and stomped around the corner to the entrance of First Federal. Her stupid-ass husband had gotten himself so deep in debt that the only way to keep him from being beat up or killed was to offer more money. After she had cooled off from the reading of the will, she knew why her mother had left the recipes to her. It wasn't the index cards that were important, it was what else was hidden in that little box on the dusty shelf. The key to the safe deposit box. *Mom did think of me. She might not have left me Big Al's, but she left me a bunch of cash. The cash will buy me time to convince Vickie to give me Big Al's or buy her out.*

"What does he look like?" Aubrey asked.

"How should I know? I've never met him. Just talked to him on the phone."

"Great. Just great," Aubrey muttered. "Let's stand outside of the bank and try not to look conspicuous." Despite the cool April air, a line of sweat ran down her back dampening her blouse. She glanced down the street and saw Mimi from the floral shop duck into the post office. *Gossipy little woman.*

"Shall we go inside and get my money?" a deep voice asked.

Aubrey whirled around and stared. The voice of Darth Vader rolled out of a large Black man wearing a suit with army boots, his hair a maze of corn rows.

"There's been a development. We can't get the money for another week."

"Why is that?"

"It's in a safe deposit box, and I don't have the key. The lawyer has it and she won't give it to me until she files the will in court and she's not doing that until Monday," Aubrey lied.

"The delay is going to cost you an extra twenty grand," the bookie said. "I'm debating whether or not to add in a few broken bones."

"You're gonna break my leg right here on the street?" Doug blurted out.

"Legs. What a dumb fuck."

"Let's walk to the Skillet. Pretend you're a lawyer and we're discussing our options."

"Afraid of being seen?"

"Damn straight. We've lived here all our lives and since my mom owned Big Al's, everyone knows us. No one knows you and people will talk." Aubrey strode down Field Street.

"Nosy little town."

The bookie fell in step with her while Doug trailed behind. "On Monday, you're going to pay me fifty thousand dollars."

"Tuesday."

The bookie raised his eyebrows.

"She's filing the will on Monday. I have no idea how long that takes and if she'll be available on Monday. Tuesday's the best I can do." Aubrey stuck her nose up in the air and walked faster. Her heart was hammering underneath her windbreaker and the roots of her hair were damp with sweat. *I need another shower.*

"Until Tuesday."

The bookie crossed Field Street and headed back north. Aubrey watched him climb into the passenger seat of a camouflage-colored Hummer. As the vehicle passed by, she caught a glimpse of the driver and shuddered. Even from this distance, she could see the scar on the side of his face and the tip of his nose was missing. The man had been in a fight or two and was no doubt the one who would break Doug's leg. Legs. "Where in the hell are they from? Indy?"

"Detroit."

"Let's get to the diner."

"Wait a minute. I think I'm gonna puke."

*   *   *

"What happened?" Aubrey stood on the sidewalk on Woodruff Street in front of Big Al's and stared at the plywood covering the window.

"Looks like someone threw rocks through it," Doug said.

"We'll go in through the back. Grab the box off the shelf. The key to the safe deposit box is in the recipe box." She marched to the back of the building and pulled out her key ring. "Who changed the locks?"

"The sheriff?"

"That bitch Vickie changed them. Come on. Let's hope she didn't change the lock on the walk-in cooler door." Aubrey brushed past her husband. Reaching the exterior door to the walk-in cooler, she breathed a sigh of relief. Same lock. Flipping through her key ring, she unlocked the heavy door, pulled it open, and stepped inside. The walk-in cooler was kept at a constant forty degrees and was pitch dark. "Wait here and hold the door open. The light switch is next to the other door. I can't see a thing." Holding her hands in front of her, she moved two food racks and walked slowly through the enormous refrigerator. Her fingers touched an ice-cold shelf. Trailing her fingers along the shelf, she rounded the corner and touched the concrete wall. *There's the light switch.*

"Got it." Aubrey flicked on the interior light and pulled open the door leading to the prep area. She crossed the room in a few quick steps. Her mom's office was on the east side of the building next to the employee break room. She flicked on the light switch and glanced at the shelf behind the desk. She froze. The recipe box was gone.

"Where's the box?" Doug said.

"Vickie must have it," Aubrey said.

"Now what?"

"Do I have to do all the thinking?" Aubrey erupted. She shoved her husband against the wall and pounded his chest. "What the fuck is wrong with you? How could you do this to me?"

* * *

Aubrey gripped the steering wheel, her knuckles white. After dropping Doug at the house to get his Explorer and go to work, she drove up and down Field Street, cruising the side streets before heading north to fly along the Five-and-Twenty. Taking the curves, a little too fast.

The bookie had scared the shit out of her. His mean, little eyes. And the guy driving the Hummer. *What the hell was his story?* Aubrey had no doubt the two men could break every bone in Doug's body and dump him in a cornfield. *Will they come after me or my kids? What did Doug get us into? Why the hell can't he stop gambling?*

Aubrey squealed through a left-hand turn and crossed the double yellow line, her foot never letting up on the gas pedal. Her father was a stupid ass. He gave away the store. Literally. All those hours. The snotty high school kids she'd trained. The thousands of sandwiches she'd made. Side by side, next to her mom. She was positive her mom would outlive her father and she and Andrew would inherit Big Al's. It would have taken a few years to buy out her brother, but it was possible he might have given her the diner. He had his rooftop wine bar. She'd have Big Al's. Now, she had nothing. A bunch of recipes she knew by heart. Writing a cookbook and selling it would take years and if people in Field's Crossing could duplicate her mother's sandwiches, no one would eat at Big Al's. A cookbook was a stupid idea. God knows she couldn't cook. Andrew inherited that gene from their mother.

How am I going to get Vickie to give me the key to the safe deposit box? Aubrey was positive Vickie knew about the extra cash stashed at the bank. *Why does Vickie need the money? Is she trying to piss me off? Or is she giving Andrew his hundred thousand dollars from the safe deposit box instead of from Big Al's bank account? What a greedy bitch. When did Vickie take the recipe box? Last night? Was she the one who broke in? The sheriff has had Big Al's sealed up since Sunday. We found out yesterday morning that Vickie gets Big Al's. I bet she went there while we were arguing in the parking lot. She stole the box. How'd she get in? Doesn't matter. The recipe box isn't in the diner anymore. It's in Vickie's house. Which means the key to the safe deposit box is in Vickie's house. How am I going to get it?*

Aubrey pounded the steering wheel. *Would Vickie let me buy her out? Where would I get the money?* The profit margins at Big Al's were decent, but some of that was due to the fact her mom never paid herself. *I'm not going to devote myself to Big Al's the way Mom did. She lost her marriage and her house. Big Al's needs a trustworthy manager. But if I hire a manager, the profit margin goes down even more. The only way to make this work is to have Vickie give Big Al's to me. No buyout. I deserve it and she knows it. She's never worked there. Doesn't know how to make a sandwich. Probably doesn't know anyone's name other than Mom and me.*

What am I going to do about the moonshine? The setup is perfect. If I have to move it from Vickie's garage, I'll have to find another place. Which means paying rent and bringing the new place into compliance. Then I'd have to disassemble and reassemble all the equipment and pass inspection from the Excise Police. So much money down the drain. No. Vickie has to give me Big Al's and let me make moonshine in her garage. What can I say to convince her? Is there some way to blackmail Vickie?

Aubrey glanced at the clock on the dashboard and did a U-turn in the middle of the Five-and-Twenty. Her root touch-up appointment was in fifteen minutes. She'd be late. Too bad. *They'll wait for me. They know who I am.*

CHAPTER THIRTY-FIVE

LAURENT GLANCED OVER her shoulder as she keyed in the code for Big Al's Diner. Her gaze traveled north along Field Street, skipping over the melting piles of snow. The door to the Skillet opened, and Laurent smiled as her two favorite old guys emerged. Art and Dutch, arguing as always. Art stabbing his finger in the air, Dutch shaking his head, both wearing the familiar green and yellow John Deere baseball hats. She waved.

Laurent pushed open the door. Big Al's carried the faint scent of onions and bacon. She poked her head in the employee area and prep room before finding the thermostat in Lisa's office. She was meeting Rina Yoshida to conduct the inventory, which would take several hours, and the boarded-up front window leaked cold air making the diner chilly. She could feel it through her jacket. Laurent clicked the heat up to seventy-two degrees and opened all the blinds, flooding the dining room with sunshine.

The cow bells above the front door clanked. "Hello? Sheriff?"

"Right here. Just turning up the heat."

"What's with the front window? Break-in?"

"Last night."

"Glad I wore an extra layer today. I hate the crossover from winter to spring. I never know what to wear. It's like we're on the verge of spring and then the temperature drops below freezing and, instead of snow, we end up with ice." Rina wiped her feet on the mat. After unbuttoning her navy-blue wool coat, the young woman hung it on a hook next to a booth and laid her briefcase on a table.

"At least it's not below zero. It's sad when twenty-eight degrees feels like a heat wave."

"You are so right. Should I set up out here?"

"What's easiest for you? Room by room?" Laurent asked.

"That's the way I had it in my head, but I haven't been here since I graduated. Is it still the same?"

"Pretty much." Laurent rolled her right shoulder. She had little twinges of pain and knew after this afternoon's physical therapy she'd hurt even more.

"I think I'll start in the smallest room and work my way up. How many rooms are there?" Rina pulled a laptop out of her briefcase, opened it, and clicked on the mouse pad.

"Six. This big dining area, the employee break area, the prep area, walk-in cooler, office, and an outdoor shed."

"What's in the shed?"

"Shovels. Snowblower, lawn mower, salt, and ice melt."

"I'll start there."

"Any idea how long you'll be?" Laurent asked.

"Most of the day. I've already imported the list of items you tagged and bagged and sent to CSU. Some of those knives are very expensive," Rina said. "I'm a little surprised the safe was empty."

"We think the murderer stole the money. There was no weekend deposit on Monday," Laurent said.

"You subpoenaed the bank?"

"A couple of days ago."

"Who's the new CEO at Farmers?" Rina asked.

"Vincent Walker. I've talked to him on the phone but haven't met him yet. He was a senior vice president under Bob Kane. Lives in Columbia."

"Bob Kane was a big loss for Field's Crossing. Just like Lisa." Rina draped her scarf around her neck. She pulled her coat back on and tucked the ends of her scarf inside. Her hands were bare. "Sheriff, if you'll name the items, I'll type them in and we'll both be out of the cold sooner."

"Don't you own a pair of gloves with the fingertips cut off?"

Rina shook her head.

"Use mine."

The shed contained very little, and the two women were back inside the diner in less than ten minutes.

"One down, five to go."

"Are you looking for anything in particular?" Laurent asked.

"There are a few special bequests in Lisa's will, mainly for the grandchildren. A couple of milk jugs, ice cream scoops, embroidered aprons, and a recipe box for Aubrey. Other than that, everything else goes to Vickie," Rina said.

"Has anyone filed a countersuit?"

"Not yet. Anyone who wants to contest the will has three months from this coming Monday to file. I image the heirs will wait for me to finalize the inventory before making a decision."

"Do you have to get a value on all this stuff?"

"Not unless someone contests the will, or the judge declares the waivers from ten years ago invalid." Rina laid her laptop on Lisa's desk and unwound her scarf.

"What's the chance of that?" Laurent asked.

"Slim to none. I read the real estate appraiser's reports. The house on Cardinal Street and Big Al's held similar values at the time the waivers were executed, so there's no unfair financial advantage."

"You're saying Keith doesn't have a leg to stand on?"

"I don't think he does, but he thinks he does," Rina said.

"What about Aubrey?"

"She's got less of a leg than Keith. The law doesn't say you have to leave anything to your kids. I assume you're looking for a motive for Lisa's murder?" Rina settled behind the office desk.

"Money is the biggest motivation of all, especially if you don't have any."

"Care to comment on that?"

"Nope. Probably shouldn't have said that." Laurent grinned at the young female attorney. She liked Rina. Efficient, professional, and pleasant. *She'll do well in her new law practice.*

"Not much in here. Shouldn't take too long."

"We confiscated almost everything in this room," Laurent said. "Especially the paperwork. You'll see in the notes on the evidence list that we gave the employees their paychecks. It was approved by Judge Jenkins."

Rina nodded. "I saw that. At the reading of the will, Aubrey said the recipe box was on a shelf in here, but I don't see it."

"Might be in another room. Let's do the employee break room next." Laurent led the way.

The break room contained tables, chairs, a few sweatshirts hanging on hooks, and boxes of paper goods. Napkins, paper towels, toilet paper, straws, and Styrofoam cups for fountain drinks.

"Walk-in cooler, prep area, and dining room. That's all that's left," Laurent said.

The walk-in cooler was easy. Nothing but food on racks and shelves. Laurent didn't point out the hidden door and wondered if Rina noticed. Or noticed and said nothing.

"What's Vickie going to do with all this food?" Rina asked.

"She's donating it to the food pantry at St. Peter and Paul. They don't have a lot of space for refrigerated goods, so the church is lining up volunteers to repackage the bulk items and take them directly to families in need."

"Good. I hate waste." Rina picked up her laptop. "Let's inventory the dining room next. It's going to take a while in there."

"How do you want to do this? Describe the painted scene? Give them a number? How many milk jugs, cans, tins, and stools do you think there are?" Laurent stood at the entrance to the area where customers ate.

A chair rail ran around the entire room. Painted barn red below, white above. Dozens of shelves held painted tin milk jugs, ranging from six to ten inches tall. On the floor and artfully arranged in corners sat large milk stools with tops. Laurent estimated fifty small jugs and thirty large stools. Interspersed between the shelves on the walls hung artwork all depicting barns.

"Some of these might have value to them."

Laurent snorted. "A painted milk can? You gotta be kidding me."

"Ever watch *Fixer Upper* on HGTV? Joanna Gaines single-handedly created an entirely new design scheme. Farmhouse. Now there's coastal farmhouse, modern farmhouse, subsets of her original farmhouse theme, and there's no sign it's letting up. This stuff could sell at auction or eBay for some nice cash."

Laurent stared at Rina. "Seriously?"

The lawyer nodded. "I brought a set of numbered stickers. We'll stick a tag on the bottom and write a brief description. That's all we need for now."

"I'll stick. You type." Laurent picked up the roll of numbers, walked to the closest shelf, and pulled down a bright yellow milk tin. Placing the sticker on the bottom, she held it up for Rina to write a description. "Heavier than I thought."

"Is it empty?"

Laurent turned the tin upside down and three rubber-banded rolls of money fell out.

Rina stopped typing.

Laurent stared at the money on the floor. Setting down the yellow milk tin, she picked up the one next to it. Turned it over. Three more rolls of money fell to the floor.

"You don't suppose . . ." Rina whispered. "What about the big ones?"

"There's only one way to find out." Laurent strode to the corner, pried off the lid on the nearest large milk stool, and turned it over. She watched as bundles of money tumbled out rolling under tables and chairs.

"Holy shit."

"They teach you that in law school?"

"I repeat. Holy shit."

Laurent pulled out a chair and dropped into it. She had opened all the blinds while waiting for Rina to arrive and now wondered if she should close them. She looked at the young attorney and saw her counting, pen poised in the air.

"Fifty-one little ones, thirty-two big ones," Rina said. "We're going to be here all day."

"Better than going to physical therapy." Laurent rubbed her shoulder. *Why did Lisa fill all these milk tins with cash?* "I think we'd better call for reinforcements."

* * *

"What money? I thought we took it all." Dak filled the front doorway of Big Al's, hands on hips.

"Pick up that tin," Laurent said. "Turn it over."

"What the hell?" Three large rolls of money lay in Dak's open hand. "These look like the one we found in her purse."

"Same amount. Three thousand dollars," Laurent said. "When I released Lisa's personal effects, I had to give that money to Keith."

"We assumed that money was Saturday's take, and Lisa was heading to the bank to deposit it," Dak said. "Maybe we were wrong."

"What did Vincent Walker at Farmers Bank say?" Laurent had picked up the money scattered across the dining room floor while she and Rina waited for Dak.

"He didn't remember Big Al's or Lisa making large deposits. A few thousand a day, more on Mondays. Enough to pay the bills." Dak hung his jacket on a hook and stuffed his gloves in a pocket. "She stuffed cash in all these tins?"

Rina looked up from her laptop. "I've added a column so I can enter the amount of money in each tin. I think we should get someone from the bank here. As executor, I'm going to open a separate account for all the money we find. But frankly, I'd like someone to check me. Verify the amounts."

"Dak. Give Walker a call. See if he's got someone he can send over."

"On it, Sheriff."

"I'm calling the Skillet and ordering lunch for the three of us. I'm not comfortable with anyone leaving the building until we're done," Laurent said.

"Agreed. I don't want to be left alone with this cash, and none of us want to be accused of impropriety," Rina said. "Tuna melt with cheddar on an English muffin with chips and a Diet 7UP."

"Dak?"

"Ultimate sub with extra bacon, French fries, and Diet Coke."

Half an hour later, the two police officers and the young lawyer were digging into their sandwiches from the Skillet when the front doorknob rattled. Dak jumped up to open the door for the CEO of Farmers Bank.

"Mr. Walker. I wasn't expecting you." Laurent held out her hand. "This is Dak Aikens, my deputy, and Rina Yoshida, executor for the estate of Lisa DuVal."

Vincent Walker was in his late fifties with a full head of white hair and bushy white eyebrows. He carried a leather briefcase in one hand and his long wool coat was unbuttoned. "My afternoon was completely open, and I'll admit I'm intrigued by what Deputy Aikens said on the phone. There's money rolled up inside the milk tins?"

Dak plucked a small milk can off a shelf, turned it over, and three rolls of money fell into his large hand.

Walker whistled. "Glad I brought sleeves and rubber bands. We're going to have to count these by hand. If they've been rolled up for a long time, the bills would jam the counting machine." He set his briefcase on a nearby table. "How do you want to do this?"

"Let's set up three tables. Rina, would you mind if Dak entered the item number and description using your laptop? He'll then pass the money to you for the first count. When you're done, you'll pass the money to Mr. Walker who will verify and Dak will enter that amount in the laptop. Mr. Walker will also do whatever the bank needs done. I'll retrieve each milk tin, put a sticker on the bottom, and return the empty to the shelf. How does that sound?" Laurent glanced at Rina.

"Efficient."

Dak and Laurent pushed three tables together in the middle of the dining room.

"Sheriff, what if a call comes in?" Dak asked.

"I texted Poulter and asked him if he could start his shift at three this afternoon. Overtime approved. He said yes." Laurent glanced at the painted clock above the front door. "Let's hope everything stays quiet for the next two hours."

Once they established a rhythm, Laurent relaxed. "Who inherits this money?"

"Vickie Wright. The money's not in a bank account, it's in the diner. She inherits the diner and all its belongings, except the recipe box and the items Lisa left to her grandchildren," Rina said.

"Whad'ya suppose Aubrey and Keith will say to that?" Dak asked.

"If they react the same way they did when I read the will, I'm going to get some nasty phone calls," Rina said.

"When are you going to tell Vickie?" Walker asked.

"I'm debating. Today's Thursday. I'm opening the probate estate on Monday, which will include this initial inventory. I'm certain the judge will ask me to send a copy of everything to all the heirs. That's standard procedure."

"About this time next week, we'll see fireworks from Aubrey and Keith for sure. Probably the girlfriend," Dak said. "This might get as bad as the Martin-Tillman feud."

"Bite your tongue. Everything's quiet right now." Laurent pulled another milk jug off the shelf, emptied it, and handed the rolls of money to Rina. She put a sticker on the bottom. "What do you want to call this one? Yellow cow with blue flowers?"

Dak typed in the description.

"Vickie asked me a few days ago if I thought whoever killed Lisa would come after her. I told her no. Now, I'm wondering." Laurent raised an eyebrow at Dak.

"You know, Sheriff, sometimes you scare the shit outta me," Dak said. "Don't you have a PT appointment this afternoon?"

"You think I'm gonna leave so I can do a bunch of painful exercises?"

"Yeah. I'd skip it, too."

*   *   *

Four hours later, Laurent replaced the lid on the last milk stool and sat on it. "And the grand total is?"

The bank CEO leaned back in his chair. "Fifty-one small tins times three thousand dollars in each equals one hundred and fifty-three thousand dollars. Thirty-two large milk stools times fifty thousand per tin equals one million six hundred thousand dollars for a grand total of one million seven hundred and fifty-three thousand dollars."

"Confirmed." Dak slouched in his chair and spread his long legs on either side of the table.

Laurent looked at Rina. She was peering over Dak's shoulder at the computer screen and shaking her head. "What are you thinking?"

"I'm asking the judge for a raise."

Laurent, Dak, and Walker laughed.

"You're going to earn every penny of your executorship," Walker said. "How long has this money sat here? She could have earned so much more with interest."

"I bet she started stashing it when she bought the place." Laurent glanced at the banker. "You walked here, didn't you?"

Walker nodded. "I've got to call the Federal Reserve. They may want to arrange a special pickup. This amount of cash puts us well over our regulatory limit."

"Dak will escort you to Farmers Bank," Laurent said. "Rina? Do you want to finish the inventory today or leave the prep room for tomorrow?"

"Tomorrow." Rina's shoulders slumped. "I've got to talk to Judge Jenkins. He's not going to believe this."

"Let's pack it up."

*   *   *

Laurent swung into her driveway and waited for the garage door to open. *Dak made a good point. Is this going to escalate into all-out war? Vickie versus Aubrey? Aubrey versus her father? What's Andrew going to do? One point seven million dollars is a lot of money. Certainly worth fighting for. And worth killing for. Who else knew about the money stashed in the milk jugs? Anyone? Did Lisa hide one point seven million dollars from everyone?* She rubbed her shoulder. *All I did was pick up a few milk tins and put a sticker on and now, my shoulder hurts like a sonofabitch.*

CHAPTER THIRTY-SIX

"WE'VE BEEN ROYALLY fucked. Did you know about this hundred grand for your son?" Monica's manicured fingernails drummed on the end table next to Keith's swivel chair. The La-Z-Boy was the only piece of furniture in the run-down living room that wasn't sagging or old. That and the flat-screen TV and sound bar. She hated this house. It was a glorified version of all the dumpy apartments she had lived in the past few years. She understood why Keith wanted to sell. No amount of work or upgrades would increase the value. *It needs to be condemned.*

"I'm not surprised. Lisa always put the kids before me even when they were little."

"Where's that money coming from?"

"The account at First Federal, not our joint account at Farmers Bank. I would have noticed that kind of money."

"How can we get the money from First Federal? How much is in there? Who are the signers?" Monica demanded.

"Aubrey made the daily deposit so she must be a signer and, of course, Lisa. Probably Vickie."

"How much is in your joint Farmers account?"

"A few thousand. Last week's paycheck. Enough to cover next month's bills," he said.

Monica looked at Keith. Part of her understood Lisa. *He's useless.* In his opinion, he brought home the bacon and didn't have to lift a finger or do anything else. She wondered if he had ever changed a diaper. Or did the dishes. *Is he expecting me to keep house for him now that his wife is dead?* She shuddered. "If Aubrey is a signer on the First Federal account, I bet she's emptying it right now. Her and that useless husband of hers. Think she'll leave her brother the hundred grand or, will she steal that, too?"

"She'll leave it for Andrew. Aubrey's not a thief."

"Maybe we could ask Vickie to give us the restaurant. She was just as surprised as we were."

"Vickie's not going to give us the restaurant. If she gives it to anyone, it'll be Aubrey."

"How can we get Vickie on our side?" Monica asked.

"She hates me. I'm sure Lisa bad-mouthed me every chance she got."

"How long has Vickie lived in Field's Crossing?"

"No clue. Why?"

"We have to blackmail her," Monica said. *Or get rid of her.*

"With what?"

"You want to get the hell out of here or not? You know the judge was going to order you to give half of your 401(k) to Lisa. Whad'ya think she'd have done when she discovered the account was empty? We faked her signature on the spousal consent form. I'm betting she could have sued you for that. Made you pay it back. Garnish your wages." Monica played with her earrings.

"It's not like there was a lot of money in the account. Even if I had to split it, she would have gotten thirty thousand or so. By taking the early withdrawal, she gets nothing."

"You dumb ass. The judge would have ordered you to pay her thirty thousand dollars. He might have thrown you in jail." Monica shot to her feet, the rocker recliner hitting the wall behind her.

Keith blinked. "Never thought of that."

"Doesn't matter. There's nothing left and no one will ever know. We need the money from the sale of Big Al's and this crappy little house to get out of here. We need a new plan." Monica paced between the living room and the kitchen. "What can we blackmail Vickie with? Think. You've lived here your entire life. Any rumors? Innuendos? Cheating on her husband?"

"Her husband died years ago."

"How?"

"Who cares? Even if she killed him, it's not going to help us get the diner. We've got nothing to blackmail her with," Keith said.

"Murderers can't inherit," Monica said. "We've got to get a murder charge placed against Vickie, either for her husband or for your wife."

"How do you know that?" Keith asked.

"Never mind." Monica knew Indiana didn't have a statute of limitation for murder. Even if Vickie's husband died years ago, a murder charge could still be brought. *I'm gonna see what Vickie's husband died from, but we'll be better off accusing Vickie of murdering Lisa.*

"Where was Vickie on Sunday afternoon when Lisa was killed?" Monica asked.

"How should I know? Isn't that the sheriff's job?"

"There's got to be something we can blackmail her with. Scare the shit outta her. Any rumors of cheating or improper audits from her firm?" Monica asked.

"If you want to find dirt on her, talk to Ralph Howard at *The Crossing* newspaper. He's got dirt on everyone," Keith said. "You said in the parking lot the recipes had value. What did you mean?"

"I know you hate your late wife, but the woman could build a phenomenal sandwich and bake up a storm. If your daughter's smart, she'll write a cookbook with Lisa's recipes and make a fortune. That'll take time. Possibly years. We need money now. Aren't you ready to get out of this cold? Think how nice and warm the Caribbean will be. Sun all day long. Sit by the pool. Walk in to town for dinner. Get drunk. Stumble home. Screw. Wake up and do it all over again. If we can't blackmail Vickie, then our best bet is to invalidate the waiver and get the hell out of Dodge. Where's the paperwork that lawyer handed you?"

"Kitchen table. Bring me another beer."

Monica snatched the empty beer bottle. Stalking to the kitchen, she silently gave Keith the finger. *As soon as we get outta here, I'm dumping him and taking his money.* She dropped the empty beer bottle into the overflowing recycle bin, grabbed a fresh one from the fridge, and twisted off the cap. She picked up the stack of papers and carried the pile to the living room. "Is that your signature?" She held up the waiver.

"Yeah."

Monica read the waiver. It was short and clear-cut. The house on Cardinal Street went to Keith and the diner on Woodruff belonged to Lisa. "How much is this house worth?"

"Three-fifty."

"Big Al's?"

Keith set his beer on the end table. "No clue."

"If we establish a huge discrepancy between the value of the house and the diner, maybe the judge will invalidate the waivers," Monica said. "Old value versus new value."

"We're going to need a lawyer for that and neither of us has a dime," Keith said. "That's where Aubrey comes in. She can get the money out of Big Al's account and pay for the lawyer. After the waivers are invalidated, Big Al's goes to me, Aubrey, and Andrew. I'll make Aubrey the manager and the three of us will share the profits. That'll work, but only if you stop fighting with her. We also might be able to stall Andrew from taking the hundred grand while we try to regain control of Big Al's. If we can't invalidate the waivers, then we've got to get Vickie to give Big Al's to Aubrey. Either way, we need Aubrey on our side."

Monica scowled. "How long do I have to put up with her?"

"Until we get our money. The other option is to take out a second mortgage on this dump, which means there won't be any profit when we sell." Keith held out a closed fist. "Guess what I have for you?" He dangled a set of car keys in front of Monica. "The police released Lisa's car to me. Apparently, both our names are on the title, so I own it. Why don't you drive the Escalade and get rid of that piece of crap you drive?"

CHAPTER THIRTY-SEVEN

OPINION/EDITORIAL PAGE
WHO INHERITS BIG AL'S DINER?

April 26, 2019
Field's Crossing, Indiana
Ralph Howard

This reporter has been made privy to the details of Lisa DuVal's will. It appears that no one in the family will inherit Big Al's Diner. Instead, the best friend of the deceased gets the popular restaurant. Victoria Scott Wright.

Why? Did Ms. Wright murder her friend to gain control of the diner? The autopsy results were made available to the public yesterday and confirmed the victim was stabbed while sitting in her catering van on Easter afternoon.

Why did Lisa cheat her husband and children out of their rightful inheritance? According to a source close to the family, Victoria Scott Wright can't cook and has never run a restaurant. The woman is an auditor, used to working with numbers, and, apparently, the auditor for the diner. What does she know? In her position, Ms. Wright would have knowledge of the financial details of Big Al's. The diner has been hugely popular for the last decade, and one has to assume, raking in the cash. Literally.

Is Ms. Wright's auditing firm in trouble? Since her husband's death has Ms. Wright run Baylor, Scott, and Wright into the ground? Does the firm need money? What would an audit of BS&W show? Is Ms. Wright going to sell the diner? What might the sale of Big Al's pay for? Does Ms. Wright need the cash? What kind of cover-up might be going on?

More importantly, why didn't Lisa leave the diner to her daughter, Aubrey Holmes, who has been running Big Al's with her mom for the last several years? Or leave the diner to Aubrey and her brother, Andrew, who owns and operates Cityscape Rooftop Wine Bar in Indianapolis? Two individuals well versed in running a restaurant.

What hold did Ms. Wright have over her supposed best friend?

CHAPTER THIRTY-EIGHT

THE CUTTING EDGE Hair Salon was quiet for a Friday morning. All the regulars were at Lisa's funeral. At Keith's suggestion, Monica had volunteered to work and DeeDee agreed. Fighting with Aubrey or being seen at Keith's side during Lisa's funeral was unacceptable, even to her.

The hair salon was empty. Monica sat in her chair at her station, Lisa's key ring in her lap. *Damn thing weighs two pounds.* Car key, two sets of house keys, keys to Big Al's, and . . . She frowned. She didn't know what the fourth set of keys were for. She pulled out a bottle of pink nail polish and dabbed a drop on the keys to Keith's house. The other set of house keys she assumed belonged to Vickie since Lisa was moving in with her. Monica detached and dropped them into the bottom of her purse. *Got no use for them. May as well dump these keys to Big Al's, too. Vickie's probably changed the locks, so these are no good. That leaves the fob for the Escalade, keys to my car, house keys, and whatever these are.* Monica detached the two mystery keys and laid them on the counter. She threw all of Lisa's key ring gadgets into the garbage can.

The front door of the hair salon opened, and Monica glanced up as DeeDee walked in.

"Can't thank you enough for holding down the fort," DeeDee said.

"No one wanted me at the funeral," Monica said.

"You're right about that. Do you wanna take your lunch break now?" DeeDee had toned down her outfit for the funeral. Every article of clothing was black including her lipstick. She tilted her chin at the two keys sitting on the counter in front of Monica's station. "Is that where you stashed all your stuff? At the storage unit?"

"My furniture's there and some other stuff," Monica lied. "I packed a few things that I really need, so, yeah, since there's no one here, I'll take my lunch now."

* * *

Monica sat in Lisa's Escalade in the parking lot behind the hair salon. The heat was cranked on high to take off the chill. She googled "storage units Field's Crossing Indiana." There were two. She put the Escalade into gear and headed south on Field Street. FC Storage was closest to Keith's house and a few blocks from Big Al's.

She parked next to the keypad and rolled the window down. She pulled out the two keys. Each had a number written on it. She punched in #234. Nothing. The gate remained closed. She punched in 5678*.

The gate creaked open.

Monica drove in. Motion sensors were activated, and overhead lights clicked on as she parked next to a set of stairs. Sliding out of the Escalade, she hit the fob to lock the doors and climbed to the second floor and stopped outside unit 234. Inserting the key into the lock, she removed the lock, bent over, and lifted the rolled-up door. The smell of mothballs wafted out.

Monica stared. The storage unit was lined with curio cabinets. *What the hell?*

She stepped inside and peered into the nearest cabinet. Little porcelain figurines smiled back at her. She tugged open the glass door and picked up a statue. Turning it over, she snapped a picture of the bottom before putting it back.

Sinking Indian style to the cold concrete floor, Monica googled the statue. Goebel. Apple Tree Girl and Apple Tree Boy. Number 1. Her eyebrows shot up. *Twelve thousand dollars?*

Monica stood and circled the storage unit. Fifteen curio cabinets, ten filled with Hummels, five with Beanie Babies, and a file cabinet. *How much money is in this room and who gets it? I forgot. The grandkids inherit this shit. That means everyone in the family knows about it. I'm going to have to move fast. Where can I stash this stuff before anyone remembers? Or should I chuck it all in my new Cadillac and take off?*

Next to the rolled-up door sat a two-drawer black filing cabinet. Monica opened the top drawer. Filed alphabetically were the names of every Hummel and Beanie Baby with the original receipt and certificate of authenticity. The bottom drawer held two three-ring binders, one with Pokémon cards, the other Yu-Gi-Oh! cards.

Monica remembered her little brother playing Pokémon games with his friends, but mostly negotiating a trade, which always ended up with someone in tears. Until the moms said no trading. After that, the tears stopped.

She googled the cards.

Monica wondered if her brother or any of his friends realized the value of those cards in today's collectors' market or if they had thrown them all away. Torn and used. Just like . . . She slammed the file cabinet as she shoved away the memories, the sound echoing in the empty corridor of the bare-bones building.

I'm taking it all.

*   *   *

Monica climbed back into the Escalade and glanced at the clock. She'd been gone longer than she'd expected. Her afternoon was completely booked including a late afternoon up-do for a high school sophomore celebrating her sixteenth birthday. *Crappy little farm town with a bunch of snobby people. I can't wait to get out of here.*

Putting the Cadillac in gear, Monica drove to the Cutting Edge Salon, parked, and entered through the rear door, wiping her feet on the mat.

"Did you get all the stuff you needed?" DeeDee poked her head out from her office. "Your one o'clock canceled. I'm not expecting any walk-ins today, so if you want to take another hour, go ahead."

Perfect opening. "I've got nothing to do. Do you want to talk about the funeral?" She hung her purse and coat on a hook and switched from her boots to black tennis shoes before settling in front of DeeDee's desk. *The woman really needs to get out of the sixties.*

"The funeral was sad," DeeDee said. "Lisa lived her entire life in Field's Crossing, and everyone knew her or someone in her family. The church was packed. I looked up in the choir loft and people were sitting in folding chairs on either side of the organist. Bet he hated that. I was okay until I saw one of her grandkids cry and then I lost it. And I wasn't the only one. By the time the pastor got to the final hymn, you know the one—'he'll raise you up on eagle's wings,' everyone was bawling. Couldn't hardly hear the soloist. What a sucky day. Thank God for waterproof mascara."

"You came back to work right after the service?" Monica asked.

"I'll pay my respects at the cemetery in private," DeeDee said. "The luncheon in the church basement will be a zoo. Those church ladies know how to cook. Sylvia always makes baked beans. Best in the area." DeeDee rolled back and forth on her exercise ball. "What are your plans?"

"Plans? What are you talking about?"

"Are you moving in with Keith?"

"Already did that. Before Lisa was killed, she and Keith had a big-ass fight and she said she'd move out before the divorce was finalized. I moved in last Monday."

"Lisa wasn't even buried, and you moved in?" DeeDee stopped rolling.

"That was the plan. All of her stuff was gone. No clothes, no cookbooks, no knickknacks. Nothing. Place looked kinda empty."

"Empty? Lisa was a collector," DeeDee said. "Wonder where her stuff is?"

"What stuff?"

"Beanie Babies. I think she inherited her mother's collection of Hummels. I bet those are worth a pretty penny these days. Keith'll probably sell them on eBay and pocket the money."

Monica crossed her legs. "There's nothing in the house. Did she take the collection wherever she was moving?"

"Most likely. I think she was planning to stay with Vickie until she found a place of her own or maybe she was gonna live permanently with Vickie in that country mansion of hers. She never said."

"I didn't realize you were that close to Lisa," Monica said. *Are there more little statues in Vickie's house?*

"The women business owners of Field's Crossing met every six weeks or so to sit and shoot the shit," DeeDee said. "We became pretty close. Lisa's the first to die. Makes you wonder."

"Wonder what?"

"Who's next?" DeeDee smiled at Monica. "You're too young to wonder about death."

"Who all was in this group? Whad'ya talk about?" Monica was curious. *A group of women became friends due to owning a business. That's weird.*

"Business mostly, but a lot of the time it was personal stuff, stuff going on at home. I knew about you and Keith early on." DeeDee paused. "You're not the first woman he's cheated with."

Monica nodded. "He's not my first either."

"Why him? Why married men?" DeeDee frowned.

For the second time that day, Monica shoved away the memories. The voices. The laughter. Her dark bedroom. Her parents not protecting her from the monster that was her brother. And his friends.

"Men are disappointing, especially young men. Most older men are married and dissatisfied and don't ask much. Easy to please."

CHAPTER THIRTY-NINE

"ARE YOU READY to finish?" Laurent watched Rina Yoshida slam her car door. With her briefcase in hand, the attorney reminded Laurent of Rina's father, the principal at the high school. Small in stature, big on brains.

"Let's hope there's no money stuffed inside cookware in the prep area. Do you think Lisa was a hoarder or just wanted to hide the money from the IRS?" Rina asked.

"It never occurred to me she might be a hoarder," Laurent said. "I didn't see any milk tins in her house when I went to do the NOK, but then again, I wasn't looking."

"Maybe she's got a storage locker somewhere," Rina said. "The will mentioned a collection of Hummels, but there was no mention of where she stored them. If they're in the house on Cardinal Street, I'll need to do an inventory there also, before someone in the family decides to do something with them. I'm assuming Keith, Aubrey, and Andrew know about this. The collection is supposed to be sold and the proceeds divided among the four grandchildren."

"I'll ask, but not today. The entire family's going to be exhausted when they get home from the funeral and the luncheon." Laurent unlocked the door, lifted the crime scene tape, ducked under, and held it for Rina. "If the Hummel collection and whatever else Lisa collected is in the house on Cardinal Street, it doesn't go to Keith even though he gets the house. It goes to the grandchildren because Lisa made a special bequest. Am I right?"

Rina nodded. "And everything inside and outside Big Al's except for the recipe box belongs to Vickie. Remind me to take it with today. I completely forgot yesterday."

"Understandable. We were all in a state of shock." Laurent flipped on the lights. Closing the door behind Rina, she pulled off her gloves and headband and dropped them on a table and hung her jacket on a chair. As she waited for Rina to power up her laptop, Laurent wandered around the eating area. She, Dak, Rina, and Walker had emptied the cash out of the milk tins and returned them to their spot on the shelves and the floor. Rina's comment about hoarding raised a few thoughts. *Who knew Lisa was a hoarder? If she was a hoarder, where was her stuff? What did she hoard? Was it worth anything? Maybe that was why she was murdered, and Big Al's has nothing to do with it. Would Lisa's collection of Hummels be worth more than Big Al's?*

"I've got a question for you. When I pull the IRS file for Big Al's and if I find Lisa didn't pay tax on the money we found, what happens? Will Vickie have to pay the IRS?"

"I'm not a tax attorney, but the inventory I file in probate will trigger a response from the IRS, especially if Lisa was under-reporting income," Rina said. "The problem is the person evading income tax is deceased, so does the unreported tax burden carry over to the heir? What does the IRS have to prove? Intent? Where the money came from?"

"I think the fact she hid it proves intent."

"I agree. I think the heir is going to have to pay a penalty and back taxes. The problem the IRS will have is how much underreporting was there? They may say the entire one point seven million dollars was underreported and taxes and penalties are due on all of it. What do they base their claim on? I think they have to have some factual cost basis and that may be hard to come by in Field's Crossing. There's no other restaurant or diner like Big Al's in the quad-county area.

"The other issue is Lisa was murdered. The life insurance company will delay payment until you prove who did it. If Vickie or Aubrey or Keith or Andrew killed Lisa, they forfeit their inheritance."

"When I chatted with Vickie, she said Lisa canceled the life insurance policy," Laurent said.

"Good to know. I've been through all the papers in Lisa's desk and didn't find anything and the bank records indicate that the last payment for a policy was several years ago," Rina said.

"After I file the inventory, the IRS will descend like the predators they are. I'm certain the first thing they'll do is freeze everything, especially the account with the one point seven million. I'll be allowed to pay utilities and property taxes and the like, but Judge Jenkins will have to sign off on every bill I submit for payment.

"If Keith intends to sell the house on Cardinal Street, he may have to wait for the IRS to finish their audit. Same with Vickie and Big Al's. Until the IRS is satisfied, no one can do anything."

"I wonder if the heirs know that," Laurent said. "If Vickie killed Lisa, who gets Big Al's?"

"Vickie would be disqualified from inheriting and the part of the estate she inherited would be divided between Aubrey and

Andrew. Keith still wouldn't be able to inherit the diner or that bank account due to the waivers. If Keith killed Lisa, then Aubrey and Andrew would split the house on Cardinal Street and the Farmers bank account, fifty-fifty. Vickie still gets the diner and the bank account at First Federal. If Aubrey killed her mom, Keith and Andrew would split the recipe box and Keith still gets the house and their joint bank account. If Andrew killed his mom, then the hundred thousand would be split fifty-fifty between Aubrey and Keith. The bottom line is Vickie inherits Big Al's unless she killed Lisa. Clear as mud?" Rina shook her head. "And I'm the attorney."

"What if Vickie is killed?" Laurent asked.

"If Vickie didn't kill Lisa and in turn is killed, then everything from Lisa's estate passes to Vickie's estate and whoever Vickie has designated as heirs will inherit."

"Vickie has no children."

"The better question is does Vickie have a will? Imagine the mess if she doesn't. It would be easier if none of the heirs killed Lisa, but if one of them did, the estate could be tied up in court for a few years." Rina exhaled. "All right. Let's get this over with."

"Follow me." Laurent walked through the dining area and paused at the entrance to the prep room.

"Other than the knives, did you confiscate anything else?" Rina asked.

"Gloves, aprons, a bit of trash. The diner was closed for Easter, so the prep area was clean and empty," Laurent said. "You want to do this the same way?"

"I'll type. You talk."

"Let's put a table right outside the door."

While Laurent dragged a table into the hallway, Rina opened her laptop and plugged it into the wall outlet.

"How come you're not in uniform?" Rina asked.

"I was supposed to meet Randi for lunch. She texted and canceled." *I hope this isn't the first in a long line of cancellations.*

"Your daughter?"

"I gave her up for adoption thirty years ago. She doesn't think of me as her mother, and she shouldn't." Laurent hunched her shoulders. She wasn't entirely comfortable talking about Randi with other people.

"But you think of her as your daughter. I met her at the voter registration drive. She's tall, like you. Does she have your musical talent?" Rina asked.

"She plays violin in the Indianapolis Symphony Orchestra and she's a math teacher at the high school level."

"Ick. Calculus. I did the minimum requirements for math in high school and in college. No math in law school, thank God." Rina scooted her chair closer to the table. "My dad still talks about the voter registration drive. He was so happy you asked to use the gym and even happier with all the high school seniors who signed up. He's planning on holding one every year, but to somehow incorporate it into the civics class everyone has to take."

"Excellent idea." Laurent was glad there was no judgment in Rina's voice about giving Randi up for adoption.

"I thought you might attend the funeral this morning," Rina said. "I drove by the church and the parking lot was full and the side streets were starting to clog up. Lot of people going."

"Dak and Poulter are handling traffic and escorting the hearse and family to Field's Crossing Cemetery. The new one on the south end of town."

"Field Street will be a mess."

"The procession will pass right by us. I'll text Dak to let us know when they leave the church. I chatted with Mimi and she's not going to the church but plans to watch the procession on the sidewalk in front of her store. Lot of the store owners are doing that. We could do the same."

"I'd like that. Dad said he was going to allow any students who worked at Big Al's to stand outside and watch from the high school as the procession goes by," Rina said.

"Lisa's gonna be missed."

*   *   *

Two hours later, Rina leaned back in her chair, clicked on her mouse, and saved the inventory spreadsheet. "Done." She rolled her shoulders. "My back is sore."

"Glad I'm not the only one with aching muscles," Laurent said. "Let me put the table and chair back. You get the recipe box."

Scrape. Laurent hated that sound. Reminded her of nails on a chalkboard, but the table was heavy and easier to pull than lift. And her arm hurt. She had missed yesterday's physical therapy session and needed to reschedule. She was hoping her shoulder would be okay without the last two sessions. *Wishful thinking.*

"It's not here." Rina emerged from Lisa's office.

"Let's check all these shelves. I didn't see it yesterday, but . . ." Laurent said, shaking her head. "You know why."

The two women pulled everything off the shelves and placed it on nearby tables. No recipe box. They pulled every cart from the walk-in cooler and emptied them onto tables. No recipe box. Every item in Lisa's office was placed on a table. No recipe box.

Laurent stood with her hands on her hips. "We've searched everywhere. Dak says he and Poulter did not inventory it or take it to CSU. I'm calling Vickie."

Two minutes later. "You've got it? Why'd you take it without telling me or Rina?" Laurent was exasperated. Vickie had wasted hours of her time to say nothing of the pain in her shoulder. "Bring it to Rina's office. It's her job as executor to handle the special bequests."

"What'd she say?"

"She took it the day the new locks were installed and was planning to give it to Aubrey as a sign of peace. She knows Aubrey is furious with her." Laurent frowned. "I remember her saying something about it, but I didn't think she had already taken it."

"Aubrey should be mad at her mother, not Vickie," Rina said. "I better get to my office. Thanks for your help, Sheriff."

Laurent locked the front door of the diner and waved goodbye to Rina before texting Dak. NO NEW SURPRISES AT BIG AL'S.

Dak's reply was immediate. I HAVEN'T RECOVERED FROM YESTERDAY. KEEP WANTING TO TELL SOMEONE.

CHAPTER FORTY

LAURENT PARKED NEAR the rear exit of the Skillet Restaurant, climbed out of the black SUV, and lifted her face to the sun. It was midafternoon and the April sun was welcome. The forecast was for rain tonight and she knew the local farmers were anxious to get into the fields. Rain equaled mud in April and none of the farmers wanted their tractors or plows to get stuck, but the sooner the crops were planted, the sooner they started growing. She wandered around the corner of the building and strolled north on Field Street.

After two days of indecision, Laurent decided to take Vern's advice and call Randi. She pulled out her phone, hit Randi's number. When her daughter answered, Laurent, without hesitation, asked, "Have you contacted your biological father?"

"I left a message with his manager, but no one's called back," Randi said.

"He won't know your name. You may have to explain the situation," Laurent said. "Even then, he may still choose to ignore you."

"Then I'll have my answer."

"What's the question?"

"Why didn't you want me?" Randi's voice cracked.

"I did want you. I had you for two weeks and I broke my own heart when I gave you up. But I couldn't do everything. My parents were dead, and no help was coming from Lucroy's family. My aunt was in the hospital, dying from cancer, Joelle was in trouble in college, and I had just been fired from the orchestra, thanks to Lucroy. No job. No money. Brand-new baby. My options were limited," Laurent said. "I thought the best thing I could do for you was to give you up and I still think I made the right decision. How was I going to get a job and afford child care? Maybe if my aunt had been healthy or able to care for you, I might have been able to keep you, but she was so weak and frail. I had to take care of her, too."

"Tell me about your parents. What were they like?"

"They both came from farm families. Dad was a tenant farmer. We moved every March 1 when he signed a new lease. I've lived all over north central Indiana. Mom's family bought land and she grew up in the same house, same school, same town. I thought they were happy. I was happy. Joelle was happy.

"But, one day, early in March, just after we moved again, my father took the shotgun he kept behind the mudroom door and killed my mother and then turned the gun on himself. Joelle and I found them in the barn after school." Laurent stared across the street, willing the tears away. *May as well get all the bad news out in the open.*

Silence on the other end.

"I'm sorry that happened to you," Randi said. "How old were you when you found them in the barn?"

"Ten."

"Aunt Joelle?"

"Eight."

"Where is she now?"

"Joelle is currently in prison for DUI and damaging public property," Laurent said.

"Do you ever visit her?"

"No."

"Why not? She's the only family you've got."

Randi's biting tone sliced Laurent in half. "We had a falling-out when I became a deputy sheriff. When she was sentenced, I asked to visit, but she refused." Laurent's guts were twisted into a knot. "Randi, I gotta ask. Why are you contacting me now?"

"I told you. Mom and Dad just told me I was adopted."

"Is that the only reason?"

"Of course."

Laurent was silent. Randi's voice didn't ring true with her. Even though they had only met twice, she heard hesitation.

"I found a copy of the police report from that night. Apparently, I was screaming so much the neighbors called the police," Randi said.

Laurent closed her eyes. "It was nighttime. I hadn't slept in almost seventy-two hours. My aunt was days away from death. I couldn't take it anymore. I put you in your crib. You were two weeks old. I sat on the couch and cried. I cried so hard I didn't hear the police knocking. I didn't hear you bawling. I looked up and there they were." She sniffed. "They took both of us to the hospital and gave me something so I could sleep. I woke up twelve hours later and signed the adoption papers and checked myself out. Two days later, my aunt died, and I had no one."

* * *

"Use this." A white handkerchief was thrust into her hand as another hand steered her toward a concrete bench along the parkway under the growing wisteria. "Sit down. Breathe."

Laurent sat, her fist pressed against her mouth trying to stifle the sobs, but tears dripped on to her pants. Using the hanky, she hid her face. After a minute she blew her nose. "Thanks. I'll get this back to you."

"No rush. I've got a drawer full of them," Vern said. "Was that your daughter?"

Laurent nodded and stared at the sidewalk, cheeks burning, eyes swollen from crying. She was glad it was the middle of the afternoon. Not a lot of people on the street.

"What happened between you and your daughter's father?"

"I was a fool."

"How old were you?"

"Twenty-two."

"Old enough to know better," Vern said. "But responsible enough to do the right thing. The asshole ran away. You didn't. Your daughter will see him for what he is."

"How can you be so sure?"

"Because she's a part of you. It takes courage to meet the past and courage to let the past go. She's got the courage to meet you. You need to trust her when she meets the asshole."

"When did you become such a philosopher?" Laurent leaned against the cold concrete bench and looked at the middle-aged farmer sitting next to her. The first time she had met Vern Martin, she was positive he was going to shoot her in the back, but since the fiasco in the forest . . . *I think we're sort of friends. How odd.*

"Ten years sitting in my cabin. The threat of Dylan going to jail woke me up. It's time for me to rejoin the human race. Even if it means eating lunch at three o'clock in the afternoon in town so I can avoid everyone."

She laughed. "That's your definition of rejoining the human race? Eating lunch alone?"

"I'll let you know the next time I'm in town for lunch. Maybe you could join me," he said.

"I'd like that." Laurent sighed. "What am I going to do? Now that I've met Randi, I want her in my life, but she may not want me."

"Waiting's the hard part."

"And if she rejects me?"

CHAPTER FORTY-ONE

"HEY, BOSS. I'VE been following up on a few items regarding Keith DuVal." Dak held up a sheaf of papers. "Isn't today your day off?"

"Not when there's an ongoing murder investigation. Can you imagine what Ralph Howard would say if I were to take a day off? Greene's probably already called his buddy at *The Crossing* to complain about me. Pull up a chair." Laurent opened the mini fridge and grabbed two bottles of water and handed one to Dak. "Did you read his column?"

"Ralph likes to stir the pot. It's his job and, sadly, he's good at it. But I'm glad he took a shot at someone other than you." Dak settled into the metal folding chair. "I chatted with HR at Columbia Hospital, and other than the one incident Ken Sakamoto told you about, Keith's record is clean. I asked about his 401(k) account and the HR chick sent me to the company. After I got the warrant, guess what I found?"

"I'm afraid to ask."

"Keith has been withdrawing money, bit by bit."

"How much did he take out?" she asked.

"Sixty thousand."

"How much is left?"

"Not one damn dime," Dak said. "The administrator of the fund sent a copy of the last five years, and up until six months ago, Keith was a regular contributor. Then, he stopped the automatic deduction from his paycheck and started taking money out."

"Six months ago? That coincides with when he started dating Monica," Laurent said. "How old is he? Didn't he get hit with a penalty for early withdrawal?"

"He did. By law, the company withheld ten percent for the penalty and twenty percent for federal taxes, but nothing for state taxes," Dak said. "The administrator also sent a copy of the spousal consent form."

"Lisa agreed to this? Wonder what was going on? Remodeling Big Al's? Big vacation?"

"I know we're not experts, but I'd like to compare signatures."

"Let me pull up a copy of the will. Her signature's on the last page." Laurent reached for the mouse. "I'll print it out."

Dak plucked the paper from the printer and handed both pieces to Laurent. He walked behind her desk and peered over her shoulder.

"I'm no expert, but that's not the same signature."

"Look how loopy this signature is and the signature on the will is tight. Tiny. No way that's the same person."

"Who do you think signed this?"

"Keith forged it or he got Monica to do it." Dak returned to the other side of Laurent's desk. "Maybe Monica suggested to Keith to make withdrawals so Lisa wouldn't get anything. Think she's that devious?"

"She's my first thought, too. Vickie told me Lisa was demanding half of Keith's retirement income and Aubrey said something similar. Why does Keith need sixty thousand dollars?"

"Buys a pretty nice car," Dak said.

"I wonder if Wes, the apartment manager, would give us a copy of Monica's signed lease agreement without a warrant?" Laurent asked. "I think we're on very thin ice if we ask the DA for a warrant, especially since we're not handwriting experts. Keith's 401(k) goes to motive in killing his wife, so that warrant's fine, but Monica's lease agreement would be a stretch."

"All you can do is ask. If Wes says no, we'll build a case for the warrant."

Laurent looked at her favorite deputy. "It could be Aubrey's signature."

"You think Keith withdrew money from his retirement account to pay for Doug's gambling addiction? I'll buy that."

"Lisa wouldn't give him a penny. That's what Vickie and Mimi told me."

"So, if Mommy won't give us the money, let's run to Daddy? Spoiled brat. You know how hard Mimi and I worked to get the flower shop up and running? How hard she still works? Who's going to take over when she can't do it anymore? She's gonna be seventy next year." Dak pushed to his feet.

"I'm with you, Dak. No silver spoon ever touched my lips."

CHAPTER FORTY-TWO

LAURENT KNOCKED ON Keith's front door and stepped to the side. Her gaze wandered down the quiet street. Lisa's funeral had been the day before, and according to *The Crossing*, it was the largest funeral and procession in Field's Crossing's history.

The front door opened.

"What the hell do you want? Haven't you caused enough damage with your insulting questions and innuendos? Accusing my daughter of stealing? What is wrong with you? You know how much crap I had to put up with yesterday?" Keith crossed his arms over a badly stained Indiana University sweatshirt. "The only person who's got it right is that reporter. Ralph Howard. Me and my family were cheated out of our inheritance, and I wouldn't be surprised if Vickie killed my wife."

"May I come in or would you like to come to the station?" Laurent was tired of Keith's demeaning attitude toward women. *Or maybe I'm just tired of Keith.*

"Make it quick."

Laurent stepped inside but left the front door open.

"You know where the kitchen is." Keith reached past her and slammed the door.

"Lead the way." Laurent followed Keith into the messy kitchen and settled into an uncomfortable plastic chair. "How was the funeral?"

"How do you think? So many people spouting nonsense about Lisa. What a sweetheart she was. How generous. What a load of crap." Keith tugged a cigarette out of the packet lying on the kitchen table, lit it, and blew a cloud of smoke directly at Laurent.

"How did you respond?" *Did Keith bad-mouth his wife on the day of her funeral?* She resisted the urge to bat away the smoke.

"I sucked it up and agreed with all those assholes. Glad that's over with."

"How are Aubrey and Andrew? Grandkids?"

"They'll get over it. Grandkids probably won't even remember her."

"That'd be a shame," she said.

Keith shrugged.

"I've got some follow-up questions." Laurent pulled out her notebook and opened it. She took her time finding the right page. "Was Lisa a hoarder?"

"Yes."

"What did she hoard? Anything in particular?"

"She inherited that pain-in-the-ass gene from her mother. The woman couldn't throw away a used paper plate."

"Lisa or her mom?"

"Her mom." Keith crossed his legs. "Lisa's mom owned Hummels dating back to World War II and she left them to Lisa."

"Where are the Hummels? I didn't see any."

"No clue. They used to sit around the house, but Andrew broke one and Lisa went nuts. Next thing I know, she packed them all up and I never saw them again."

"How old was Andrew when he broke the figurine?" she asked.
"Three."

"Long time ago. Then what?"

"Lisa replaced the Hummels with Beanie Babies. Guess she thought those wouldn't break. Instead of ceramic figurines, now there's little stuffed animals everywhere. With tags on. It's not like she let Aubrey and her friends play with them."

"Where are the Beanie Babies? Does Aubrey have them now?"

"I don't know where Lisa stashed them. I got so fed up with the damn things sitting everywhere, I threatened to rip off the tags." Keith smirked. "Smartest thing I ever did. They were gone the next day."

"When was this?" Laurent asked.

"Right after she bought Big Al's."

"Do you think she sold them?" *I'm giving this task to Dak. He can search the internet. Where could Lisa have sold them? I wonder how long eBay has been in existence.*

"Probably. I always wondered where she got the money for the down payment for the diner. I didn't give it to her and she didn't take it out of our joint account." Keith ground his cigarette in the overflowing ashtray, ashes and butts spilling on the already-filthy kitchen table. "Let me show you something." He threaded his way through the living room, up the stairs, and opened a door at the end of the hallway. "This is supposed to be a fourth bedroom. Can't use a goddamn inch of it."

Laurent peered in. "What's in all the bags?"

"Lisa bought crap every day and tossed it in here. Sometimes, I'd find her scrounging around for stuff. Why didn't she just put it away when she bought it? I bet there's five gallons of Windex and hundreds of rolls of toilet paper."

"What are you going to do with it?"

"Go through it. Keep what I need and return the rest. I bet I make a thousand dollars on returns."

"Don't you need the receipts? Won't the merchants credit it back to the card it was charged on?" Laurent asked.

"Receipts are in the bags, and I'll put up such a stink, they'll write me a check on the spot." Keith rocked back on his heels, arms folded across his chest, huge grin on his face. "Might be two grand in there." He closed the door and Laurent followed him back to the uncomfortable chair in the kitchen. "And thanks to my dearly departed wife, I got another three grand from her purse. Had to be money from the diner and Vickie can't touch it."

"We've discovered you've taken sixty thousand dollars out of your 401(k) in the last six months. Can you tell me why?"

"I'm buying a new car."

"Who signed the spousal consent form?" Laurent asked. *Why won't he look at me?*

"Lisa."

"Are you sure?"

"Of course I'm sure," Keith snapped. "If you've got something to say, spit it out. Quit beating around the bush."

"We're having the signatures analyzed. No results yet." She paused. "What do you know about Aubrey and Doug's financial situation?"

Keith looked away. "Doug's got it under control. All he needs is for Aubrey to stop hounding him and spending so much money. Why does she need to spend two hundred dollars on a haircut? If she'd quit hassling him, he'd get his gambling under control."

"The money from your 401(k) wasn't to help Doug pay off his bookie?" *Shot in the dark.*

"Like I said. Doug's got it under control. The money is for me."

Laurent glanced at her notebook. "Aubrey made the daily deposits for Big Al's. She claims she deposited every dime. What do you think?"

"If that's what she said, that's what she did."

"Are you sure?"

"Positive."

"What did you use to smash in the front window of the diner?"

"What? I didn't smash it in and I'm sure as hell not paying for it. Vickie inherited the diner. She can buy a new window. Serves her right. Hope it costs a bucket of money." Keith rubbed his hands together.

"If you didn't do it, who did?" Laurent asked.

"My money's on Stacy Simmons. She's still ticked at Lisa for outbidding her on Big Al's."

"That was a long time ago. Why would Stacy still be upset?"

"'Cuz, I fucked her and every one of Lisa's bridesmaids the week before our wedding."

Laurent's head snapped back. "Stacy was one of your bridesmaids? Why'd you do it?"

"Challenge from my brother." Keith smirked. "He did it before he got married."

"Did Lisa find out?"

"Who cares? Lisa knew who she was marrying. After Aubrey and Andrew were born, she didn't give a damn about me."

"How long have you been having sex with women other than Lisa?" Laurent asked.

"Years."

"Names?"

Keith pulled out another cigarette and tapped it on the table. "Before Monica, there was Ruby Rae, and before that I don't remember."

"Ruby Rae Evans? One of Lisa's employees?" Laurent wiggled in the plastic chair. Her butt was numb.

"Ruby Rae's the one who suggested the IRS audit."

"Why would she do that?"

"Everybody knew Lisa and me were getting a divorce," Keith said. "Ruby Rae went on some website and looked at Big Al's tax returns. Because she's one of the Moonshine Mamas, she realized Lisa wasn't reporting all the money Big Al's took in and if I wanted more money in the divorce, I had to get the IRS to check Big Al's books."

"Why does Ruby Rae care how much money you get in the divorce?" Laurent's brow furrowed.

"She thought if Lisa was audited, it would show Big Al's real income, which would be much higher than mine, and Lisa would have to pay alimony to me," Keith said. "Ruby Rae said Lisa was small potatoes and Ruby Rae wanted to make more moonshine, which meant more money for everyone. She's the one who called the IRS. I've never seen Lisa so scared."

"When was the last time you spoke with Ruby Rae?" Laurent asked.

"Months ago."

"So Ruby Rae sicced the IRS on your wife hoping to make more money and you went along assuming Lisa would have to pay you alimony," Laurent said. "Why'd you break up with her?"

"Younger's always better."

*   *   *

Laurent paused on the top step of the DuVal home, flipped through her notebook, and reread her interview with Ruby Rae Evans. *Ruby Rae is the whistleblower and she's angry with Keith. But why kill Lisa? How does Ruby Rae benefit from Lisa's death? Ruby Rae wasn't going to inherit the diner, but like everyone else, she probably expected Keith to inherit and if not Keith, then Aubrey. What would Ruby Rae do to make more money? Kill Lisa?* Laurent remembered Vickie telling her that Lisa didn't manufacture all ten thousand gallons of moonshine allowed under the FDSP. *I need to have another chat with Ruby Rae and Aubrey.*

Laurent trotted down the stairs and leaned against the rear bumper of the police SUV before writing a few notes to herself. The bedroom was filled with bags and bags of stuff. Lisa bought something every day. *Lisa transferred her hoarding to the diner. Wonder what Keith's reaction will be when he finds out about the milk tins? Wonder how Aubrey will feel about the $1.7 million in cash right under her nose?*

Gazing at the DuVal house, Laurent saw a curtain fall back in place. *Keith's nervous. Good. Should have told him I'm interviewing Ruby Rae Evans next.*

CHAPTER FORTY-THREE

LAURENT DROVE NORTH on Field Street before turning right on Webster Street. She counted houses. Ruby Rae lived thirty-four houses away from the park. *Ruby Rae's a runner.* Laurent parked opposite the Evans' home, shut off the engine, and gazed around the neighborhood.

Webster Street ran parallel to the Five-and-Twenty. The homes were small, many of which looked to be original to the area. Cornfields were one block to the north. Laurent opened the driver's door and slid out. She inhaled. *Lilacs. My favorite.* She pulled her sunglasses from the top of her head as she strolled across the street and up the front sidewalk. Climbing the stairs, she knocked.

The front door whipped open, and Ruby Rae's red face glared at Laurent. "Now what? Haven't you got better things to do?"

"Would you like to talk on the front porch or at the station?" Laurent narrowed her eyes at the Moonshine Mama.

"Get in. I don't need the neighbors telling my husband you were here." Ruby Rae slammed the door behind Laurent and crossed her arms over her chest.

"Tell me about the IRS audit for Big Al's."

Ruby Rae's gaze dropped to the floor, and she took in a big breath. "I was an idiot. I assumed after the audit that Lisa would be bankrupt. Broke. Have to sell. Maybe go to jail. If that was the case, I figured Keith would hire someone to run the diner and I told him I could increase profits at Big Al's. Lisa didn't make all the alcohol the FDSP allowed. She left money on the table. If the Moonshine Mamas manufactured all ten thousand gallons, we'd double our take-home pay."

"What were you going to do if the IRS just fined her?"

"She'd still have to come up with the money for the penalties and back taxes," Ruby Rae said. "Either way, the audit would force Lisa to make more moonshine."

"Who knows you're the whistleblower?" Laurent asked.

"Me and Keith."

"Why were you trying to increase Keith's potential alimony?" Laurent asked. "Did you think he was going to marry you?"

"I don't give a rat's ass about Keith's alimony. I need to make more money," Ruby Rae said.

"What would you have used this money for?"

"Divorce my husband."

"Is he abusive?" Laurent asked.

"Dismissive. Like I don't exist. I bring in more money than he does, and he still thinks he's the king of the house. Wish I'd never married him."

"Why'd you sleep with Keith?"

"Revenge. I was hoping my husband would sit up and notice me. He didn't bat an eye."

"How'd he find out?" Laurent asked.

"I told him."

"How'd you feel about Keith dumping you?"

"Knew it was gonna happen. I used him for what I needed."

"Did you kill Lisa?" Laurent asked.

"No."

"Where were you on Easter Sunday afternoon?"

"Here. Making dinner. I told you that."

"When I speak with your husband, what's he going to say?"

"Same thing. He may not know I exist, but he knows when dinner's not on the table."

Ruby Rae has no alibi.

CHAPTER FORTY-FOUR

LAURENT BARELY HAD time to knock on the front door when a pissed-off Aubrey flung it open, shouting in her face. "Do you know what my father did? Do you know what my dumb-ass father did? He gave Mom's Escalade to that skank."

Laurent stepped inside and decided to respond as if Aubrey had asked a rational question. "Both of your parents' names were on the title. The vehicle now belongs to your dad. Once the coroner released the body, I was able to give your mom's personal effects to the next of kin, your father."

"Everyone in town's laughing at me. There goes Aubrey. Her mother gave the diner to her best friend and then her father gives his dead wife's car to his girlfriend. And we all know who Ralph's 'source close to the family' is. That bitch, Monica. I'm gonna sue her for defamation of character and I'm gonna sue Ralph and his stupid newspaper. I don't care if he ran his column on the opinion page."

"I doubt people are laughing at you. Most people don't have time to think about anyone other than themselves," Laurent said. "If anything, people feel sorry for you, getting the short end of the stick."

"What's worse? People laughing at me or feeling sorry for me. This town sucks." Aubrey slammed the front door and stalked to the kitchen. "I'm gonna call Rina when we're done. She needs to work harder. I haven't heard anything since the will reading. What in the hell is she doing and what happened to the diner? Who smashed in the front window?"

"I know for a fact Rina inventoried the diner this week and that took a lot of time. As for the front window," Laurent said, "we'll catch whoever did it." She settled on the same stool at the counter. "What are your boys up to? I see their backpacks on the floor."

"They're sleeping at the neighbor's house tonight so Doug and I can have a free evening. God knows we need one."

"What did they pack?" Laurent waited as Aubrey picked up a backpack, pulled out a Ziploc bag of candy, two water pistols, and a swimsuit.

"Boys." Aubrey sighed. She zipped the backpack shut and picked up the other one. "Same. They're planning to eat themselves sick and run through the sprinkler and shoot each other with Nerf water guns."

"It's a bit cold for running through the sprinkler," Laurent said. "I've got a few follow-up questions. First, why did your mom give everyone a key to Big Al's?"

"I asked her the same question. God knows she was there all the time. Opening and closing every day. She didn't need to give every employee a key, especially the high school kids. I don't think she knew why she did it."

"Was Big Al's ever robbed?"

"Never."

"Even though the diner was cash only?" Laurent asked.

"You'd think we'd be a prime target, wouldn't you? But, no, never, ever robbed."

"What happens if the cash register is too full, and the drawer doesn't close?" Laurent asked.

"Depended on how many people were in line. Mom was all about not waiting in line. I don't know how many times I heard her say I shouldn't have to wait for someone to take my money."

"There's some truth in that. But with Amazon and buying online, there's not much waiting anymore," Laurent said.

"I was at the register for lunch, Monday through Friday, eleven to three, except if the kids had the day off school," Aubrey said. "When the drawer was full, I'd empty all the twenties and half of the tens, fives, and ones, and drop them into the drawer underneath the register. Then, before I left for the day, sometime around three or three fifteen, I'd scoop it into the deposit bag and go to the bank and make the deposit."

"Did you count the money before you went to the bank?"

"No. All the tellers know me. I'd hand the bag to the teller, and she'd sort the paper bills and run them through their counter. You know, the one that rifles through the money fast. Same thing with the coin counter. Took less than five minutes, and if the bank didn't have any other customers, even less. To sit in Mom's office and count the money would have taken at least an hour."

"What about at night when the diner closed?"

"Mom put the money in the safe in her desk at night or she made a night deposit," Aubrey said.

"Did you ever check the balance in the account?"

"Mom took care of all that. Paying suppliers, ordering inventory. She refused to use QuickBooks for payroll or taxes or to pay vendors. She said she didn't trust electronic money."

Aubrey wouldn't need to check the balance in the checking account because she stole the money before it was deposited.

"What about the cash withdrawals you made?" Laurent asked.

"Sometimes the register was short, and we needed coins or singles or fives or tens. I'd run down to the bank and withdraw whatever we needed in that denomination."

"Did you deposit every single dollar?" Laurent gazed at Aubrey. The woman had calmed down considerably since opening the door. *Poulter's research had shown no large withdrawals. Maybe that's because Aubrey knew her mom used this account frequently and might have noticed a bunch of money missing.*

"You asked me that last time." Aubrey picked up her purse dog, Dolly, and stroked her. "I repeat. Every single penny, every single dollar bill was deposited, every day. Check the bank records. Big Al's takes in roughly fifteen hundred dollars in cash every day. Give or take five hundred."

"I know you only worked at lunch, but can you be more specific about the nighttime closing procedures?" Laurent said. "Big Al's closed at seven, Sunday through Thursday, and nine on Friday and Saturday night. Correct?"

"Yes."

"Did any of the high school employees handle the cash?"

"Mom trusted all those kids. After a couple of them were trained on the register, she left them alone. When the register was full, they put the overflow cash into the drawer just like me."

"Did your mom think any of her employees stole from her? Did she say anything?"

"She never complained about anyone. I think the high school kids liked working there, especially the boys. She made them free sandwiches."

"Teenage boys have hollow legs," Laurent said.

"What did the kids who closed on Saturday night say?" Aubrey asked.

"They cleaned the dining room, emptied the trash, wiped down the tables and chairs, mopped the floor, washed the windows, refilled the salt, pepper, sugar, ketchup, and other condiments," Laurent said.

"Where was my mom when they were doing all of that?"

"All four claimed your mom was in the prep area getting ready for Sunday."

"So, any or all of them could have taken the money out of the drawer?"

"I asked that exact same question and they all said your mom took the money and put it in the safe before they started cleaning up," Laurent said. "She had a roll of cash in her purse when I found her. I made the assumption she was planning to make a deposit at the bank but hadn't gotten there yet."

Aubrey frowned. "So, when you gave my dad the keys to Mom's Escalade, you also gave him the three grand that was in her purse? Dad got the weekend's take from Big Al's?"

"We're assuming that's where the cash came from," Laurent said.

"It probably was. I'd check the amount deposited on that weekend with other weekends to see how much they stole."

"Did that." *Aubrey thinks her mom made evening deposits, but records show the only deposits were from Aubrey. Lisa stuffed the milk tins but left enough in cash for Monday's deposit and to pay bills. Wonder how much Big Al's really took in on the weekends?* "So, you didn't know how much money was in the diner's account at any given time?"

"Mom kept the checkbook. I never looked to see how much money the diner had in the bank."

According to Stacy, you stole a few twenties every day. Why would you check and see how much was in there? You could take whatever you wanted. "Do your father or Andrew know the closing procedures at Big Al's?" Laurent asked.

"Dad doesn't. Andrew probably has his own procedures since he owns a wine bar and apparently is opening a moonshine bar," Aubrey said. "I'll never understand why Mom gave him so much money and developed new recipes just for him. Talk about having a favorite."

"Sounds like you're jealous of your brother," Laurent said.

"I had Dad, Andrew had Mom. Made it easy all the way around."

"You're your father's favorite? That doesn't surprise me," Laurent said. "Fathers and daughters; mothers and sons. Did you and Lisa fight a lot?"

"Same as everyone else. Teenage rebellion. I've got a few years before my boys start."

"If Vickie reopens Big Al's, will you work for her?" Laurent asked.

"I don't know, but I can tell you, she better not use my mom's recipes. Mom left them to me, not her."

"What if your mom left copies in Andrew's house or Vickie's house or Stacy's car or anywhere else?"

"Mom left me the recipe box with the original recipes she wrote down on three-by-five index cards. Her intention is clear. She wanted me to have the recipes, copies and all." Aubrey placed Dolly on the floor and stood up. "Where is the box? Who's got it?"

"Vickie gave it to the executor, Rina Yoshida."

"When is she going to get here and give it to me?" Aubrey snapped. "What the hell do lawyers do all day? Sit on their ass?"

"Was there anything else in the recipe box?"

"No."

She's lying. What can you hide in a box designed to hold three-by-five index cards?

"You believe the originals and all the copies belong to you?" Laurent asked.

"Damn straight they do. Mom was very clear about her intent. She wouldn't have left the recipes to me if she wanted Vickie to use them in the diner."

"Why do you think she left the diner to Vickie and not to you? Will Vickie be able to operate Big Al's without the recipes?"

"That's Vickie's problem, not mine. I don't know why Mom separated the lock from the key. It was stupid of her. She should have left it all to me or me and Andrew. I'm the one who worked there every day. I'm the one who took orders from customers. I'm the one who drove to the bank every day. Mom couldn't have run the diner without me. What was she thinking?" Aubrey plopped onto the bay window seat.

"If the judge rules that copies of the recipes that are in Vickie's house or your dad's house or anywhere outside of the diner belong to the property owner and not you, what will you do?" Laurent asked.

Aubrey's head jerked up. "I'll fight tooth and nail. Don't think I won't. Those recipes and everything else in that box belong to me."

Everything else. There's something in the recipe box that Aubrey knows about and isn't saying. Maybe Vickie took something.

"Can you tell me what your financial situation is? Are all your bills paid? On time? Outstanding credit card debt?"

"We're fine."

No, you're not. You've got fifty thousand in credit card debt, a mortgage, and two car payments. Does Doug handle the finances and Aubrey really doesn't know? Not in today's world. More like Aubrey handles the money and gives Doug an allowance.

"What can you tell me about Doug's gambling?"

"It's none of your business. He's got it under control."

Laurent stared at Aubrey. The woman's cheeks were red, lips pressed into a thin line, her arms folded across her chest. *Not going to get another word out of her on that subject.* "What can you tell me about your mom's collectibles? Hummels and Beanie Babies?"

Aubrey let out a sigh. "Grandma collected these statues called Hummels. Apparently, they were expensive and made someplace in Europe after World War II, and Grandma thought they'd be worth money someday. Crazy old bat. She was definitely wrong about that. Mom picked Beanie Babies and some kind of cards, like baseball cards, but . . . Ask Andrew—he'd know more about the cards. In any event, it was all junk. Dad got fed up with it lying around the house. He called them 'dust collectors' and threatened to throw them out or donate them to Goodwill, so Mom rented a storage unit and stuck them all there. I've never been to the storage unit. I don't think anyone in the family has. It'll be the last thing we get rid of. Nobody buys that shit."

"Which storage facility did your mom use and who's got the key? I suspect Rina will have to inventory that as well," Laurent said.

"I have no idea which place she used. There's only two in town. The key is probably in the junk drawer at Dad's house."

* * *

Frustrated, Laurent climbed into the police SUV and slammed the door. *What if the key to the storage unit was in the recipe box and that's why Vickie took it from Big Al's? Maybe Vickie stored something in the unit and wanted to get it before Rina inventories it. Maybe Vickie and Lisa shared the unit. Wonder what's in there? What if the key to the storage unit was on the key ring that I had to give to Keith? Did I take a picture of the keys?*

She started the engine. *Lisa didn't make any deposits on Saturday or Sunday. Ever. The bank records show that. Aubrey thinks her mom made a weekend deposit, when, in reality, it looks like Lisa stuffed a milk tin or stool with the cash. Is there more money stashed in the storage unit? Rina's not going to like this. I need to give her a call.*

Laurent put the SUV in gear and pulled away from the curb. *Keith's a cheater. Doug's a gambler. Aubrey's got a huge entitlement attitude. Ruby Rae was dumped by Keith for a younger woman. What's Vickie's problem? Maybe Vickie's auditing firm is in financial trouble. She said she was set for retirement. Did she lie to me?*

She drummed her fingers on the steering wheel. *What would a cheater, a gambler, an entitled mom, and a jilted lover do to keep their lifestyles?* An old saying drifted through her mind. *Ambition and revenge are always hungry.* Kind of appropriate for a diner.

CHAPTER FORTY-FIVE

"YOU'RE KEEPING THE diner? Why? You hate it. You've never made a sandwich. You don't even like to cook. You've spent your entire career as an auditor for Baylor, Scott, and Wright and ever since your husband died, you've been running the show. You're going to give that up to run Big Al's?" Aubrey laid her phone on the marble countertop, tapped the SPEAKER button, and clenched her fists, silently pounding the stone surface.

"I don't hate Big Al's. Your mother was a great cook. I'm not. Let's just say I was intimidated and knew I could never measure up to her standards, so I didn't try," Vickie said. "I know you're disappointed."

"Disappointed? I'm not disappointed. I'm mad at my mother. I've worked at Big Al's since high school. I've developed some of her signature sandwiches. All she left me were the recipes and I know them by heart. What am I going to do with three-by-five index cards sitting in a box? Big Al's should be mine. What did I do to make her so mad that she didn't leave it to me? I don't understand why she left it to you."

"Neither do I, but I'm going to honor your mother's wishes."

"What does that mean?" Aubrey asked.

"I haven't decided what to do. Keep Big Al's and hire a manager, sell, or learn how to run it myself."

"You'd leave your job to run Big Al's? You'll be closed in less than six months. You just said you can't cook, and Mom left the recipes to me. How are you going to make a sandwich? I'm not giving you permission to use her recipes. Why can't you give me the diner? You don't want it. You've got a pile of money sitting in the bank. You're a millionaire several times over."

"What makes you think you know my financial situation?"

"Oh, please. We all know how much your firm charges and how you've got the lock on all the farmers in the quad-county area." Aubrey's jaw ached. She and Vickie had been talking for the last half hour, and she had to stop herself from grinding her teeth. She had been a fool to think Vickie would give her Big Al's. Her father was right. Deep down, the woman was greedy.

"I don't need your recipes," Vickie said. "Your mom left copies at my house. I'll bet your dad's got copies at his house. You better hope his girlfriend doesn't find them."

"You can't use them. It says so in the will. Mom left the recipes to me."

"No. Your mom left the recipe box to you. Copies outside the box aren't yours."

The sheriff was right. "I'll sue you and anyone else who tries to use my mother's recipes. They belong to me."

"No, they don't."

"My mother was murdered, and the sheriff has no idea who did it. She's gonna be asking you a whole lot of questions," Aubrey snapped. "How about this: I'll run the moonshine business and you run the diner."

Vickie laughed. "No way. You're not going to cheat me the way you cheated your mom. Everyone in town knows you stole from her."

"Who said that?"

"You sat in your car in front of the bank and took money out of the deposit bag and shoved it in your purse. Dozens of people saw you."

I hate this town. "Did you kill my mom?" Aubrey demanded.

"No. How could you ask that? I loved your mother. Maybe I should ask—did you kill your mother?"

"How dare you accuse me of murdering my own mother. You ought to be locked up just for asking."

"And yet it's okay for you to question me? You're such a hypocrite."

"Hypocrisy would be working for you at Big Al's. The diner belongs to me, not you," Aubrey shouted at the phone lying on the countertop.

"You'd cut your brother out of his share?"

"He doesn't need the money."

"And you do?"

"Bitch. I wouldn't work for you if you doubled my salary." Aubrey stabbed END on her phone and stamped her feet. *Those recipes belong to me. I'll never let her use them. I'm going to find every single copy Mom made and burn them. Burn them all. Even the originals, so I'm the only one who knows the recipes. That'll show her. I'm not giving up Big Al's without a fight. The diner is mine.*

Aubrey took in a huge breath and let it out. She touched her cheeks and felt the heat. *What am I going to do? We don't have the money to hire a lawyer to contest the will. Maybe I can find a lawyer who'll work on commission or wait to get paid after the lawsuit is settled. Why didn't I take more cash? Okay. Breathe. Laurent said the attorney has the recipe box. Thank God. I thought Vickie had that, too. I can't wait for that lawyer to call me. I'll have to go to her office and get the recipe box and the key to the safe deposit box. I'm getting the cash now.* Aubrey gasped. *Wait a minute. Vickie gave the box to the lawyer. What if Vickie stole the key before giving it to the lawyer? Why didn't I think of that? What am I going to do if Vickie stole the money from the safe deposit box? We have to have that money before Tuesday otherwise Scarface will beat the crap out of Doug. Goddamn him, putting me in this position!*

CHAPTER FORTY-SIX

AUBREY SHIFTED HER Porsche into gear and peeled out of the driveway. She touched a hand against her warm cheek and looked in the rearview mirror. Her face was red. *Wonder what my blood pressure is?* She headed south onto Corn Belt Road and stepped on the gas. The two-lane country road was black, and the orange lattice fences used to stop drifting snow were still up.

How can I convince Vickie to turn Big Al's over to me? If I accuse Vickie of stealing the key to the safe deposit box, she'll deny it and there's no way for me to prove it. But, if the judge rules that anything in the safe deposit box belongs to me because the key was in the recipe box, then Vickie stole from me. And I will definitely press charges. She could end up behind bars. I'll threaten her with that. And then, in exchange for dropping the charges, I'll ask for the diner and the cash from the bank box. That's fair.

Aubrey pounded the steering wheel. She had a plan.

* * *

Aubrey braked and turned into Vickie's driveway. She drove past the house and continued down the lane to the rear of the property.

There she is.

The rear doors to one of Big Al's catering vans was wide open.

Aubrey parked behind the van. Pulling on her gloves, she slid out of the Porsche, stomped to the side door of the moonshine garage, and punched in the security code, kicking the snow shovel out of the way. The six-car moonshine garage was more secure than the diner.

"What are you doing here?" Vickie asked.

"I want to talk, face-to-face. I'm asking you to give Big Al's to me. I know I got a little hotheaded earlier on the phone. I'm sorry. I'm just so upset." Aubrey strolled to the kitchen area where Vickie was emptying the dishwasher. "I was wondering if you knew where the key for the safe deposit box is? You know that's why Mom left the recipe box to me. It was her way of making sure my family was financially okay."

"I don't know where your mom kept her key for the bank box, and I have no idea how many keys there are or how many people knew. Did you know?" Vickie asked.

"There's a bunch of people who know about that key. Dad, Andrew, you, me, Mom, and Stacy, but Mom was the only one with the key. If you don't have it and I don't have it, it has to be at Dad's house or Stacy or Andrew has it. I'm betting Stacy's the one who busted up the diner," Aubrey said. "Probably used that baseball bat of hers."

"If she has the key, the bank won't give her access," Vickie said. "The only people your mom listed are you and me, so the key is useless to her."

"Does she know that?"

"I don't know," Vickie said. "Are you going to help me load the van?"

"I think you should call the bank and warn them." Aubrey walked to the closest garage door, bent over, pulled out the pin, and lifted the door.

"There's no need. The bank won't let anyone in without the executor. Both banks, Farmers and First Federal, put a hold on everything the minute Lisa died."

"Will the bank let us know if Stacy tries to get into the safe deposit box?" Aubrey asked.

"My guess is they'll call Rina and tell her about the attempt at unauthorized access. It'll be up to Rina to press charges on behalf of Lisa's estate."

"Will the bank confiscate the key?"

"I don't know."

"Before you gave the recipe box to Rina, did you look inside? Was the key in there? Did you try to get into the safe deposit box? What did you take that legally belongs to me?" Aubrey asked.

"The key wasn't in the box."

"You're lying. I think you took the recipe box and the key inside and emptied the bank box. If you give me the contents of the safe deposit box and Big Al's, I won't press charges. Do you really want to lose a lawsuit and wind up behind bars?" Aubrey said. "The bank will have a recording of you opening the box."

"Opening a safe deposit box is a private matter. The bank doesn't record anything unless there's a problem or they think there will be a problem."

"So you did take the money," Aubrey said. *I know Mom kept that key in the box, but Vickie's called my bluff. Now what?*

"Are you deaf? The key wasn't in the box."

If I can't get the cash out of the safe deposit box, then I've got to get Vickie to open Big Al's and let me run it. Aubrey drummed her fingers on the stainless-steel countertop. "How long before Big Al's reopens?"

"Months, probably close to a year."

Aubrey stared at Vickie. "We don't have months."

"Sure, we do. The insurance company is coming out the end of next week to assess the damage to the diner and then it'll be a month before they issue a check, which will go into an account that only Rina has access to. Or Rina and the judge. Then I'll have to get Rina to authorize the repairs because she'll have to pay all the invoices."

Aubrey saw Vickie's mouth moving but couldn't hear over the roar in her ears.

"Like I said, it'll be months before Big Al's reopens." Vickie settled two growlers in the little red wagon and pulled it to the open garage door. She stepped to the rear doors of the van and lifted the growlers, one at a time, into the specially carved holders.

Aubrey followed her. "You have to open sooner. The employees need the money."

"You mean you need money."

"What's that supposed to mean?" Aubrey's cheeks burned.

"How much did he lose this time?"

"None of your business. How long have you known?"

"Since it started." Vickie slammed the rear doors of the catering van and returned to the garage. She motioned Aubrey inside, rolled down the garage door, and relocked it. "I'm done. This is the last batch of moonshine."

"What are you going to do with it?" Aubrey asked.

"I'm dropping it at Stacy's. She's calling some customers to get rid of it and asking them to tell everyone we are shut down for at least six months."

Aubrey leaned against the stainless-steel counter and crossed her arms over her chest. "Why don't you let me run Big Al's for you? I'll get the insurance company here tomorrow and the money into the executor account. I'll do it all and you won't have to worry about a thing."

"I want to hold off reopening the diner as long as I can. I need time to decide what to do." Vickie walked to the lockers and retrieved her jacket.

"It's all about you, isn't it? You never gave a shit about my mom." Aubrey yanked open the side door and grabbed the snow shovel lying on the ground.

"Why don't you and Doug go to the bank and get a short-term personal loan based on your inheritance?" Vickie flicked off the lights and turned toward Aubrey.

Crack.

Vickie screamed. The blow struck her in the arm, and she lurched sideways, cradling her arm.

Aubrey swung again at the hunched-over form. The edge of the shovel sliced into Vickie's neck and blood shot out as she crumpled to the floor.

Dropping the shovel, Aubrey stumbled back against the wall. Sliding down, she wrapped her arms around her knees. And stared.

Vickie lay on her side, blood spurting from a slash in her neck, the spray beating with the heart. Aubrey crawled along the wall, grabbed the door handle, pulled herself up, and stumbled outside. Bending over, she sucked in huge breaths.

I killed Vickie.

CHAPTER FORTY-SEVEN

AUBREY STARED AT the side door of the six-car garage. Part of her was expecting Vickie to stumble out holding her broken arm, but the door remained closed. She staggered to her Porsche and flicked the heating vents on high. *What if she's not dead? Should I check? I don't want to go in there again.* An image of a crazed Vickie, shovel in one hand, broken arm dangling, blood oozing from her neck, filled Aubrey's mind. She touched the phone button on the steering wheel and dialed Doug's cell phone. "I killed Vickie."

"What? How? Where are you?" Doug asked.

"Moonshine garage."

"Don't move. I'm on my way."

"Hurry." Aubrey touched the six-way power button on the side of her seat and reclined back until she was looking at the sky through the moonroof. She rolled the window down and closed her eyes and tilted her face to breathe in the fresh air. She had no energy. She picked up the Starbucks coffee from the holder. Empty. *I could use some caffeine. What am I gonna do? Think.*

Doug's the only person who knows I'm here and he'll never rat me out. No one can see this part of Vickie's property from Corn Belt

Road. What would happen if I set fire to the moonshine garage? Or blew it up? Aubrey raised the back of the driver's seat and stared at the brick building. She tapped her fingers on the steering wheel. *I wonder what happens to Big Al's now. It should go to me. How do I make that happen?*

Aubrey lowered the heat blowing from the vent and rolled up her window. *I drove here to ask Vickie to give me the diner and she said no. And she lied about the key to the bank box. I need to search the house.*

Crunch.

Aubrey whipped her head around at the sound of a vehicle creeping down the gravel road. It was Doug. She shut off her car and hopped out. The shock had worn off and now she was pissed again.

"Are you sure she's dead?" Doug asked.

"No, but I'm not going back in there," Aubrey said.

"What's the code for the garage? I'll check."

"While you're checking, look around for the key to the bank box. Vickie said she didn't have it, but I don't believe her." Aubrey watched Doug enter the code, poke his head inside, and immediately close the door.

"Why didn't you look for the key?"

"Aubs. There's blood right inside the door. I didn't want to step in it. We need to call the police," he said.

"No." She grabbed his hands. "I've had time to think. No one knows I was here except you. We both wore gloves so there's no prints anywhere. And just like the diner, there's a bunch of people who know the code to the garage. Any one of them could have killed Vickie. All we need to do is find the key to the bank box.

Tomorrow, I'll drive the catering van to Stacy's, empty it into her garage, and repark back here. Stacy's got customers coming to her house for the last batch of moonshine. No one will miss Vickie until Monday morning. That's two days from now."

"Does Stacy know who was supposed to deliver this batch?" Doug asked.

"I'll tell her Vickie called me and wasn't feeling up to it and I offered to do it."

"We need to think this through," he said. "What did Vickie say about the safe deposit box key?"

"She gave the box to the lawyer and said there was no key in it. She lied." Aubrey looked at Vickie's country mansion. "I know Mom kept a bunch of extra cash she didn't report to the IRS. I think Vickie stole the key and emptied the safe deposit box at Farmers Bank before anyone knew there was money in it. Then she gave the recipe box to the lawyer, minus the key."

"Why'd you come out here?"

"To reason with her. I asked Vickie to give me Big Al's or let me manage it. I told her I'd have the diner up and running in a month and she said no. She wanted to keep it closed for at least six months. Do you know what that would have done to us? Even if we could have lasted six months, Vickie'd make the daily deposit. She'd probably count it right there at Mom's desk. There'd be no way I could skim off a few twenties."

"How much were you taking?" Doug frowned.

"I never counted. Maybe a hundred a day."

"Aubs, that's two thousand dollars a month."

Aubrey was quiet. She knew she took more than that but wasn't going to tell her stupid-ass husband. They both enjoyed the finer things in life, and she knew Doug loved to boast about his mother-in-law and Big Al's like he owned the place.

"How'd you kill her?"

"I picked up the shovel and hit her."

"She looks like she's got a broken arm and a slice in the side of her neck," Doug said. "You hit her more than once?"

"I think so."

"Aubs, this is bad."

"I know. I know. But no one else has to know."

"What do you want to do?" Doug asked. "You want to break in and search the entire house? It'll take hours."

"Do you want broken legs or would you rather search the house for the money Vickie stole? Besides, people who live in the country don't lock their doors." Aubrey glared at her husband. "It's your gambling problem that got us here in the first place. Suck it up. We've got to find that money." She marched up the stairs to Vickie's back door.

"What are we gonna do if the sheriff finds the place is a wreck?" Doug trudged after his wife.

"The sheriff won't know we trashed the place," Aubrey said. "In fact, we might be able to make it look like a random burglary. Someone killed her in the garage and then came and destroyed the place. We're going to steal a few things. Break some furniture. Pound on a few walls."

"We can't keep the stuff," Doug protested.

"We'll dump it in a cornfield," Aubrey said. *Does he really think I'm that stupid?*

"What about the kids?"

"Jake and Justin are sleeping at the neighbor's house tonight." Aubrey looked at her husband. "What did you tell them at work?"

"That you were having a breakdown and I needed to go home," Doug said. "If Vickie took the money, where do you think she hid it? Are we looking for ten bucks or ten thousand?"

Aubrey resisted the urge to slap her husband. "Shut up and start looking."

*   *   *

Aubrey sank into the chair next to the fireplace. They had found the key. She picked up a throw pillow from the floor and hugged it to her chest. Even with a sweater and a roaring fire, she was cold. And tired. She and Doug had searched Vickie's country mansion for hours without finding any cash, but the key to the bank box was sitting in a ceramic bowl by the back door along with a set of car keys. *Vickie lied to me. I'm glad I killed her. We'll be able to pay the bookie.* "How much did you steal from her purse?"

"A few hundred. I stuck the flat-screen TV and the sound bar in the garage and covered them with a blanket, but we need to get rid of them ASAP. We can't risk one of the boys finding that stuff." Doug perched on the edge of the couch, his hair sticking straight up. "Helluva day."

"You think?" Aubrey didn't bother to disguise the sarcasm. "A week ago, we had a normal life even with your gambling addiction. Now look what we've got. Mom's dead, Vickie's dead, and we have no money. What you make as a service manager at the dealership barely pays the bills. I can't steal from the diner anymore, and we can't get to the cash Mom kept in the safe deposit box until Monday morning. Did I miss anything? Oh yeah, your bookie's gonna break both your legs and arms on Tuesday if we don't pay him fifty thousand dollars."

"If Vickie emptied the safe deposit box, she could've stashed the cash in her office or in one of her firm's accounts. If she did that, we'll never get it back. What are we going to do then?"

"Could you try for one minute to be positive?" Aubrey snapped.

"Maybe your mom emptied out the safe deposit box and stashed the cash somewhere."

"That'd be great." Aubrey sat up straight. "What if she stashed it in the house or at the storage unit where she kept all those dust collectors?"

Doug grabbed the poker, embers flying. "We have to search your dad's house and the storage unit. Where's the key to the storage unit?"

"I have no idea," Aubrey said. "I'll search Mom and Dad's house first."

"You can't do it tomorrow. You have to drive the catering van with the last batch of moonshine to Stacy's. Monica and Keith will be at the house all day. You're gonna have to wait until Monday morning after your dad leaves for work and then you have to make sure Monica's gone," Doug said. "I hope the money's at your mom's house."

"What if Dad found it? Or worse—Monica?" Aubrey shuddered. "Let's hope Mom stashed the money in her storage unit. I'll call the manager and tell him about Mom. See what we can do if we don't have a key."

"When you call, just ask him what unit number she had. Let him assume we have the key. We'll buy a bolt cutter and a new lock."

Aubrey snapped her fingers. "Excellent. Tomorrow I'll drive the van to Stacy's and on Monday, I'll go to the bank and check the safe deposit box. If the money's not there, I'll search Mom and

Dad's house. While I'm searching, I'll look for the key to the storage unit. After I find the key, I'll search the unit. The money has to be in one of these places. If the collectibles are in the storage unit, we'll sell the ones that are worth something and tell Andrew that's all we could get for them. I'll go through it before that lawyer does. The kids will never know, and Andrew doesn't give a shit about them. He broke one when he was little, and I think he hates that crap. Besides, he doesn't need the money. Mom left him a hundred thousand dollars." *And on Tuesday, we'll pay off the bookie, and I'll stash the rest of the cash where Doug can't find it.*

"Where are you going to sell that crap? eBay? Facebook Marketplace? That's the first place Andrew or anyone will look. Maybe even your dad."

"I wonder if there are collector clubs. People who only buy Hummels or Beanie Babies or whatever. Maybe they're private groups, and if I join with pictures or samples, I can sell them there," Aubrey said. "What if some of that crap Grandma collected is worth something? Wouldn't that be great? We could take a cruise or head to Disney World this summer."

"It's worth a try. How soon can you get this done?" he asked.

Aubrey sprang to her feet and grabbed her husband's shirt. "If you ever gamble again, I'm gonna be the one to break your legs."

CHAPTER FORTY-EIGHT

"How's your arm?" Vern asked.

"I hate physical therapy. I go in feeling only mild discomfort and I come out screaming in pain." Laurent stood at the library's return book counter. Vern was ten feet away, checking out a stack of books. Even though it was Sunday, she was planning to re-interview Stacy Simmons. The woman had lied to her. Laurent wasn't sure she had recovered from the bombshell Keith dropped on her yesterday about sleeping with the bridesmaids from his own wedding.

"How much longer for PT?"

"Another week." She slid the last book into the chute and wandered to the checkout counter.

Vern shoved his pile of books into a black backpack and slung it over his shoulder. "What are you here for?"

"Same as you. Can't play my cello much, so I thought I'd get some reading done, but with the situation at Big Al's, I'm not checking anything out today," she said.

Laurent and Vern exited the library, trotting down the three steps. Crossing Oak Street, she hit the fob for her little red truck and unlocked the door.

Crash.

The sound of a fender bender rang in the air. Sighing, she glanced east along Oak Street. In the middle of the street, the front end of a big old Lincoln Town Car sat in the back end of Big Al's catering van. Laurent pulled out her cell phone and stepped into the street. Smoke streamed from the sides of the crumpled hood of the Lincoln.

Laurent walked faster.

A lick of fire shot out from under the hood.

Laurent ran. She grabbed the door handle of the old car.

Boom!

The rear of the catering van exploded.

Laurent flew backward landing on the soggy grass of the library, her head bouncing off the concrete sidewalk, her cell phone flying out of her hand. *Owww! My head!* She rolled onto her stomach and pushed to her hands and knees.

The back of the van was engulfed in flames.

The driver of the Lincoln was buckled in, head against the window.

Laurent wobbled to her feet and jogged unsteadily toward the car.

Boom!

Laurent fell onto the street and crawled to the Lincoln. Grabbing the door handle, she yanked it open and pulled herself up. Stretching across the unconscious driver, she released the seat belt.

The fire was five feet away and the heat scorched her face. Out of the corner of her eye, she saw Vern open the van's front door and pull a body out. He had lost his baseball hat.

Laurent grabbed the left arm of the driver and pulled, falling back on her butt. The driver was halfway out of the car.

Boom! The back doors of the van blew off.

Laurent curled into a ball, one arm over her head as debris rained down. After a few seconds, she flipped onto her back, sat up, dug in her heels, and yanked the dead weight of the driver again. The driver came free. *I'm gonna need more physical therapy.*

Boom!

What was exploding in the back of that van? She heard sirens.

Rolling to her feet, she grabbed the driver of the Lincoln by the wrists and dragged her over the curb and onto the grass. The area was littered with debris. Broken glass, pieces of burnt plastic. Black smoke poured from the engine of the Lincoln. The entire van was in flames.

Laurent saw Dak's cruiser scream around the corner of Fourth and Oak. The young deputy leaped out, shouting into his radio.

Boom!

Laurent threw her body across the unconscious driver, hands over her head. She flinched. The back of her leg was burning. Rolling off the driver, she scooted to a nearby puddle and laid her leg in the water. Her gloves were black and bits of burnt plastic and ash clung to her jacket and pants.

"Stay here. You look like you're hurt." Dak squatted in front of her. "I'm calling for extra ambulances. There's two more people over there." He pointed to figures sitting in the grass.

"Vern pulled the driver of the van out. Can you see if he's all right?"

"Will do. Poulter and Ingram are here. So's the fire department." Dak stood. "You look like shit. Don't move." He stepped next to the unconscious driver lying in the grass. "Of the four of you, she looks the worst. I'll ask the paramedics to start with her."

Laurent glanced at the driver of the Lincoln. *Old lady Parks.* She pulled the fabric of her pants away from her leg and was relieved to see she wasn't burned.

"Jhonni. You okay?" Vern knelt next to her, one hand on her shoulder.

"I'm fine."

Vern stood and waved at the paramedics. "Old lady Parks is hurt worse than the driver of the van and you and me. I think the driver is Lisa's daughter, Aubrey. Said she ain't waiting. She's not hurt. She's heading home. I heard her tell Dak; he knows where to find her."

"She is bossy," Laurent said. "We ought to charge her with leaving the scene of an accident. Wonder why she's in such a hurry."

"She's had a lot of shocks lately. I'd leave her be. Let's sit on the steps and watch your guys do their job. Can you walk?" Vern reached down.

"Give me your hand." Laurent grasped Vern's hand and let him pull her to her feet. She was a little woozy. She felt his arm tighten around her waist and leaned into him before sinking onto the cold, concrete steps of the library.

Vern sat next to her.

Neither one spoke.

Laurent watched as Dak took control of the situation. Deputies Poulter, Greene, and Ingram snapped to his orders. Crime scene tape was tied from tree to tree and bystanders were moved back. She saw Caleb Martin's crew hop out of the orange public works trucks and grab the barricades from the back of Caleb's truck. Both ends of Oak Street were blocked off, traffic redirected onto other residential side streets.

"You got your boys well trained," Vern said.

"I was thinking the exact same thing," Laurent said. "You don't see my cell phone anywhere, do you?"

"Whoever cleans up this mess will find it."

"Thanks for your help. There's no way I could've gotten both drivers out in time. I barely got this one." She glanced down the street. "You dropped your backpack."

"Look at me."

Laurent turned her face toward Vern and felt a tug on her head.

"You've got little pieces of black stuff in your hair." He handed her one.

Laurent pulled her braid over her shoulder and held it up to her nose. "I smell like smoke."

"Don't bother trying to wash your clothes. Stick them in a bag and drop them off at the dry cleaner. He's got special stuff for smoke," Vern said.

"How do you know that?"

"Had a fire at the farm. Once."

"Uh-oh. Here comes Dak." Laurent tried to stand, but Vern held her arm.

"Thank you, Mr. Martin."

Laurent looked up to see Dak glaring at her, hands on hips. "Does this look like desk duty to you? 'Cuz it doesn't to me. What were you doing here?"

"Returning books."

"Damn it, Jhonni. You scared the crap out of me. Don't either one of you move until the paramedics from Alexander County arrive. Our boys have their hands full." He stomped off.

Laurent stared after her deputy. "What the hell?"

"Cut him some slack. Your deputy cares about you. There's lots of folks in Field's Crossing that care about you," Vern said.

"I have no energy left. Sitting on this ice-cold step is kind of nice." Laurent leaned against the black wrought iron railing.

"Then, we'll sit for a spell."

The smell of burning plastic mingled with the blooming lilac trees lining the west side of the library. She tried to settle more comfortably on the concrete steps as pieces of burning ash drifted down. Behind her, the front doors to the library were propped open, warm air cascading over her back. She heard the high-pitched chatter of the head librarian as she talked on her cell phone.

The scene in front of her was controlled chaos. The fire department had blown foam over the Lincoln and Big Al's catering van and Oak Street was white, mixed with bits of black plastic and shiny glass. On the far side of the library parking lot, Laurent saw mothers holding babies or toddlers as they gazed on the accident. A few had settled in to watch from their porch swings.

Pieces of the destroyed Lincoln and catering van were strewn over the damp grass and on the hoods and roofs of cars parked in the library's lot. One of the rear doors of the catering van had landed in a windshield. The other one lay in the middle of Oak Street. Patrons huddled on the sidewalk in front of the library, clutching their checked-out books in one arm while pointing with the other. Laurent listened to snippets of conversations floating past her.

"How long do you think Oak Street will be closed?"

"Was anyone hurt?"

"Isn't that old lady Parks' Lincoln?"

"Why's the sheriff sitting down? Is she hurt?"

"Who's car is that? The one with the door in the windshield? Who has to pay to fix it?"

"Can't wait to see the pictures and read about it in the paper."

At that last comment, Laurent noticed Ralph from *The Crossing* and a photographer with a long-range lens snapping pictures. Ralph was talking to bystanders while scribbling in a notebook.

"Somehow, Ralph will make this my fault." Laurent pointed to the newspaper reporter. "And you can be sure, he'll criticize my department."

"He is an ass," Vern said. "Have that photographer snap a picture of you and post it on the internet. Beat Ralph to the punch."

Laurent glanced at Vern. "Do I look that bad?"

"Sheriff. Your eyes are glazed over. I'm not sure if you're in shock or in pain. You've got bits of stuff in your hair. Half of your pant leg is burned off and your gloves are black. You're hunched over like your shoulder or arm hurts. Your face has a sheen of ash, and you smell like smoke. So, no, you don't look good." Vern's blue eyes crinkled at the corners.

"Don't pull any punches, Vern," Laurent said. "You've got black stuff in your hair, too."

"No one gives a shit about how I look," he retorted. "Let Dak talk to the press. He'll set that pain-in-the-ass Ralph straight." He picked up a piece of glass from the van explosion. Part of a Mason jar. "You know what was in the back of the van, don't you?"

"Moonshine. That's why it blew sky high." Laurent shook her head. "It never occurred to me that the Moonshine Mamas would continue making and transporting it, especially since Big Al's is closed. What were they going to do with it?"

"Sheriff? Mr. Martin? Dak says we're to check you both and not to take flak from either one of you," Keke King said. "I know you're kinda feisty, Sheriff, but you've got blood in your hair. Mr. Martin, I'm hoping you're more reasonable. Sir, if you'll climb into the ambulance with the boys from Alexander County, they'll check you out. Sheriff, you're with me." Keke pointed to his ambulance.

Laurent looked at Vern. "Feisty? You? Me?" She grabbed the railing and pulled herself up. "If I go, you go."

*   *   *

Half an hour later, Dak handed Vern's backpack to him. "Thanks for your help, sir. How are you? Is the sheriff still with Keke?"

"I've heard some arguing."

"By who?"

"You know who."

"Are they gonna take her to the hospital?" Dak asked.

"Not if she has anything to say about it." Vern slung his backpack over one shoulder.

The rear door of the ambulance opened and Laurent stepped down.

"What's the prognosis?" Dak walked to the ambulance.

"I'd like her to go to the hospital because she may have a slight concussion, but the sheriff has agreed to go home and stay home and have someone come and stay with her tonight," Keke said. "She has to see her specialist about that shoulder. I think she's reinjured it."

"Where's your sling?" Dak asked.

"In my truck."

"I'll get it," Vern said.

Laurent waited until Vern was out of earshot. "How's he doing?"

Dak snorted. "Helluva lot better than you."

"Keke called Starr and you know she's gonna pack like she's staying for a week."

"Ingram will drive you home," Dak said.

"I can drive." Laurent patted her pockets looking for her car keys.

"Sheriff, you promised." Keke pointed at her. "No driving. No nothing for the next twenty-four hours."

Laurent sighed. "Goddamn men ganging up on me."

Vern returned, one hand holding the sling. He dropped his backpack on the ground and waited. "Need help taking off your coat?"

Laurent glared at him before unzipping her jacket and shrugging out of it. "Trade."

Dak grabbed her jacket.

Vern handed the sling to Keke.

"All right. All right. Help me like I'm a little old lady."

Vern grinned. "That's more like it. I'll drop you off on my way home."

"Thank you, Mr. Martin." Dak pointed a finger at Laurent. "Don't give him any shit, Sheriff. He's on your side."

CHAPTER FORTY-NINE

LAURENT CREPT DOWN the lane past Vickie Wright's house and pulled up between the two six-car garages, Dak's cruiser in front of her. She slid out of the SUV and joined her deputy.

"Are you supposed to be here? Yesterday, you almost got blown to bits, and Keke said you have to rest for twenty-four hours. How's your head? Shoulder? Any other body parts hurting?" Dak demanded.

Laurent glared at her deputy. "Did Starr text you?"

"Don't get mad at me. She only texted once. Said you slept like a baby when she let you sleep. You scared her, Sheriff. You scared a lot of people yesterday."

"I'm a mass of bruises and my hair still smells like smoke. I washed it three times. Starr's taking my clothes to the dry cleaner this morning. She wouldn't let me in my own house. Made me strip in the mudroom. But she did have a toasty grilled cheese and one of those weighted, heating blankets ready for me when I got out of the shower." Laurent sighed. "It's been twenty-two hours and I feel fine. No headache. And Starr was driving me crazy. Treating me like I was an invalid. I love her to bits, but she can be a mother hen."

"You need a mother hen."

She punched him lightly. "Do not. So, Mr. Weatherman, how much snow did we get last night?" April in Indiana was always a mixture of rain and snow and sleet.

"About half an inch."

"Those big footprints are yours and the ones from that vehicle to that door and to your vehicle belong to whoever you've got in the back of your cruiser," Laurent said.

"Stacy Simmons. Those tire tracks are hers, too." Dak pointed to the other six-car garage. "According to Stacy, the Moonshine Mamas parked in that garage and worked in this one."

"Where's Vickie's footprints? The killer's? Tire tracks?" Laurent looked from the garage, along the tree line, up to the house and back. No prints or tracks in the overnight snow.

"That means Vickie's been here since sometime yesterday," Dak said. "There's only two sets of tire tracks. Me and her." He jerked his thumb toward his cruiser.

"Both garages are empty?"

"This garage has the victim, that garage has Stacy's car and what I'm assuming is Vickie's car."

"What about the house?" she asked.

"I didn't check."

"Let's go."

* * *

Ten minutes later, Laurent locked the rear door of Vickie's country mansion and followed Dak down the sidewalk. "Whoever trashed the house was looking for something and they did it before last night's snow. The flat-screen TV and the sound bar have been stolen, but other than that, I couldn't say. I was only in the house once."

"Any idea who's Vickie's next of kin?" Dak asked.

"Call Marissa and have her contact one of the partners at Baylor, Scott, and Wright. They'll know," Laurent said. "I know her husband is deceased, and she mentioned a brother-in-law and mother-in-law, but that's all I got. We may never know the extent of what was stolen if Vickie doesn't have a close relative nearby."

"Random burglary?"

"No way. Whoever killed Vickie ransacked the house, trying to distract us."

The two officers stopped next to Dak's cruiser.

"Why was Stacy here?" Laurent asked.

"She was expecting the catering van with a shipment of Sweet Tea Moonshine. I guess that's where Aubrey was headed yesterday when the van blew up. When the van didn't show, Stacy tried calling Vickie. No answer. This morning, Stacy decides to drive to Vickie's. She doesn't check the house. She goes directly to the moonshine garage, keys in the code, and there's Vickie, dead on the floor."

"She didn't check the house first?" Laurent said. "Like she already knew where to find her."

"My thoughts, exactly," Dak said. "I stuck her in the back of my cruiser while I waited for you and the coroner."

"I'm gonna poke my head inside the garage." Laurent pulled on gloves and followed Dak to the side door. "What's that? Murder weapon?"

"Looks like. After I checked her pulse, I bagged it. Blood all over it. Like it caught her in the neck," Dak said.

"Severed the carotid artery," Laurent said. "The height and angle of the shovel may give us an approximate height of the assailant. Is the coroner on the way?"

Dak nodded, punched in the code, and stepped back. "Stacy gave me the code. There's only going to be a handful of people who have it so our suspect pool is limited."

The smell of blood filled Laurent's nostrils as she stood in the doorway. The victim lay on her side directly in front of her. Dried blood covered Vickie's neck and had seeped into her hair and matted it to the floor before congealing on the concrete.

What a mess. There was no question Vickie had been murdered and a few suspects popped into her mind. Stacy topped the list.

She stepped back. "While we're waiting for the coroner, I'm going to talk to Stacy." Laurent walked to Dak's cruiser, opened the rear door, and motioned to Stacy.

"About time. Your deputy wouldn't let me leave. Said I had to sit here and wait for you. Can I go now?"

"I need to ask a few questions first," Laurent said. "Are you okay standing here?"

"Can I smoke?"

Laurent looked at the coarse woman leaning against Dak's cruiser, fingers shaking, and nodded. "Who has the access code for the garage?"

"Me, Lisa, Vickie, Aubrey, Ruby Rae, Hannah, and Diane. Maybe Keith or Doug or Andrew."

"What brought you to Vickie's house this morning?" Laurent started a new page in her notebook.

"The van was supposed to be driven to my house yesterday between eleven and twelve," Stacy said. "Then when I was at the Walmart, I heard about the accident in front of the library, so this morning I was checking to make sure the moonshine garage was empty and that's when I found her."

"What was going to happen with that last batch?"

"Some of our customers were coming by my house and picking up three or four growlers. You better watch out for pissed-off old ladies, Sheriff. All their aches and pains are comin' back. People get bitchy when they're in pain."

"You can't distribute moonshine from your house."

"If the van hadn't blown up, I'd have had all those growlers sold and out of the house in less than two hours. You never would have known," Stacy said. "It was the last batch. No sense dumping it down the drain."

"And what were you going to do with the money?"

"Vickie said to keep it."

Laurent rolled her eyes. "What time did you get here and what did you do when you arrived?"

"Got here 'bout nine. I parked in my usual spot." Stacy pointed to the six-car garage on the west side of the driveway. "Then I walked to the moonshine garage and punched in the code and there she was."

"Did you enter the moonshine garage?"

"Hell, no. There was blood everywhere. I shut the door fast and called nine-one-one." Stacy had finished one cigarette and was lighting another one. "Goddamn. I can't get the picture of Vickie laying on the floor out of my head."

"Why didn't you check the house first?"

"Never been in the house. Why would I? All the work's in the garage and I wasn't looking for Vickie. I was checkin' on the moonshine," Stacy said.

"Vickie didn't oversee the making of the moonshine?"

Stacy snorted. "Hell, no. We four did it all. Vickie didn't do a damn thing. Neither did Aubrey."

"If Vickie didn't do anything, why was she out here?"

"My guess is she was loading the last van," Stacy said.

"How'd you feel when you heard Vickie inherited Big Al's?"

"I was glad. We all was. Aubrey's a bitch. And who knows? Maybe Vickie would have kept us on the same way. If the licenses and permits transfer to Vickie, then we're only out six months' pay."

"One last question." Laurent looked at Stacy. "Why'd you sleep with Keith the week before he married Lisa?"

"I was drunk. I think I slept with all the groomsmen that week. Had a great time."

Laurent closed her notebook. "That's all for now. Would you please drive to the station and give your statement to Deputy Poulter? It'll take him a day to type it up and then you can review it and fix any errors."

"I got to do this all over again?"

"I'm afraid so. I'll tell him you're on your way." Laurent pulled out her phone.

"Fuckin' wasting my time."

CHAPTER FIFTY

"WHAT DID SHE say?" Dak had propped open the side door of the moonshine garage with a fifty-pound bag of sugar.

"Stacy was expecting the last batch of moonshine yesterday. When it didn't show up, she drove here to see what was going on." Laurent joined him outside the door and smiled. Dr. T'ara Romero was here.

"How many people do you think Lisa gave the access code to?" Dak asked.

"Eight or nine," Laurent said.

"Better than the twenty-nine keys we confiscated from the diner," he said. "How can you be that lax about security?"

"Anything you can tell me, Doc?" Laurent brushed past Dak, stepped around the victim, and stood in the middle of the six-car garage.

"A couple of things," Dr. Romero said. The petite rookie coroner crouched next to the victim. "The shovel Deputy Aikens bagged is most likely the murder weapon. The first blow caught the victim on the left side on the arm and the second blow struck the neck, severed the carotid artery, and the victim bled out. The other thing I can tell you is the body has been here for twenty-four to forty-eight hours.

"I checked the thermostat. It's set at seventy-two degrees Fahrenheit, and there's a lock box over it. The only person who can change the temperature is the person with the key. I don't know how to make moonshine, but I'm guessing that, at some point, there needs to be a constant temperature. The body has cooled to the surrounding temperatures. Cooling takes about a day and rigor mortis has started to disappear. My preliminary time of death is from Saturday afternoon to yesterday morning."

"From the angle of the shovel, can you estimate the height of the attacker?"

"No. The blow to the arm was fairly level, kind of like swinging a baseball bat, and I'm guessing the victim bent over to grab her arm when the second blow was struck. Anyone taller than thirty-six inches could have struck both blows."

"But right-handed?"

Dr. Romero nodded.

"And they were facing each other?"

"The victim was facing the door and the blow came from her left side, so, yes, I think they were facing each other."

"Vickie knew who killed her. Same as Lisa," Laurent said. "Dak, contact the alarm company and ask what time the access code was punched in and if the door automatically locks when it closes. If it was locked, what time was the code punched in again. Get a list of everyone with the code. Ask if the garage had remote video or any other security."

"Ten-four."

Laurent glanced at Dr. Romero. "How much longer will you be?"

"I'm ready to bag the body."

* * *

Half an hour later, Laurent and Dak donned shoe coverings, masks, and gloves and left their jackets in Laurent's SUV. Both officers carried markers and evidence bags, and Dak had tucked the clipboard under one arm.

"Let's get started." Laurent slipped past the open door, stepped inside, and waited until Dak moved the bag of sugar and closed the door behind him.

"The alarm company sent me the list, but they did mention most people forget to add the names of the people they give the code to," Dak said. "This is a perfect example. The only names on the list are Lisa and Vickie, both of whom are dead."

"I'm not surprised," Laurent said. "What else did the alarm company say?"

"There was a key punch on Saturday at nine in the morning and another key punch around five thirty. If the door was propped open the way we did, another key punch isn't necessary. The door was disarmed on Sunday morning at nine," Dak said. "The alarm company says the weekend logins were very random, but Monday through Friday there was a consistent pattern. They're sending me a report for the last forty-eight hours and a summary for the rest of the year."

"Did everyone have the same code? Is there any way for the alarm company to know who keyed in the code?"

"Same code. And there are no external or internal cameras."

Laurent stopped in front of one of the rolled-up garage doors and pointed. "Every one of these doors has another lock. It looks like all you have to do from the inside is pull out the pin. Dak, go outside and see if you can open this door."

Laurent waited until she heard the garage door rattle.

"Can't open it from the outside and there's no exterior locks on the individual garage doors," he said. He rejoined Laurent by the closed roll-up door.

"The only way to get inside the building is through the side door or if one of the rolled-up doors is open," she said. "Pull that pin out and see if you can open the door now." Laurent watched as Dak removed the pin, bent over, and opened the door. "You have to know a passcode to get inside and you have to be inside in order to roll up these doors."

"Simple but effective."

"So, the building would be locked unless they were loading the van," she said. "That limits the number of suspects. The catering van exploded in front of the library yesterday around eleven in the morning. The van must have been loaded either on Saturday or early Sunday morning. Did it snow Saturday afternoon or night?"

"Nope."

"How long do you suppose it took to load and who loaded it?"

"Depends on how many people were working," Dak said. "Big Al's opened at eleven every morning except Sunday, which means the van had to leave by ten forty-five to be at the diner when it opened and then the moonshine had to be transferred into the diner."

Laurent circled the inside of the moonshine garage. "There's no laptop, no paperwork of any kind. How'd they keep track? Which set of growlers were ready? Was it a simple rotation? Have they worked here for so long they don't need notes? How'd they know when to order supplies? Tell Poulter to have Naomi look at the laptop we confiscated from Lisa's office. Maybe there's something on there. Some kind of schedule. The Excise Police had to require reports of some kind. Dak, call them and ask about the regulations for securing the building and who had to register to make the moonshine. Apparently, Lisa didn't have to be on the premises."

"Ten-four."

"Did you know about the Sweet Tea Moonshine?" Laurent watched as her deputy's cheeks turned pink.

"Mimi likes it." He raised his hands. "I never asked where she bought it. Ever had it? It's more sugar than booze. Tastes great, especially on a hot summer day. Ice-cold."

"How much for a growler?"

"I have no idea. I didn't buy it for her. I'm not really sure how she got it," he said.

"She probably walked down the street."

"She can't carry a growler."

"Your grandma's stronger than you."

Dak chuckled. "Mimi's going to like that."

"Let's close the door. No need to freeze while we search," Laurent said.

As Dak rolled down the door, Laurent backtracked and started by the side door. She opened all the lockers and bagged and tagged the contents. "Start dusting for prints at the side door. They should match up with the ones we already have from the diner. Dust the shovel and these lockers. We'll pile the evidence bags next to the side door."

"Do you think the same person killed both Lisa and Vickie?" Dak asked.

"We've certainly got enough suspects," she said. "Keith and/or Monica kill Lisa to get control of Big Al's, and when they don't, they kill Vickie. Easiest solution, closely followed by Stacy Simmons. Stacy killed Lisa on a promise from Keith to run or buy

Big Al's. She doesn't have an alibi for Easter Sunday afternoon and her prints are all over Big Al's and the van and I'm guessing out here. In fact, any of the Moonshine Mamas could have killed Vickie. Dr. Romero gave a huge time span for time of death, but Stacy found the body. The doc said the first blow was fairly level like a baseball bat. Who's the softball home run champion in Field's Crossing?"

"Stacy Simmons," Dak said. "I'm going to dust the kitchen area next, and I'll finish up with the stills. After that I'll start logging in the evidence and boxing it up." He walked past her. "Maybe Ruby Rae Evans killed them both."

"Another strong possibility. I think she's the one who broke into Big Al's the other night," Laurent said. "Ruby Rae had an affair with Keith, called the IRS, has access out here, and her alibi for Easter Sunday is her husband. She told me he doesn't know she exists. She could have left the house, killed Lisa, and returned home without her husband knowing. She lives a mile or two from the diner."

"What if Stacy and Ruby Rae are in this together?" Dak asked. "A conspiracy? Two of Keith's rejected lovers. Stacy's pissed at Keith. Ruby Rae is pissed at Keith. But Lisa is killed. What's the connection? Why didn't they kill Keith?"

"I don't think it's a conspiracy," Laurent said. "Stacy wouldn't want an IRS audit. She'd want to continue the cash under the table that Lisa paid to the Moonshine Mamas. Ruby Rae wanted the audit to force Lisa to sell Big Al's or make more moonshine to pay the fines and penalties or whatever the IRS levied. Ruby Rae wanted to make more money. Stacy wanted revenge. Did Keith make a deal with either Stacy or Ruby Rae or is it him and Monica?

I think it's the same person or persons. Stacy said Vickie was never out here and she wasn't sure who loaded the van yesterday."

"Was Vickie supposed to drive the van to Stacy's house?" Dak asked.

"I didn't ask, but Vern pulled Aubrey from behind the wheel," Laurent said.

"I bet whoever loaded the van killed Vickie and she was dead before the van exploded. Did Aubrey kill Vickie?"

"God, I hope not." Laurent stared at the chalk outline on the concrete floor.

"Just because Aubrey drove the van doesn't mean she killed Vickie," Dak said. "Maybe the van was already loaded, and Aubrey parked and switched vehicles without going inside the garage."

"It's possible." Laurent frowned. "Aubrey practically ran from the accident. Vern said she was in a hurry and didn't want to wait to give a statement or have the paramedics check her for injuries. I assumed she didn't want to get charged with transportation of moonshine.

"I need to talk to Aubrey again. And Stacy. And Keith. They're all hiding something."

Aubrey knew the garage code. It's not a far jump to assume that Doug knew it, too. It'll be interesting to see whose prints are on the shovel and in Vickie's house. There's no way we'll get any prints off the burned-out van.

CHAPTER FIFTY-ONE

AUBREY KNOCKED AND opened the door to Rina Yoshida's office.

"Mrs. Holmes, how can I help you?" The young attorney emerged from behind her office door.

"Thank you for meeting me. The key to my mom's safe deposit box at Farmers was in the recipe box," Aubrey said. "I called the bank to make an appointment and was told that all my mom's accounts, including her safe deposit box, were locked and that I'd have to talk to you. I was wondering if you'd accompany me to empty the contents."

"Please sit down," Rina said. "I'm not sure who receives the contents of the safe deposit box, and, in fact, I was wondering where the key was. The bank sent a list of all your mom's accounts, and I noticed the box."

"Mom's intention was clear. The key was in the recipe box and has been for years. Mom left the box to me. She wants me to have whatever is in the safe deposit box, especially since she didn't leave me Big Al's."

"That must have hurt."

"Like being stabbed in the back. All the years, making sandwiches, training employees. I don't understand." Aubrey swiped at a fake tear. *You catch more flies with honey.*

"What do you think is in the safe deposit box?" Rina asked.

"I'm pretty sure that's where she kept her important papers and possibly Al Sr.'s or Al Jr.'s recipes," Aubrey lied. "But most likely, another milk tin painted by some no-name artist."

"Let me call the judge," Rina said. "Either way, I have to inventory the contents. It'll be up to the probate judge to decide who inherits the contents."

"Sounds good."

A few minutes later, Rina reappeared carrying her coat. "The judge has agreed to let me inventory the contents, but he wishes you would relinquish the key to me."

"I'm keeping the key."

"I anticipated your answer and he agreed—all I can do is ask. You don't have to give it to me."

"Thank you." Aubrey let out a sigh of relief. *So far, so good.*

"Vincent Walker, the new CEO, will meet us. He has also agreed you may accompany me and view the contents, but I am not to release any of the contents until the judge reviews the will and applicable law. There is a case to be made for the contents going to the estate."

"I understand. Thanks so much for your help." Aubrey's brow furrowed. *The safe deposit box was filled with cash. I need fifty thousand of it. Somehow, that cash has to end up in my pocket without Rina seeing.*

"Is there any way I can view the contents by myself?" Aubrey asked. "Just in case she left me something personal."

"Let me talk to Mr. Walker."

*   *   *

A few minutes later, Vincent Walker opened the door to a small, private room and Aubrey stepped inside.

"As per our agreement, all four security cameras will be recording this," Walker said. "I don't want any lawsuits from anyone regarding our procedures. It's my job to protect Farmers Bank."

Aubrey nodded. If she couldn't steal the cash outright, she'd ask the probate judge to allow the attorney to disburse half of the funds to her. *That's fair. But I won't have the money by tomorrow. Goddamn bookie's going to break Doug's legs and ask for more money.*

"Ms. Yoshida and I will be on the other side of the door when you're ready for us." He cleared his throat. "I'm so sorry about your mom. She's going to be missed by the community. I hope she left you something you'll treasure."

Aubrey let a tear slide. *Let Walker think there's something of sentimental value in the box.*

She waited until the door clicked shut and then took off her coat and laid it next to the box on the table. She pressed a hand against her stomach. *Please, please, please.* She pulled the key out of her purse, inserted it, and lifted the lid.

Empty.

CHAPTER FIFTY-TWO

AUBREY SLID OUT of her Porsche and walked quickly to her parents' garage. She keyed in the code, ran back to her car, parked in her mom's space, and closed the door. She didn't want anyone to know she was here. She had stormed out of the bank and snarled at the president. The box was empty. She threatened him with a lawsuit and had enjoyed the look of panic on the man's face.

Unlocking the back door of her parents' house with her old key, she poked her head inside. "Dad?"

No answer.

She wasn't expecting one. Her father should have left for work hours ago. Who she wasn't sure about was Monica. She listened. No TV. No hair dryer. No creaking. She let out a sigh of relief. She could search the house without worry.

Aubrey sat down on the bench in the mudroom and took off her shoes. Habit. She hung her jacket on a hook and stepped into the kitchen. *What a mess. Mom would be furious.* The kitchen had always been spotless. In less than ten days, her father and Monica had trashed it. The sink was full of dirty dishes, pots and pans sat on the top of the stove, unwashed, and the table held the remnants of last night's spaghetti dinner. The faint smell of sour milk hung in the air.

Don't worry about the kitchen. Where would Mom hide the money?

Aubrey knew her parents hadn't slept in the same bedroom for years. She started upstairs in her old bedroom. *Goddamn it! The skank had taken over her room.* Aubrey dashed to the closet and yanked open the door. None of the clothes in the closet belonged to her mom and the top shelf was empty. She ran her hand along it and came away with dust. She stood with her hands on her hips. The room only had one dresser, a bed, and a nightstand. She opened the top drawer of the dresser. *The skank's underwear. I ought to rip it all to shreds. But then she'll know someone was here and if the money was in this room, the bitch already stole it. What if I ask the sheriff to look at Monica's bank account? That won't work. Laurent will ask why and I can't tell her about the money Mom stashed in the safe deposit box. She'd tell Rina.*

Aubrey stalked down the hallway to her father's bedroom. *What a pigsty.* Hamper overflowing. She knelt and looked under the bed. And sneezed. Only dust bunnies and a sock. She rifled through the chest of drawers. Underwear, T-shirts, sweatpants, socks. She slammed the drawers shut and spun around. Marching to the closet door, she opened it, stood on her tiptoes, and pulled everything off the shelf. Old T-shirts, a carry-on suitcase, box of old high school yearbooks. She picked through everything, but the dust on the boxes told her her father hadn't looked or used anything on the closet shelf in years.

Aubrey marched down the hallway, past her brother's bedroom, and opened the door to the unused fourth bedroom. It was exactly as she remembered. Bags and bags of stuff, bought but never used.

Her mom had a buying/hoarding obsession for as long as Aubrey could remember. *I bet the money's in here somewhere.*

Aubrey heard a car door slam. Picking her way through the piles of bags, she peeked out the window and was surprised to see her brother, Andrew, jogging up the back stairs.

Aubrey trotted down the staircase to meet him. The siblings hadn't talked the day of the funeral. Too many people.

"Aubs. What are you doing here?" Andrew asked. A backpack was slung over one shoulder.

"I could ask you the same thing."

"Mom left the new moonshine recipes to me, and I came to pick them up."

"Mom left me jack shit," Aubrey said. "How come you get a hundred thousand dollars and I get nothing?"

"How much money have you skimmed off Big Al's without telling or asking Mom? Don't deny it. Mom knew you were stealing."

"Stealing? That wasn't stealing. Mom paid me the same as the rest of the staff, but I deserved more because I did all the work."

"You're upset because Mom treated you like an employee at Big Al's and you wanted to be treated as someone special," he said. "Wasn't the money enough?"

"Mom should have paid me more. The Moonshine Mamas made buckets more money than I did. She paid them cash under the table. Whatever money I didn't deposit was the same as what she paid them." Aubrey was mad. She was the daughter of the owner and should have made more money than all the Moonshine Mamas put together. And she should have made it without having to steal.

Andrew hitched his backpack higher on his shoulder. "I think the real reason Mom left Big Al's to Vickie is Doug's gambling problem."

"Doug doesn't have a gambling problem."

"You've always been a loyal spouse, but Aubs, Doug asked Mom for money at least once a month."

"How dare you."

"Why would I lie? I want you and Doug to be successful in life. I want Jake and Justin to go to college. But your husband is putting all that in jeopardy. No one in the family's going to give Doug a dime and neither is Vickie."

"Vickie's dead."

"What? When?" Andrew's backpack slipped off his shoulder and thudded on the floor.

"I don't have any details. It looks like someone killed her at the moonshine garage. The sheriff was pretty tight-lipped," Aubrey said. *I'm not supposed to know that.*

"How do you know?" Andrew asked.

"The grapevine starts with Stacy," Aubrey said. "I was supposed to deliver the last batch of moonshine to her house yesterday, but old lady Parks rear-ended me, and the van blew up. Stacy called me this morning. She found Vickie dead in the moonshine garage."

"Oh my God. Who gets Big Al's now?"

"I don't know." Aubrey stared at the floor.

"Why are you really here, Aubs?" Andrew asked softly.

Aubrey burst into tears. "There's not one thing in this house that I want or is worth a single penny. It's a crappy, old, run-down house."

"But it's home, Aubs."

"Go to hell, Andrew. You know nothing about me or my life. You married Michelle and money. I married Doug and stayed in this dinky little town. I waited years for Mom to give me the diner and I got nothing. Nothing."

"Aubs, don't cry." Andrew awkwardly patted Aubrey on the back.

She wiped her eyes. "Where did Mom put your new recipes?"

"In the nightstand next to her bed."

"The skank took that room. Hope you got copies because she probably stole them," she said.

"I'll ask Dad."

Aubrey glanced at her brother. Patches of gray hair were beginning to grow at his temples and a cowlick at the crown of Andrew's head grew in every direction. "I've been thinking about Mom and Grandma's collectibles. Do you know where the key to the storage unit is?"

"I thought she sold off Grandma's stuff and used it as the down payment to buy Big Al's." He picked up his backpack. "If Mom still had all that stuff, the key to the storage unit is probably on her key ring. You remember how she liked to look at all that stuff?"

"She was a hoarder. The upstairs bedroom is still full of bags," Aubrey said. "I hope Dad took Mom's key ring because the bitch is driving the Escalade."

"Dad will give you the key. What are you going to do with that stuff?" Andrew asked.

"I'll go online and check the value and if those dust collectors are worth anything, I'll sell them and put the money in an account for the four grandkids. They'll earn more money than sitting in a storage unit."

"Aubs. Those little statues are nothing. Let them sit. You've got more to do than worry about that stuff."

"Like what? It's not like I have a job."

CHAPTER FIFTY-THREE

"When was the last time you saw Doug?" Laurent was sitting in Aubrey and Doug's living room. Aubrey had called, hysterical, claiming a bookie had kidnapped Doug and was going to break his legs.

"Last night. I know. I know. It's been twenty-four hours. Doug worked at the dealership from six in the morning until two thirty in the afternoon and was usually home after I picked up the kids at four. Well, he wasn't home yesterday afternoon, and I didn't think twice about it. I was just hoping he wasn't gambling. Trying to fix a gambling problem with gambling."

"You told me Doug didn't have a gambling problem," Laurent said.

"So I lied. Get over it."

Laurent refrained from rolling her eyes. "What did they say at work?"

"He called in sick for today and the other service manager worked the entire day. It happens sometimes. No one at the dealership thought anything about it, especially with my mom dying." Aubrey plucked a tissue. "When he didn't show up for dinner, I was ticked off. But by the time I put the kids to bed, I was worried, so I called a few of our friends to see if anyone knew where he was or had seen him. You know, maybe a bunch of the guys went out drinking."

"And?"

"Nothing. None of his friends have seen or heard from him since the funeral."

Aubrey's long blonde hair was twisted in a ponytail, the ends damp from being chewed on. "We were supposed to have the money this morning. Fifty thousand."

Laurent's eyebrows shot up. "What the hell did he bet on?"

"Some stupid college basketball game. Well, at first it was only thirty thousand, but we didn't have it so we made a deal and the bookie gave us another week, but it cost us another twenty thousand. If I had inherited Big Al's and the bank account, none of this would have happened. Wonder if my mom thought of that."

"Where was Doug supposed to meet his bookie?" Laurent asked. *What were Aubrey and Doug going to do if Lisa hadn't died? Did either one or both of them kill Lisa to pay off the bookie? How much money was in the diner's bank account? I need to recheck that.*

"I don't know." Aubrey rearranged the candlesticks on the mantel and made a tiny adjustment to the picture hanging above the fireplace.

"Doug was supposed to meet his bookie this morning and hand him fifty thousand dollars. Instead, he ran away?" Laurent asked. "And never said a word to you?"

Aubrey nodded.

"I suppose it's better than getting beat up and landing in the hospital."

"What about me? Jake? Justin?" Aubrey cried.

"What do you know about the bookie?" Laurent pulled out her notebook.

"He's got Darth Vader's voice and he wears a suit with army boots. He made a snarky comment about what a rinky-dink little town this is."

"You met him? When? Where?"

"Doug talked to him before the will was read and promised to have the money last Thursday morning, so his bookie met us outside Farmers Bank on the sidewalk. Scarface sat in the car."

"Who's Scarface?"

"The guy who was driving the Hummer. The tip of his nose was cut off and he had a scar running from his forehead to his chin. I nicknamed him Scarface."

"What color Hummer?"

"Camouflage."

Laurent pulled out her cell phone. "I'm calling the CEO at the bank and asking him for the outside surveillance video from last week and this week."

"The bank taped us?"

"You can't walk anywhere and not be surrounded by surveillance cameras. That's how they found the Boston Marathon bomber," Laurent said.

"That's creepy."

"And yet it will probably help us find who took your husband."

"Do you think Doug's bookie knows where we live?"

"Yes."

"What am I gonna do?" Aubrey sank down on the couch.

"Aubrey, I need you to focus. We've got to find Doug before his bookie and Scarface. Where would Doug hide? Someplace special?

Where's his car? Where do his parents and siblings live? Someone from high school or college?" Laurent said.

"He didn't go to college."

"Work associates?"

"Wait a minute." Aubrey jumped up, ran through the kitchen and mudroom, and flicked on the garage light. "Yes. It's gone."

"What's gone?"

"The camping equipment. The tent, the portable heater. All of it. It's gone. Thank God." Aubrey wiped her eyes with the heels of her hands. "He's at the abandoned campground by Turtle Lake."

"I'll send someone."

"No. Don't. Let him stay there."

Laurent stared. "You place a nine-one-one call for the disappearance of your husband and now you don't want us to find him?" *Is Aubrey going to let Doug live at the campground until they have the money to pay the bookie?*

"Thanks for your help, Sheriff, but I'll deal with my husband."

CHAPTER FIFTY-FOUR

LAURENT TAPPED HER fingers on the steering wheel. She was driving on the north side of Field's Crossing on the Five-and-Twenty and thinking about Aubrey's strange response last night. Aubrey was positive Doug was hiding in the forest on the southwest side of Turtle Lake at the abandoned campground and wanted him to stay there. *Maybe Doug was safer there than at home or work. Aubrey and Doug owed the bookie thirty thousand dollars last Thursday and fifty thousand on Tuesday. Lisa was killed four days before Doug had to pay his bookie. When did he find out how much he owed? He had to know that going in. Did he kill Lisa to pay off his gambling debt? Did Doug really think there was thirty thousand dollars in the diner? Obviously, he didn't know about the money in the milk tins. Did Aubrey know? If she did, why didn't she take the money? Lisa must not have told anyone.*

Laurent swung right on Turtle Lake Road and drove past her house. She lived on the northwest side of the lake and skied the thirteen-mile perimeter several times a week during the winter months. The east and south sides were surrounded by Emmit Martin's and Neal Tillman's farms. She turned left on Bees Creek Road and pulled off the side of the road. Twisting in her seat, she frowned at the forest. She didn't know what she was looking for. Smoke from a campfire? Aubrey said Doug had taken the propane heater.

She picked up her phone and dialed Beaumon's Hardware store. After a minute, Brett Kessel, the manager, spoke. "What can I do for you, Sheriff?"

"Did you sell a lot of propane gas recently? The kind used in a portable camping heater, not the kind used for a gas grill."

"Yes, we did. In fact, I placed a rush order this morning for three cases. Whoever bought it took the lot."

"Would your video cameras record the buyer?"

"Most likely. If not in the aisle where it's sold, certainly at the register."

"Even the self-checkout?" she asked.

"Especially the self-checkout. Do you need to see it?"

"Yes."

"Let me check the SKU. I should be able to get a day and time sold, which will narrow down the video search. Give me an hour," Kessel said.

"Thanks. Call me back on this number." Laurent tapped the red END button.

A knock on the passenger window startled her. Vern.

He walked around the front end of the police SUV and waited for Laurent to roll down the window. "You okay? What are you doing out here staring at the trees?"

"So many questions." She glanced at the tractor, idling at the end of a row, plow attached. She slid out of the SUV. "I've got a PT session later today that I'm dreading. I'm afraid he's going to say I reinjured my shoulder and need more treatment before he'll clear me for active duty."

Vern leaned against the SUV. "You probably did. Pulling dead weight out of a car and across the street ain't easy. How's your head? Any headaches? Blurred vision? Vomiting?"

Laurent laughed. "What are you? My doctor? No to everything. Starr finally left this morning."

"What's so interesting about the trees?"

"Have you seen anyone?"

"I only started plowing this field today. Been here since sunup. Somebody lost?"

"More like hiding."

"Care to explain?"

"I've got a question for you. When you pulled Aubrey from the van, how did she seem to you?"

Vern pulled off his John Deere baseball hat and ran one hand through his hair. "She brushed me off like a fly. Said she wasn't hurt and that she'd walk home. She was definitely in a hurry and didn't seem to care about the van or the exploding moonshine. Maybe she thought if she disappeared fast enough, you wouldn't charge her with transporting hooch."

"How long will it take to plow this field?" she asked.

"I'll be plowing this side of Bees Creek for the next couple of days. I'll keep an eye out when I'm heading this direction. If I see someone, I'll radio Emmit to call you."

"Still no cell phone." Laurent looked at the middle-aged farmer. His brown Carhartt jacket was worn and faded at the elbows. "How are you feeling?"

"Same. Nice to get back in the saddle. I missed farming more than I realized."

"Are you going to buy your farm back from Emmit?"

"Nah. We formed a partnership for these acres and left it all to Caleb, Morgan, and Dylan. This way Emmit's gotta handle all the paperwork."

"That's very smart of you."

"Not really. He uses a laptop most days, and I don't think he wants me to touch it."

Laurent opened the driver's-side door and propped one foot on the running board. "You're never going to touch a computer, are you? Or a cell phone?"

"That's my plan."

*   *   *

Laurent's cell phone rang. *Rina. She must've filed the inventory in probate. Wonder if she's received any threatening calls.* Laurent climbed into the SUV and waved to Vern.

"Hey, Sheriff. How's your shoulder?" Rina asked.

"Why is everyone concerned about my shoulder?"

"Because we don't want Mike Greene running things."

"If I couldn't work, I'd put Dak in charge. I don't care if Greene has seniority." Laurent did a U-turn in the middle of Bees Creek Road and headed into town. "What can I do for you?"

"I filed the inventory and application for Letters of Administration in probate today and when I got back to my office, Aubrey Holmes was waiting for me. Vickie had dropped the recipe box off at my office, and according to Aubrey the key for the safe deposit box was in the recipe box. Lisa left the recipe box to Aubrey, so she automatically assumed she gets whatever's in the safe deposit box."

"I'd make the same assumption."

"It's going to be another point of contention, along with copies of the recipes," Rina said. "It's a logical assumption, but the law is not always logical. A claim can be made that the key and anything else in the recipe box belongs to Aubrey, but what the key opens is part of the estate. The contents of the safe deposit box weren't in the recipe box."

"What does Judge Jenkins say?"

"He won't comment unless someone files a lawsuit," Rina said. "But he allowed Aubrey to view the contents and Vincent Walker recorded it."

"Do you know what was in it?"

"Nothing."

"Lisa left Aubrey a key to an empty safe deposit box?"

"Aubrey says she didn't get the key until a week after her mom died. She practically accused Vickie of stealing whatever was in there. She was spitting mad when she stormed out of the bank."

"Would Vickie have been able to get into the safe deposit box? Who was allowed access? Anyone who had a key?" Laurent asked.

"You have to have the key and be on the list. The bank keeps a record of who enters the vault."

"And?"

"You'll need a subpoena for that record."

"Will do," Laurent said. "Think there was more money in there? How much cash would it hold?"

"It's not my job to speculate, but I suspect there was an emergency fund in there. Rolls and rolls of cash."

"Thanks for the info. I'll get that subpoena today." Laurent ended the call and pulled into a parking spot at Big Al's. *Who emptied out the box and why and what was in it? Aubrey's searching for money. What would she do to keep Doug alive? Better yet, what would Doug do to stay alive? After Lisa died, he probably made the same assumption as Aubrey. That she'd inherit the diner. Did Doug kill Lisa? I need to recheck his alibi. If there were more rolls of cash in the bank box and Vickie took it, where would she put it? Her house was ransacked. Did the intruder take it? If the intruders were either Doug or Aubrey, they would have paid off the bookie, so either the money wasn't in Vickie's house or Doug and Aubrey weren't the thieves. What if Vickie stashed the money in one of Baylor, Scott, and White's bank accounts?*

CHAPTER FIFTY-FIVE

LAURENT PARKED ON the side of Turtle Lake Road and switched off the headlights on her little red truck. She rolled down the window and listened. The night breeze was quiet, no rustling in the trees, but under the dead leaves on the forest floor, she heard the scuttling of small animals. She turned off the interior lights, slid out of her truck, and crouched next to the front tire. Fifty feet in front of her was Pot-hell Path, which led to the abandoned campground. Earlier in the day, Caleb had told her the road was not maintained by the county and was one pothole after another. Only fishermen used it now.

Rising, she jogged along the road before turning onto Pot-hell Path. She was dressed in all black and under her jacket she wore her shoulder holster. Laurent stopped at the first oak tree. If Doug was there, had he heard her? Was he armed? She assumed he owned a shotgun. Most people in Field's Crossing owned a weapon and could shoot. Even the townies.

The night was black, and the overhead tree canopy kept out the moon. Laurent aimed her flashlight at the forest floor. She didn't want to twist her ankle. *All I'm going to do is confirm that Doug is here, hiding out. I've got no evidence to arrest him for murder.*

She sniffed. Campfire smoke?

Laurent stopped and listened. Someone was talking. Only one voice. Whoever it was, was talking to themselves or on the phone. A branch snapped to her right and she bolted behind a huge honeysuckle bush. She clicked off her flashlight. Who else was out here? *God, I hope that was a deer settling in for the night.* She peeked out from behind the huge bush.

A shadowy figure crouched next to a tree.

Laurent caught her breath and watched as the shadow slipped behind another tree and moved closer to the muttering voice.

She knelt, one knee on damp leaves, twenty feet behind the dark figure.

The shadow stopped. A knee on the ground, arm resting on top of the other knee. He spat.

Laurent frowned. Male. He was watching Doug. *Who else besides Aubrey knew Doug was here? Was it the bookie? Scarface? How'd he find him?*

The dark figure crept closer to the campfire and settled next to a bush.

She waited.

He didn't move.

Is he going to sit there all night? Laurent decided to back away and circle around the campground until she was directly opposite the crouching figure. Maybe with the help of the campfire and knowing where he was, she'd be able to see his face. She looked down and stepped and exhaled. She might be an expert marksman, but she wasn't a stalker or a tracker.

Another step. Another.

Crack.

Laurent froze.

The crouching figure slowly swiveled and looked right at her.

Laurent's heartbeat shot up. Sweat ran down her back and her armpits were wet. Her heart slammed in her chest. *Why didn't I wear a vest? When Dak finds my body, he'll say I deserve what I got.*

She shifted her weight and eased behind a tree. Where was he? Had he seen her?

Poking her head out from behind the tree, she quickly scanned the forest. There he was. On the opposite side of the path, directly across from her.

He jerked his head to the side.

Laurent didn't move.

He pointed a finger in the direction of Turtle Lake Road and stepped that way, turning his back to her.

She yanked the Glock out of her holster and aimed at the man's back. *What the fuck?*

At the end of Pot-hell Path, he stepped onto Turtle Lake Road. "Sheriff, you're making me nervous."

"Vern? You asshole!" she hissed. "What are you doing here? You scared the shit outta me." Laurent holstered her gun.

"I saw you circle by at least a dozen times today and I figured you'd try tonight after dark. Looks like I was right," Vern said. "You ain't got no deputies with you, do ya?"

"That's none of your business. I could've shot you."

"I'll take my chances."

Laurent stalked back to her truck and sat down on the rear bumper. Vern joined her.

"What's so important about this guy?" he asked.

"He's a murder suspect."

"Why's he hiding out in the woods?"

"He owes his bookie fifty grand."

"You thought I was the bookie, come to get my money and beat the hell out of that guy." Vern nodded. "I get it."

"Damn straight I did," she said.

"You come here all by yourself to arrest him?" Even in the dark, Laurent heard the anger in Vern's voice. "Haven't you got any regard for your own life?"

Laurent heard the crunch of tires. She shoved Vern off the bumper and into the ditch before crouching behind the tire on her truck. Headlights lit up the front end of her truck. The driver shut them off before opening the door.

"Sheriff, you all right?" Dak whispered. He slid out of the police cruiser and crouched next to the open door.

Laurent stood.

So did Vern.

Dak whipped out his gun and aimed at Vern.

"Look who found me." Laurent didn't bother to keep the sarcasm out of her voice.

"Mr. Martin, why don't you just join the force and stop scaring the crap out of all of us?" Dak slid his gun back in. "Is it Doug?"

"I didn't get close enough to see. Vern beat me here." She glared at him. "My heartbeat is finally slowing down."

"I saw him. You got a picture?" Vern asked.

"Dak, pull him up on your computer."

A few minutes later, Vern said, "That's him. Does this mean we can all go home now?"

* * *

After calling Aubrey and assuring her Doug was hiding at the campground, Laurent drove home. Followed by Vern. And Dak. Both tooted their horns as she turned into her driveway. She stuck her arm out of the window and waved but was tempted to give Vern the finger.

Laurent slid the dead bolt on the mudroom door, hung her jacket on a hook, and sat on the bench to pull off her boots.

Doug's hiding from his bookie. But is he also hiding from a murder charge? Mimi had told her Doug asked Lisa for money several times a year and Lisa said no every single time. *Why would he expect a different answer? Maybe he wanted to scare Lisa, threaten her, and the knife slipped? Nope. A knife doesn't slip upward and diagonally for ten inches. The stab wound was deliberate.*

She climbed the stairs to her bedroom and stood at the huge window overlooking her front yard. Yesterday, she noticed her bleeding-heart perennials were four inches tall and the row of lilac trees on the east side of her house had bloomed. The pointed shoots of all her hostas were sticking out of the ground and the clematis had begun its long climb upward. Spring had finally arrived in central Indiana.

Laurent unbuckled her holster harness, wrapped it around her Glock, and placed the gun in the bottom drawer of her nightstand. Vern's question was bugging her. "Haven't you got any regard for your own life?" *Why would he say that?* She unbuttoned her shirt, unclasped her bra, and tossed both into the hamper before slipping into her oversized pajama T-shirt. After her jeans went into the hamper, she pulled on warm fuzzy socks and settled into the chair next to the window.

Pulling her braid over her shoulder, she began the familiar, soothing motion of loosening her hair. She sighed and gazed at her reflection in the window. She didn't think she looked fifty-two years old, but didn't all women want to believe that about themselves? That they were years younger than their actual age.

As Dak, Vern, and Laurent had climbed into their vehicles to leave the campground, Dak paused by her window and asked, "Why is he here? How'd he find out?" Laurent explained about her conversation with Vern earlier in the day and how she had circled Turtle Lake too many times.

"He's smart. But I don't know why he felt he had to be here. I didn't tell him I was coming tonight."

"He's got you figured out, Sheriff," Dak had said.

"What does that mean?"

Dak had climbed into his cruiser and left without answering. She frowned at her bedroom window. *Was Dak implying Vern had a romantic interest in her? Dak needs a girlfriend.*

CHAPTER FIFTY-SIX

"WHEN WAS THE last time you saw Vickie alive?" Laurent stood uneasily on Stacy's front porch. She wasn't sure if it would hold together or if she'd fall through one of the rotted boards.

"Friday morning."

"Where?"

"At the garage. She waved as she headed off to work," Stacy said.

"Why were you at the garage?"

"Finishing up."

"Finishing up what?" Laurent asked.

"The moonshine. Ain't no sense in letting it go to waste."

"Do you mean you continued to manufacture moonshine after Lisa was killed?"

"We didn't start any new batches. I was just finishing up what we had already started," Stacy said. "I told you that already."

So many violations. "Where were you from Saturday morning until you found the body on Monday morning?"

"Home, mostly. Went to the batting cages both days. Been sitting around doing nothing. No work. Nothing to do. Just me and Mooch," Stacy said. "I don't know if this is relevant, but I got a job offer from Andrew."

"Lisa's son? Doing what?"

"Andrew offered me a job in Indianapolis to make his moonshine recipes on the premises, you know, so people can gawk at you. He's applying for another liquor license. It has to include the making of moonshine in the same building. There's a lot of codes and venting and fire hazard stuff that has to be worked out."

"When did Andrew offer you the job?"

"Yesterday. He stopped by his dad's house to pick up the recipes, but they weren't there. He said he had copies on his phone. He drove up, parked, and we talked for about a half an hour."

"Was this before or after you found Vickie?" *If he has copies on his phone, why does he need the paper copy?*

"After," Stacy said. "I left Deputy Poulter and came home. Andrew pulled in a few minutes later."

Andrew had been in Field's Crossing the same day Stacy found Vickie dead at the moonshine garage.

"How much did Andrew offer you?" Stacy had no reason to worry about money and no reason to kill Vickie. She might have lost her cash under the table, but she had an offer of legitimate employment. *But the offer came after Vickie was dead.*

"Enough."

"Enough for what?"

"To move out of this dumpy little town," Stacy snapped.

Laurent jotted a note to have Poulter dive into Andrew's financial situation. He wasn't high on her list of suspects because she assumed his rooftop wine bar was successful. The image of Andrew's Lexus flashed through her mind. What if he needed money? Lisa left her son one hundred thousand dollars. *Who needs more than that?* Aubrey said Andrew and Michelle and their kids were at her house all day Easter Sunday and they didn't leave until six o'clock. *Andrew has no reason to kill his mother or Vickie. What am I missing?* "What did you tell him?"

"I told him I'd think about it, and he said don't think too long." Stacy crossed her arms over her chest. "Got a weird call from Keith. Said he got a bunch of papers from the lawyer, Rina. Wanted to know how to stop the IRS audit."

"What did you say?" Laurent asked.

"Got no idea. Then he told me about Ruby Rae finding the diner's tax returns and adding two and two, which didn't make four. I think Ruby Rae sicced the IRS on Lisa and now Keith wants it stopped because he knows his wife hid a bunch of money and he wants that money."

"Thanks for letting me know."

"What happens to the van that was in the crash?" Stacy asked.

"From looking at it, I'm sure it's beyond repair. Why do you ask?"

"I bet Vickie chewed out old lady Parks. She was delivering the last of the moonshine to my house. I had people showing up for two days asking if there was anything left."

"Why would Vickie chew out Mrs. Parks? Aubrey was driving," Laurent said.

"My mistake. I thought Vickie was driving the last batch to my house. Aubrey did call and say she was going to do it."

"When was this?" Laurent asked.

"Day before the crash."

"I thought Aubrey didn't have anything to do with the moonshine."

"She was probably just helping Vickie. Trying to get in good with her. Who gets the diner now?"

"I have no idea."

CHAPTER FIFTY-SEVEN

"YOU PLANNING ANY more night visits to the forest? You and Vern and Doug were the highlight of last night," Dak said. "What did Aubrey say?"

"She told me to leave Doug there." Laurent was dressed in soft clothes. Dak and Poulter were meeting her before her next PT appointment. She had downed several ibuprofen with lunch.

"The nights are pretty damn cold," Poulter said. "She must be really angry with him."

"He's hiding from his bookie," Laurent said. "Aubrey told me he owed fifty thousand dollars for betting on a basketball game, and they were supposed to pay the bookie on Tuesday morning and neither one showed up."

"Which means we've got two suspicious characters running around town," Dak said.

"Not only that, but we're going to have fireworks soon. Rina filed the inventory in court on Monday and received the Letters of Administration from the judge," Laurent said. "She mailed certified copies to Keith, Aubrey, Andrew, and Vickie on Tuesday. If the post office is on time, several people are going to be upset when they read the inventory."

"Vickie's dead," Poulter interrupted. "How's that work?"

"Rina mailed everyone before she knew about Vickie. She's resending everything to Vickie's brother. Apparently, right after Vickie learned she inherited Big Al's, she wrote a new will. Rina did it. Vickie's new will is one week old and her brother is the executor."

"Has Rina left town?" Dak asked.

Laurent smiled. "I told her to call if anyone got out of hand or threatened her. Poulter, make sure you circle the block a few extra times today."

"Do you think Doug's bookie will show up at Rina's office?" Dak asked.

"Doubtful," she said. "The one point seven million dollars is in the bank, but I wouldn't put it past Aubrey or Keith to pound on Rina's door."

"Who gets all that dough?" Poulter asked.

"According to Rina, Vickie inherits everything inside the diner."

"Did Vickie leave everything to her brother?" Poulter asked.

"I'm guessing Vickie's will is complicated. Don't forget she owned Baylor, Scott, and Wright. I'm speaking with the other partners after Vickie's funeral. Since she was a part owner, her will probably outlines who gets her share of the company, but I doubt BS&W cares about her house or personal estate."

"How much is she worth?" Poulter asked.

"Without Big Al's, a few million. With Big Al's . . ." Laurent said.

"You think someone from her office killed her?" Dak asked.

"Not really. She was found in the moonshine garage. It's got to be one of them."

"Or someone they gave the code to," Dak said.

"This entire mess starts with Lisa," Laurent said. "Everyone expected Aubrey to inherit the diner, so when she didn't, the killer had to improvise and get rid of Vickie. Is gaining control of Big Al's the motive?"

"Who else knew about the money Lisa stashed in the milk tins?" Dak asked. "That's who we should be looking for. If Aubrey knew about the cash, she'd have stolen it and paid off Doug's bookie. If Keith knew about it, he'd have told Monica and they both would have flown the coop."

"As far as I can tell, Lisa was the only one who knew about the money she stashed in the milk containers. Stacy told me Lisa wouldn't let anyone dust the shelves in the dining room. Lisa told the staff she'd do it. She found it relaxing," Laurent said. "There is something satisfying about dusting, especially when you can write your name in the dust." She laughed at the baffled looks on Dak's and Poulter's faces. "Ever dusted before?"

Both deputies shook their heads.

"My dust bunnies love me," Dak said.

"When I interviewed Stacy at her house, I was afraid I was going to fall through the front porch. So many rotten boards. If she knew about the cash, she didn't use it to fix up her house," Laurent said. "Poulter, run deep financial checks on Aubrey and Doug, Andrew and Michelle, and Stacy. I know you already did one on Keith."

"What did he say about the 401(k) withdrawals?" Poulter asked. "I verified with the life insurance company that Lisa canceled the policy. The last premium paid was back in 2017."

"Keith claimed it was Lisa's signature on the consent form and he didn't bat an eye when I said I was having the handwriting analyzed." She sighed. "I wonder if Lisa realized the mess she left behind. If Aubrey had inherited, would Vickie still be alive? Vickie asked me after the reading of the will if I thought the killer would come after her. I told her no."

"Don't go feeling guilty about it," Dak said. "There's no way you could have known."

"Would Aubrey have kept things the same?" Poulter asked. "We're making that assumption. When did Aubrey find out Doug owed fifty thousand to his bookie?"

"I never asked that question," Laurent admitted. "Her answer might refocus this investigation. I never really considered her or Doug as the murderers. If either of them killed Lisa, then Vickie had to die, too."

"I think Lisa's killer is either Keith or Monica or both. Like you just said, when Vickie inherited Big Al's, she had to die, too," Dak said. "The only Moonshine Mama who wanted Lisa to die was Ruby Rae Evans. What Ruby Rae really wanted was to make more money and she thought Lisa would have to manufacture more moonshine to pay the IRS." He ran a hand over his bald head. "Where were Keith and Monica from Saturday afternoon to Sunday?"

"Monica worked until six on Saturday," Laurent said. "They claim to alibi each other for Saturday night and all day Sunday. Same alibi as when Lisa was killed."

"And we've got no way to check it," Poulter said. "Especially if they say they stayed inside."

Laurent nodded. "What about Stacy Simmons? Her alibi for Lisa's murder is thin. But, she's got a job offer from Andrew to run his rooftop moonshine bar in Indianapolis, so now, she doesn't need the cash-under-the-table money."

"When did Andrew offer the job to Stacy?" Dak asked.

"Monday afternoon. Stacy might have killed Vickie before Andrew offered her the job," Laurent said. "I interviewed her

Monday morning, and at first, she was shaky, but then she became belligerent. I think she's a very angry woman."

"I like Keith and Monica as Lisa's killer and I like them as Vickie's killer, especially after the will was read." Poulter held up a finger. "One, Lisa wanted half of his 401(k), which he emptied out. Two, there's still a mortgage on the house, and he's now solely responsible for it. The diner is paid off. Keith said he didn't know Big Al's didn't have a mortgage, but I'm not sure I believe him. Three, Monica. Gotta keep the girlfriend happy or she'll leave."

"Before the will was read, Keith and Lisa were having a huge argument in court about the division of assets. Keith wanted Lisa to pay him alimony," Laurent said. "Keith said Ruby Rae contacted the IRS. With the audit, Keith would be able to prove Lisa made more money and should pay him alimony."

"That's pretty damn mean."

"I can see Monica and Keith murdering Lisa and then going on to kill Vickie," Dak said.

"The minute Monica found out Keith didn't inherit the diner, she started working on Plan B," Poulter said.

"Lisa is killed on a Sunday. Vickie is killed on Saturday or Sunday. The hair salon is closed on Sundays," Laurent said. "To me, that points to Keith and Monica. Whether they did it together or separately, doesn't matter. The only flaw in the plan, and that goes for everyone, is that no one knew the contents of Lisa's will, which is why Vickie had to die. The killer had to improvise."

"Now that Vickie's dead, who gets Big Al's?" Poulter asked.

"With Vickie gone, I automatically assumed the diner would revert to Keith or Aubrey or Andrew or any combination of the three. It wasn't until you said something that I realized Vickie's will took over, not Lisa's will. What if the killer made the same mistake? Maybe Keith or Monica killed Vickie assuming they'd get Big Al's back," Dak said.

"You've got a point," Laurent admitted. "I made the same mistake until Rina set me straight."

"Lisa is killed. Vickie inherits the diner. Vickie is killed. Maybe whoever killed Vickie made the mistake of assuming the diner would revert to the DuVal family," Dak said. "Which goes back to my theory that Lisa's killer is a family member. Vickie's killer could be a family member or someone who made the same misinterpretation that we did."

"My biggest problem with Keith and Monica killing Vickie is the catering van crash," Laurent said. "Stacy said Vickie was supposed to drive the van to her house and then she changed her story and said Aubrey called her and said she was driving the van over. Who loaded the van and when? That's who we need to find, assuming it wasn't Vickie. I'm going to check phone records."

"Stacy could have made a mistake," Dak said.

"In what universe? We've got nothing but liars, cheaters, and gamblers," Poulter said. "Just watch, Baylor, Scott, and Wright are going to inherit Big Al's. They'll sell it to some out-of-towner who'll change everything." He held up a hand. "I've got something else. Monica's done this before."

"Done what?" Dak asked.

"Picked up an older, married man and drained him of money," Poulter said.

"Keith is vain enough to think he's the main draw. I think Monica's a shark. I'm betting she found out Keith was married to the owner of Big Al's and decided to go after him. He made it easier by being stupid and gullible. I bet the first time he sat in her stylist chair, he spilled his guts and she was right there, mopping up the tears, and commiserating with him. Yes, his wife's a bitch. She doesn't deserve my money. She's got enough of her own. That sort of thing," Laurent said. "Mimi told me Lisa said she'd never leave the diner to Aubrey because of Doug's gambling problem, so if the killer is a family member, it still could be Aubrey or Andrew."

"Or Doug or Michelle."

"I never really considered Andrew," Poulter said. "And, Michelle, no way."

"I pulled his license plate and his wife's plate and ran them through the tollway authority," Laurent said. "He didn't use either vehicle to drive from Indianapolis to Field's Crossing using the highways. There's nothing to say he didn't take the back roads."

"I don't peg him as a killer," Dak said. "He was getting what he wanted from Lisa. New recipes and a hundred thousand dollars and he runs a successful rooftop wine bar."

"We know he was at Aubrey's house all afternoon on Easter Sunday," Laurent said. "But I'm with you. I don't peg him as killing his mom or his mom's best friend and then running back to Indianapolis."

"I think Doug is more than a slim possibility. When he found out his wife didn't inherit Big Al's, he lost it and killed Vickie," Poulter said. "But his alibi for Lisa's death is solid."

"Here's what we're gonna do. Dak, I want you to concentrate on Keith and Monica. Get proof that one or the other is the murderer. Poulter, you work on Ruby Rae Evans and Stacy Simmons. Same thing. Prove or disprove them as murderers. I'll take Doug and Aubrey."

Dak stood up. "You've got to get to PT and I've got to get out on the street. What are we gonna do about this bookie and his sidekick?"

"If you spot him, Scarface, or the Hummer, call for backup first," Laurent said. "I don't want a shoot-out on Field Street. The state's going to rotate a couple of officers nearby for the next few days. Don't approach the vehicle or either individual until backup arrives. Assume they are armed and dangerous. I've informed dispatch, so they're ready, too."

"Armed and dangerous?" Dak snorted. "I bet they carry semi-automatics in the back seat."

CHAPTER FIFTY-EIGHT

LAURENT GLANCED UP at the knock on her office door. Deputy Poulter poked his head inside.

"Got a minute? The judge's ruling came down this morning," he said.

"Do I want to know the outcome?" Laurent tossed her pen on the desk and leaned back in her chair. She had returned from physical therapy and immediately downed four more ibuprofen. Her shoulder was killing her.

"Yep." Poulter scooted into her office and closed the door. "The judge is allowing the security video from Bubba's Steakhouse because the owner offered it voluntarily. You didn't ask for it. Your attorney didn't subpoena it. Apparently, it means more when someone comes forward. The owner's wife was cleaning the table next to Greene and Ralph and got a glimpse of the paper with your passwords. When she read the story in *The Crossing*, she contacted the judge and he's admitting it into evidence."

"Does Greene know yet?" she asked.

"He will in the next hour."

"How'd you find out so soon?"

"A buddy of mine is a clerk. I asked him to keep an eye on the case," Poulter said. "Is Greene working today?"

Laurent nodded. "What happens next?"

"Depends if Greene wants to keep fighting. The video is a nail in his coffin. He already knows that if the judge allows the video, the union will back you. The question he has to ask himself is all about money. Lawyers are expensive and he's going to lose, but how much money is he willing to part with to save face or does he toss in the towel and retire with his benefits?"

"What do you think he'll do?"

"He'll drag it out for a month or so, but in the end, he'll resign," Poulter said. "I will personally review his retirement options with him. He's got thirty years in. Let's hope he doesn't blow it trying to get revenge."

"What if he gets the money from somewhere else?" she asked. "What if Ralph and Greene decide to wage war?"

"Ralph's not going to lend him a penny. He's a greedy bastard. They'll sit in a bar and Ralph will buy the drinks, but in the end, that's all."

Laurent peered at her deputy. "I suppose I have to take his gun and badge when the time comes."

Poulter nodded. "We'll record that conversation and I'll be here as a witness. And, Sheriff, you've got to hire more deputies. We're getting tired."

CHAPTER FIFTY-NINE

"This ain't my problem. I pay you all that money every month so my customers can use their credit cards in my store. You fix it and you fix it now. I'll wait."

Laurent glanced at Mimi. She had never heard the floral shop owner use that tone of voice and certainly not on the phone. The tiny grandma winked at her and put a finger to her lips.

"You done yet?" Mimi asked. "I ain't got all day and my favorite customer just walked in. You better have that internet working in the next two minutes or I'm charging you for a lost sale."

Laurent slid onto a stool next to the cash register.

"It's fixed? Let me check."

Laurent watched as Mimi punched a few buttons on the credit card machine. "You done good. Now don't let it happen again."

"Sounds like you have a love-hate relationship with the internet," Laurent said.

"How can they get away with crap like that? It ain't my fault if they can't keep up. He kept mumbling something about bandwidth. There's not enough of it. I told him I pay for the most they got and they better keep it up all the damn time," Mimi said. "Last time this happened, it turns out the customer's credit cards had hit their limit. I chewed out the internet company that time, too. But I called back and apologized. I don't want no reputation for being a cranky old lady."

"Was this when Doug's credit cards didn't work? He paid cash?"

Mimi nodded. "You any closer to figuring out who killed Lisa?"

"Getting there. I've got my suspicions, but no proof. Yet."

"Here's somethin' you may not know. DeeDee over at the hair salon fired that hair stylist Keith was dating. She's the one who spouted nonsense to that asshole reporter at *The Crossing*."

"I figured her for that, but thanks for the confirmation."

"You gonna tell me who killed Lisa and Vickie?" Mimi spread her feet wide and planted her hands on her hips.

"Not today. Talk to you later." Laurent slid off the stool and left the florist. She paused on the sidewalk. *Where next?* She had decided earlier in the morning to stroll the downtown business district. The walk would give her time to think.

She crossed Field Street and walked into Farmers Bank. After a minute, Walker's secretary motioned her into the CEO's office. "I won't take much of your time. Thanks for the video. We were able to capture a still and now my deputies know who to be on the lookout for."

"Anything to help," Walker said.

"I do have one question for you," Laurent said. "How would you describe Aubrey's reaction when she found out the safe deposit box was empty?"

"Shocked and angry. Like she was expecting there to be something in it. It made me wonder what her reaction was when she read about the one point seven million dollars."

"I would have liked to have been a fly on that wall," Laurent said. "When did she discover the box was empty?"

"Monday morning."

"Who had access?"

"Lisa DuVal, Aubrey Holmes, and Victoria Scott Wright," he said.

"I subpoenaed the bank's record showing who had requested access to that particular box and Vickie Wright was here last Wednesday, the day Lisa's will was read."

Walker nodded. "Her name was on the list, and she had a key to the box. There was no reason to suspect anything illegal. We had no way of knowing about Lisa DuVal's will. If we had, I would have frozen the deposit box that day. Vickie beat us to it. If there was anything in it, she either took it or it was already empty. Safe deposit boxes are a private matter. We don't videotape people opening their boxes or the contents. Standard operating procedure."

"So, there's no way to know if Vickie opened an empty box or if there was something in it?"

"Correct."

"Why'd you let Aubrey open it?" Laurent asked.

"Several reasons. First, she does stand to inherit from her mother's will and there is a case to be made for the contents of the box belonging to her. She could have walked in here with an order from the judge and I would have had to comply. Second, Aubrey agreed she would take nothing from the box until the judge ruled on who was to inherit. She signed an agreement stating that, and, third, she had a key. I taped the whole thing to protect the bank, but it wasn't necessary because there was nothing there," Walker said.

"Would you forward a copy of that consent to my office?" Laurent shook hands with the bank president. "Thanks for your time." *Now I've got Aubrey's signature.* After exiting, she cut through the bank's rear parking lot to County Street and entered the police station from a side door. She climbed the stairs to her office, settled behind her desk, powered up her computer, and reread her notes. And made some new ones. *I'll subpoena Vickie's personal bank accounts, but for BS&W, I'll need a warrant.*

Who killed Vickie, and would finding Vickie's killer lead to Lisa's killer? Laurent decided to follow that line of thinking. She picked up her office phone and, after several minutes, she was viewing Vickie's cell phone statement. Stacy had told her Vickie was driving the catering van to her house on Sunday morning, but Vern had pulled Aubrey from the vehicle. *When did Vickie change her mind? When did she call Aubrey?* There was no call from Vickie to Aubrey in the last few days. Laurent accessed Aubrey's statement. The statement showed a long call on Saturday from Aubrey to Vickie. *Right after I left. Certainly, enough time for the two women to decide who was going to drive the last batch of moonshine to Stacy's house. That's not proof.*

Laurent picked up the phone and called the park district. A minute later, her email dinged. She opened the attachment. Stacy had signed in for the batting cages from eight until eleven on Sunday morning and the attendant's email confirmed it. The attendant reloaded the balls three times. While she and Vern were sitting on the steps of the library, Stacy was at the batting cages and Aubrey was in the accident. *If either of them had killed Vickie, they did it on Saturday.* The attendant at the batting cages had also confirmed that Stacy was there on Saturday morning. Again, eight until eleven. Where was Stacy the rest of the day?

Laurent pulled Andrew's business card out of the slip pocket in her notebook and dialed the home phone number.

"Hello?"

"Andrew DuVal, please."

"Speaking."

"This is Sheriff Laurent. We met last week in the parking lot after your mother's will was read. I've got a few questions for you."

"I'm listening."

Laurent paused. What did she really want to know? "I understand you were in Field's Crossing recently. May I ask why?"

"To pick up the new recipes for my moonshine bar from Mom's house," Andrew said. "I ran into Aubrey, and we chatted for a while."

"Where did you run into your sister?"

"At Mom and Dad's house."

"Why was she there?"

"I didn't ask. I'm guessing she was searching for some token or small remembrance. She was very upset because Monica had taken over Mom's room. I think she was also sad about Vickie. She said Stacy had called her and told her Vickie had been found dead at her home."

"What time were you at your folks' home?"

"Around ten," Andrew said. "I dropped the kids off at school and drove here."

Laurent circled the number ten. *Check with Dak. Did he allow Stacy any phone calls while she sat in his cruiser? Had he taken her phone? Check Stacy's phone record. How did Aubrey know Vickie was dead? I was still questioning Stacy at ten and then I sent her to the station to give her statement to Poulter. What time did they finish?*

"Any other reason you came to Field's Crossing?"

"I offered Stacy Simmons a job in Indianapolis."

"Doing what?"

"Making moonshine," Andrew said.

"What was her response?"

"She said she'd think about it."

"What else?"

"Nothing. The recipes weren't in Mom's room, but I've got copies on my phone. I drove back to Indianapolis after I spoke with Stacy," Andrew said.

"Why'd you want the paper copy?"

"Nostalgia."

"Thanks for talking to me." Laurent hung up the phone. She clicked open Vickie's file and located the autopsy report. The stomach contents of the victim were listed as 50 ml of partially digested food. *Breakfast? Vickie was killed between Saturday afternoon and Sunday morning. The van blew up on Sunday. It snowed Sunday night. No tracks except Dak and Stacy. Was Vickie alive on Sunday morning when Aubrey picked up the last of the moonshine? If she was, the finger points to Aubrey, unless Aubrey picked up the moonshine on Saturday. No. That doesn't work. The accident was on Sunday morning and the lengthy phone call was on Saturday afternoon. What if Aubrey killed Vickie on Saturday afternoon and she was the one who ransacked Vickie's house and then on Sunday, she drove the van to Stacy's house but got rear-ended first. What was she looking for? Money. The key to the safe deposit box. Rina told me Aubrey surprised her with a visit on Monday and Aubrey had a key to the box. But it was empty. What was Aubrey expecting to find? Cash?*

Laurent leaned back in her chair and stared at the ceiling, imagining the scenario. Her office phone rang. "Yes?"

"Manager at FC Storage on line two."

Laurent punched a button. "Sheriff Laurent. How can I help you?"

"I'm the manager at the storage facility south of town and I rented a unit to Lisa DuVal several years ago. I understand she is now deceased."

"Correct."

"This morning, her daughter, Aubrey Holmes, came in and wanted me to tell her what unit her mother rented. So I did. She said she had the key but had forgotten the unit number."

"Got it."

"I watched the security cameras. She didn't have a key. She used a bolt cutter. She lied to me."

"Did she remove anything?" Laurent sat up straight in her chair.

"No. I switched on the audio, and I could hear breaking glass. The cameras don't look into any particular unit. They monitor the hallways and other common areas," the manager said. "She didn't carry anything out."

"Please send me a copy with time and date stamp," Laurent said. "Has anyone else been in the unit?"

"Lisa came in every afternoon between two and three."

"What'd she do?"

"No clue. All I have is the daily record of who used their passcode to get in. What they do is none of my business unless they try to sleep here," the manager said. "Everyone creates their own code for the main gate and the sliding doors and they put their own locks on the units. Am I in trouble?"

"Not with me." Laurent hung up. *Aubrey's still looking for money.* She called Rina. "You sent the probate papers via certified mail, right?"

"Of course. Why do you ask?"

"Who signed for them at Aubrey and Doug's house?" Laurent asked.

"Aubrey's signature is on the green card."

"Thanks." *Maybe Aubrey didn't read the inventory.* Laurent pulled her chair closer to the desk and opened the file that held the crime scene photos. She also opened CSU's report. *Was it too late to get DNA on the dog poop?*

Another call. This time to the tech at CSU in Indianapolis.

"I'll run the test ASAP, but I can tell you the specimen came from a little dog. Their poop is like rabbit pellets."

Aubrey's dog. Dolly. Fits in her purse. Stacy's dog is a beagle. Mooch.

"Hey, boss. You got your thinking face on." Deputy Poulter stood at the entrance to her office. "Solve the murders?"

"Almost. Would you call the Ford dealership and ask what hours Doug worked on Saturday afternoon?"

"Ten-four."

Laurent pushed away from her desk. "I'm taking a walk. Text me the answer."

"Gonna share?"

"Not yet."

*   *   *

Laurent exited the police station and strolled to Big Al's. She paused on the corner of Woodruff and Indiana Streets. *What's the most direct route to Aubrey and Doug's house from Big Al's?* She glanced at her watch and headed west on Woodruff. Six blocks later, she turned left onto Cardinal Street and stopped. Eight minutes. At a leisurely pace. Add in another minute to reach the Holmes' residence. Nine minutes each way, eighteen minutes total. Maybe twenty because the dog pooped in the circular drive at Big Al's.

Laurent walked west on Cardinal Street, looking at the houses on the opposite side of the street from Aubrey and Doug's house. She wasn't exactly sure who or what she was looking for. A curtain twitched. *There she is.*

*   *   *

"I gotta tell you, Sheriff. I don't sleep so good no more and my chair by the window's kinda comfortable and I can sleep sitting up so that's where I sit. Got to keep watch on the neighborhood. You like your tea strong or sweet?"

"Strong." Laurent was amused. The elderly occupant of the house across the street from the Holmes' residence was the quintessential busybody. Nothing to do but sit and stare out the window all day long. Napping on and off. Her mind, sharp as a tack. "What did you do on Easter Sunday?"

"I'm Jewish. Easter don't mean nothing to me. I was sitting here when I seen Doug walking that little purse dog his wife loves so much. Never seen him do that before. He was going kinda fast. Dragging the poor thing along. I don't care for pets myself, but I felt sorry for the dog."

"Wouldn't it be normal to walk the dog?"

"Doug ain't never walked that dog before. He hates that dog. I heard him say more than once, he'd like to kick it from here to Shinola."

*   *   *

Did Doug get a call from his bookie on Easter and panic? Thought the bookie was going to show up at his house while his wealthy brother- and sister-in-law and their kids were there? Did he make the excuse to walk the dog, but really intend to steal from Lisa? Was his intent to kill her? Only Doug can answer that one.

Laurent stopped at the crosswalk and rocked back on her heels. In her mind's eye, she saw Aubrey emptying the dishwasher. Putting knives in the block. One knife lay on the counter. The block was full. Was that the murder weapon? Did Aubrey know? *Do I have enough to get a warrant for all the knives in the Holmes' kitchen?* She quickened her pace. *Or did Doug kill Lisa immediately after the Easter egg hunt and then go home? No. Doug had Jake in his Ford. Aubrey took Justin in her car because he was muddy and filthy. Maybe Doug dropped off Jake, sped to the diner, stole the money from the safe in the desk and the cash register, and killed his mother-in-law. That works.*

Laurent crossed Sycamore Street and retraced her steps to Big Al's. *Aubrey made a comment to her brother, Andrew, about Vickie being dead, but Dak told me that he didn't allow Stacy to make any phone calls. So how did Aubrey know Vickie was dead unless she killed her? Am I going to find that big flat-screen TV in the Holmes' garage? Where was Aubrey on Saturday? Doug?* Laurent frowned and narrowed her eyes. Nerf guns. Candy. *Aubrey and Doug's kids had a sleepover at the neighbor's house on Saturday. Did Doug kill Lisa and Vickie or were Doug and Aubrey in on both murders? It's time to talk to Doug.*

Her phone vibrated. Text from Poulter. Doug left work at two on Saturday.

CHAPTER SIXTY

"IF HE RUNS, tackle him."

Laurent didn't think it would take much to bring Doug in for questioning for the murder of his mother-in-law and Vickie Wright. She and Dak crept along Pot-hell Path to the abandoned campground while Poulter was stationed at the corner of Bees Creek and Turtle Lake Roads. Greene was parked at the big bend of East Road and Bees Creek. Doug was surrounded on three sides by the sheriff and her deputies and on one side by ice-cold Turtle Lake.

"Not going to run through the forest after him?" Dak asked.

"That's why I brought you along," she said. "Your legs are longer than mine and I'm pretty sure you run faster than I do."

"Getting smart in your old age, huh?"

"Let's call it learning to delegate."

The sun would be down in an hour, Laurent noted, and she wanted Doug behind bars before the day was over. She wound her way through the oak trees surrounding the campground. There was no need for stealth. She paused at the edge of the clearing to Doug's campsite and scanned the area.

The clearing was rectangular-shaped with Doug's tent anchored slightly to her left. A campfire sat twenty feet away from the front flap of the tent, and along the rear edge of the campsite sat a tiny tent. Port-a-potty. On the picnic table sat a propane stove with two burners and extra propane tanks were stacked underneath. A large Yeti cooler was perched next to the table.

Slowly, Laurent circled the area until she was opposite the front opening of Doug's tent. She touched her earpiece. "Dak. Got anything?"

"Looks quiet. Can you see him?"

"Not yet."

"Poulter?"

"All's quiet."

"Greene?"

"Nothing north of Bees Creek. Looks to me like Vern or Emmit's plowing, south of Bees Creek. Want me to tell them to turn around?" Greene said.

"Negative. The suspect won't get that far. We'll take him in the woods if he tries to run."

"Ten-four."

Laurent crouched behind an oak tree and considered her options. Where was Doug? Had he abandoned camp? Why didn't he take the tent? Where was his Explorer? It wasn't in the garage when Aubrey called her to report Doug was missing. She remembered going out to the garage when Aubrey thought Doug might have taken the camping stuff. Only one car in the garage. But there was no vehicle parked near the campsite. *I suppose Doug could have driven his Ford home and then Aubrey dropped him off. Maybe with a load of groceries. How long was Doug planning to camp out? He'd be fired if he didn't go to work, but maybe that's better than getting beaten up by the bookie and Scarface.*

Laurent wanted to walk over to the fire and check the embers, but she hesitated and mentally reviewed her plan. It was simple. Find Doug at the campsite. Arrest him. Return to the station. Do the paperwork. Go home. She made the mistake of assuming he'd be here, waiting, ready for her. *I'm an idiot. Nothing ever goes to plan.*

A branch snapped to her right. Laurent crouched behind an oak tree and peered out. Doug appeared carrying an armful of branches and sticks. He dropped them next to the fire pit and sat down on an upright log, brushing dirt and twigs off his jeans. He picked up a charred stick and poked at the fire.

Laurent stepped out from behind the tree.

"We've got a problem." Dak's voice murmured in her ear. "Look to your left. Slowly."

Laurent stepped back and peeked around the oak tree. And froze. Emerging from the forest between her and Dak were the bookie and Scarface.

CHAPTER SIXTY-ONE

"Look who I found."

Laurent heard the deep voice from across the campsite and watched Doug jump to his feet, the log seat falling over behind him.

"How'd you find me?"

"Followed your wife. Watched her bring you supplies. You're such a dumb fuck." In one hand, the bookie held a baseball bat, the other hand shoved in his pocket. The man was large, tall and broad-shouldered, jeans tucked into army boots, camouflage jacket buttoned up, blending into Turtle Woods.

"Please. I can explain." Doug's hands were in front of him, pleading.

"I'm not interested in explanations anymore," the bookie said. "Only one thing interests me. Money. And you owe me a bunch. Fifty thousand."

"Yes. Yes. I know. Things didn't go as planned."

"No shit." The bookie swung the baseball bat at a nearby tree. *Thwack!* Big chunks of bark flew off.

"No. Let me explain. Please." Doug was crying, tears rolling down his face. "My wife was supposed to inherit the diner, but she didn't. She only got the recipe box, which had the key to the safe deposit box where her mom always kept a bunch of cash. When she got to the bank, it was all gone. We think we know who took it, but then she was killed, and we searched her house, but couldn't find the money. My wife searched her mom's house, but she still hasn't found the money, but we still have to look in the storage unit. The money's here somewhere. I promise."

The bookie stepped closer to Doug; baseball bat clenched in a large fist.

Laurent pulled out her Glock. Quietly. As far as she could tell, the bookie and Scarface hadn't seen her or Dak. She whispered into her radio.

Scarface stepped forward.

Another step.

Scarface halted at the edge of the clearing, a gun dangling from his hand. His arm rose.

Laurent put a bullet in the tree behind his head, the roar of the Glock ripping through the quiet forest.

Doug bolted into the trees.

CHAPTER SIXTY-TWO

LAURENT PRESSED HER back against the oak tree and closed her eyes. The tree shook with bullets fired from Scarface's semi-automatic. Gunfire raked the ground on both sides of the tree and bullets kicked up clouds of dirt and leaves around her. *Another shoot-out in the woods.* She heard the roar from Dak's gun. "Did you hit the bastard?" she shouted into her radio.

"Negative."

"You got eyes on Darth Vader?"

"Ten-four."

"What's Scarface doing?"

"You mean other than trying to shoot down the tree you're hiding behind?" Dak said. "He's backing up step by step. I think they're trying to get away. Darth Vader just tripped and fell into a pothole. His baseball bat went flying into the woods."

Why didn't Vader fire? Maybe he didn't carry a gun. Just the bat. Laurent dropped to her stomach and crawled on the floor of the forest using bushes and mounds of fallen leaves to keep hidden. Reaching the next tree, she poked her head up for a quick look.

Scarface was spraying the trees around Dak. Leaves and branches rained down.

He's not trying to kill us. Why? He's trying to get the bookie out alive and in one piece. Firing on a police officer is not as bad as killing one.

Laurent slowly raised her head again and watched as the bookie crawled toward Scarface, the semiautomatic never stopping. *Stay down, Dak.*

The bookie hid behind Scarface.

Laurent fired. Scarface dropped the semiautomatic and grabbed his shoulder. From across the campsite, she saw blood streaming between Scarface's fingers.

The bookie grabbed Scarface's gun and sprayed Doug's campsite. *Boom!*

The bookie hit the propane tanks. The picnic table exploded. The pile of wood caught fire.

"Dispatch," Laurent shouted into her radio. "Call the fire department. Woods around abandoned campground southwest of Turtle Lake are burning."

Laurent peered from behind the bullet-riddled oak tree. The bookie and Scarface were gone. She heard them crashing through the forest.

"Dak, you okay?"

"Fit as a fiddle. You?"

"Great."

"Where's that little wimp?" Dak asked. "Did Scarface mow him down?"

"Doug ran for the trees. Right now, we gotta get out of here without getting shot or burnt."

"Sheriff, what the hell's happening?" Poulter's voice rang in her ear.

Laurent's gaze swept the clearing. She touched the radio on her shoulder. "Doug's running through the trees. Apprehend him. Be on the lookout for two men, big guy with camouflage coat and army boots, and one missing the tip of his nose. Scarface took a bullet to the arm, but Vader's got a semiautomatic." She pushed through the brush, heading toward Bees Creek Road. "And the forest is on fire.

"Dak and I are following through the woods as fast as we can. Doug's trapped unless he's got a vehicle stashed somewhere in the forest or another part of the campground."

"I got eyes on the suspect." Greene's voice broke in over the radio. "He's hiding behind a tree at the edge of Turtle Woods. Now, he's creeping out."

"Take cover!" Poulter's voice shouted in her ear. "Hummer with two men just sideswiped me. Bastard shot at me."

Laurent ran. She heard Dak a few feet to her right, crashing through the woods with her. *God, I hope I don't trip and fall flat on my face.*

"Doug's running across Bees Creek Road. He's heading for the tractor," Greene shouted.

"Dispatch." Laurent touched her radio. "Get Emmit Martin on the phone or on his walkie-talkie. Tell him to call whoever's plowing south of Bees Creek to take cover. Stop plowing and get down."

"The Hummer's flying on Bees Creek," Poulter said. "Wait. They stopped. They're shooting at Doug. I'm fifty feet behind the Hummer."

"Do not engage, Poulter. You've got no cover," Laurent ordered. "Where's Doug?"

"Behind the tractor," Greene snapped. "The Hummer's shooting out the windows on the cab."

Laurent slowed as she approached the edge of the woods and stopped behind a tree. Dak hid behind another tree. She spotted

Greene. He was hunkered down behind the cruiser's engine, weapon pointed. Poulter's cruiser was parked fifty feet behind the Hummer. All she saw were feet. *Good.* She took a deep breath.

"Greene. Can you see Doug?" She exhaled into her radio.

"Ten-four. He's crouching behind one of those big-ass tires. He's in a better spot than me and Poulter."

"What about the driver of the tractor?"

"Cab windows are all shot out. I can't see anybody," Greene said.

"Ten-four. Stand down. Let the Hummer go. Greene, get the plate," Laurent ordered. "Dispatch. We need an ambulance at the big bend on East Road and Bees Creek. Advise possible gunshot wound. Fifty-year-old male."

"Ten-four."

"Dispatch. Alert state troopers. Hummer with Michigan plates heading north on East Road. Armed and dangerous. Wanted for attempted murder of police officers."

"Ten-four."

"Look out!" Laurent shouted. "Greene. He's heading right for you. Take cover. Dak. Poulter. Open fire on the Hummer."

Three guns roared across the open field.

An arm appeared from the driver's window of the Hummer firing a semiautomatic. Laurent dropped to a knee. She emptied her Glock into the fleeing vehicle, glass exploding. Dak lay on the ground in a trench next to her, shooting. Poulter fired from behind the driver's door of his cruiser.

The Hummer fled.

CHAPTER SIXTY-THREE

LAURENT FLEW ACROSS Bees Creek Road and yanked open the door to the cab on the tractor. Vern's blue eyes peeked from under his Carhartt jacket. "You okay?" Unexpected tears welled up.

Vern nodded. "Did you get the bad guys?"

"Only one." Laurent holstered her weapon. "How's it feel getting shot at? Don't move. Let me get this glass off you." She climbed into the cab and started plucking glass off Vern's jacket and the back of his head.

"Been a while since I've been this scared," Vern said.

"You and me both."

"Got anything to do with that guy hiding out in the woods?"

"He's the reason all of us got shot at today."

"Ow."

"You're going to need a few stitches in the back of your neck. There's a piece of glass stuck in partway." She swatted his hand. "Don't try and pull it out yourself. Wait until Keke gets here."

"He can stitch me up. Or Emmit."

"You are a stubborn old coot." Laurent stepped down the ladder on the side of the tractor and waited for Vern to back out. "Take off your coat. Let me shake it out."

"Look who's talking about being stubborn." But he handed her his jacket as he brushed off his jeans. Vern bent over, hands on his knees. "Damn. My neck hurts."

"Sit. Put your head between your knees. It should take some stress off the wound." Laurent waved to the ambulance as it bumped through rows of tilled soil. "Keke's here. So's Emmit."

Laurent waited until Keke set his massive toolbox of medicine on the ground next to Vern. "I'll be back. Gotta check on a few things."

"That asshole's gonna pay to fix my tractor." Emmit pointed to a handcuffed Doug before he dropped to one knee next to Vern.

Dak had handcuffed Doug, sat him in the middle of a plowed row, and was squatting in front of him. Laurent heard him reading Doug his rights. Poulter and Greene stood on either side of Doug, hands on hips, glaring at him.

"Well done, everyone," she said. "Thank you for not getting shot."

"What are we gonna do about the bookie and Scarface? Assholes got away," Greene said.

"Let's hope the state troopers in Indiana or Michigan catch them," she said.

"If they're smart, they'll take the back roads all the way home," Poulter said. "Who was in the tractor? Vern or Emmit?"

"Vern. He's got a piece of glass stuck in the back of his neck and wants Emmit to remove it. He's going to need a few stitches," Laurent said. "Stubborn old coot won't go to the hospital."

"Pot. Kettle. Black."

CHAPTER SIXTY-FOUR

"NEED HELP WITH that?" Laurent parked lengthwise across the end of Aubrey and Doug's driveway.

"Don't sneak up on me like that," Aubrey snapped.

"I arrested your husband for the murder of your mother."

"How dare you! Go arrest that skank my dad's been drooling over. She took off with Mom's collectibles."

"We've already picked her up and charged her." Laurent stopped a few feet away from the open trunk of Aubrey's Porsche. "Nice flat-screen TV. Must have been pretty easy to kill Vickie. Shovel right there."

"She had it coming," Aubrey said. "None of this would have happened if my mom had given Doug the money. Mom and Vickie, dead, all for thirty thousand dollars."

"You probably shouldn't say another word," Laurent said. "Your lawyer won't be happy."

"Who gives a fuck? I wish Mom had never bought the place. I was in elementary school when she started working here, but when she bought it from Al Jr., everything changed. She was never home. She didn't go shopping with me for my prom dress or wedding dress. She drove Dad into the arms of other women. All so she could be the big fish in a little pond." Aubrey sank onto the bumper of her car. "What did she do with the money?" She pounded the heel of her hand on the rear bumper. "It wasn't in the safe deposit box. It wasn't in Vickie's house. It wasn't in Dad's house. The storage unit's empty. But the lawyer found it. Where was it?"

"Your mom hid the money right under everyone's noses," Laurent said. "You know those milk tins and jugs and stools she used for decoration? Every single one was stuffed with cash."

"You're shittin' me."

Laurent shook her head.

"How'd you find it?"

"I helped Rina inventory the contents of the diner. When I picked up one of the little milk jugs off the shelf, it felt heavy. I opened it and the money rolled out."

"One point seven million." Aubrey stood and kicked the tire. "Did Vickie take the cash out of the safe deposit box?"

"There's no way of knowing what, if anything, was in the bank box," Laurent said. "Vickie had access and the contents are private. The bank doesn't know what's in any of those boxes."

"Which means there's no way for me to prove there was money in there, so I can't sue," Aubrey said. "No diner, no Mom, no Vickie. I've lost it all." A tear slid down her cheek. "What's gonna happen to my kids?"

"Who'd you name as guardian? Your brother?" Laurent said.

"That white trash Michelle is gonna raise my kids. What's she gonna tell them? Your father killed your grandmother, and your mother killed her mother's best friend. Helluva story."

"Kids are tough."

"Will I get out before I die?"

"That's not up to me." Laurent pulled out her handcuffs, grabbed Aubrey by the elbow, and spun the angry woman around. "Aubrey Holmes, you are under arrest for the murder of Victoria Scott Wright."

CHAPTER SIXTY-FIVE

"SHERIFF, YOU LOOK tired."

"It's been a rough two weeks." Two days ago, Laurent had asked Mimi to contact the business owners on Field Street to meet with her at the Skillet on Sunday morning at eleven. She raised her voice. "Folks. Everyone got coffee? I don't want to take too much of your time, but I did want to update you. As business owners, you deal with the public day in and day out and I'd like to squelch the rumors before they begin."

"Thank you, Sheriff. Me and Dutch appreciate it," Art said.

Everyone laughed. The two retired farmers were often accused of gossiping and spreading rumors, which they vehemently denied. Laurent knew the accusations rankled both farmers. She was surprised to see Vern sitting between Art and Dutch. *Maybe he really was trying to rejoin society. Little by little.* She nodded to him.

"Who killed who?" a voice shouted from the back of the restaurant.

"Doug Holmes has admitted to killing his mother-in-law, Lisa; and Aubrey has admitted to killing Vickie." Laurent paused and waited for the chatter to die down. "We have signed confessions from both."

"What'll happen to their kids?" Mimi asked. "You can't let the state take 'em."

"Andrew and Michelle DuVal are taking Jake and Justin." She didn't mention the boys' grandfather, Keith, refused to raise them. "The boys want to finish the school year in Field's Crossing. Child Services has granted temporary guardianship to their neighbors. After the school year is done, Jake and Justin will move to Indianapolis with their cousins, and Andrew and Michelle will receive permanent guardianship until the boys reach the age of eighteen."

"Andrew and Michelle have to teach four teenagers how to drive. Yuck," Dutch said.

Laurent smiled. "Amongst other things."

"How long will Doug and Aubrey be in jail?" Art asked.

"As you know, Indiana has the death penalty, but the prosecution has assured me they won't be pursuing that avenue. Unfortunately, Doug killed with intent to steal. He stole the cash from the safe in the office. He could get up to sixty-five years. I expect Aubrey's sentence to be less, possibly forty-five years. They could be out in half that time with good behavior." Laurent sighed. "Either way, they're both looking at twenty years minimum."

"Who gets Big Al's?"

Rina stood up. "I'll take that question. Let me start from the beginning. Lisa left Big Al's to Vickie. The day after Vickie inherited Big Al's, she came to my office and drew up a new will. Vickie left Big Al's to Aubrey. However, murderers can't inherit. I spoke with Judge Jenkins yesterday and he agrees with me. Vickie's entire estate goes to her nearest blood relative. Vickie's parents are dead. She has no children. Her husband is dead, but she has one brother. By law,

Vickie's brother inherits the diner, the house on Corn Belt Road, and her share of Baylor, Scott, and Wright and everything else."

"That don't seem right."

"Vickie's brother is financially well off and doesn't want Big Al's or the money. This morning he signed documents turning over Big Al's and all its contents and bank accounts to Jake and Justin to be administered by Andrew until both boys reach the age of twenty-five," Rina said.

It took several minutes before the assembled crowd quieted.

"Do you know what Andrew is planning to do?" Art asked.

"In my conversation with him this morning, Andrew said that as soon as the sheriff releases the site, he'll have the health department do an inspection and bring everything up to code. And, yes, he's planning to use his mother's recipes."

"Who's he gonna get to run it or is he planning to move back to Field's Crossing?" Dutch asked. "Or commute from Indianapolis?"

Before Rina could answer, Stacy rose.

"Andrew has offered me the position of manager and overseeing the updating of the diner," Stacy said. "I can't tell you how grateful I am for this opportunity. Give me a few months and we'll be back in business."

Mimi stood and faced the crowd. "Everybody, get on the phone and call the trustees on the town council. Get those liquor licenses and permits transferred to Andrew DuVal ASAP. I want my Sweet Tea Moonshine."

"Any other questions?" Laurent stood next to Rina. "If not, Rina and I'll be here for the next hour. The sheriff's office is buying coffee and doughnuts. Help yourselves."

An hour later, everyone had left.

Laurent glanced up to see Vern and Art and Dutch walking toward her, Styrofoam coffee cups in hand. She reached for her jacket.

"Good job, Sheriff. We're sorry to see it end this way." Dutch set his coffee on a nearby table and transferred his cane to the other hand.

"What's with the cane? You getting old?" she asked.

"I got arthritis creeping up my spine. Some days it hurts like hell. Doc said I had to use this so I don't fall down," Dutch said. "I don't need it, but I got these two nagging me all the damn day so just to shut them up, I use it."

"We ain't the only ones nagging. Your wife's pretty good at it," Art said. "Let's go. My wife gave me a list for the grocery store."

Laurent caught Vern's eye and hid a smile. She waited until the door closed behind the two old farmers. "How's your neck?"

"Ain't the first time Emmit stitched me up. Thought Keke was gonna have a heart attack right there in the cornfield. You finished for the day?"

Laurent nodded.

"It's afternoon. Time for lunch." He pulled out a chair. "Join me?"

BOOK CLUB
DISCUSSION QUESTIONS

1. The whole town was shocked by Lisa DuVal's will. How did you originally feel when she left her seemingly most valuable asset to her friend, not her family—particularly her daughter, Aubrey?

2. Lisa's relationship with her daughter, on the surface, seems "normal." How do you think they communicated on a day-to-day basis? Do they address the underlying issues about theft and Doug's gambling problems—or simply avoid talking about them?

3. How did Lisa's relationship with her son differ?

4. What "IRS" problems was Lisa facing? And how do you think she planned to handle the "cash in the pots"?

5. Did you think there was much value in the collectibles that Lisa kept in storage? What do you think prompted her to keep these?

6. Were you familiar with the moonshine laws in Indiana? Were you surprised to learn how it was made in Vickie's garage?

7. In small-town Indiana, did you expect the aggressiveness of gambling debt collectors?

8. What is your prognosis for Laurent's relationship with her daughter? Has the perception of an illegitimate child changed over thirty years in a small town? For the mother? For the child?

9. Were you surprised at the ultimate ownership of Big Al's after all the inheritance laws were decided?

10. Do you think that Aubrey's children will be okay with her brother and his wife?

NOTE FROM THE PUBLISHER

We hope that you enjoyed *Cracks Beneath the Surface*, the second in Mary Ann Miller's Jhonni Laurent Mystery Series.

The first in the series is *Bones Under the Ice*. The two novels stand on their own and can be read in any order. Here's a brief summary of *Bones Under the Ice*:

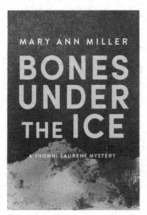

Jhonni Laurent is the first female sheriff of Field's Crossing, Indiana. Murder is rare in farm country, but when Jhonni discovers the frozen body of a high school senior under a fifteen-foot pile of snow and ice, she's thrust into her first homicide investigation. With an election looming and an opponent threatening to oust her, Jhonni must do more than find a killer—she has to save her job, too.

"Set in rural, blizzard-frozen Indiana, Mary Ann Miller's *Bones Under the Ice* launches a chilling police procedural series. From page one when Jhonni Laurent brushes snow off a frozen hand, the reader will be rooting for this likeable sheriff."

—Vinnie Hansen,
author of *Lostart Street*

We hope that you will enjoy reading *Bones Under the Ice*, Mary Ann Miller's prior novel, and that you will look forward to more to come.

For more information, please visit her website:
https://www.maryannmillerauthor.com

If you liked *Cracks Beneath the Surface,* we would be very appreciative if you would consider leaving a review. As you probably already know, book reviews are important to authors and they are very grateful when a reader makes the special effort to write a review, however brief.

Happy Reading,
Oceanview Publishing
Your Home for Mystery, Thriller, and Suspense